The Whisper of Calaresp

by
Kate Campbell

Hi Gemma,

I hope you enjoy delving into the world of Calaresp

Love
Kate Campbell

The Whisper of Calaresp

First published in 2021
by Wallace Publishing, United Kingdom
www.wallacepublishing.co.uk

All Rights Reserved
Copyright © Kate Campbell

The right of Kate Campbell to be identified as the author of this work has been asserted in accordance with section 77 and 78 of the Copyright Designs and Patents Act 1988.

This book is sold under condition that it shall not, by way of trade or otherwise, be lent, re-sold, hired out or otherwise circulated in any form of binding or cover other than that in which it is published and without a similar condition including this condition being imposed on the subsequent purchaser.

This is a work of fiction. Names, characters, businesses, places, events and incidents are either the products of the author's imagination or used in a fictitious manner. Any resemblance to actual persons, living or dead, or actual events is purely coincidental.

Typeset courtesy of Wallace Author Services, United Kingdom
www.wallaceauthorservices.weebly.com

Cover design courtesy of Steve Williams
http://saa.co.uk/art/stevewilliamsart

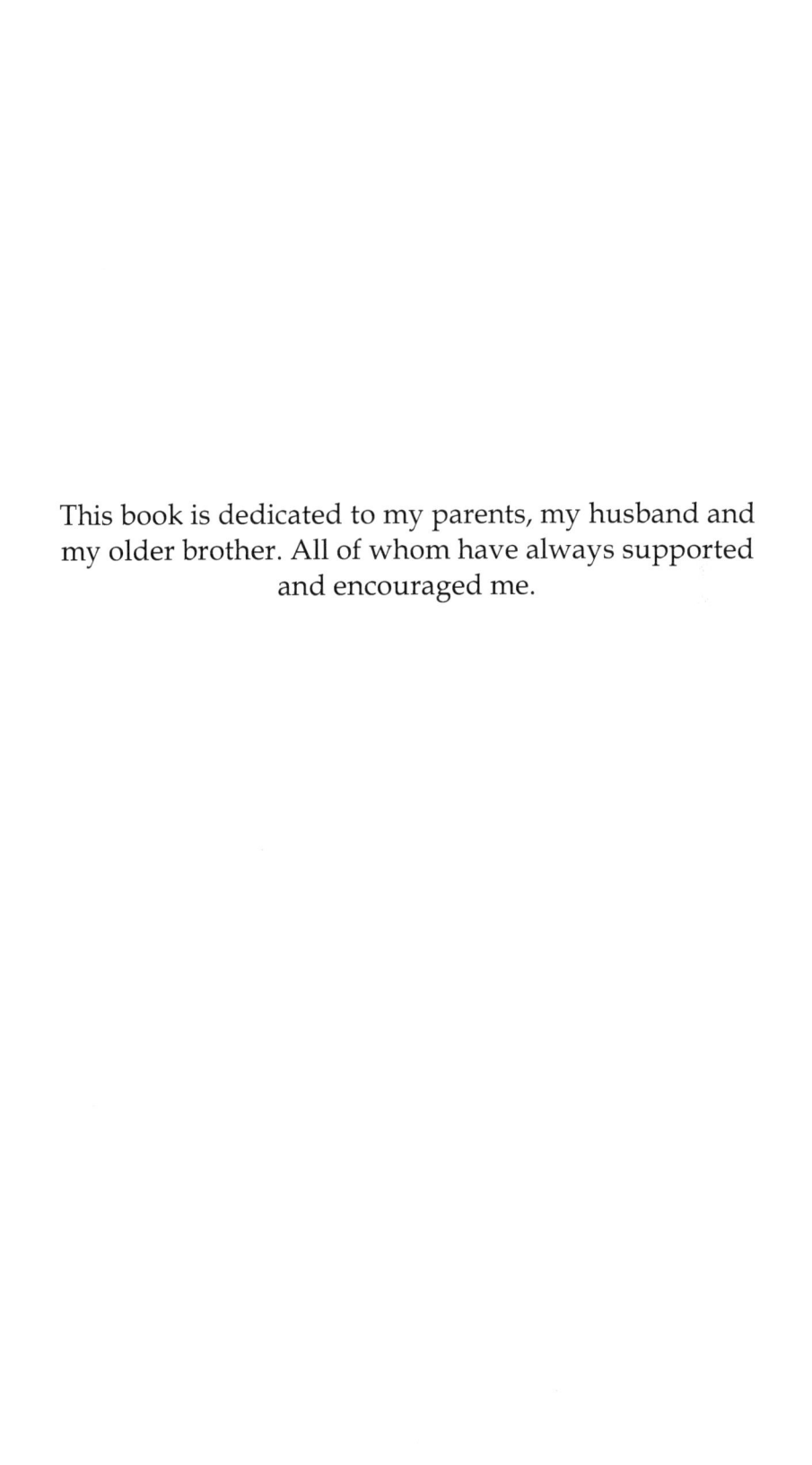

This book is dedicated to my parents, my husband and my older brother. All of whom have always supported and encouraged me.

Chapter One

It had been a bitterly cold and blustery winter, and the Scottish Borders had been hit repeatedly with wild snowy blizzards, leaving in their wake a white wintery world. As Louise stepped out of her old, battered car she was hit by a wall of freezing air that momentarily took her breath away. Straightaway, she felt a barrage of snowflakes striking her face; it felt as if she were being attacked by hundreds of small wasps determined to sting. She tucked her light auburn hair into her scarf, then pulled it higher up around her face, leaving only her eyes vulnerable to the wild weather. Louise opened the boot and without a second thought, Barney, her floppy-eared, black and tan dog, charged out with delight and immediately sank into the deep snow. After eating a mouthful, he bounded off up the path, eager to get started on their walk. She quickly closed the boot, locked the car, and followed him, struggling against the force of the furious snowflakes that seemed determined to make her turn back.

After ten freezing minutes of walking, the intensity of the falling snow began to subside; becoming wonderfully delicate flakes that danced their way gracefully to the ground. At first, she couldn't bring herself to uncover her face, not quite able to believe that the ferocious storm had calmed. When she eventually did, Louise was taken aback by the beauty that surrounded her. She'd seen these woods covered in snow before, but today there was something different in the air—almost magical. It became apparent that not a single person had ventured up this path for some considerable time, as there wasn't even a hint of a footprint. The woods spread out in front of her, the branches bowing under the weight of the layers of snow that rested on top of them. As Louise made her way further up the path, a small smile spread across her face, and she felt a small flutter of excitement as she allowed herself to truly appreciate the scene in front of her.

For as long as she could remember, Louise loved being out and about, walking the hills and woods. She had been raised in beautiful countryside by an older woman named Martha, who had found her alone and lost, walking the streets of Edinburgh as a young child. Louise had no memory of where she'd come from or who she was, and even after an extensive investigation, the mystery of her origin was never resolved.

Martha had adopted her and the two of them had moved into a remote cottage in the Scottish Borders. After many happy years together, Martha's health began to deteriorate. So, Louise spent a lot of her childhood looking after her, escaping the world whenever she could by walking. Not long after Louise's eighteenth birthday, Martha passed away peacefully in her sleep. Being her only family, the loss had been devastating. In her will, she had left everything to Louise, which had been a tremendous relief as it meant she could remain in the beautiful cottage she'd grown up in. In the years that followed, she was able to forge a somewhat successful career as a writer, earning just about enough to pay the bills.

Despite her isolation, Louise wasn't alone for long; on a rainy spring day, she'd walked out into her front garden and heard a soft whimper. After searching the bushes and flower beds, she had found a small, helpless puppy that couldn't have been more than six months old. She conducted an extensive search, but no one came forward to claim him, and so she kept him as her own, naming him Barney. It made her immeasurably happy that she was able to do for Barney exactly what Martha had done for her. Now, Louise smiled as she watched her faithful friend joyfully bounding up the path.

As she walked, Louise could feel her legs beginning to ache with the strain of walking through the deep snow. A sudden gust of ferocious wind took her breath away as it went straight through her warm clothing, reaching right into her core. She shivered and pulled her coat closer, generating as much warmth as possible. There must have been an interesting smell travelling on that cold gust of air, as Barney froze. He stuck his nose up into the air and perked up his normally floppy ears. At first, Louise didn't take too much notice as this was a relatively common occurrence on their walks. What did catch her attention was the sight of him bolting off into the woods, nose in the air and hackles slightly raised. This was so unlike Barney that before she even knew what she was doing, Louise was chasing after him, jumping over fallen branches and darting between the thick trees. Desperately trying to keep up with him.

As the wood became increasingly dense, the branches got lower and lower until eventually, they created thin barriers, scratching her face and hands as she ran through them. She barely had time to notice the wounds she was receiving, desperate to keep Barney in her sights. The trees were now so close together that no snow-covered the ground; just a layer of dead pine needles, branches and mud. Ahead of her, Barney came to an abrupt stop, hesitating, as if unsure as to which way to go next. Louise knew this was the perfect opportunity to catch up with him; her body, on the other hand, had other ideas. Involuntarily she too came to a stop, resting her hand against the nearest tree. She bent over, desperately trying to get her breath back.

'Barney!' she shouted through gasps of breath. 'Come here! NOW!'

For a second it looked as if he was turning back towards her, and she felt a surge of relief. However, without warning, he looked away again, his nose back in the air, and to Louise's horror he continued to run in the opposite direction. Obviously, he had once again picked up the scent of whatever he was following. Groaning, Louise took one last deep breath and continued her pursuit, becoming increasingly angry and frustrated. As they continued through the wood, the trees stood further apart, allowing the snow to penetrate the thick canopy, once again coating the ground. This made it incredibly slippery underfoot and Louise almost fell over on several occasions. Her voice was becoming hoarse from shouting Barney's name — which was proving to be entirely pointless as he wasn't paying her the slightest bit of attention.

All of a sudden Barney stopped and Louise darted towards him, determined to take this opportunity to finally catch him. As she did, however, she slipped and landed face first in the snow, barely inches away from the trunk of a particularity large tree. She flicked her head up to make sure that Barney was still there and quickly pulled herself back up to her feet. As Louise approached him, she saw Barney slowly sink to the ground, staring off into the distance, hackles raised. Something about his demeanour made her stop in her tracks. No longer was she worried about reaching him. There had been a strange shift in the atmosphere that filled her with instant dread. An uneasy feeling consumed her, and she froze, too afraid to move. She scanned the woods around her, suddenly certain, that she wasn't alone. Louise forced herself to keep walking and she nervously approached Barney, keeping a close eye on her surroundings. The closer she'd got to Barney, the greater the feeling of dread had become. So extreme was this sensation that now she'd caught up with him, she found herself instinctively crouching down as low as possible next to him.

'It's alright boy,' she whispered into his ear, 'I've got you.'

She clipped the lead onto his collar and as she did, she pulled him towards her and gently stroked the top of his head comfortingly. Even though she was desperate to leave, Louise found herself reluctant to move. A sensation, deep in her gut told her something or someone was lurking in the trees around her. Something evil.

Louise stayed in the same position for at least ten

minutes, with Barney glued to her side. Fearful, she saw everything that went on around her. Every bird that delicately darted through the trees, every shadow of light that leaked through the dense foliage, and every falling clump of snow that had become too heavy for the branch it had been resting on. After a while, she realised how ridiculous she must look, hiding for so long with absolutely no proof there was anything out there. Louise shivered; her clothing drenched in snow and mud, dampness penetrating deep into her body. She chastised herself for getting into such a state and decided that it was time to leave. Louise found she had to physically force herself to stand up and to stop searching her surroundings. She shivered again but couldn't say whether it was just a result of the cold or a part of her body telling her that she was in a great deal of danger. She tugged on Barney's lead to try and get him moving, but he wouldn't budge. She could feel panic rising within her. All she wanted to do was to get out of these woods and back to the safety of her nice warm house.

    Swearing quietly under her breath, she leaned closer towards him and whispered harshly, 'For God's sake Barney! Come on!' She then tugged on his lead slightly harder than she anticipated and in doing so, she accidentally pulled him right off his feet. Although she felt a pang of guilt, the shock did at least pull him out of his fear-driven state of temporary paralysis. He gave her a begrudging look, had a quick shake to remove drops of melted snow from his fur, and began to follow her back the way they came.

Chapter Two

Every now and then, as they walked, Barney would suddenly freeze, prick up his ears, and stick his nose back in the air. He would then stare transfixed in one direction, as if certain he could see someone off in the distance. Instinctively, Louise would also stop, follow his gaze and stand there for a while, staring at the seemingly empty horizon. She would then come to her senses, laugh at herself for allowing her imagination to run so wild, and continue on her way. After a while, if Barney tried to stop, Louise would force herself to keep going, refusing to give into her paranoia.

After walking somewhat aimlessly Louise hesitated. It was slowly dawning on her just how lost they were. When she'd been chasing Barney, she'd been so consumed with worry that she hadn't given a second thought to her surroundings. Now, absolutely nothing looked familiar. The woods had once again closed ranks, the trees standing side by side, as if regimented. Louise paused as she scanned the horizon, desperately hoping to see something familiar. Her heart sank when she realised that every direction looked identical, there was nothing to suggest that one way may be preferable to another. Louise sighed as she realised that she was just going to have to pick one and hope for the best. She decided to keep going in the same direction and hope she didn't somehow start walking in circles or worse, further into the deep woods that she knew stretched for miles. She continued on.

All of a sudden, she heard a strange sound forcing its way through the quiet woods; it made the hairs on the back of her neck stand bolt upright, and her heart seemed to stop dead in her chest. It was the howl of an animal, but like none she had ever heard before. It began quite quietly, as if miles off in the distance, then it started to build up as if it were moving closer, until it became so loud that Louise had to put her hands over her ears whilst Barney ran in frenzied circles around her. She looked around, terrified. Certain that any second she would see some sort of monster leap through the trees towards her, with razor-sharp teeth and thick pointed claws. When the sound abruptly stopped, she couldn't quite believe her ears. Slowly she brought her hands back down and waited, barely allowing herself to breathe as she listened closely. The only sound to be heard, however, was the occasional roar of the wind as it hit the tall trees.

After a while, she began to doubt whether she'd really heard that blood-curdling roar. She wondered if it may have been her already overactive imagination misinterpreting the sound of the wind crashing into the trees. She desperately tried to believe this was true, but it didn't stop her from moving much faster as she continued on through the woods. After another fifteen minutes or so of walking, Barney once again stopped.

Determined to keep going, Louise kept her eyes ahead and pulled him onwards. As she took another step forward, she gasped as something flashed past her through the woods to her right. She stopped and stared into the trees. Subconsciously holding her breath as she listened intently, but all she could hear was the sound of her own heart, beating loudly in her chest. Then, she saw something moving just ahead of her. Squinting, she realised that it was the silhouette of a person covered in a dark cloak, making their way through the trees. Louise hesitated; she couldn't quite believe that anybody else would be stupid enough to be so far into the woods on such a cold and wild morning. As the figure moved away, Louise followed, keeping a reasonable distance, unsure as to whether she should reveal herself or not. Barney seemed to be just as hesitant, sticking close to her side.

The figure ahead of her stumbled over the roots and dead branches scattered across the ground. They slumped forward slightly; arms stretched around themselves as if in pain. As Louise continued to watch, she realised that something was terribly wrong with this person; they seemed to have little or no control over their own feet as they dragged them across the ground. Eventually, the figure's foot got caught on the root of a large tree. They didn't seem to notice, however, as they did little to protect themselves as they crashed into the mud below them. Before she even knew what she was doing, Louise bolted out of her hiding place and headed toward the mass of cloth now lying in a heap on the floor, Barney, right by her side.

As Louise drew closer to the figure she hesitated for a moment. The hood of the dark blue cloak had fallen during the tumble and Louise was now able to see a mass of long silver hair spread across the ground, and the shape of a small woman huddled up into a ball. She was cradling her face in her hands and as Louise approached, she could see the shape shaking slightly, which led her to think that the person was silently crying.

'Excuse me,' she asked in a quiet voice, wary that her sudden presence may alarm the injured woman. There was no response or indication she had even heard. Louise took a step closer and bent down towards the woman, then in a slightly louder voice said, 'Excuse me? Are you alright?' There was a pause, and then the woman began to slowly move. She didn't look at Louise straight away. Instead, with her head facing downwards, she used the arm she'd been leaning on to push her body upright.

Her long hair fell around her shoulders and almost touched the ground. It was a wonderful, bright silver colour that almost seemed to glisten in the dark woods. It took Louise's breath away; she'd never seen anything quite like it before. The woman slowly lifted her head towards Louise, and as they made eye contact it became obvious that in her youth, she had been outstandingly beautiful. The thing that stood out above all else were her vibrant light green eyes; they bore into Louise as if she could see right through to her soul. Her porcelain skin seemed to almost glow, and perfectly complimented her unusual hair. She had a small delicate nose that was slightly pointed at the end, and below that, a small, gentle-looking mouth that would have brightened up any room once it spread into a smile. The closer she looked at her face, the more aware

Louise became that she had obviously fallen victim to the ever-constant changes brought about by time. It wasn't however, just age that had marked her, as multiple scars implied she had suffered a great number of hardships. As Louise's gaze settled on the woman's eyes again, she noticed that there was now a small sparkle of life in them. A broad smile appeared on her face—the type of smile you'd give a good friend that you hadn't seen for years.

'It's you!' she said, raising a hand towards Louise whilst the other wiped away the remnants of the tears she'd cried. 'You found me! I wasn't sure if you'd be ready.'

Louise gave her a puzzled look, then decided to ignore the comment, sure that the woman was confused, perhaps even delirious. 'Are you alright? You looked injured?'

The mysterious woman simply stared at Louise in wonder, before pulling herself back a little to lean against the trunk of the nearest tree. One hand weakly fell to the ground, whilst the other clasped the side of her stomach. The thick, dark blue cloak still hung over her shoulders, neatly tied around her neck. As she studied it closer, Louise noticed it was decorated with small, silver, sparkling stars, creating an uncanny similarity to a clear night sky. Her eyes moved to the woman's other garments, and she realised her whole outfit was quite unlike anything she'd seen before. She wore a fitted light green dress that stretched right down to her feet, covering a pair of petit leather shoes. Across the stomach of the dress were a series of vibrant gold panels that ended just at the hips before they spiralled down to the hem. At her waist, there was a dark blue belt, attached to which there was a small empty sheath that looked as if it had once held a dagger. The dress was splattered with mud and soaked through from the woman's fall. As she looked closer, however, she noticed that it wasn't just mud staining the dress, there was also a much darker and thicker substance. Louise was overcome with an overwhelming urge to throw up as it dawned on her that the unidentified substance gradually spreading across the dress was blood. Louise rushed forward to the woman and cried out in alarm, 'You're bleeding! What the hell's happened to you?'

The woman looked down at her stomach and moved her hand slightly to get a better look at her wound. Dismissing the horrific condition she was in, the woman merely smiled, 'Nothing can be done about that now. And anyway, there are far more important matters to discuss.'

'What on earth are you talking about!? You're bleeding, you could be seriously injured! What could be more important than that?' Louise asked with an incredulous look on her face.

'We don't have as much time as I would have liked,' the woman said, ignoring Louise's concern. 'But nothing can be done about that now.' She then gave Louise an earnest look. 'You really don't know anything, do you?' Louise felt a sudden rush of anger towards this infuriating woman, not sure whether to be insulted or not. But before she could say anything, the woman continued to talk. 'I had hoped you'd have remembered more. I mean, you are now well above the necessary age. But your true life is obviously still hidden from you!'

At this point, it was all becoming a little bit too much for Louise, she stared straight into the woman's face, hoping to finally get through to her. 'You are injured!' She said in a clear and simple voice. 'You clearly don't know what you're talking about. I need to get you to a doctor, or a hospital... Somebody who might be able to help you.' As she spoke, she pulled off her scarf, feeling an instant rush of cool air on her bare skin. 'There,' she said to the woman, pushing it hard onto her wound. 'Now keep some pressure on that, it may help stop the bleeding a little bit, at least until I think of what to do next.'

The strange woman did as she was told, and grimaced as she increased the pressure on the wound. She then looked back up at Louise as if studying her, a knowing smile spreading across her lips. 'My name is Clarris. You and I used to know each other very well. In fact...' She stopped at that moment, because a blood-curdling howl once again rang through the deep woods. Louise lifted her hands back up to her ears, wincing at the ear-piercing sound as it reverberated through her entire body. The howl became distinctly louder as if it were drawing closer, and as the sound intensified, the pain in the woman's stomach appeared to mirror it. Clarris doubled over, letting out a harrowing cry. Louise reached for her hand to try and comfort her. The second their skin made contact, she felt a strange sensation in her hand, almost like a surge of warmth, it lasted only for a second before disappearing. Not long after that, the howl gradually began to quieten until the woods were once again silent. Louise looked back down at Clarris and was surprised to see that she was now even paler than she

The Whisper of Calaresp

had been before, and somehow, she looked even older.
'We don't have much time,' she whispered in a small voice. 'He's coming.'
'Who is?' Louise demanded, temporarily distracted from the woman's bleeding wound.
Clarris raised her hand, looking around as if she'd heard something and Louise immediately fell silent. Eventually, she turned back to Louise, a determined look spreading across her pain-stricken face. 'I'll have to do something to hide us from him, to make it more difficult for him to track us. At least for a short time.'
Slowly, Clarris raised her hands into the air. Completely neglecting the scarf that had previously been pushed up against her wound, it fell to the ground drenched in blood. Louise went to pick it up but stopped as Clarris moved her hands in front of her, palms flat. A fine golden powder now spread evenly across them. Her eyes were shut and she quietly mumbled incomprehensible words under her breath. As she did so, the powder glowed, then slowly darkened. Louise edged closer towards her, not quite able to believe what was going on. All of a sudden, the powder transformed into a small black cloud, floating just above her hands.
Slowly but gradually, more and more of the substance seemed to be materialising out of nowhere, until it had tripled in size. Clarris turned the palms of her hands until they were facing away from her. As she did the black cloud remained in place. As Clarris spread her hands outwards it grew even bigger, Louise fell back in alarm as it quickly engulfing them both. Louise could still see out of it, but now, the surrounding wood appeared blurred and misshapen,

as if it wasn't really there. As if everything around them were just a vague and unclear dream.

'Now, anyone outside of this circle won't be able to see us,' Clarris said, smiling slightly at the look of shock on Louise's face. 'They'll have a vague idea that there's something here, but their eyes won't allow them to concentrate on this spot for long enough to actually identify it. If I weren't so weak, I would have been able to hide us completely, but this should do the trick. In fact, we're lucky that these woods are as thick as they are, as the darkness will work in our favour.' Clarris grimaced for a few moments as the pain momentarily became too much for her. She took a deep breath before she continued talking. 'It won't hide us for too long, I don't think I can hold on for much longer, if I get any weaker the spell will disappear.'

Louise was suddenly brought back to her senses. She reached over and picked up the scarf. Kneeling beside her, she pushed it into the ever-darkening wound. Clarris took a few seconds to catch her breath, obviously in a great deal of pain. As she did, Louise thought about what had just happened, and to her surprise, she realised that although she'd been taken aback at first by what she could only describe as magic, the more she thought about it, the more familiar it seemed. At that moment she was swamped by an overwhelming sensation that there was something very important about her past she'd forgotten. As she looked back at Clarris, she had an almost desperate desire to hear everything that this woman had to say. A part of her still felt the need to try and get help, but she knew, deep down, there wouldn't be time. She perched next to the injured woman before she said in a quiet, sympathetic voice, 'What do you want to tell me?'

Clarris looked back at her and despite the pain she was experiencing, she smiled. 'Well, as I said, my name is Clarris, and you and I once knew each other very well. In fact, you once recognised me as what you would call a nanny. In Calaresp, where we are from, we would say…'

'Alat,' interrupted Louise, confused as to how she had known.

'Yes, that's right,' Clarris said with an even wider smile on her face. 'You'll find yourself remembering more and more now that you're in the presence of this.' She reached underneath her cloak and pulled out a silver chain with a small pendant at the end. Clarris briefly cradled in it her hands, before holding it up to allow Louise to take a closer look. It was a small, silver pendant, one side of which was circular, with some form of mark etched into it, whilst the other side was flat with a silver rim, the centre was pitch black. As she stared Louise felt sure she could see a small bright light appearing in the darkness. Then as quickly as it appeared, it had vanished. Louise reached her hand out to touch it, but Clarris pulled it back and once again cradled it in her only free hand.

Clarris looked back up at Louise with an apologetic smile. 'Before I let you touch it, in fact before I let you have it, there is more I wish to tell you. You may find this hard to believe but I come from another world, a world that runs parallel to this one, you have come to call home. It's a world called Calaresp, and it's where you are originally from. It's a truly tremendous world filled with magic, mysterious creatures and terrifying monsters.' Clarris coughed, then took a few moments to catch her breath before she continued talking. 'These two worlds run so closely together that they occasionally collide, and when they do, windows are created. Whenever this happens you get a brief glimpse into each alternative world. That is pretty much where how legends of this world originated.' She paused when she looked at the confusion on Louise's face. 'Sorry, I'm not explaining this very well. Let me give you a few examples,' Clarris paused and seemed to consider. 'The Loch Ness Monster,' she said suddenly, looking back up at Louise with a smile. 'In Calaresp, we have humongous sea monsters that freely roam the wild North seas. They have occasionally been glimpsed through these windows, and so, on Earth, a myth was created.'

A small laugh of surprise escaped Louise. These exclamations may have seemed farfetched, but somehow Louise knew this woman was speaking the truth.

Clarris carried on talking, ignoring Louise's interruption. 'Another example's fairies: here they are deemed to be pure myth, fantasy even. In Calaresp, they can be seen everywhere. We know them as Krystics. At some point, however, they will have been seen through one of these windows and are therefore etched into the Earth's history. There are hundreds of examples like this, but I'm afraid that I don't currently have time to delve into the matter any further. We have far more important things that we need to discuss, and quickly. You, Louise, are originally from Calaresp. You are the last remaining member of the Clarest family who once ruled over the Northern regions and a large majority of the Southern regions.' Clarris was now speaking quickly, the pain almost becoming too much for her. 'About twenty years ago there was a great rebellion led by a man named Brisheit, who had once been the General of your parents' army. He and his followers killed your parents and then tried to kill you. A few of us however, loyal to the throne were able to smuggle you out and bring you to this world. I placed a spell on you so that you would forget your old life, at least until you were reunited with this.'

She once again held up the necklace and Louise was startled to see that the centre was no longer black; the light she had thought she'd seen before was now very clear and it swirled around through the darkness, leaving behind it a trail of light creating a strange flame-like symbol. Clarris watched as Louise stared at it.

'This pendant is called the Whisper and it has been an heirloom in the Clarest family for hundreds of years.' said Clarris. 'It's believed that you're great-great-great-grandmother created it to increase her own abilities and in doing so became the most powerful woman of all time. She misused this power and in turn, it corrupted her and turned her into a cruel and selfish leader who instigated many bloody and brutal wars right across Calaresp. Her son stood up against her and almost died in the process, but he did finally manage to stop her. Once he did, he removed the pendant and cast a spell using the very oldest of magic which bound her powers. He then banished her from the Kingdom. At first, it's believed that he was reluctant to use the pendant in case it corrupted him, as it had his mother. He needn't have worried though, for as soon as his mother left the kingdom, the pendant which had previously shone brightly turned black as night and remained like that for years. However, it was still common knowledge that the pendant had the potential to wield unimaginable powers. So, to keep it safe, it has been passed down from generation to generation. Then to everyone's disbelief, on the day you were born the pendant began to change; light appeared in the darkness and as you got older, the pendant shone brighter. It soon became evident that you held a power within you quite unlike any that had been seen for many years. It was decided that the 'Whisper' was going to be passed down to you from your mother as soon as you reached sixteen, when your abilities would begin to appear. Sadly, she died before she had the chance. But, a group of us who still refuse to be ruled by Brisheit have kept the Whisper secret and hidden from him, for all this time.'

Suddenly a memory, long forgotten, flashed into Louise's mind; the memory of her as a small child, wearing a beautiful vibrant blue dress, her hair neatly tied back into a plait. She was laughing. Beside her there stood a man wearing a blue shirt almost identical to her dress and a pair of plain dark trousers, a sword sat neatly in its sheath at his waist. He too was laughing and looked lovingly between Louise and the woman to her side, a beautiful woman wearing a deep violet dress that reached right down to her feet. It had intricate lace sleeves that looked so delicate they could have been spun by spiders. Although the memory only lasted for a second, she instantly knew that the two people she'd seen had been her parents.

'What would he do with this Whisper if he had it?' Louise asked, once she had recovered from the image that had just burst into her mind.

'This pendant holds an incredible amount of power and somehow Brisheit has discovered that he can unlock this power is by soaking the pendant in the blood of a worthy descendant.' At this point, Clarris looked at Louise with a sympathetic look on her face. 'You are the only member of the Clarest family that the Whisper has responded to for a very long time. You are the only one with the potential to wield this magnificent, yet terrible power and so you are the only one who can unlock it.'

Chapter Three

Louise once again heard the awful howling pierce her surroundings, fortunately, the noise was muffled by the dark cloud protecting them. Clarris paused for a second, clasping the scarf closer to her wound, then looked back at Louise and continued to talk. 'For years Brisheit has been content being a self-proclaimed Emperor. He gave little thought as to what had happened to you, presuming you to be dead and so he didn't think it worth his time looking for a pendant that would never work. A rumour began to circulate that you were still alive, safely hidden, and when this news reached Brisheit, he immediately began to investigate. He captured one of my closest allies…' At this point, Clarris's eyes began to glisten, and she took a second to collect herself before carrying on. 'Apparently, he tortured her to the point of death before she eventually told him the truth. He is renowned for using brutal and unimaginable techniques. She must have suffered excruciating pain before finally giving in to him. The first thing he did was try and get hold of the Whisper, but fortunately, I got away. Some of the others were able to create a decoy, giving me time to pass through a window to get me here. Brisheit however, realised he was being deceived, and he sent what seemed like his entire army to capture me. He must have known I was making my way to you. A few of his men caught me off guard and stabbed me with a knife poisoned with deadly potions. I was just able to escape.'

'How did you know I was going to be here though?' Louise asked. 'I only ended up here because Barney ran off. And how did you get through to this world, if the portals between the two worlds are only temporary?'

'There are powders that can be bought in Calaresp that can create temporary windows. They don't last long and they are extremely difficult to get hold of, Brisheit has his own personal supply. As for you being here — of course you were going to be! This is your destiny; fate would always have led you to this exact point at this exact time whether your charming dog had been involved or not.'

Another howl erupted around them, this time it was joined by a second. Even through the cloud, it was obvious they'd become louder and it seemed as if they were considerably closer. A look of horror spread across Clarris's face and a small, involuntary whimper escaped through her lips.

'They're here,' she whispered. 'You must flee.'

Without warning the protective cloud that had enshrouded them fell to the ground like droplets of rain. The woods returned to normal and the howls became almost deafening.

Louise felt her heart beating in her chest, as fear spread through her, a sense of emptiness and loss welled up within her as she grabbed the woman's shoulders.

'I can't leave you! I can't just leave you here to die!'

'Here, take this; it will help you to unlock your forgotten memories. Wait until it's safe and then return to this same spot. You have to go back to Calaresp, you aren't safe in this world anymore. He'll find you. You must return home where there are still people eager to help you, to protect you.' She said quickly, 'When you return to this spot, you'll be able to create a portal. Once in Calaresp head north towards Pologor, you'll find help there. Now you have to leave!'

'But I can't leave you. Please let me help you!' Louise pleaded.

'No,' Clarris replied firmly. 'The wreag's already have my scent. If they catch me, they'll catch you too and then both of these worlds will be in unbelievable danger. Run! Brisheit and his army are coming. Don't let them find you. The poison coursing through my veins is killing me anyway. Nothing can be done for me. Now go!'

As the howling sound became almost unbearable, Louise gave Clarris one last fleeting glance before submitting to the dying woman's wish. She turned on her heels, grabbed Barney's lead, and bolted through the woods away from the sound. When she'd run a reasonable distance, she flung herself behind a large tree and looked back at the spot in which Clarris lay. The injured woman was just within her sight. Still reluctant to completely abandon Clarris, Louise turned around, her back pressed against the trunk of the tree. She was filled with an extreme sense of foreboding, somehow aware that what she was about to see would change her life, her world, forever. Nevertheless, she couldn't bring herself to move. What was now a chorus of howls struck through the woods like a dagger. She could feel Barney shaking and he hid his head behind her leg as if certain that Louise was able to protect him.

Louise took a deep breath and tried to force herself to look around the tree to see what was going on. Every time she tried, however, she found that her hands began to shake, and her heart fluttered nervously in her chest. Aware that if she were to look, she'd finally see what horrific creatures were capable of making such an unearthly sound.

It was at this point that the howling stopped, almost as abruptly as it had started. As if a spell had been broken, Louise began to regain control of herself. Her curiosity got the better of her and before the crippling fear could catch up with her again, she slowly and cautiously moved her head alongside the trunk of the tree until she could look back at the spot where she had stood moments before. A huge part of Louise's brain was screaming at her to turn and run, but she forced herself to stay where she was. She didn't even notice the wet snow being absorbed into her jeans as her knees pressed into the ground. As soon as her eyes rested on Clarris the howling began again. Louise automatically gripped the tree. As her fingertips dug further into the ancient bark, she didn't even notice the small collection of young woodlice crawling out from the depths of the tree and across her fingers. The woods seemed to get darker and the air around her chilled until Louise could feel her entire body erupting in goosebumps.

The body of Clarris remained slumped lifelessly against the tree. Louise tried to squint to see whether the injured woman was still breathing, but she was just too far away to know for sure. Something else in the distance caught her eye and Louise saw the outline of a large, bear-like creature, slowly approaching. It raised its large head, revealing a long, sharp snout and howled.

Being in such close proximity, made the already awful sound a hundred times worse as it seemed to resonate and fill every orifice of her body. She flung herself back behind the tree, terrified that the wreag had seen her. She felt like screaming and had to force her hand over her mouth to stop herself from involuntarily submitting to the overwhelming urge.

When the woods were once again silent Louise gingerly took her hands from her mouth. Carefully she poked her head out from behind the tree and immediately, her eyes fell on the form of a monster in front of her. Nothing could have prepared her for what she saw.

Making its way towards the injured woman was the creature Clarris had referred to as a wreag. Its body was shaped like that of a wolf, but its size was more comparable to that of a small bear. A shard of light pierced through the dark woods, lighting up the ground as if a spotlight had been turned on. As it stepped into the light Louise found she was incapable of stopping her mouth from making a barely audible gasp. Almost as quickly as it had happened, she threw her hand up to cover her mouth to prevent any further involuntary outbursts. The beast had thick, coarse black fur so dark that when it stood in the shadow of the trees you could barely see it. Poking through were strands of an incredibly pointed and visibly sharp undercoat. The wreag lifted an alarmingly large paw as it stalked towards Clarris, razor-sharp claws protruding through its thick fur. Louise could see Clarris stir, then open her eyes wide in alarm at the sight of the beast in front of her.

The wreag growled and Louise could see a set of fierce, long, and particularly sharp teeth reflecting in the sunlight. It had two abnormally long fangs, stretching down below the edges of its mouth. The largely white fangs were stained with a deep rich red, that Louise knew deep in the pit of her stomach to be blood. It wasn't fresh blood though: these stains had obviously built up over a long period of time, from countless victims.

The beast thrust its gruesome face right up to Clarris's. The woman turned her head to the side, desperately trying to keep away from those large blood-stained fangs. The wreag lowered its head, sniffing deeply until it found the deadly injury at her side. It pushed its muzzle into the wound, still sniffing. Groaning with pain, Clarris feebly tried to push the beast's muzzle away, but it seemed to enjoy the smell of her blood and so continued even more intensely.

Louise had to force herself to stay where she was, as every particle of her being screamed at her to rush forward and help. Even though she barely knew her, she had felt an inexplicable link to the woman. It was for this exact reason she didn't allow herself to intervene in the events unfolding in front of her; she knew deep down that Clarris was beyond help, that she was going to die no matter what she did. She simply had to allow the woman to continue down the road she was destined to travel and allow her to have her last request.

A new sound echoed through the woods and Louise finally found herself looking away from the torturous scene. It was a strange sound, similar to that of a whistle only lower and louder than any whistle Louise had ever heard. The wreag immediately stepped back from Clarris, threw its head up into the air and howled. The sound was joined by others until the great chorus began again. Louise quickly put her hands over her ears, only blocking out a fraction of that horrific sound. This time, however, she didn't hide behind the tree, she scanned the horizon waiting with bated breath to see just how many more creatures there were. The howling stopped and the woods grew silent. The wreag remained perfectly and eerily still, whilst Clarris writhed in pain.

The sun suddenly vanished, and the woods became colder and darker. Through the darkness, Louise was able to see a pair of bright red eyes appear on the horizon. It was quickly joined by a second, then a third pair, until eventually the entire far side of the woods seemed to be filled with red. All at once, they began to move forward, getting closer and closer to Clarris until she was surrounded by at least eighteen more wreags. They continued to approach in a long line until, just a couple of feet away from her, they all stopped simultaneously, as if they had hit an invisible barrier.

The wreag that had been next to Clarris moved away until it stood just in front of the others, where they remained, perfectly still, as if waiting. Louise pushed herself slightly further from the tree, desperate to see what was going to happen next. Her hand moved to the ground, allowing for a better view. She was so intent on seeing what else was going to join these horrible creatures that she barely noticed her hand slowly slipping in the wet, cold mud; suddenly, she lost all balance and crashed to the ground. Heart racing, she remained perfectly still, lying in her bed of mud, snow and twigs. She found herself desperately praying that the pack of ferocious wreags hadn't heard her. Out of the corner of her eye, could see Barney facing her, still lying flat to the ground but attempting to edge towards her, away from the relative safety of the tree. Louise raised the treacherous hand that had led to her fall, to signal to the dog to stay, whilst quietly mouthing the command. Fortunately, he seemed to understand and plonked his head back onto the forest floor, watching her.

    She remained where she was for a little longer, but every fibre of her being longed for the comparable safety of the tree trunk. Slowly but surely, she turned and raised herself from the ground very slightly and began edging herself back to Barney. Louise concentrated on her original hiding place and nothing else. She barely noticed the state of her hands, covered in a thick layer of mud with dabbles of blood from branches and small stones tearing into her palms. When she reached the tree, Louise rolled onto her back and waited for a few moments to allow her beating heart to steady itself. She was painfully aware as to how noisy her fall had been and she felt sure that any second now one of those monstrous wreags would appear and she would come face to face with those sharp, deadly fangs.

Chapter Four

After a few long minutes, Louise finally began to consider the possibility her fall may have gone unnoticed. Peeking out from her hiding place she was relieved to find the wreags had remained where they were, guarding Clarris. Movement beyond them, in the darkness of the woods, caught Louise's attention and she squinted to get a better look at the shapes drawing closer to the injured woman. It almost looked as if the entire wood had upped sticks and begun moving. Louise felt an intense stab of fear as she saw a long line of large and frighteningly muscular soldiers step out of the darkness.

Each soldier wore thick, dark metal armour that covered their chests and arms. They had what seemed like leather padding across their legs. Across their waists, they each had belts into which various weapons were stored. Some had sheathed longswords, others had small daggers hanging on both sides of their hips, and a few had large, dirty axes, their sharp edges sticking out precariously from the top of their belts. The soldiers were battle-worn, covered in mud and blood. Many of the men had deep scars etched across their faces, some were even missing eyes and ears. They were almost the epitome of the old Saxon warriors.

All of a sudden some of the men in the centre of the line moved to the side, creating a large gap in their ranks. A few seconds later a dark shape, considerably larger than any of the others, stepped through. The men bowed their heads slightly as he passed and he stepped forwards into the light. Louise may have thought that the army looked ferocious, but they were nothing in comparison to the presence of this one man.

He too wore armour, but his was significantly superior to those around him. His, was a deep dark red, like that of blood. It covered his chest, legs and upper arms. On the lower part of his arms, he wore pitch black gauntlets with matching gloves. On his feet, he wore substantial black leather boots. A thick black belt sat at his waist with a large, sheathed sword hanging on his left-hand side, on his right, there was a highly decorated dagger. He had thick, shoulder-length, dark grey hair and a large, bushy, well-kept beard of the same colour. On his head there rested a platinum crown encrusted with sparkling green jewels.

He stepped out from behind the line of men and looked at Clarris lying on the ground. A loud booming, bark-like laugh burst from his cruel mouth echoing through the woods. She saw Clarris weakly lift her head so that she made eye contact with the towering man. They stared at each other and suddenly something clicked with Louise—she became certain that this man must be the notorious Brisheit. She was filled with a staggering feeling of dread. Even though she had no memory of it, the thought that this man had killed her parents, her family, caused her a stab of pain and she felt tears prickling her eyes. He laughed again and then turned away from her to talk to one of his men.

Louise felt Barney move even closer, trembling. Glancing down, to make sure he was alright, she rested a reassuring hand on his back. When she looked back up there was another man stood next to Brisheit, whispering into his ear. Louise hadn't noticed him at first, because, in comparison to the army of monstrously tall and deranged-looking men, he wasn't remotely intimidating or interesting. He was small and fat, and rather than having a weapon at his side he had a thick black whip curled around at his overweight waist. On the other side of him hung the carcasses of three dead animals that looked similar to rabbits apart from the fact that they were twice the size and covered in dark orange fur. He had a small face that looked distinctly odd in comparison to the fat body upon which it was perched. He had small beady eyes, a long nose covered in dark ugly warts, and a small thin-lipped mouth that moved very slightly as he whispered into his leader's ear. Judging by his demeanour, it was obvious that he wasn't a soldier. Louise suspected that he was in charge of the horrible wreags, with a whip to control them and animal carcasses presumably to feed them. The sheer thought of these beasts eating was enough to send a shiver down her spine.

Louise was distracted when the short man pointed a short, dirty, podgy finger just to the right of her position. Louise felt her heartbeat quicken. She forced herself to follow the direction of that sickening finger and had to clasp a hand over her mouth to stop herself from letting out a scream. The beast which had previously been stood over Clarris was now heading in Louise's direction. The horrible creature's nose was pointed upwards smelling its surroundings and its large, clawed paws were padding towards Louise's hiding spot. Fear took over her entire body and as she realised exactly how much danger she was in. Panicked breaths left her in short and shaky gasps which she desperately tried to control. She didn't want to do anything that wouldn't attract the wreag's attention. She crouched further to the ground, hoping that it would prevent her from being so visible. Louise was painfully aware that there was nothing she could do about the smells that drifted invisibly from her own body.

It stepped closer and she could feel herself fill with an overwhelming urge to run. Sudden movement behind the approaching beast caught her attention: Brisheit was interrogating Clarris. He bent towards her and slapped her hard across the face. Louise clenched her fist, her anger causing her to temporarily ignore the danger of the slowly approaching wreag. She'd only just met this strange woman, but she knew deep down that Clarris had been an important figure in her life. So, with every strike from Brisheit she too felt a bolt of pain, wishing in desperation there was some way she could help.

Subconsciously, Louise's hand had moved to her pocket and found the small pendant that Clarris had given her. Unbeknown to Louise, as she grasped the Whisper in her hand it slowly began to glow. To start with it looked like the small flame of a candle at the end of its wick, about to go out. As her grip tightened and the more impassioned Louise became the brighter the Whisper grew.

Oblivious to Louise, the Whisper had begun to create a protective bubble around her, blocking her scent from the nose of the horrible beast stalking towards her. Louise saw the wreag, mere feet away from her, suddenly stop in its tracks and raise its head, looking confused and disorientated. The men behind the wreag looked up and began watching the bemused creature. Brisheit let out a frustrated roar, clearly having hoped the wreag had picked up on an important scent. In response, the small fat man darted forwards clumsily. He ran straight towards the wreag, unwrapping the whip from his waist. As he approached the creature, he dramatically cracked the whip, the end of which smacked into the wreag's back end causing it to yelp and jump around again, teeth bared. The small man simply lifted the whip into the air threateningly and as he did, the wreag submitted, closing its mouth, hiding away the bulk of its sharp, bloodied teeth. It then crouched low to the ground, submitting to the man's authority.

He opened his mouth and spoke quietly to the beast. Louise couldn't quite make out what the man had said but the beast gave one begrudging look back towards Louise's hiding place, before returning to the other wreags. Louise was able to see Brisheit's mouth moving as his attention returned to the barely conscious Clarris. From the safety of the tree, all she could hear was the repulsive man mumbling. She was desperate to find out what he was saying. Louise edged herself further forwards as if an extra few inches would make the slightest bit of difference. She saw Brisheit once again move in and slap the woman. Clarris barely reacted as his thick, dirty hand collided with the side of her face.

Chapter Five

Louise's grip tightened around the Whisper, and once again it began to glow, understanding her desperate desire to hear what Brisheit was saying. As magic emitted invisibly from the pendant the voices slowly became clearer.

'Well,' said a gruff voice, so close, Louise almost jumped out from her hiding place.

'You must have known you'd never escape us, especially with that wound,'

Louise was momentarily confused as to how she could suddenly hear him, but was soon distracted when she saw him draw a small dagger. He slowly put the edge close to her face and pressed it into her skin. Louise could see the look of defiance on Clarris's face as she refused to be intimidated.

Brisheit stared at Clarris with a wry smile. 'By now, the poison in that wound will be fully absorbed into every single inch of your body.' He paused as if to let her take that news in. 'You and I both know that you won't be able to escape us this time.' He slowly dragged the dagger down her face, leaving an indented, bloody trail down her cheek. He moved his face so close that their noses were almost touching, and he whispered, 'You may as well tell me where the Whisper is.' He raised the dagger again and did the same on the other cheek. 'Then you can tell me where I can find the princess.'

Clarris opened her mouth as if to talk, but she was overwhelmed with a fit of coughing. Louise could see her raising her hand and wiping her mouth. When she brought her hand back down again, she could see it was stained with a dark purple liquid. She seemed to take a few moments to recover, then she opened her mouth again and, in a grasping, rasping voice she whispered, 'Never.' With that, she spat out more of the dark substance in his face.

Immediately, the wreag closest to Brisheit leapt forward. Filled with anger and fury, it snarled at Clarris, who flung her face backwards away from the revolting, sharp, blood-covered teeth. Saliva dribbled from its mouth as it growled angrily at her. Louise could hear a quiet whimper escape from Clarris's tight lips as it edged closer and closer. Brisheit eventually held a large dirty hand up; the wreag gave him a begrudging look but almost immediately turned away and stalked back into the ranks.

Brisheit waited until the beast had settled before turning his glance back towards Clarris and a smile once again spread across his ugly face. He chuckled slightly before saying: 'Well, that is a shame. If you had helped me, I might have been able to help you. As it is, you only give me two choices.' Brisheit stood upright, moving slightly away from Clarris. He balanced the dagger between the palm of one hand and the tip of the index finger of the other, before he threw it in the air and caught it again. He then looked back at Clarris, swinging the dagger around with his hand as if it were just a child's toy. 'I could either let you die naturally from the poison that is seeping through every vein in your body...' he pointed the dagger towards her wound, 'or I could leave you as a nice snack for my beloved wreags.'.

As he spoke, three wreags stepped forward, staring at Clarris hungrily. One of them moved forward until it stood beside Brisheit, whose large hand moved to the creature's head and affectionately patted its harsh fur. The beast continued to stare at Clarris, occasionally letting out a quiet snarl in which its lip would curl back to show its horrendous teeth.

Louise shuddered involuntarily, whilst Clarris appeared to be unperturbed, she maintained a look of defiance as she stared straight back at Brisheit. An evil smile spread across his face, creasing his eyes and making them look even more sinister. He studied her for a second and then, leaning towards her, he said in a cruel and malicious voice: 'You know that they'll rip you to shreds, piece by piece?'

He raised a hand to the air, then slowly curled his outstretched fingers into a large fist. As he did, every single wreag began to move forward, licking their lips and murmuring in hunger. Just as one got close enough it looked like it was about to take a bite, Brisheit uncurled his fist. Even though the beasts weren't facing him they somehow knew the command had been made and simultaneously stopped their advance.

'Now,' he said, 'leaving you to die from the poisons in your body would be relatively painless. At least, in comparison to them.' He smiled and looked at the wreags waiting hungrily beside him, still staring at Clarris.

'I will never tell you!' Clarris replied. 'I would rather die than tell you, and I don't care how, I'm dying anyway!'

Brisheit's smile vanished. He wrapped a large, dirty hand tightly around her small throat.

'I know why you're here,' he said through gritted teeth. 'I know you brought the Whisper into this world, and I know the only person you would have given it to is the princess. If, of course, you know where she is.' He laughed lightly and slackened his grip on her throat, leaving her to gasp and wheeze as she slumped back against the tree. 'If you give me the Whisper and tell me the location of the princess, all of this pain and fear that you are experiencing will be over.'

A look of amusement broke out on Clarris's face. She then let out a quiet yet sharp laugh that seemed to erupt from her delicate, injured body. 'Never. I lived my life for the Calaresp family, and I will gladly die for them.' Once again, the dying woman was overcome by a fit of harsh and chesty coughing.

Brisheit watched her with a look of utter contempt. His hand flew quickly forward and grasped the side of her cheeks until her lips were scrunched together. With the other hand, he pulled his dagger forward and with remarkable speed, sliced it deep into her cheek. Blood streamed down her cheek, red to begin with but quickly turning purple as more oozed out.

'Tell me where it is!' he screeched in her face, spots of saliva firing out of his mouth. 'Tell me where it is!!'

Louise felt a sudden stab of unease spread through her body as her heart gave an unexpected and intense flutter. She began to worry that despite her resolve, Clarris could very easily give in to the brutality of this man. Her grip tightened on the locket as if she were protecting it.

Brisheit stared at Clarris for a few moments longer, then sharply turned back to his men.

'Search her!' he screamed, flicking a hand carelessly in the air. Within a few moments, two of the larger men in the army stepped forwards. One's nose had obviously been broken as it leant to one side quite dramatically. The other had a large horrific scar stretching from his right eyebrow, through his eye, and right down to the corner of his lip. Both men had their small beady eyes fixed firmly on Clarris. They approached her hungrily, the one with the broken nose roughly pulled her up by her arm. She almost immediately collapsed to the ground, despite his firm grip. The other man briskly reached down and grabbed her other arm, pulling the remainder of her upwards. Their spare hands unceremoniously groped every inch of her body, searching for the missing Whisper. As they searched, jeers shot up from men behind them. Louise shut her eyes and looked away; she had no desire to see Clarris being manhandled so cruelly.

She looked back just as they finished their search. As soon as they were done, they let her go and she immediately collapsed to the ground in a crumpled heap. She lay where she was for a few seconds and then slowly began dragging her broken and dishevelled body back against the tree. The purple substance was now gushing from the wound on her waist.

Meanwhile, the two soldiers turned abruptly away from her and signalled to Brisheit that they had found nothing by raising their empty hands towards him. The one with the large scar said in a brisk low voice, 'She had nothing on her, Sir.'

Brisheit simply nodded and indicated for them to move back into rank with a quick hand gesture. He moved to Clarris in two quick strides, and just as she had gotten herself back into position, he grabbed her by the shoulders and picked her up as if she were a rag doll. He shook her violently and all Louise could see was her head flicking backwards and forwards uncontrollably.

'Tell me where it is, you pathetic woman!' Brisheit screamed with streams of spit and saliva cascading from his mouth. He stopped shaking her and pulled her face right up to his. 'Whether you tell me or not, you *know* I'll find her.'

Clarris opened her mouth to protest but gave in to the pressure being put on her body and her head slumped forward as she fell unconscious. Brisheit let go of her body and for the second time, she went crashing lifelessly to the ground. Clarris was now facing Louise's hiding place allowing her a clear view of her face. Louise stared in horror as she realised that Clarris's face was now covered in dark blue bulging veins.

Brisheit turned away from her and walked back towards his men. In a remorseless and cold voice said, 'Let the wreags feed. They deserve a good meal.'

The short, plump man in control of the beasts stepped forward nervously, and in a stuttering voice said: 'But sir! Will the poison not harm the wreags if they were to eat her!?'

Brisheit laughed deeply and looked at the wreags

with almost an affectionate look. 'A normal wreag, yes, it would probably die. But these beautiful creatures...' he stoked the head of a wreag affectionately. 'You should know by now you foolish man, that these creatures are unlike any wild wreag. They are far more intelligent, brutal and cunning. They can see perfectly in both night and day and they can track the faintest scent. Their teeth are capable of breaking through practically anything.' At that point, he moved his hand to the creature's lip, lifting it upwards to show its horrendous teeth. 'Their skin is impossibly tough and even the sharpest sword couldn't break through it. Their immune to all poisons and toxins. So, no, this pathetic woman won't be able to harm them.'

Brisheit looked down at the squat little man with a look of disgust. 'I hired you because I thought you understood these beautiful creatures. If you're not up to the job, then you know what will happen to you.' The stout man squealed and ran back to hide in the mass of huge soldiers. Brisheit looked back at the wreags and in a quiet and surprisingly gentle voice, he said 'Eat.'

The wreags moved so quickly that Louise didn't get the chance to look away before she saw one of the wreags wrapping its razor-sharp teeth through the top of Clarris's left shoulder, whilst another pierced its teeth through her left shin. Louise heard a horrific crunch as the teeth penetrated the bone. Louise launched herself back behind the tree, ferociously wishing that she had just left when Clarris had told her to.

Chapter Six

Louise knew she'd stayed for too long; it was time to go. She took a final look around the tree, in the hope she would find the perfect opportunity to get away unnoticed. The wreags were still ripping apart what remained of Clarris, whilst Brisheit watched them with a hungry expression, as if he desired to join them.

Without instruction, the large man with the broken nose — who Louise presumed to be Brisheit's second-in-command — moved to his leader's side. He seemed reluctant to disturb the foreboding man, to interrupt him whilst he was enjoying the wreags feasting.

Eventually, Brisheit looked around at the man waiting beside him, pulling his gaze from the bloodshed.

In an intimidated and quiet voice, the man said: 'Excuse me Sir, what do you want us to do now, regarding the Whisper and the princess?' He was reluctant to make eye contact with his leader and it wasn't until he finished his question that he looked up.

An expression of sheer rage flashed across Brisheit's face as he glared angrily at the man. 'She is no princess. How many times do I have to tell you?' As he spoke, he gently slapped the man on the cheek as if trying to pound his point through the man's skin. 'The Clarest monarchs are no more, I killed every single one of them, apart from that one girl. So please tell me how she can be called a princess if there is no Clarest family?! The girl is nothing, she has nothing. The only thing of importance about her is her blood.' He looked down at the blood on his hands and to Louise's disgust, he raised one of them to his mouth. He stuck his unnervingly broad, long tongue out as far as possible and with the very tip of it, he licked it off. He paused and then stared back at where the wreags were finishing off their meal. Then, in a more controlled and confident voice he said, 'Once I have killed her, I'll have her blood and the power of the Whisper. Then I will be the greatest leader Calaresp has ever known. Nobody will remember the Clarest family, all they'll know is me.'

As he finished his sentence, the wreags finished eating their meal. There only remained a few signs that Clarris had ever even been there, as all that was left were a few scraps of clothes and the dark purple stain of the blood that had leaked from her waist. Louise wasn't aware she had begun to cry until the tears began trickling down her face. She was so overwhelmed with grief that she momentarily stopped paying attention to Brisheit and his army.

A change in the men's tone of voice pulled Louise out of her trance-like state and she promptly chastised herself for getting distracted. Brisheit was now stood in front of his men, addressing them, his voice filled with absolute anger and hatred.

'Well, if she didn't have the Whisper on her then

there can only be two other options.' As he spoke, he walked slightly away from his men, scanning the horizon with sharp eyes. 'Either she hid it somewhere in these woods, between our first encounter and here...' He rubbed his beard as he considered this option before turning back to his men to say, 'or perhaps she did find the young Clarest girl? And safely delivered the Whisper to her.'

The men grumbled and growled as they considered the prospect that they hadn't successfully stopped Clarris from reaching her target.

Brisheit raised his hand in the air and they immediately fell silent.

'It could just be possible,' he said in a low, contemplative voice, 'that we can find both the Whisper and the girl all in one fell swoop. Then I will have the final two pieces of the puzzle.' A malicious smile spread across his face and he opened his mouth and let out a roar as he screamed: 'GO! Find her!!'

In one slow and forthright movement, the men and the wreags stepped forward. Louise panicked, throwing herself back behind the tree. Her eyes scanned her surroundings in a frenzy as she considered her options. She could either stay where she was and pray that they didn't notice her — the odds of that were incredibly slim, or alternatively, she could run but risk getting spotted. Eventually, Louise decided that the best thing to do would be to crawl away as quickly as possible, and then, once she was a suitable distance, she'd be able to make a run for it.

She pushed herself onto all fours, gently pulled on Barney's lead and the pair of them made their slow escape. When she looked back, she realised in horror that they weren't going fast enough; they were gradually catching up with her. It was then Louise became aware that she was still tightly gripping the Whisper. She carefully placed it into her raincoat pocket, hoping that with her hand free she would be able to move that little bit faster.

Had she been aware of the protection the Whisper had still been giving her, she would never have removed it from her hand. The second she did, the glow vanished, and the wreags instantly picked up a strange smell they didn't recognise. The smell of a woman not too far from their exact position. With their noses in the air, they began moving as one, towards Louise. Excitement spread through the army as the men realised that they had picked up a scent, and the pace increased.

Instinctively Louise knew that she was in grave trouble and that she had to run. She pulled herself up from the ground and as quickly as she could began to make her way through the trees. Barney following obediently at her side, equally as terrified. She couldn't quite explain it, but something was telling her that she no longer needed to be quiet because they already had her scent, they were already following her. Barney seemed aware of this as well, as he increased his speed quite significantly. Louise maintained a firm grip on his lead, determined that she wasn't going to let him get away from her again.

As they crashed through the close trees Louise used trunks to propel herself further. As she ran, Louise desperately studied her surroundings, trying to find something that looked familiar. She began losing faith as she realised, she didn't recognise anything, She dared a glance behind her and let out a small scream as she saw the army and the wreags were even closer on her trail. Evidently, they weren't certain enough that the beasts had picked up the right scent to let them loose, as they were still kept closely in check by the small man.

Louise had been so occupied with trying to get her bearings that she didn't notice Barney attempting to pull her gently to her left. When she finally did realise, she stopped for a fraction of a second as she contemplated whether to follow him. The sound of a wreag howling was enough to help her make up her mind. She lurched to the side and followed her trustworthy dog as he practically dragged her through the woods.

Barney seemed to be leading her into an even thicker section of wood. She hesitated for a moment, then, just as she was about to pull him back, she saw something up ahead and she felt a spark of delight. He had led her to a minuscule trench through the trees in which a tiny little stream ran delicately through the woods. She crouched underneath the last remaining branches that blocked her path and ran into the stream, barely noticing as the water seeped through her shoes, soaking her socks. Now, the path ahead of her was without obstruction, she was able to hurl down the decline at an even faster pace. She didn't dare turn around to see how close the army was.

As Louise began to tire, she felt another surge of hope as she saw an opening in the trees ahead of her. When she finally reached it, Louise noticed that the small stream she'd been following was now no more than a trickle. A stretch of bare land stood in front of her, lined by trees on the other side. With a jolt, she realised that beyond the far trees, she could just about make out a small segment of the path, covered in a thick layer of snow. From this distance, she wasn't able to make out which part of the path she was looking at, but all that mattered was that it would lead her back to the safeness and security of her car, and then her warm house.

Once again, she flung herself forwards, Barney following her loyally. She was hit by a painfully cold blast of wind and knew she was back out in the open once again, vulnerable to the elements from which the thick woods had previously shielded her. She automatically lowered her head in an attempt to protect herself from the sharp blasts.

Louise ran through the open stretch of land. As the strong winds blew into her face. A sudden thought sent shivers down her spine as she realised the wind was working in favour of the formidable enemies following her, sending her scent right into the long gruesome snouts of the horrible wreags. Telling them exactly which direction she was taking. She heard them howling in the distance with excitement. When she finally reached the trees on the other side, she took a final look behind her and was met with a horrific sight. Just at the edge of the treeline a muzzle appeared, followed closely by a large head raised high in the air, following her scent. Louise didn't wait long enough to see the other wreags appear.

As she ran, the back of her cold and wet coat snagged on an outstretched branch. The force pulled her backwards and she couldn't stop herself from screaming as she automatically thought that holding onto her coat were the teeth of those formidable beasts. Looking back, she felt an instant rush of relief, realising it had just been a branch. This moment of calm vanished almost as quickly as it had appeared as she remembered what was hunting her.

Chapter Seven

The stretch of woods that led to the path she so desperately needed to reach was situated at the end of a steep, slippery slope. Having experienced such extreme terror when she'd been caught by a mere branch, Louise was spurred on by the prospect of how frightening it would be to be caught by the wreags themselves. She, therefore, gave little thought to the treacherous snow-covered slope she now hurtling down.

The steepness of the slope meant her speed increased so dramatically that she was barely in control of her own body. As she saw the edge of the woods approaching, she tried to stop herself, or at least to slow down. This was when Louise began to really struggle. The ground below her feet was unpleasantly slushy, meaning that it was almost impossible to stop. The more she tried, the more she found the snow disappearing under her feet.

Louise automatically let go of Barney's lead, allowing herself to use both hands to grab as many tree trunks and branches as she could in the attempt to slow herself down. Barney ran off ahead of her, then stopped and waited at the edge of the wood, watching her clumsy descent. Fortunately, by grabbing everything that she could, Louise was able to slow herself quite considerably. However, despite this, she was still taken by surprise when she reached the treeline at the bottom and found a sheer drop on the other side. The section between the path and the woods had been dug out, presumably by the Forestry Commission when they were undergoing maintenance works.

'Damn it,' Louise said quietly, under her breath. She now knew exactly where she was, and although it was of great relief, she also knew how steep the drop was. Normally, she wouldn't have even attempted to climb down it. It was, however, set upon an open section of path which meant that as the snowstorm had hit, this one section had been struck hardest. This worked in Louise's favour, as it meant that it wasn't quite as steep as it normally would be. The snow had lined the edges of the crater, making it more of a slope than a sheer drop. Although this was fortunate for Louise, she had no idea as to how stable the build-up of snow was, or how far she'd sink into it if she were to set foot on it. Louise allowed herself to stop for a second, to see whether there were alternative ways onto the path.

All of a sudden, she heard the sound of branches snapping and breaking behind her. Then she heard a thud as large paws crashed into the ground, alarmingly quickly. Louise automatically turned around, then cursed under her breath. Behind her, there stood a lone wreag. She paused for a second and the beast did the same. It sniffed the air as it tried to reassess what direction to take. Louise crouched to the ground in the hope that it wouldn't see her. She scanned the horizon, expecting dozens of more wreags to appear behind this one, but they didn't. She began to suspect that it had strayed ahead of the others.

It was in that split second that Louise realised that the slope was her only option. She wouldn't have the time to take an alternative route, and if she were to even try, she would only draw the attention of the wreag. Barney was now crouched down beside her. Slowly and steadily, she placed a hand on his collar and used it to pull him close to her face.

Whispering as loudly as she dared, Louise said into the dog's ear, 'Right Barney, DOWN, go!'

As before, she wasn't sure whether or not he'd understand. However, she was pleasantly surprised to see him respond immediately. Remaining low to the ground, the dog moved away from her, his lead trailing gently behind him, leaving behind the smallest indent in the snow. As soon as he had reached the ledge, Barney edged down, picking up speed but remaining impressively quiet. Once he was at the bottom, he turned around and waited for her.

Once she knew Barney was safe, Louise turned back to contemplate how to deal with her own predicament. The wreag moved its head away from Louise, presumably to check on the location of the rest of its pack. Louise took this as her opportunity to escape. She raised herself a fraction, turned back to the steep slope and raised a foot, placing it tentatively on the snow.

Suddenly, another gust of wind swept towards her. Louise could feel it swirling around her body then filtering past her, dying out as it entered the thick wood. Even though the wind itself couldn't quite penetrate the wood, Louise knew that it would be enough to confirm to the wreag which way she was going.

Just as Louise began to edge her way down the slope, she heard the beast behind her, inhaling through its long, revolting snout. After one especially long intake, it made a quiet, satisfied, snapping sound with its jaw. She looked back at it, just in time to see it hurtling towards her, joyful to be back on track.

Louise was instantly forced to give up trying to descend the slope carefully and steadily. Instead, she moved quickly and clumsily. At first, she made steady progress — it wasn't until she was about a quarter of the way down that she began experiencing difficulties. She could feel her feet sinking deeper and deeper into the soft, unstable layers of snow. With her next step, she found herself sinking so deeply into the snow that it reached her knee. Snow immediately clasped around her thigh like thousands of tiny hands grasping her with icy cold fingers. She automatically stepped forward with her free leg, in an attempt to pull her stuck leg out. Straight away, that leg was also enveloped in the snow and Louise was stuck fast.

Her heart beat loudly in her chest and Louise's breath came in short sharp bursts. She felt as if she were losing control of herself. She tugged harshly on her legs, desperate to get them out of their prisons. This method, however, was only making things worse and they began to sink even further into the snow. Louise knew she had to calm herself and take her time. She quickly assessed the situation and then placed her shaking hands flat on the snow, parallel with her legs. She pushed as hard as she could against the shockingly white surface. Slowly she was able to ease her almost numb legs out of their casts.

As soon as she was free, Louise continued her descent, ensuring she now took her time, carefully placing her feet on the snow. Using this method, Louise was able to successfully make it to the bottom of the drift. Barney ran towards her, merrily wagging his tail, delighted she had made it.

Louise placed her foot on the comfortingly solid foundations of the path. As she did, she lowered a hand to fondly stroke Barney. She turned her head to look back at the edge of the wood, desperate to know if the beast had followed her. Initially, a small smile formed as she scanned the horizon and realised there was nothing there. Just as she was about to turn her head, something caught the corner of her eye.

A few seconds passed before she could pinpoint where she'd seen the movement. Then, she spotted it. The wreag stood boldly and confidently at the top of the slope. The horrific beast looked her square in the eye. Panic spread through Louise, paralysing her momentarily. Then, regaining her senses she turned and ran off down the path, Barney by her side. She now knew exactly where she was, as she'd walked this section of the path hundreds of times before. With that knowledge, Louise knew that the car was still around five minutes away from her current location.

The wreag still stood by the edge of the trees looking down at her, its mouth hanging open to reveal its sharp, dagger-like teeth. It watched as she ran off, not moving a muscle. Almost as if playing with her, having now located her, it allowed her to create some distance between them before it pursued. Eventually, it raised its head and emitted the blood-curdling howl that Louise had come to recognise and fear. Then, without questioning the stability of the snow leading to the path, the wreag launched itself downwards.

It was at this point that Louise turned her head back and wished with all her might that the wreag would experience as much difficulty as she had. That it too would fall into the snow. If she'd looked in her pocket, Louise would once again have seen the pendant glowing. She didn't know it, but the longer she held onto the Whisper, the stronger their magical bond was becoming. It was now becoming connected to her very thoughts and as she wished for the snow to collapse below the wreag, the Whisper made it happen.

The wreag was still paying no attention to the ground beneath its feet, it was purely focused on catching its prey. With every step it took, its feet began to sink. In the very centre of the slope, a section of the snow had become so soft that the slightest impact would cause it to collapse in on itself. As the wreag reached this section, it instantly fell downwards. Soon, the creature's legs were encased in the same prisons that had briefly held Louise. Almost immediately, the creature was stuck. It looked down at its torso, filled with frustrated confusion. It tried to wrench its feet free, but this only made things worse. After a while, it gave up and, filled with overwhelming anger, it began snapping at the snow, trying to free its lodged paws.

Louise, still completely oblivious to her magical capabilities, had no idea that she had played a part in delaying the beast. She wasn't even aware it was no longer pursuing her, as she was far too frightened to glance back, forcing herself to concentrate on the path ahead of her. Which curled to the left, running alongside the wood's edge, large fields appearing on the other side of her as she ran.

She knew that once she reached that corner, there was just one more turn and then she'd finally be able to see her car. At that moment, Louise was hit by a wall of exhaustion. She'd been filled with such an extreme rush of adrenaline that she hadn't felt even remotely tired until now. However, as she was getting closer to safety, she was starting to realise how long she'd been running for. Louise began to feel a stitch developing in her side, her lungs seemed to burn with the pressure of having to inhale so quickly and with such veracity. She desperately longed to stop and catch her breath, but she knew that those waiting behind her were considerably worse than a mere stitch. So, although she wasn't running quite as fast as she had been previously, she continued onwards.

Barney kept bounding ahead, stopping and turning back to look at her, as if urging Louise to hurry up. They had been fortunate, as the pursuing wreag had been detained long enough to have put a reasonable distance between them. In fact, the wreag had found itself incapable of escaping its shackles, its fury and clumsiness had simply made its situation worse. It wasn't until the wreag's master and the majority of the army had caught up with them that they quickly and carelessly dug him out. It didn't help matters that the frustrated wreag was snapping at the hands of those helping him, as if they were responsible for the monster's situation. As soon as it was free, they continued their pursuit of the Whisper and Louise.

Meanwhile, Louise's stitch was becoming

increasingly painful. She tried to distract herself by concentrating on one single thought: reaching her car, throwing herself inside it, and driving away from these nightmarish woods.

The last turning of the path was just ahead of her and as she reached it, she desperately longed to stop and double over to allow more oxygen to flood into her lungs. But she knew that even now she was nearing her goal, she couldn't afford to stop; she couldn't afford to allow them to catch up with her. Instead, a heartfelt sob burst out of her small and unbelievably tired frame. With a pathetic and desperate struggle, Louise pushed herself forward.

Barney, who was was still running ahead of her; eventually reached the car. He turned back towards her, whining and pawing the ground anxiously. The fact he had reached the car spurred Louise on. With the last bit of energy she could muster, she began to run faster.

Hand-stretched out in front of her, Louise was barely able to believe that she had finally made it. She wouldn't allow herself to believe that they were there until she felt her hand rest against the cold boot of the car. Everything she had gone through seemed to catch up with her all at once; she had thought she'd been in pain before but that had been nothing compared to the pressure her body was now under. She was completely soaked through, her clothes drenched in equal measures by sweat, mud and melted snow, chilling her right to the core. She didn't notice any of this, instead, her exhausted body felt as if it were on fire.

For a split second, Louise's exhaustion took over and despite a few feeble attempts, her body refused to move another muscle. She was woken from her trance-like state when the eerily familiar howls boomed through the air, coming from behind her. This time the sounds were entangled with the shouts and cries of thousands of men, their boots crashing so loudly on the ground that the closer they got, the stronger their reverberations became, making the ground beneath Louise's feet rumble.

She glanced back along the track. Despite the sounds crashing towards her, the land itself was empty. The only thing that stood out in the picturesque scene before her were the wild and sporadic footprints that she'd left behind as she'd run to her car. Satisfied that they hadn't yet caught up with her, Louise turned back to her car and felt a new sense of dread as she realised that she didn't yet know where her car keys were. The exhaustion suddenly disappeared as a new type of fear took its place. She frantically searched her pockets, desperate to feel the familiar points of her keys hidden away in a small crevice of her pocket. Visions suddenly passed through her mind as she contemplated the possibility that they may have slipped out of her pocket on one of the numerous times she'd fallen over. The longer it took, the more frenzied her searching became, meaning that the likelihood of her finding the keys was becoming increasingly slim. Her hand simply pushed the contents of her pocket from side to side.

She suddenly felt her loyal friend press his body against her knees. She could feel him shaking violently against her. Barney stared back towards the track. Slowly and reluctantly, Louise turned her head to follow his gaze. At first, there was nothing there, but then she saw something bound around the corner at such a speed that it almost crashed into the ground. The Wreag used its powerful back legs to quickly steady itself and then, driven forwards by its undeniable strength, it bounded towards her. With renewed momentum, it continued towards its prey.

The frenzied search for those all-important car keys became ever more desperate. She stopped, took a deep breath in an attempt to calm herself. Then, on a whim, she tried the rarely used inside pocket of her jacket.

She was suddenly filled with an indescribable blossom of relief as the tips of her fingers felt the familiar shape of her keys. She quickly grasped onto them as if scared they may suddenly disappear and with a quick triumphant cheer, she pulled them out. Louise pressed a small button situated in the middle of the key. This was followed by a sound she had never truly appreciated until this moment — the sound of the car unlocking.

Knowing that she wouldn't have time to put Barney into the boot of the car, Louise yanked open the driver's side door. Barney instinctively jumped inside, bounced across the seat, and settled on the floor of the front passenger's seat. Louise flew in after him and slammed the door behind her. With one glance in her rear-view mirror, she could see that the first wreag was almost upon them, followed by at least another six.

As the engine roared into action, she was immediately overwhelmed with a feeling of gratitude for her old wreck of a car. Putting it into first gear, Louise forced the old car forward, carefully navigating the thick snow that covered the ground. She held her breath, concerned that they might get stuck in the beautiful, yet treacherous snow. This fear intensified when she felt the stationary wheels spin slowly on the spot. Thinking quickly Louise reversed it a few inches and then tried to move forward again.

The lead wreag was now mere feet away from her car, she revved the engine and quickly jolted the car forward. This happened just in time, as the wreag had finally caught up with them. The beast placed a heavy, strong claw onto the side of the boot and it plunged its five sharp claws into the car's casing. Louise felt the back of the car jolt forcefully, but it soon dissipated as the wreag lost its grip, slid off the car, and then fell back to the ground. Louise hit the accelerator and started putting as much distance as possible between herself and her pursuers.

Much to her surprise, the fallen wreag picked itself up off the ground and remained exactly where it was, nose raised to the air as if sniffing. As the car reached a corner, she took one final glance back at the stationary wreag. She could see that it had now been joined by the rest of the pack. They were all over the place, sniffing their surroundings feverishly, almost distressed because they seemed to have suddenly lost her scent. As she turned the corner Louise didn't allow herself to believe that she was finally safe, so she drove home much faster than she normally would in such treacherous conditions.

Had Louise known the truth — that the Whisper had bonded even closer to her than before — she probably wouldn't have driven so ruthlessly. Once she had entered the car, Louise's subconscious had used the security of her car and the precious pendant to shield her from the incredibly powerful noses of Brisheit's hunting beasts. They now paced in every direction, desperate to rediscover which direction their prey had taken. Quiet howls escaped their great muzzles as their frustrations increased. They had been so distracted; they hadn't even seen the car disappearing around the corner.

As the car moved onwards, Brisheit and his men finally caught up with the wreags. The men had immediately understood that they had lost track of their prey, and they knew exactly how Brisheit was going to react. With this knowledge, they hung back from the huddle of confused beasts and when Brisheit approached, they lowered their heads, keen not to make eye contact with their formidable Commander.

Brisheit quickly read the scene in front of him and emitted a roar. A roar considerably louder and far more horrific than that of the wreags. Its every syllable filled with loathing and hatred, it opened a window right to his inner soul, demonstrating the true evil that dwelt within his core.

As Louise drove on, she was certain she heard a ruthless cry following her. She was going so quickly, however, she couldn't hear the full power of the roar. Despite the distance, the cry still invoked an involuntary shudder that travelled through her entire body like a ferocious wave smacking into the shore of a bare and vulnerable beach.

Chapter Eight

Louise barely remembered any of the journey home, her mind seemed to separate itself into two. One part subconsciously concentrating on navigating the treacherous roads and the other was in a blind panic, trying to process what had just occurred. Barney had remained crouched in the footwell on the passenger's side, his head resting on the seat. He stared up at Louise as if concerned. Before she knew it, Louise could see her small house with its quaint little garden. She slowed down as she approached and allowed herself a few moments to truly appreciate how beautiful her little house was. It was a soothing contrast to the events that she'd witnessed and experienced in the last few hours. She drove into the small gravel driveway, turned off the engine, and sat back. She took in a few deep breaths, Barney remaining where he was.

Louise slowly placed her hand in the top pocket and drew out the formidable locket that was the cause of so much trouble. With the chain wrapped around her fingers, the locket sat comfortably in the palm of her hand. As she stared, she tried to make herself relax, her hand shaking violently, she couldn't stop reliving what had happened in the woods.

She couldn't help but dwell on the death of that kind and beautiful woman she'd met. Contemplating how brutally she had died and how the sole reason had been to reunite her with the strange pendant. She was so absorbed in the past that she barely noticed the first tear as it rolled down her cold face. It wasn't long before tears were streaming, blurring her vision as she allowed the emotions, she'd kept under control, loose. Louise slowly lent her body forwards as she pressed her hand, pendant enclosed, against her mouth and held back a deep and sorrowful sob. She rested her head against the steering wheel and continued to silently cry for a few more moments.

Barney then moved up onto the seat beside her and gently licked the hand that was still resting on the handbrake. Without looking up, she moved her hand up to his head and caressed his ears gently. Louise sat back again, she took a deep breath and closed her eyes for a second as she tried to compose herself. She put the locket back securely in her top pocket, intending to deal with it later. She then put all her concentration into motivating her now exhausted body to move.

Louise barely noticed her surroundings as she walked down the path towards her house. She didn't spare a glance at the bird table, which she'd normally monitor regularly, checking to see whether they had finished all of the food. She had always loved the little birds in her garden. Today though, she didn't have enough space in her brain to contemplate even looking.

She slowly staggered towards her door and

somehow managed to fit the key into the lock. Then, as soon as they were inside, she pushed the door shut and stopped for a second, staring at it. The thought of the wreags flashed through her mind, and of Brisheit and his terrifying army. She quickly locked and bolted the door.

Barney had wandered into the kitchen to drink some of his water, equally as knackered. He went over to his bed and with a great exhale, he collapsed clumsily into it. Louise gradually made her way up the stairs until she reached her bedroom, wherein she too collapsed on her bed.

Louise had to use every inch of her remaining energy to pull off her wet clothes, now clinging to her as if they were another layer of skin. With every move, she felt as if the muscles in her limbs were ripping in two. Every time she brushed her numerous scratches against her wet clothes, or the dry bed covers, she winced with pain. Although none were deep or serious, some, were still prominent enough to be painful.

After having to struggle with her own body for a while, she kicked her wet clothes off the edge of the bed and with just as much effort, she pulled on some dry pyjamas. Her cold and shaking body still felt damp against the stark dryness of her pyjamas, but she was too exhausted to even contemplate fully drying herself off. Instead, she crawled underneath the covers and wrapped them around herself as tightly as she could, so only her head poked out. She closed her eyes and let herself go, allowing the exhaustion to take over.

Immediately she felt herself ebb away, she reached the brink where you balance between consciousness and the unknown realms of sleep. As she tried to tip the scales towards the latter, she found something was holding her back.

Reluctantly, she opened her eyes and let out a quiet sigh of exhaustion. Her eyes flickered around the room with frustration as she tried to work out what was keeping her awake. Eventually, they rested on the ripped and wet coat that lay on the ground. Louise forced her body to awaken once more and she crawled out of her bed towards the dismissed garments. Once her fingers had curled themselves around a corner of the damp coat, she pulled herself back towards the bed. Being careful not to pull the coat too close to her dry duvet.

Slowly she pulled the Whisper out of the pocket. Then she clasped it in her hand as she settled back into bed. Unclasping her hand, she allowed herself to sink into her soft embracing pillows to stare at the unusual object. She studied the back of the small, round silver pendant, rubbing her thumb across it, expecting it to be completely smooth. Instead, she was surprised to find her thumb was met by several small bumps and ridges. Frowning, she lifted the Whisper closer to her face as she studied it. She was amazed to find the bumps created a symbol; together they formed a small single flame, rising out from a flat surface. It had two small singular dots inside of it, and four lined up perfectly below. She brushed her finger lightly against it. There was something familiar about it, but the memory was just out of reach. Her entire body was gradually shutting down, and almost involuntarily, she found herself pulling the covers right up to her shoulders. She sank her body into the comfort of her bed and fell asleep.

It wasn't long before her sleep was interrupted by a terrifying nightmare. She heard something crashing up the stairs towards her bedroom. A wreag knocking the door right off its hinges and bursting in. It didn't pause as it entered the room; it turned to its left with unimaginable speed and came at her, mouth open, heading straight for her face.

Louise awoke with a start. Sitting bolt upright, it took a few seconds for her to realise it had just been a dream. That was until she heard something slowly moving up the stairs. As the sound stopped on the other side of the door, there was a moment's silence and Louise, heart racing, held her breath, trying to anticipate what the intruder was going to do next. The gentle sound of a small paw scratching on the other side of the door put her mind at rest.

Louise got out of her bed and quickly threw open the door, a small smile spreading across her face. Just as she'd expected, standing on the other side, looking decidedly pathetic, was Barney. Crouching down to his level, she placed a comforting hand on the top of his head to gently scratch behind his soft ear. Barney automatically wagged his tail appreciatively.

'Are you alright, my boy?' she asked in a barely audible whisper. 'Are they haunting you too?'

Barney replied by way of a small, whine that even Louise's ears struggled to hear. Louise felt a sense of relief at the realisation that she wasn't the only one whose mind was still dwelling on the events of the day. She opened the door fully to let Barney in, and without a moment's hesitation, Barney trotted in and jumped onto the end of the bed, curled up, and fell asleep. Louise found herself comforted by the presence of her old friend, the sense of vulnerability that had swamped her ever since she'd returned was gradually disappearing. She closed the door and made her way back into bed.

Almost as soon as her head hit the pillow, Louise felt her eyes closing. She couldn't have stayed awake, even if she had wanted to.

Louise initially slipped into the welcome darkness of sleep. However, this soon changed. Her dreamless sleep suddenly sprang into action and dreams began to take over. Slowly she realised that she was stood in a beautiful courtyard, filled with vibrant, blossoming flowers. She noticed a figure to her left and turning, she saw a tall handsome man. His smiling face looked down at her and then across, to her other side. Louise followed his gaze and saw a beautiful woman with long red hair, her blue eyes glistening in the sunlight as she stared back at the man lovingly. Louise looked at each of them in turn, filled with the strange sensation that she knew who these two people were. They were important, incredibly important to her. The man to her side stepped forward and the image in front of Louise changed.

This time, she was stood beside what looked like stables. The man she had seen before was once again in front of her, and just behind him was an elegant white horse, upon which sat the beautiful woman. They were both looking at her again. The man began talking but it was as if she were underwater, as she could only vaguely make out a quiet mumbling. All of a sudden, as if she weren't in control of her own body, Louise felt herself stepping towards the man and hugging him. It was at this point she noticed how short she was, how much bigger the world around her was, almost as if she were a child.

Then, with a gentle hand, she found herself being lifted upwards onto the back of a large chestnut horse. The scene switched again and this time she was cantering, her hair blowing behind her, the horse grunting and huffing as it pushed itself. Ahead of her was the woman, who looked back and laughed. Beside her was the man and as she looked at him, Louise saw something around his neck, glistening and glowing as if the sun had caught it. There was something strangely familiar about its shape and she found herself almost certain it was some sort of pendant.

All of a sudden, everything went black. She glanced around, feeling disorientated and suddenly terrified. She wrapped her arms tightly around herself, aware of how vulnerable she was. Flickers of light appeared around her and she was soon able to identify them as the flickering flame of torches. Someone was tightly gripping her wrist, she was with the woman with red hair, being pulled urgently through a castle. She thought she could hear the muffled sound of screams somewhere in the background. As they reached the end of the hallway, the man appeared, he hugged the woman, and then Louise, tightly and lovingly. He grabbed Louise's other arm and the three of them kept running.

Then everything moved abnormally fast, as if it had been sped up, furniture and figures becoming blurs of colour and movement. The protective grips on her arms disappeared, as they did Louise was filled with a sense of foreboding and dread. Then, she was outside, all around her had become dark and cool, and as she looked up, Louise saw a large, beautiful silver moon. There were now new figures running alongside her, encouraging her to move faster. One of them looked like the woman she'd met in the woods, Clarris, only she was significantly younger. Her expression was one of complete fear and her eyes flickered from side to side in a panic. Louise found herself wondering where the woman with the red hair had gone, her absence creating a spasm of pain and fear within her. Louise heard a sound behind her, the sound of heavy breathing, of even heavier footsteps. As she turned around, she was taken aback, as she saw a large and repulsive wreag flying through the air towards her, its huge mouth open, its large and bloodied teeth preparing to bite into her.

Chapter Nine

Her eyes opened with a snap, and as she stared up at the white ceiling above her, it took her a few moments to realise who she was and where she was. Rubbing her hand across her eyes, she tried to get her senses together, to fully wake herself up. Barney, meanwhile, was still at the bottom of her bed, only now he was lying on his back, legs sticking up into the air, tongue hanging out ever so slightly between his front teeth.

Louise lay back and closed her eyes again, overwhelmed with the need to go back to sleep. She was reluctant however, her dreams were so confusing, terrifying and familiar. Filled with frustration, she opened her eyes and her gaze moved across to the window. It was now light outside, which must have meant that she'd been asleep for well over twelve hours. She groaned, annoyed that even though she'd been slept for so long, she still felt exhausted.

A quick and convulsive shudder spread across her entire body, she pulled the duvet so that she was entirely covered. As she did, the small pendant fell from the folds onto the empty pillow beside her. She stared at it for a few seconds, as it wasn't instantly recognisable to her. It wasn't long, however, before the events of the last twenty-four hours, her own experiences, and the dreams that had run rampage throughout her sleep came swarming back to her. She was filled with a strange mixture of emotions, ranging from fear due to the terrifying Brisheit and dread at the thought she'd managed to get involved with such a hellish group. The strongest feeling that consumed her though, that outweighed any fear, was one of startling excitement.

She felt as if a thick veil of fog had been lifted, revealing events from her own life that had previously been hidden. Events that portrayed an entirely different past to the one she'd thought she'd always known. It was extraordinary, beyond anything that she could have ever imagined. Still holding the Whisper in her hand, Louise tried to remember every detail of the dreams that had consumed her throughout her long sleep. Her thoughts were interrupted by yet another shiver, which spread throughout her body. It took control of every limb, causing them to move and jerk quickly and sharply. She gently rubbed her arms, suddenly realising just how cold she was. As she felt her chilled and clammy skin, she had a flashback to the night before—wet and cold, getting straight into bed without even having dried herself.

'No wonder I'm so cold!' she said quietly, chastising herself.

As she reluctantly pulled herself out of bed, Barney flung himself the right way up and watched as Louise left the room, his head slumped on the duvet. Other than that, he made little attempt to move, seemingly happy where he was. Louise, meanwhile, made her way into the bathroom and began to undress. This proved a far more difficult task than normal as each part of her body felt as if it were twice as heavy.

She stepped into the shower and turned it up as hot as she dared. Louise felt instant relief as the warm particles of water splashed down onto her cold skin. She stood there, ensuring that every inch of her body benefited from the soothing effects of the shower. Louise, reluctant to leave, tilted her head backwards, allowing the water to fall directly on her face. She let her mind drift back to the dreams that had taken over her sleep, desperately trying to make sense of the truth that had only just been revealed to her.

As hard as it was to believe that the dreams she'd found so harrowing and amazing could be true, there was an undeniable familiarity surrounding them. Something told her that to try and persuade herself otherwise would be pointless. She thought about the woman who had died in the woods less than twenty-four hours before; Clarris, the mysterious stranger who she had quickly recognised as her Alat. Now that the fog had lifted from her mind, everything was starting to become clearer—her true past. She could see herself as a young girl, playing games with the man and the woman she'd seen in her dreams, all of them laughing heartily. The image shifted suddenly as the woman she had met in the woods joined them, wrapping her arms around Louise with a warm embrace.

As all of these emotions built up, the memory of this woman being ripped apart by the wreags once again crept into her mind. The tears that began to trickle down her face mingled with the water from the shower; the sob that escaped her merged with the sound of the droplets hitting against the shower floor. She tried to pull herself together, but the feeling of unimaginable loss had hit her so hard, she felt as if her heart had been ripped in two.

Whilst she remained vulnerable to the feelings of pain and loss, she found her mind drifting to the death of her parents. Or rather, to their murders. Their faces flashed into her mind and the feeling of loss that had surrounded her intensified alarmingly. Collapsing down onto the floor of the shower, she continued to weep; to mourn for those she'd forgotten, for those whom she had once loved so dearly.

It was a long time before Louise stopped. It was as if she was releasing a lifetime of emotion. Eventually, she stood up and, still not ready to leave the warmth of the shower, she forced herself to think of something else. She raised her hands to her face and looked closely at them. She had barely thought about one truth she'd just discovered; the fact that she had powers. A small laugh escaped her, as she instinctively disbelieved this could ever be true. No matter how hard she tried, she couldn't recall ever having used magic. The actual ability, the magic that others had believed to be so strong within her, was still a complete mystery.

As a long shot, but Louise stretched her right hand out in front of her and concentrated on a bottle of body lotion sitting on her bathroom cabinet.

'Move,' she said quietly to herself, wondering whether her powers could include telekinesis. After a few minutes, the body lotion still hadn't budged. Louise let her hand fall back to its natural position. She watched the bottle for a few more seconds and then smiled to herself, feeling daft. Calrris told her that everyone had believed her to be the most powerful member of the Clarest family since her great-great-great-grandmother. She didn't, however, have any recollection of powers, so she began to wonder whether they may have been wrong.

Begrudgingly she turned the shower off. As the flow of water stopped, Louise remained where she was for a few moments, water trickling off her hair and down her body. The longer she remained, the cooler the droplets felt, so she stepped out of the shower. As she reached for the towel and wrapped it around herself, she stood still for a few moments and enjoyed the warming comfort it provided. When she'd fully dried herself, she pulled on a fleecy dressing gown, wrapped her hair up in her towel, and returned to her bedroom.

Louise suddenly felt very lethargic. She considered getting changed and getting on with her day, but she couldn't quite muster the energy. She removed her hair from the towel and gave it a quick dry. Lazily, she let the wet towel drop to the floor and made her way back into bed. Dressing gown, wet hair and all.

As she got into bed, she picked up the Whisper and slumped back onto her pillows. Carefully holding it between her thumb and index finger, Louise brought the remarkable pendant up to her face and studied the small markings. As she did, something unusual on her hand caught her attention. Between the joint of her thumb and her wrist, she saw a strange marking embedded on her skin; she rubbed it with her left thumb to see if it would disappear. It didn't budge, Louise put the pendant gently on the bed and brought her right hand even closer to her face to study it in more detail.

The marking looked as if it had always been there, as it was indented into her skin. It had somewhat of a shine to it too, like an old burn scar. She was certain that it formed a shape, but it wasn't quite defined enough for her to identify it.

Licking the thumb on her left hand, she wiped it slowly across the marking, desperately hoping that it would disappear. Frustrated, she began to rub harder. Eventually, she was pressing so hard that the skin surrounding the marking was becoming alarmingly red. The marking itself, however, didn't change at all; it didn't even redden like the rest of her skin. This simply made it stand out even more.

Louise felt a knot form in the pit of her stomach. She was desperate for it to just disappear so she wouldn't have to stare at it anymore, as she knew deep down that it sign that everything was about to change. She was no longer just Louise, the struggling writer who lived with her dog in the middle of nowhere. Now an entirely different past had been brought to life; a past that no matter how hard she tried, she simply could not ignore.

Completely absorbed by these thoughts, she got to her feet and went through to the bathroom. She paused for a second, then moved over to the sink, turned on the tap, and shoved her hand underneath. The water was alarmingly cold, but desperate to see if she could remove the mark, she kept her hand where it was. At long last, she conceded and withdrew her hand. Not surprised to see the mark was still there.

The feeling of nausea intensified alarmingly, in what

could only be described as a state of panic. Louise despondently turned off the tap and then looked at herself in the mirror, she was surprised to find tears slowly edging their way down her freckled cheeks, her green eyes were red and blotchy. The prospect of what had occurred the previous day, the dreams that had consumed her throughout the night, and now this bizarre mark on her hand — it was all becoming far too much for her to take, and exhaustion was beginning to take control of her entire body. She threw open the door of the bathroom cabinet just above the sink and frantically began to root around inside. She knocked over boxes of cough sweets, creams and various medications, some of which fell into the sink. Louise ignored these until she found what she was looking for, a box of skin-coloured plasters. She rooted around in the box, looking for the right size. Completely ignoring the mess she'd made; she diverted her attention to placing the plaster over the mark on her wrist and carefully smoothing it down. She then forced herself to ignore her hand from that point on.

Chapter Ten

Feeling as if her entire body was ready to shut down, Louise made her way back to her bedroom. She lazily slumped into the bed, head falling straight onto the pillow. Every second she spent dwelling on her true past and family history, the more her head began to pound. She closed her eyes, tight, hoping it would help her headache, and before she knew it, she'd fallen asleep. This time her sleep was undisturbed, too exhausted to even dream.

Louise awoke later that day with Barney fidgeting at the bottom of her bed. She looked down at her watch and saw it was 3 p.m. which meant that she'd been sleeping for about four hours. Barney continued to fidget, rolling from his back to his front as if he were obscurely trying to scratch an inaccessible itch. Louise raised her hand to the top of her head, resting it on her now wildly unkempt hair. She was finding it difficult to keep her eyes open; they kept rolling shut against her will. She took a deep breath and as she exhaled, the air that left her body was broken and short, as if it were catching in her throat. Slowly leaning forward, she made her way over to the dog at the end of her bed and fondly scratched behind his ears. He stretched his head at an awkward angle, demonstrating to his owner his appreciation.

Once she felt she'd shown Barney some well-deserved attention, she slowly pulled herself out of bed and placed her feet on the floor. In doing so, the covers she'd so determinedly wrapped around herself before falling asleep fell back onto themselves messily. As they fell, something glistened lightly within them. She carefully pulled the Whisper and its chain away from the bed and into the safety of her hand. Without being entirely aware of it, Louise smiled, pleased to have her newly-found family heirloom.

As she stared at it, a thought popped into her head. She raised her right hand and peeled back the plaster that covered the strange mark. The skin was no longer as alarmingly red as it had been after her frantic cleaning session. The strange mark however, remained; if anything, it seemed more noticeable than before. The indented skin seemed even lighter, so much so that it almost appeared to shine. Raising the Whisper with her left hand, she turned it until she could see the engraving, she'd spotted the previous night. It didn't surprise her that the two markings were perfectly identical. Unsure as to what it meant she simply pulled the plaster back down over her hand. So much was going on, changing, she simply couldn't dwell on it.

Without hesitation, she lifted the chain, allowing the pendant to fall to its natural position. Undoing the clasp, she pulled it up to her face, paused for a moment to look at it one last time, and then put it around her neck.

Standing up, Louise stepped over to the chest of

drawers and pulled on a warm knitted jumper and a pair of comfortable old jeans. As soon as she'd finished, Barney raised his head. As she met his gaze, he sat up and gave her two quick wags of his tail. She could see his excitement bubbling, obviously anticipating the next step to be a walk. Louise, still exhausted, could only meet his excitement with a half-smile. As she turned to leave the room, Barney launched himself off the bed, running past her and down the stairs.

When she reached the bottom, Barney was already waiting, staring up at the front door. She pulled on her walking boots and coat, grabbed her house keys and Barney's lead and unlocked the door. Just as she was about to open it, she hesitated, hand remaining on the latch without moving. What if that heinous army that had pursued her so mercilessly the day before had followed her home? The wreags had been creatures from out of this world — what was to say they couldn't track her, even over so great a distance?

Whilst Louise knew it was very unlikely, she couldn't stop herself from peering cautiously through the small window. Looking outside, her eyes took a few moments to adapt to the blinding reflection of the sun against the startlingly white snow. Her gaze flicked across the frozen wonderland that was her garden and she let out a small involuntary sigh of relief. The garden was completely empty and still, the ground was also untouched as a fresh layer of snow had blanketed the world outside. Once she was satisfied that they were still alone, Louise pulled open the door and released Barney into the unsuspecting world.

As she stepped outside and walked down the pathway, Louise became increasingly aware of every sore and tired muscle in her body screaming at her to return to the comfort of her bed. She simply had to get out of the house, and although she wasn't going to go for a long walk, she felt sure that a bit of fresh air would do her the world of good. Instead of heading to the car, she left her garden and turned to the right, towards the fields that surrounded her little house. She took deep, rejuvenating breaths as she tried to clear her mind. She knew she had some important decisions to make, and soon.

Chapter Eleven

The next few days were spent in much the same fashion—walking, sleeping, and trying to sort out exactly what she was going to do next. She wasn't able to decide this until five days after that notorious day in the wood. It was impossible to say what had changed; she'd simply woken up on that fifth day and her mind felt clear. She was no longer conflicted—she knew who she was, who she had been, and the truth of her family's demise. With this clarity, Louise knew that she had to return to her homeland. She hadn't yet decided what she was going to do once she'd returned, but she knew that it was her responsibility to go back. If nothing else, she could at least try and find those who had known Clarris—those who had been loyal to her parents—and let them know what had become of their friend.

That morning, Louise rooted around in her cupboard and didn't emerge until she found her old backpack. Into this, she shoved a spare pair of clothes and a few other essentials. She had given a lot of thought as to what she was going to wear and had settled on a pair of simple, black trousers and a dark maroon shirt. Louise had also found an old, but incredibly warm knitted jumper which she pulled on over the shirt.

Just as she was about to leave her bedroom, a thought sprung into her mind. Returning, she placed her backpack on the bed and walked over to the chest of drawers. Opening the top drawer, she rooted around in the mass of old scarves and socks. Eventually, her fingers tightened around a small wooden object and, smiling with satisfaction, Louise pulled out her old pocketknife. Rather than placing it in her bag with her other items, she felt it was more appropriate to have it close to hand. As such, she tucked it away in the top pocket of her shirt.

Heading downstairs, Barney followed her; not quite certain what was going on, he satisfied his curiosity by watching her every step of the way. When they entered the kitchen, Louise routed around in various cupboards collecting supplies. She needed to make sure she'd have enough to last a few days but not too much to make her bag unpleasantly heavy. She also had to ensure she had food Barney could eat.

Once she'd decided that she'd packed enough, Louise made her way into the hall and pulled on her walking boots, grabbed Barney's lead, and her warmest jacket. It was at this point she had to stop and take a breath, wondering for a moment whether she was making the right decision, abandoning the comfortable life she had always known.

As doubt threatened to overwhelm her, she realised her hand had somehow found its way to the Whisper, still hanging around her neck and this seemed to give her some much-needed resolve. Pushing all thoughts of uncertainty to the back of her mind, Louise and Barney headed outside. She quickly walked across to the car and got Barney and herself into it before she had a chance to dwell on what she was about to do.

Louise hadn't formulated much of a plan at this stage, she'd simply decided to try and retrace her steps to the spot in which Clarris had died. She didn't know what would happen once she got there and if truth be told, she didn't want to think about it. The sheer thought of finding a window into Calaresp, let alone entering it, was not only ludicrous but terrifying.

The journey passed by remarkably quickly as the roads were once again quiet and still. As she had before, Louise pulled into the car park, ensuring the car would quickly and easily pull out in case she needed to make another quick escape. The ground was untouched; any tracks that may have been left by other dog walkers had been covered by a fresh layer of snow.

Pulling the keys out of the ignition, Louise paused for a moment. She thought about her little house just a few miles away — her gorgeous farmhouse kitchen and the little writing room she'd made for herself. Doubts as to whether she wanted to leave that life behind drifted forcefully into her mind. The more Louise thought about it, the more it seemed like a terrible idea. She slowly put the key back into the ignition. Just as she was about to let the car roar back into action, to go home, a new thought struck her.

'Have I ever felt truly happy here?' she asked herself in a quiet voice. She paused and without realising it, she pulled the key back from the ignition. Although she'd built a good life for herself, she had always felt there was something wrong, something missing. She'd never felt she'd belonged here. The prospect of this new life was the opportunity for a real adventure and a chance for her to be genuinely happy. With what could only be described as a renewed spring in her step, Louise got out of the car and grabbed her backpack. Once the boot was open, Barney bounced out and bounded off to start sniffing his surroundings. Ensuring the car was locked, Louise pulled her scarf close around her face and followed him.

Chapter Twelve

As they headed up the path, Louise couldn't stop herself studying the ground around her, looking for any traces of Brisheit or his army of men and wreags. Just like in the car park, however, the ground had been blanketed by a fresh layer of snow. The countryside was a blank canvas, there wasn't a footprint or paw print in sight and the isolation was strangely comforting to her.

Louise had decided to walk in the same direction she had prior to Barney running off. By doing this, she felt she would be able to create a vague idea as to which way they had gone.

They hadn't walked for long when Louise noticed Barney sniffing intently at something ahead, just off the path. Frowning, she sped up, quickly making her way over to him. The dark mess on the ground that had so fervently grabbed his interest was a stark contrast to the bright, clean, sparkling snow. The closer she got, the more unpleasant the object looked. Eventually, Louise realised it was the savaged body of an animal, surrounded by dark blood that had been absorbed into the snow.

'Barney!' she shouted sternly. 'Get away from that!' Automatically, he looked up at her and begrudgingly moved away. Although she was reluctant to approach the carcass, curiosity got the better of her. Which she immediately began to regret, as the closer she got, the more revolting the scene became.

Louise was fairly certain that the long-deceased creature in front of her was a deer, although all that was left of it was its skeletal frame, the skull, and a few small patches of fur and dried blood. On her walks, Louise had seen many a dead creature, primarily deer. They had either been shot by deer stalkers or had died from natural causes, providing a great feast for many a passing animal.

This particular carcass was very different. It had been ripped open savagely and in Louise's estimation, this amount of damage could only have been done by a large creature, with powerful and substantial teeth. Louise froze, eyes wide, she took short, sharp breaths and she began to feel her own heart beating deep in her chest. Louise had seen brutality like this before.

'Wreags.' she said quietly to herself. She whistled gently for Barney, then walked quickly onto the path and continued on her way. Although the sight had been unspeakably frightening, it had also been somewhat of a comfort. The animal had undoubtedly been killed recently, but probably not within the past three days. Louise felt sure that one or more of the wreags must have killed and eaten it after she'd escaped. Perhaps Brisheit had been forced to let them hunt in order to pacify the bloodthirst he'd unleashed when they had pursued her.

Louise shuddered in revolution and tried to push the thought to the back of her mind. She was almost certain they weren't around anymore and it was vital she paid attention to where she was going so she could retrace her footsteps. Then suddenly, just as before, Barney bounded off unexpectedly into the woods. Eyes widening, Louise didn't stop to consider what she was doing and followed. Her instincts told her that Barney somehow knew where he was going and that the best thing she could do was follow him.

As soon as she stepped between the line of trees, Louise realised that her hunch had been right. Not far in front of her, Barney was waiting. As soon as she caught up with him, he bounded off again, maintaining a steady pace that Louise was easily able to keep up with. As they walked, Louise began to recognise more of her surroundings until she knew exactly where she was.

Ahead of her, Barney finally came to a stop by a tall tree. As Louise approached, she knew it was the same tree that Clarris had leant against, and the ground in front of it was where she had so brutally been killed.

Initially, she was filled with an almost overwhelming sense of remorse as she was reminded how Clarris had suffered so greatly. These emotions were soon usurped as something else caught her attention. Wonder erupted within her as she noticed that the ground surrounding the old tree — which had once been full of decaying leaves and mud — was now covered with a delicate soft moss that had small, beautiful flowers poking through it. They were unlike anything she had ever seen before. Their petals were dark purple with a streak of white shooting through the centre which fragmented into several smaller streaks at the end, almost like a flurry of small lightning bolts. Louise gently ran a finger along the edge, admiring its beauty in such a morbid setting.

'Oh Clarris,' she said under her breath, 'what do I do now? Where do I go from here?' As she stared at the spot in which her only connection to her past had died, Louise didn't notice a small tear trickle across her cheek. It made its way down her nose and then fell to the ground. A few moments after it landed, something inexplicable happened; at the point of penetration, the ground began to glisten, until small golden lights appeared, like minuscule fireflies. They were so mesmerising that it took a few moments before Louise realised they were moving and spreading, almost as if they multiplied as soon as they touched a new piece of moss. Eventually, it was everywhere, until it began to spread upwards. It was a wondrously magical moment that took Louise's breath away. It wasn't long before she was surrounded, swallowed by this cloud of golden lights that floated gracefully in the still air.

The sparkling lights unexpectedly stopped, fell to the ground, and vanished. Louise was left in a trance-like state and remained so for a few minutes. When she finally came around, Louise stared at the moss where the lights had vanished a few moments before.

A sense of confusion crept into her mind. She still had no idea what she was supposed to do, she had no idea of how to get into Calaresp. She and Barney were once again left alone. Then all of a sudden, Barney, who had been waiting patiently beside her, barked loudly. Louise jumped violently and looked up towards him, a little frustrated that he had disrupted her whilst so deep in thought. She quickly understood why he was barking though, as right in front of him were small clumps of glistening lights, hovering just above the ground. They seemed to create a path leading off into the woods, as there was a cluster every eight foot or so.

Amazed, Louise slowly got to her feet. As she approached the first cluster of lights, As she placed her feet on either side of it and knelt to get a closer look. She immediately identified them as the same lights she'd seen near the tree. Mere seconds later, they disappeared, just as they had before. At the same time, the next set seemed to grow brighter and Louise was drawn on towards them. As she reached them, the same thing happened; the lights closest to her quickly vanished and the next set grew brighter. After a while, Louise didn't even stop at the lights when she reached them. Instead, she simply kept moving onwards, Barney close behind her. When she turned back, it was near impossible to differentiate the tree from all those surrounding it. Nevertheless, Louise continued onwards, certain that Clarris had somehow left the lights as a way for her to return home.

Louise came to an abrupt stop when she couldn't see the next set of lights. She began to panic, thinking she'd perhaps gone the wrong way or missed the next clue. Her worry worsened when the light she was stood beside suddenly went out. She had no idea where she was or how she'd get back to the tree, let alone where she was meant to go next. Barney came to a stop beside her and waited patiently. Louise looked down at him — he had always been a very well-behaved dog, but he seemed to be surpassing himself. His presence and loyalty calmed her.

Suddenly a wave of exhaustion took over and Louise knelt to the ground, deciding to rest whilst she contemplated her options. She held her face in her hands as she forced herself to concentrate on finding a solution, becoming increasingly frustrated when no ideas presented themselves. A sound left her lips, a combination of a moan and a scream that made Barney jump slightly. She was quickly running out of ideas and was aware that the day was gradually disappearing. Subconsciously, she picked up a small clump of mud and rocks and threw it to the ground in front of her. It knocked into a small pile of sticks and Louise noticed something hidden between them.

Leaning forward, she found a small, dark purple fabric bag, which she gingerly picked up. Feeling a slight weight to it, she emptied some of the contents into the ground. What fell out was a small collection of tiny purple balls. On closer inspection, she found they had a very faint black centre. She pushed herself forward. Her instincts, although cautious, told her that there was no threat from the small purple pellets. Besides, the only way to know for sure if they were a threat was to touch them and considering her lack of other options, it seemed the best plan.

With her right hand, she held one between her thumb and middle finger and carefully studied it. Squeezing the purple pellet gently, she found it to be softer than she'd expected, almost like a berry. She increased the pressure. She could feel the pellet beginning to give way and eventually, it burst open. Louise had expected there to be a liquid substance inside and was surprised to find that instead, the whole thing had turned into small purple granules. Which fell neatly into a pile in her hand.

Her instinctive reaction was to turn her hand over, let the granules fall to the ground, and then quickly wipe her hand to ensure none had been left behind. However, something told her that it still wasn't of any threat to her, and she was becoming increasingly certain that it was somehow important to her progression into Calaresp. Louise brought up her left hand and picked up some of the dust with her fingers, rubbing it gently. She was surprised to find that the granules were rock hard and unexpectedly harsh against her skin. Returning them to the pile in her hand, she was startled to find that not all of it had left her fingers—some of it locked onto her skin, almost like small shards of glass.

Still unsure as to what exactly the powder was, Louise began to feel concerned. She rubbed her hands against the ground to try and rid herself of it and was alarmed when this didn't work. Desperately, she raised them to her face and fiercely blew at her fingers, hoping this would finally rid her of the strange substance. She was surprised when the granules lifted off her hands and drifted into the air in front of her. Filled with relief, Louise was about to turn her attention back to the larger pile when she noticed something strange.

The purple granules that were floating in the air suddenly vanished, and just as they did, the view in front of her shifted. It moved slightly, like it was caught in a heat haze. However, it was almost -5 degrees—there was no chance of a heat haze here. Louise raised her hand in front of her and reached out at the point the granules had vanished. She was strangely disappointed to find that nothing happened. It didn't feel any different than the rest of her surroundings.

On the brink of deciding it had simply been her imagination, Louise repeated the process with some more of the granules. This time, she watched carefully. Just as before, they drifted gracefully into the air and as soon as they reached that same point, they vanished. Louise brought the entire pile up to her face, took a deep breath, and blew all of the substance off her hand.

Everything in front of her turned black as the particles travelled through the air, some darting straight forward, and some getting caught in a slight breeze so that they danced in front of her eyes. When they reached that same point, the same thing happened. This time, however, there were so many more impact points. It spanned across a far larger area, and it was at this point, Louise noticed that it was forming an oval-like shape, growing slightly taller and more defined with every second.

Louise raised her hand to gently touch the air in front of her, curious as to whether it would be a solid shape. When her hand was mere inches away, she suddenly froze. The oval shape quickly turned jet black, alarming Louise and making her pull her hand back. As she did, a small white spark appeared in the centre. It quickly began to grow, until it filled the dark oval. It shone so brightly that it wasn't long before Louise was forced to avert her gaze. Even with her eyes shut, she could sense the light glowing brightly and noticed immediately when it subsided. Louise opened her eyes a fraction to ensure that it had definitely gone, then she opened her them fully.

It took a few moments for Louise's eyes to adapt to

the much darker woods. The outline of the oval was evident in front of her, illuminated by a series of small golden lights. Instead of darkness inside, it now appeared like a window. The closer she looked however the quicker it dawned on her that the trees appearing within the oval were very different to those growing around her. Instead of large pine trees, the trees in the oval had larger trunks, and from what she could see, it looked as if the bark was a deep red colour. Louise was thoroughly confused and before she could stop herself, she was peering around the side to ensure it wasn't just an obscured version of the trees ahead of her. As she'd expected, the two scenes were totally different. Looking back, Louise almost kicked herself for having taken such a long time to realise what the oval actually was. It was exactly as Clarris had said — it was a window into another world; a window into Calaresp.

Chapter Thirteen

A burst of excitement and relief erupted inside her as she realised that this was the answer to all of her questions. Thrilled by the thought that she was now looking at her homeland, she studied the scene more thoroughly, preparing herself for the world she was about to enter. The trees were reasonably far apart, allowing plenty of space to walk between them. From what Louise could see, there wasn't any snow on the ground there. Instead, despite the shadows caused by the large looming trees, long and luscious grass grew almost as if it were springtime.

Louise looked across at Barney and found herself smiling broadly.

She let out a sigh of relief as she spoke.

'Well, it seems we've found our way into Calaresp!'

She kept the smile on her face as she looked back at the window in front of her. As she considered the last hour, she knew that none of the events that had led her to the window had been a fluke. Somehow, she had been led to that exact spot. It could have been a result of memories locked in her subconscious, leaking out, guiding her. The alternative and more probable option was that Clarris had somehow ensured that when Louise returned to her point of death, this would be how events were supposed to unfold.

'Well,' Louise said quietly to herself. 'I suppose it's now or never.' Rising to her feet, Louise swung her backpack over her shoulders and adjusted the straps to ensure that it was comfortable and secure. She always kept Barney's lead loosely around her neck, but now she pulled it off and clicked it onto Barney's collar. An idea popped into her head and she crouched back down to the ground. Searching carefully, it wasn't long before she found more of the purple granules scattered around her. She scooped up as many as possible and safely tucked them away in the pocket of her shirt, on the opposite side to where her knife remained hidden. She then carefully gathered Barney into her arms and held him close.

Louise stood back up and took a deep and unsteady breath as she prepared herself. She hesitated for a few moments and then she thought she saw the oval wavering. She felt a sudden panic as she realised that she had no idea how long this window would remain open for. Terror began to seep back through her and with this pumping through her veins, she forced herself to step forward.

Lifting her right foot into the oval, she felt as if she'd dipped her foot into an ice-cold bath. For a split second, she hesitated, then forced herself onwards, allowing her right foot to find solid ground. She then allowed the rest of her body, and a seemingly unperturbed Barney, to pass through the window. Every part of her body froze as she stepped through. When her face followed, she automatically forced her eyes shut, instincts telling her that some elements of the cold window were similar to that of water and could affect her eyes if she tried to keep them open.

Louise rushed forward until the freezing wave of water had left her entire body and the atmosphere began to feel normal again. She opened her eyes and her mouth fell open. The window had worked; she was now on the other side, her surroundings entirely different. Now, for as far as she could see, there were large, red-barked trees with low, leaf-covered branches. She looked down at her feet and moved the soft, vibrant grass around with her right foot. It was a stark contrast to the wintery scene she had left moments before.

Carefully, Louise placed Barney onto the ground. He didn't seem remotely surprised to find himself somewhere entirely different. Louise bent towards him and gave him a gentle pat on his head. Barney wagged his tail.

Louise looked up at the sky. Through the leaves of the large trees, she could see that it was blue, without a single cloud. She looked back at the window and saw the wood she'd been in just moments before. A world engulfed by winter. Where she was now, was warm, dry, and alive with spring.

The window wavered once again, and the golden edges of the oval darkened. They began to move inwards, causing the window to shrink. The view into her world was quickly disappearing until the lights met in the middle, where they sparkled for a few seconds before vanishing completely.

Chapter Fourteen

Louise starred at the spot in which the window had been. Her home for the best part of her life was gone. Unless she were to waste the granules in her pocket, she was now at the point of no return. Just to make sure it had vanished, she waved her hand through the spot in which it had been, finding nothing but air. She sighed to herself, nervousness replacing the fear and excitement she had felt before.

Now the window back had vanished, she became increasingly aware of how overdressed she was. On the other side, the temperature had been below zero, yet here it was a balmy spring day. She was beginning to feel unpleasantly warm and stuffy, so before doing anything else, she took her backpack off and placed it on the ground. She quickly took off her jacket, keeping a keen eye on her surroundings, slightly paranoid that something could creep up on her unexpectedly. She took off her winter clothes and placed them in her backpack for later, in case it grew cold at night. She then rolled up her sleeves and lifted the bag back onto her shoulders.

Louise turned and examined her surroundings. The beautiful grand trees stretched for as far as she could see, and there was nothing to suggest the best route to take in order to find some sort of civilisation. It was then that she noticed Barney sat just to her right, patiently looking at her. She stared at him for a few moments.

'Let me guess,' she said, studying him as she spoke. 'You know which way we should go?' At which point, he gave a wag of his tail, hesitating only for a second as she removed his lead. Barney turned and began to walk away from her. After a few paces, he stopped and turned around, an action which Louise took as a sign he wanted her to follow. As soon as she caught up with him, Barney trotted just in front of her. She couldn't understand how, as a dog, he seemed to know exactly what he was doing. However, with all the strange events that had unfolded over the past few days, and the prospect of Brisheit's army trying to hunt her down, Barney's increased intelligence was the least of her worries.

The scenery didn't change that much as they continued onwards, with each tree looking the same as the first. Louise wondered whether she should have marked the tree in which the window had been, but it was too late for that. If she wanted to go back, she'd have to find another way.

Louise followed Barney through the woods. As they went, the grand trees that had initially struck Louise as being mysterious and strikingly beautiful were now eerie and strangely frightening. At first, she thought it had merely been a coincidence that the branches on the trees seemed to be in identical places, but then she realised that it was more than that. Every single branch, leaf, bulge and indent on every tree was situated in exactly the same place. They continued walking and as they did, Louise stepped closer to one of the trees to obtain a better look. She noticed a small clump of purple moss merged within the bark. It delved into the natural crevasses of the bark, creating the impression that it ran so deep that it struck the very heart of the tree. She moved onwards to the next tree, eager to find out if that had the same patch of moss. She wasn't surprised to find that it did, as did the tree after that one, and the one after that.

Despite the warmth, Louise felt a chill pass through her. Although the woods were technically beautiful, the replication of the trees made it seem distinctly unnatural. She was also beginning to notice just how quiet it was. Although she didn't know anything about the wildlife of Calaresp, she still expected some sounds; a birdsong, an animal's call, or even the occasional sound of something scampering across the ground. Instead, all Louise could hear were the sounds of the contents of her backpack rustling and knocking against one another, whilst the bag itself gently bumping against her back. Her feet, on the other hand, didn't make a sound as they stepped into the marvellously soft ground. It was almost like walking barefoot across a soft carpet.

As they continued onwards, Louise forced herself to ignore the continuous stream of identical trees. It was a difficult thing to do as they surrounded her, so by way of a distraction, Louise tried to recall what Clarris had told her in regards to the rebels and where she would have been most likely to find them.

Louise was so deeply engrossed in her own thoughts, that she didn't notice Barney abruptly stopping ahead of her, she almost tripped over him, but quickly found her balance again. A split second later, Louise realised why Barney had stopped. Just ahead of them, there was a large clearing in the wood. It was so obvious that Louise couldn't believe she hadn't noticed it before.

It was a large path about ten feet wide that split through the woods. To Louise's right, the path curved around the corner, whilst on the left-hand side, it stretched onwards for a while and then took an abrupt turn to the right. Louise studied the path with interest. It was a stark contrast to the wood that surrounded it, which was emphasised by the way the trees and even the grass stopped abruptly in a disciplined symmetrical line outlining the path.

Stepping towards it, she hesitated, filled with a feeling of unease. The line was so distinctive that she felt like she wasn't supposed to cross it. As always, her curiosity took over and she had stepped onto it before she even knew what she was doing. This perspective made the woods seem even more ominous — trees lined up next to one another on either side, staring down at her like soldiers. She looked around, keen to ensure there wasn't anyone else nearby and that she wasn't being watched. There were hundreds of places in which someone could hide but Louise was fairly certain she was alone. She bent down towards the ground, looking for tracks or something that would give her some clue as to who or what used this path. Although she could see some indents on the ground, the majority of the path was covered with white and grey dust that obscured any tracks.

A loud thunderous sound suddenly pierced through the still air and the ground began to vibrate. Looking either side, Louise had the distinct impression that the sound was that of something approaching — something large, moving very fast. Louise was filled with a deep sense of unease, and her instincts screamed at her to get off the path, to hide and quickly.

Barney obviously had the same impression, as he looked over at Louise and whined softly. She rushed over to him, grabbed his collar, and retreated back into the trees. A part of her wanted to keep running to get away from whatever force was storming towards her. After a couple of steps, however, she hesitated, then threw herself and Barney behind a tree. She wanted to know who used the path; whether they could be trusted or if they worked for Brisheit. The tree they hid behind was far enough from the path to shield them from, but still close enough to allow Louise the chance to get a good look at whatever was approaching.

Eventually, as the vibrating ground beneath her began to intensify, she noticed a cloud of dust forming at the end of the path. It wasn't long before she could see legs and hooves piercing through it. Seconds later, their bodies followed and as the riders came into view, a small gasp escaped Louise's mouth. On top of the black and brown horses sat large men wearing armour identical to those she'd seen in the woods just days before. The same armour worn by Brisheit's men.

Panic spread throughout Louise's body and the urge to run became overwhelming. However, even if she'd wanted to give in to those desires, she wouldn't have been able to. Her entire body was paralysed with fright, it took all of her concentration just to move back behind the tree. She pressed her hands against the bark and they instantly stuck to it as if they'd been covered in glue.

The approaching soldiers were moving at such an alarming rate that they were soon passing right alongside the tree she was hidden behind. Louise carefully looked out from behind the tree, keen to get a better look at their faces. It proved to be an almost impossible task as they moved so fast. They rode two a breast and as they passed, Louise tried to keep count, keen to know exactly how many there were. The whole world shook as they galloped, armour and weapons glistening in the sunlight.

Even though her entire body was filled with paralysing terror, she found the entire thing utterly mesmerising. By the time they had passed, Louise had counted twenty-two in total; a large cloud of dust remained, particles drifting through the air like a fog. Eventually, the dust settled, and with half a notion to follow them—in the hope they'd lead her to some sort of civilisation—Louise prised herself away from the tree. She took a deep breath and quietly moved across the wood towards the path. Just as her first foot was about to land on the ground, a force smacked into her left-hand side, painfully knocking her onto the ground. All Louise could see was a blur of blue and black. When the world finally stopped moving, a hand stretched out and grabbed her.

'Quick,' said a quiet, low voice, 'you need to get back!'

Chapter Fifteen

The stranger lifted her off the ground and unceremoniously flung her behind a tree; the impact spread from her back to her stomach, causing her to gasp loudly as she was winded by the force. Taking a few deep panicked breaths, Louise looked back at whoever had attacked her. Beside her was an imposingly large man who wore a light top that was neatly tucked into a pair of dark brown cargo-style trousers. Stretched out below him were a pair of black boots, pushed so forcefully into the ground he had managed to uproot some of the grass, showing the dirt underneath it. She looked up at his face, but he was turned away from her, so all she was able to see was the back of his head. From here, she could see he had dark brown messy hair.

Panic spread through her body and mingled with the pain he'd caused her. Was this man her friend or foe? He had been so rough with her, she couldn't begin to believe that he was going to help her. Louise slowly raised her hand and brought it up to her shirt pocket. Fumbling with the flap, she brought out the small knife she'd stowed there. She flipped it open and pointed it towards the man.

'Who the hell are you?' she hissed. 'What do you...?'

He moved so quickly she had little time to react, as, one hand harshly clasping her mouth whilst the other covered the hand holding the knife, forcing it away from her. He brought her body right next to his, bringing her head beside his own and with a harsh, angry voice he whispered, 'Will you be quiet before you get us both killed!'

His grip around her mouth intensified and ignoring the pain, Louise forced air uncomfortably in and out from her nose. She tried to wriggle free but his sheer size and strength gave him the advantage. Through the panic, she heard a noise, a vibration on the ground. Louise immediately stopped trying to break free and her eyes flashed to the side, trying to see what was happening. She recognised the approaching sound and knew it must be more horsemen riding along the path.

As if he knew she'd acknowledged the greater threat, the man let her go, and he turned his back to her to look at the path. Louise did the same, hands pressed against the tree. On the ground between them lay the small knife; it had fallen from her hand as soon as he had let go and neither of them were concerned about getting it. They just wanted to ensure that the passing soldiers didn't notice them.

By the time Louise had turned, they were already starting to pass their hiding place. As soon as she saw them, Louise's mouth dropped. She'd thought the last group had been intimidating, but this time there were twice as many men going twice as fast. They were so loud and the vibrations on the ground were so intense that it felt like the entire world was caving in on itself. Unlike the last time, Louise had no desire to count the number of men passing or to get a better look. She simply wanted to ensure they couldn't see her, whilst simultaneously refusing to turn her back to the strange man that had saved her in what could only be described as a brutish manner.

After what felt like a tremendous amount of time, the world was still again. Louise ventured to look up and was relieved to find they had finally passed and remained unaware of the three of them hiding in the trees.

Louise noticed Barney emerging from the tree to her left that she had originally hidden behind. He held his head low and his gaze was fixed on the stranger. Whilst the man kept his back to Louise, she slowly and carefully picked up her knife and moved away in Barney's direction. The soft grass meant that she made next to no noise and she became increasingly confident that she'd get away unnoticed.

'So, this is how you thank the person who saved your life is it, by sneaking away?' the man suddenly asked, still watching the path.

Louise froze, panic spreading through her body as she considered her options. She could try and run away, although she wasn't certain she'd even be able to run faster than him. Alternatively, she could stay and discover whether he was a friend or foe.

'Who are you?' she asked curtly. 'What do you want from me?'

He finally turned around to look at her and a smile spread across his face, although Louise didn't think it was necessarily a friendly one. His brown eyes stared straight at her, his brow furrowed as if perplexed by the situation. He let out a short, sharp laugh and leant back against the tree, folding his arms against his chest and crossing one leg over the other as he stretched them out in front of him. The expression on his face combined with the way he'd positioned his body screamed an arrogance that made Louise's blood boil. Simply looking at him filled her with an instant dislike.

'Once again, is this how you treat the person who just saved you from almost guaranteed torture and eventual death!?' He looked up at her and raised an eyebrow, giving her a smug look.

Louise was just about to retort with a scathing remark when she realised exactly what he had just said.

'Torture?' she asked in a quiet voice.

He studied Louise carefully with a questioning look and then jumped to his feet.

'Jamsen,' he said with a smile. 'And you are?'

The question sent Louise into a mild panic. She had no idea how common the name Louise was and for all she knew, Brisheit could have banned anyone from using it to single her out if she were ever to return. She decided to risk it.

'My name is Louise,' she replied, watching him carefully for some sort of reaction. If he did have any suspicions, he hid it effectively as the smile on his face widened. Then he looked to Louise's right and his expression quickly changed to one of shock and alarm. As Louise followed his gaze, she realised that Barney was now stood at her side, head down, hackles raised, watching him closely. Now Jamsen was looking back at him, Barney slowly curled his lip, baring his teeth and allowing a quiet growl to escape.

'Woah, steady there, my friend!' he said, his expression becoming slightly less confident.

Louise smiled, immediately comforted by Barney's wary reaction. She looked up at Jamsen filled with renewed confidence.

'Steady Barney,' she said, raising a hand to keep him where he was. 'Now, tell me what exactly is going on?' she asked. 'Why would they have tortured me?'

Once again Jamsen gave her a quizzical look, then watched her for a moment before asking, 'Do you really not know where you are?'

Louise didn't say anything, becoming increasingly infuriated. She felt like he was trying to wind her up. He watched her closely and as the smile left his face, he raised his eyebrows.

'This is the Whalsp Wood.' He paused as if expecting her to recognise the name. When she didn't, he let out a half-whistle of disbelief before continuing, 'This is the enchanted wood, the private property of Commander Brisheit. No one is meant to enter them other than his own men, and even they have to remain on the path.' He paused for a second, the cocky edge was creeping back despite the presence of Barney. 'You mustn't be from around here if you don't know about Whalsp!'

'I'm not,' she replied, perhaps a little too quickly. 'I come from a small village quite far from here, so I don't know too much about this area.'

He eyed her suspiciously and replied simply with a, 'Uh-huh." Louise felt a flare of paranoia, worried that this stranger couldn't be trusted and that he may work out who she was. She had already decided that if she were to meet anyone here, she wouldn't reveal her identity, not when there were so many people that would probably want her dead. However, this meant that she had the impossible task of deciding whether or not somebody could be trusted.

She looked at him indignantly and said, 'The village I grew up in was very small. We had little to do with the outside world, the troubles it tangles itself up in, and the politics. It made for an easier life.' Louise had rehearsed this speech in her mind time and time again and as she watched Jamsen's reaction, she felt she had pulled it off successfully.

His look of suspicion vanished and the arrogance once again took its place. 'Well, despite your sheltered upbringing, I presume that you know who Brisheit is?'

Louise nodded, 'Yes, of course we know of him.'

'Well, as I've said, these are his woods and they are steeped in secrets and magic, hence the fact they call them enchanted.'

'What sort of magic?' Louise asked, her attention grabbed.

'Don't know,' he replied. 'Nobody really knows too much about them. The woods stretch for miles, and anyone who enters them gets torn apart by the wreags that are left to roam them, or they wind up caught by soldiers. Anyone who enters them doesn't escape to tell the tale.'

'Why do they torture them?' Louise asked.

'Simple. To discover why they are in the woods, who sent them, and whether they learnt anything whilst being there.' He said this in such a nonchalant manner that Louise felt herself becoming increasingly suspicious and almost frightened of him.

'So, are you a soldier?'

He seemed taken aback by this question, and when he replied, it was in a more subdued voice.

'No, I am not a soldier.' He averted his gaze, choosing to look at the ground beside her.

'So, if no one is meant to be here, why are you?' Louise felt her grip tighten on the small knife in her hand that she had so far kept hidden.

At this remark, he lifted his head again, any uncertainty in his expression replaced by his usual attitude. 'I am not like most people!' he said, a grin spreading across his face. 'I come to the woods on occasion to hunt. So far, I haven't been caught. I am an exception to the rule. As it seems, are you!'

Louise studied him, looking for any sign of creatures that he may have caught. It was at this point that Louise noticed a black, rather tatty satchel that had been thrown carelessly against a tree not far from him. Next to it, there sat a dark wooden bow and a dark green quiver filled with black arrows with bright white points. Hanging at the bottom of the quiver, tied by a small piece of rope, hung a small, dark grey, fluffy animal. It looked remarkably like a rabbit, but with short, almost non-existent ears.

Meanwhile, Jamsen had knelt to the ground and was looking directly at Barney. He stretched out his arms and in a quiet, non-threatening voice he said, 'It's alright pal, I'm not going to hurt you.' He opened up his arms towards the dog. 'Come here,' he said gently.

Initially, Barney merely stared at the stranger, then as his arms remained extended, he cautiously began moving forward. He remained totally still as Barney approached, allowing him to sniff and investigate him as much as he wanted.

Jamsen slowly moved one of his hands, careful to ensure that Barney could see what he was doing. The dog simply watched him and when the hand reached the top of his head, he allowed Jamsen to stroke him. Barney raised his head and some of the tension left his body. He manoeuvred his head away from Jamsen's hand and he trotted back to Louise's side, still watching the stranger; he had clearly decided that he was not a threat but didn't fully trust him either.

'A good companion you have there, what's his name?' asked Jamsen, getting back to his feet and heading over to his dropped pack.

'Barney,' Louise replied, still watching him.

He nodded acknowledgement whilst moving his weapons into a comfortable position. Once he finished, he stepped over to Louise and brushed past her. She watched as he moved to the tree she'd first hidden behind and pulled out her old backpack. He gave it a slightly quizzical look when he first saw it and then walked back over to Louise and passed it to her. She took it without hesitation but kept the knife in her other hand.

Louise pulled her bag onto her shoulders and took a few minutes to make sure that it was secure. When she looked back up, she was surprised to find Jamsen standing right beside her, watching her. Louise automatically took a step backwards and tripped on a tree root as she did so.

She prepared herself for the impact of another harsh landing, but it never came. Instead, she felt a hard grip on the top of her arm as she was pulled upright, only letting go when she was stable again. She looked up and found Jamsen holding onto her, a smile on his face.

'So,' he asked, 'what are you planning on doing now?'

It took a few minutes before Louise could answer, purely because she really didn't know herself. She was trapped in a wood she apparently wasn't supposed to be in, she couldn't follow the path, and she didn't really know which direction to take. The uncertainty must have shown on her face as he smiled sincerely for the first time.

'Where were you going?' he asked, gently prompting her for some sort of answer.

Louise looked up at him, her mind was racing as she tried to think of a convincing answer. 'I was heading to the Pologor. My cousin lives there, but I haven't seen her since I was a young girl.'

'I presume you aren't entirely confident of the way, otherwise, I doubt you'd have ended up here.'

Louise was just about to answer when she thought she saw his gaze flickering to her neck. Instinctively, she brought her hand up to where the Whisper hung, paranoid that it might be on show. But as her hand reached her chest, she felt it safely tucked away underneath her shirt. The only part he could have possibly seen was the chain and that was of no concern to her. Louise had decided when she'd first put the Whisper on that the best thing to do would be to keep it hidden. She had no idea whether it would be widely recognised, nor whether people's loyalties would lie with her family or with Brisheit.

Jamsen didn't wait for her to answer. 'How about we leave together? I'm heading to a village called Shorot, it's not far from Pologor.' He stopped fidgeting with his pack and looked at her intently.

Louise's mind was going a mile a minute. A large part of her didn't want to trust this stranger, but an even larger part of her wasn't convinced that she'd be able to find her own way there. She'd only managed to get as far as she had through chance and Barney's inexplicable guidance. Although she still had her doubts about this Jamson, he did know how to get to a village that was close to Pologor. He also knew the dangers of the land far better than she did, so sticking with him could potentially be safer.

Louise could feel Jamsen staring at her, deep in thought. Once he realised that she was watching him, his expression quickly changed back to the broad smile that now looked forced. He raised an eyebrow expectantly.

'Tell me, why are you so keen for me to join you?' she asked sternly.

'I've been travelling alone for a while; I can imagine worse things than to have a bit of companionship for the next stretch.' He paused and looked away from her awkwardly as if trying to work out the best way to word his next sentence. 'I would also never forgive myself if I left you here and you were caught. They would make your torture very public, to warn others away.'

Louise wasn't sure whether the concern in his voice was genuine or whether it was all an act. She didn't believe there was any chance that he knew who she really was, or that he'd care if he found out. Even though she didn't particularly like this man, she couldn't see how he could be a real threat to her.

'Okay, I'll come with you,' she said, still intending to keep him at arm's length as a precaution. Despite feeling uneasy, she decided that she should show some gratitude considering he did technically save her. Feeling the blush rise instantly to her cheeks, she turned away from him before saying 'thank you' in a quiet, almost inaudible voice.

Jamsen must have heard as he smiled once again. He turned to his right and made his way to the path, placing the quiver and bow onto his shoulder as he moved. Louise opened her mouth to ask where he was going but the look of concentration on his face made her close it again. Instead, she watched him, transfixed.

Standing stock-still in the centre of the path, he raised his head to the air, listening. He remained like this for a few minutes, then slowly knelt to the ground and placed his hand on it. He abruptly rose to his feet, brushing off the dust that had stuck to it. He then looked over at Louise as if only now remembering she was there, his usual smile appearing as he moved towards her.

'There aren't any more patrols approaching, at least not for the moment,' he said, looking at their surroundings.

'Isn't it still too dangerous to walk on the path, they approach so quickly?' Louise asked, feeling rather naive in these strange new surroundings.

'We won't walk on the path, we'll stick to the woods. But to get out of the woods as quickly as possible, I think we should remain close to the path as it's the fastest way out. If we remain in the woods, we can duck behind the trees relatively quickly if we hear anything. We'll just have to be careful of wreags.'

Louise couldn't think of anything to say in response. It seemed a sensible enough plan, so she just nodded her head and the two of them turned and began to move on. Louise fell back until she was walking just behind him. She couldn't help but remain distrustful of the young man, despite his smiles and seemingly good-natured temperament. She couldn't shake the feeling that to trust him so quickly would be foolish. He automatically turned to look at her, but as soon as he had realised what she was doing, he seemed to accept it and continued onwards.

Chapter Sixteen

They walked for around ten minutes, the same replicated tree surrounding them, the quiet empty path always to their right. Louise was beginning to feel increasingly awkward. The silence was becoming oppressive and despite how little she knew of him, she felt she should make some effort to fill the emptiness.

'So, how far do we have to walk before we leave these woods?' she asked, raising her voice to ensure that he heard her.

'It's about twelve miles and we should be out.' He turned, stopping abruptly to look at her. 'No offence intended but I think it would be a good idea for us not to talk. Just until we're out of the woods.' He saw the slightly insulted expression on her face before he continued in a whisper, 'The wreags have superb hearing and have the capability to hear us from miles away. The closer we get to the edge of the Whalsp Wood, the more likely there'll be patrols with wreags. I don't know about you, but I don't want to run the risk of catching their attention by talking.'

Louise considered what he'd said and was just

about to reply when she thought better of it. Instead, she just nodded her head. The two of them then continued in silence.

It was a few hours later before they stopped. The sun, which was just visible through the trees, had moved from in front of them to behind them. Louise was beginning to grow tired, her legs becoming increasingly heavy. Through the course of the day she had walked quite a substantial distance and was now unsure of how much further she could continue without a break.

When the exhaustion eventually became too much, she took an extra step forward to tap Jamsen on the shoulder. He looked surprised as he turned around as if he had almost forgotten that she was there. Maintaining the silence, he cocked his head to the side and inquisitively raised his eyebrow.

Louise was conscious of remaining quiet, so she stepped as close to him as she comfortably could, and then, in a quiet voice, she asked, 'Would it be possible for us to stop for a break? I've walked miles so far today and I'm getting quite exhausted.'

At first, he looked frustrated at her request, seemingly eager to get out of the woods. The look of exhaustion on her face must have been enough to convince him, however, and he nodded. He gestured deeper into the wood, and Louise realised that he wanted them to have their rest further from the path, where they would presumably be safer. They walked for another ten minutes before finally stopping. Jamsen, keeping his bag on but removing his quiver and bow, settled himself against the trunk of the tree, facing away from the direction of the path. Louise hesitated, unsure where to sit; she was keen to be hidden from the path but the only place that offered this concealment was the tree that Jamsen had settled behind.

A few moments later, he looked up at her and seemed to quickly become aware of her dilemma. He moved over so that he was resting right against the edge of the tree, leaving just enough space for her to do the same. Louise hesitated for a second, but the longing to sit down took over and she pulled off her backpack and slumped herself against the tree. Barney settled himself by Louise's feet, keeping a watchful eye on Jamsen. When she had finally settled, Louise quickly became aware that her arm was resting against his. She subtly tried to move so that they weren't touching but with the size of the tree trunk, it was very difficult to achieve.

Louise turned away, feeling a blush rising to her cheek. Jamsen was undeniably an attractive man and being in such close proximity to him made her feel decidedly awkward. Jamsen, on the other hand, didn't seem to notice a thing as he leant back, stretching his legs out and shutting his eyes. Bow and quiver resting against his legs. Louise brought her bag up next to her and searched inside it. Eventually, she found what she was looking for and brought out bread and cheese, quickly making herself a sandwich. Just as she was about to take a bite, she looked over to Jamsen.

'Umm, would you like something to eat?' she asked him quietly.

He opened his eyes and looked at the scruffy, quickly made sandwich being offered to him. He took it in his hand.

'Hmm,' he said, a quizzical look on his face, 'it looks

quite unlike anything I've eaten before! What's this yellowish stuff?' he asked, pulling out the cheese.

A look of shock spread across Louise's face. 'You've never eaten cheese!?' she asked.

Jamsen shook his head and took a large bite from the sandwich. After the first few chews, his eyes widened.

'This is amazing! Delicious!' he said, spraying small half-digested pieces of food across himself.

Louise couldn't stop the smile that spread across her face as she rummaged in her bag and made herself another sandwich. She leant back against the tree as she took her first bite; it was the first thing she'd eaten for hours and at that moment, it seemed like the most delicious thing she'd ever tasted. Louise was, however, careful to leave a bit for Barney, who wolfed it down eagerly. Once they'd finished, she dug in her bag again and brought out a flask of water. After taking a good long sip, she offered it to Jamsen, then cupped some in her hand and let Barney have a good drink.

Rested and fed, it was Louise who stood up first and pulled her bag back on.

'Should we get going?' she asked Jamsen, who had once again leant back and shut his eyes. As a response, he let out a long and exhausted sigh and brought himself to his feet. He led them back to where they'd been walking, just parallel to the path, and they continued onwards in silence. Barney loyally at Louise's side.

The sun was slowly setting and as the surrounding wood was plunged into darkness, the trees began to change. It was so subtle at first that Louise barely noticed it. The edges of the leaves began to light up — a gentle blue light, almost as if they were lined with thousands of minuscule stars. The darker it became, the further it spread, until the entire leaf was covered. They weren't overwhelmingly bright, but it was enough to illuminate their surroundings and let them see where they were going. Without knowing what she was doing, Louise found herself drawn to one of the leaves, transfixed by it. She brought out her hand and gently lifted one, taking a better look at it.

Jamsen, having walked a few paces ahead, noticed she'd stopped and turned to look at her. Louise saw a smile spreading across his face as he watched her study the glowing leaf. He walked back until he was stood beside her.

'Not many people get to see the Whalsp trees at night—not close up, anyway. Those passing can see it from a distance but as none of them come into the woods, they are rarely seen at such close proximity.'

Louise didn't reply. Instead, she looked up at the tree, taking in every inch of the beautiful sight in front of her.

Jamsen followed her gaze. 'It's truly beautiful, isn't it?' he quietly asked.

'Yes, yes, it is,' Louise replied. 'I've never seen anything like it, never seen something quite so stunning before.'

Jamsen looked down at her and smiled, 'Come on, we need to keep moving.'

Louise took one last glance and then followed him onwards, filled with awe for the world to which she'd been born and ripped away from.

It wasn't long before Jamsen turned to her and in a barely audible voice, said, 'Take care, we're almost at the edge of the wood. There will be patrols here that are particularly vigilant.'

They slowed considerably to make as little noise as possible, which was relatively easy on the soft forest ground. They were so quiet that Louise became certain that every breath would give away her position; the more she dwelled on the matter, the louder it seemed to become. She became so concerned, Louise found herself holding her breath, which consequently made things worse, as the breaths she let out were even louder.

Louise was so absorbed by this that she didn't notice Jamsen had stopped just in front of her. She bumped into him so forcibly that she almost fell over. Luckily, Jamsen grabbed her just in time. She opened her mouth to thank him, but he promptly put his finger to his lips and whispered 'shh' in her ear. He kept a firm grip on her as he looked all around them.

His gaze lingered behind them and after a few moments, his grip intensified.

'Quick!' he said in a louder, more urgent voice as he shoved her onwards. 'There's a patrol nearby and I think their wreag's have picked up on our scent. Run!'

For the first few steps, Louise was hesitant, trying to comprehend how he could possibly know these things when the woods were still so quiet. Realising she wasn't moving at the required speed, he darted back and grabbed her arm, pulling her onwards. Louise could see Barney bolting past them a few seconds later and before she knew it, she too was running as fast as she could, at which point Jamsen finally released her arm. If she had found the wood of identical trees disorienting whilst they were walking, it was nothing in comparison to running through it. Louise found it impossible to register how fast they were going when the surroundings were forever the same.

As time passed, Louise began to doubt whether they were actually being pursued. Just as she turned to Jamsen to question him, a sound echoed through the woods—a sound she knew all too well. The piercing howl ran straight through her and threatened to paralyse every bone in her body. The first howl was joined by a second and then, in quick succession, a third and fourth.

'Damn it!" Jamsen shouted, obviously no longer concerned about remaining quiet. 'They're in pursuit! Follow my lead and run as fast as you can!' He didn't even wait for a response; he simply ran on at a pace that Louise struggled to keep up with.

Chapter Seventeen

A few short minutes later, Jamsen suddenly took a sharp turn to the right. Louise and Barney instantly copied. Just as she was about to question Jamsen as to where they were going, he stopped. As Louise caught up to him, he crouched to the ground and she immediately followed suit. Barney came up beside them and lay on the ground as low as he could.

Jamsen brought himself next to Louise and whispered gently in her ear. 'Stay perfectly still and don't say a word.'

Before he could move away, Louise whispered back, 'We can't have lost them, their senses are far too good for that. Surely they'll be able to smell us.'

Jamsen nodded before replying, 'I'm just trying to get my bearings. I've set several safety points in these woods, a precaution for occasions such as this.'

'How often does this happen to you?' Louise whispered back.

He didn't reply, and as Louise opened her mouth to repeat the question, he grabbed her arm and pushed her in the direction she needed to go. She was just about to object when another series of howls filled the emptiness around them, making her run once again.

They ran at a good speed and seemed to cover a lot of distance before Jamsen, who was running just ahead of her, came to an abrupt halt. She had only been a few paces behind but by the time she had caught up with him he was already crouched low to the ground, carefully studying the floor just below one of the many glowing trees.

'What are you doing?' Louise whispered, trying to hide her frustration.

He didn't reply. Instead, he continued to stare at the ground. Louise glanced behind her, expecting one of the wreags to appear in the distance at any second and make a beeline straight for her. However, the horizon remained empty. She looked back at Jamsen, who was now scrambling at a small spot on the ground as if hoping to find something buried there.

'Don't you think we should keep running?' Louise asked him, not even attempting to keep the urgency out of her voice.

'It should be here, I'm certain this is it!' he replied in a quiet voice, not even acknowledging her question.

Louise stared at him, trying to decipher whether he was insane or not. She began to consider running on without him if he didn't snap out of it soon. She looked at her surroundings and tried to decipher which direction would be best to run.

'Yes!' Jamsen suddenly exclaimed in slightly too loud a voice. As Louise looked back towards him, she found him grinning at her triumphantly, holding back what looked like a large patch of ground. To begin with, Louise was so puzzled that she almost forgot that there was a patrol hunting them down.

'Come on, get it!' Jamsen said in a hurried voice.

For a moment, Louise simply stared back at him, bemused by the entire situation. All of a sudden, she realised what he had done. Jamsen had pulled back a part of the ground at the base of the tree, revealing underneath it a small hole that was probably big enough to fit three or four people. The section of ground he had ripped out wasn't actually ground, but a window-sized door, the top of which was covered with grass to camouflage it.

Louise cocked her head to get a better look into the hole when Jamsen jumped in, 'Come on! You need to get in!' he said urgently, staring at her with a desperate look on his face.

'Barney, come on,' Louise whispered at the dog. 'In you go!'

Barney obediently got into the hole and just as Louise was about to follow suit, she realised just how dark it was in there. Hurriedly, she turned around and ran to one of the trees slightly further from them, keeping a keen eye on her surroundings in case she needed to make a hasty retreat. Once she reached one of the trees, she stretched up and picked a few of the leaves situated just within her reach. With four in her hand, she turned back and ran to where an impatient Jamsen waited for her. She threw herself into the hole and as she did so, Jamsen pulled the false door over the hole and plunged them into darkness.

'What the hell were you doing?!' he asked her in a harsh whisper, clearly annoyed by her little venture.

Rather than reply, Louise smiled in the darkness and brought her hand up to her face, unfurling her clenched fist to reveal the leaves. The small pulses of light that the leaves generated were enough to chase the darkness in the centre to the sides of the hole, creating wild and obscure shadows.

Jamsen raised his eyebrows, seemingly a little impressed. 'But why didn't you just take them from this tree?' he asked. 'Why did you waste time and put us both in danger by going to one further away?'

Louise gave him an incredulous look, surprised he didn't already know the answer to this. 'These trees are all identical. I thought four missing leaves may look a little suspicious and so would be better found on a tree other than the one we're hiding beneath.'

He nodded his approval and smiled at her.

'So, what is this thing?' Louise asked. 'Will it stop the wreags from finding us? Haven't they got an incredible sense of smell?'

Jamsen nodded and replied in a quiet voice, obviously still concerned that they could be overheard. 'To be honest, I don't quite know how it works. I stumbled across one of these holes about six years ago when I was hunting. I had dropped an arrow, and as I bent to pick it up, it got caught on the trapdoor and dislodged it. It was quite late at night and so I thought it was the ideal place to safely get a little bit of sleep. I was awoken early the next morning by the sound of feet hurriedly stomping on the ground above me.' He sat back, getting himself comfortable before continuing. 'I obviously panicked, presuming they had found me. I remained as far from the trapdoor as possible, my bow ready to take a shot at whoever opened it. But nothing happened, the footsteps moved on. I was confused, I can tell you that much. So, I did something somewhat reckless. I opened the trapdoor — just a fraction, mind — and took a sneaky peek outside.'

'What did you see?' Louise couldn't stop herself from asking, transfixed by the bizarre tale.

'There was a large patrol with at least eight wreags, but they were heading away from my location. I opened the door a little further and it was at that point I saw one of the wreags freeze and raise its muzzle to the air. It had obviously picked up my scent and just as I was closing the door once again, I saw it turn to face my direction.' At this point, Jamsen let out a quiet chuckle. 'I can tell you, the next few minutes were possibly the most terrifying moments of my life. I was certain I'd given my location away. I heard vibrations above my head; at least three wreags had returned to investigate the smell. And then, nothing.'

'What do you mean, nothing?' Louise demanded, becoming increasingly confused.

'Exactly what I said: nothing. The patrol left. I remained in this hole for a little longer hoping by then it would be safe to move on, and it was. I was out of the woods about an hour later. I've found quite a few of them throughout the woods and have been using them to sleep in and to hide from patrols ever since.'

'So how do you think they work, how do they hide you so well?'

Instead of answering her question, Jamsen raised a finger to his lips and pointed to the trapdoor above them.

Louise had been so intrigued by this mysterious hole in the ground that she had forgotten about the patrol that had been hot on their trail. Now she could hear the distinct sounds of heavy-booted feet and large paws thumping loudly against the ground. Louise pushed herself against the base of their hiding place, keeping herself as far from them as possible. Instinctively, she raised her spare hand over the glowing leaves, once again allowing the darkness to spread through their hiding place. As she did, she stared intently at the edges of the trapdoor, half expecting small rays of light to suddenly pierce through, shining on them like hundreds of small spotlights.

Heart beating heavily in her chest, Louise waited with bated breath as she became increasingly anxious. Muffled sounds of the men talking leaked through into their shelter. Louise concentrated, trying to interpret exactly what they were saying. No matter how hard she tried, however, she simply couldn't understand them.

All of a sudden, the voices above them stopped, then the sound of footprints began moving away from them until they were once again consumed by silence.

Louise let out a soft sigh of relief. Moments later, Jamsen did the same. As Louise revealed the glowing leaves once again, she realised that he was looking at her, a content smile on his face.

Jamsen raised his hand towards the top of the shelter. 'See,' he said. 'Some sort of magic protects these shelters; it masks scents, ensures they blend in perfectly to the surroundings and who knows, perhaps they wouldn't hear us if we were talking either. That's something I've never been too keen to try out!'

Louise smiled back at him, finally beginning to feel more comfortable in his presence. Despite any doubts that might have remained, she could feel herself beginning to trust him.

'Well, whatever it is,' Louise said in reply, 'I like it! What should we do now, stay here or head off?'

He seemed to consider their options for a while and leant back casually as he replied. 'We're probably best waiting here for a while, just to be sure they're not lingering around in the hope that our scent will reappear.'

Louise opened her mouth and yawned widely as she felt sleep beginning to creep up on her.

'Why don't you try and get a bit of sleep. It won't be for long but you might feel a little refreshed.'

A small part of her felt a little uncomfortable about falling asleep in this shelter, leaving herself so vulnerable. Barney then pressed himself against Louise's leg, reminding her that he was there. She felt her eyes slowly closing as sleep crept up on her and before she knew it, she was asleep.

Chapter Eighteen

Louise was woken by a hand gently shaking her arm. To begin with, she couldn't remember where she was or why she was asleep on such an uncomfortable surface. Memories then began to trickle back into her mind and once she remembered the patrol, she sat bolt upright. The room around her was now pitch black and Louise desperately tried to scan it for Jamsen. Once he had stopped shaking her to wake her, he seemed to have melted into the shadows.

'Where are you Jamsen?' she asked in a quiet voice. 'What's happened to the light, where are the leaves?'

From out of the darkness a voice replied, pinpointing his location in the black shelter. 'I'm here. It's alright. The leaves only remain lit for a certain amount of time; it seems that without the tree's energy flowing through them, they are unable to maintain that light.'

'How long was I sleeping for?' Louise replied, trying to regain her composure.

'Not too long, probably about an hour.' he said, a large yawn overcoming him.

'Do you want to get some sleep now?' Louise asked sympathetically.

'No, I'll be alright. It's been quiet outside for a while now, so I think it's best we try and take this opportunity to escape the woods,' Jamsen answered.

Louise didn't reply straight away. Instead, she rummaged around to find her rucksack and on finding it, she checked the clasps and zips to make sure that it was all closed. She then gave Barney a quick stroke before finally replying to Jamsen, 'Right, well I'm ready to go when you are!'

'Let's get going then,' Jamsen said.

As he spoke, Louise could hear him beginning to move. She soon heard a rustling sound above her and it wasn't long before shards of dim light began to pierce their shelter. Louise was able to see a striking silhouette of Jamsen reaching out into the wood above them. He remained stationary for a few moments, and Louise presumed he was checking their surroundings to ensure that the patrol had left.

'It's clear. Come on, let's get going,' he said in an even quieter voice. With that, he stepped out of the shelter and vanished from Louise's view. Both she and Barney quickly followed suit. On stepping out, Louise's eyes took a few moments to adjust before she realised the sun had been replaced by a bright full moon. The trees still effectively lit up the woods and Louise located Jamsen standing a few paces away from her, calmly scanning his surroundings.

He indicated for Louise to follow and quietly whispered, 'Let's go, it's this way.' With that, he headed off into the wood, Louise and Barney following close behind.

They made their way silently through the woods, constantly eyeing their surroundings for fear of being caught. It wasn't long before Louise saw an end to the continuous run of trees, beyond which, all she could see was a sea of darkness. She felt relief flow steadily through her body and the paranoia that had gnawed away at her soon began to ebb away. It was then something happened that almost made her stop in her tracks; the howl they had dreaded so bitterly was once again spreading through the woods.

Jamsen looked around at Louise in shock and dismay.

'How did they find our scent again so quickly!' he whispered. He quickly scanned the woods around them, trying to pinpoint exactly which direction the patrol was approaching from. He looked back at her with a strange look of suspicion. Then stepped towards her and harshly grabbed her arm, pulling her towards the edge of the woods.

As he did so, he whispered somewhat harshly in her ear, 'Have the wreags chased you before?'

Louise tried to reply but found herself stumbling on her words, 'Oh, well they…'

'Have they known your scent before, have they pursued you?!' he asked, the tone intensifying and volume increasing.

'Yes!' Louise hurriedly replied, hoping he wouldn't ask for too much detail. 'A few days ago, they caught my scent and pursued me for a while. I escaped by the skin of my teeth.'

Jamsen cursed under his breath, still pulling Louise along. 'You should have told me this before!' he replied in a harsh voice.

'What difference does it make?' Louise asked, beginning to feel frustrated with Jamsen's attitude towards her.

He didn't get the chance to reply, however, as the howls once again filled the silence surrounding them. Just as they reached the edge of the woods, Jamsen yanked her harshly and pushed her down against one of the trees. He ignored the protests that flooded from her and began to rummage in his bag.

Louise, who was desperate to continue running from the patrol, was filled with fear that any second now they could be pounced upon by a wreag. She tried to get up on several occasions but Jamsen simply pushed her back down whilst he continued to look for some unknown object.

He brought out a small black vial, which he immediately shoved towards Louise. 'Here!' he said. 'Put one drop behind each ear and one on each wrist.'

Louise, having seen the drastic alteration of his mood, immediately did as he asked. Whilst she did this, he kept watch, ensuring that they weren't caught unaware. She then carefully placed a few drops on various points on Barney's fur. Brushing them through his coat with the tips of her fingers. Jamsen finally looked back as she passed him the vial and he slipped it into his pocket. At the same time, he pulled Louise to her feet and pushed her onwards. Barney ran just a few paces ahead of them, equally as eager to escape the woods.

Jamsen didn't explain to Louise what he had given her and she was certain that this wasn't an appropriate time to discuss it. Instead, followed by the chorus of howls, they ran through the trees, and it wasn't long before they reached the end of the woods. What had previously looked like a sea of darkness, now became clearer. With the leaves behind them, Louise could see the stunning countryside lightly illuminated by the glow of the moon.

They paused and Louise found herself taking a few minutes to look up at the sky, immediately delighted by the array of stars shining brightly above her. It was a night's sky quite unlike any she had seen before; instead of the usual light white, the stars here were a multitude of subtle, gentle colours consisting of red, blue, green, yellow, and even light purple. It made for a truly beautiful sky.

Whilst she admired the spectacle above them, Jamsen had been scanning the edge of the woods, ensuring there weren't any further patrols that could threaten them. Once he seemed sure that the only patrol in the vicinity was the one pursuing them, he nudged her arm indicating that it was safe for them to move on. Since Louise had doused herself with whatever had been in the vial, Jamsen had appeared much calmer and friendlier towards her.

'Right, let's get out of these woods before they catch up with us,' he said, no longer feeling the need to whisper.

'Won't they just follow us? I mean, they'll easily be able to spot us out there!' Louise said, speaking at a normal volume too.

'No, we should be okay. The patrols aren't supposed to leave the wood; if we get far enough away before they reach the edge, they shouldn't continue to pursue. We can use those crop fields below us to obscure their view.'

They stepped out of the woods and ran down a gentle decline that skirted around the Whalsp Woods and led straight to the fields just below them. Louise was desperate to ask more questions but as they ran increasingly faster, she found the deep breaths she was required to take limited her ability to talk. The howls that had surrounded them so completely whilst they'd remained in the woods now seemed to be considerably further away, although Louise was still certain they were pursuing them.

As they reached the edge of one of the multiple fields that stretched before them, Jamsen led them to one filled with crops that were taller than her. The thick stalks were positioned closely together but there was just enough space for someone to walk between them. In the moonlight, Louise couldn't see exactly what the crops were, but could just make out a circle of thick leaves at the top, with something circular growing in the centre.

Jamsen suddenly put his arm around her and pulled her into the field. Louise followed without protest and they squeezed themselves between the tall plants, still trying to maintain a reasonable speed. As a result of this, they were considerably louder than they had been previously, carelessly knocking against the stalks and the tops of the large leaves which were bent downwards so that they gently grazed against their heads as they ran. Once they were surrounded by the crops, Jamsen began to slow down and gradually came to a stop. Louise stopped beside him, breathing heavily.

She looked up at Jamsen as he stared back in the direction they'd just run. She could see he was carefully studying the edge of the wood, which, with the advantage of his height, he was able to see through the tops of the plants. Louise's view was blocked by the thick stalks and so she had to trust him to check where the patrol now was.

'They've reached the edge of the wood,' he said in a quiet voice. 'But they don't seem to be coming any further and I don't think they will now, especially if they can't see us.'

'Well, let's keep going,' Louise replied. 'I want to get as much distance as possible between us and that patrol!'

Jamsen nodded and smiled, the first time he'd done so in a while. Louise looked at him, watching his reaction as she asked, 'Why was it so important to know whether I'd been tracked by wreags before? And what exactly was in that vial you handed to me?'

He seemed unfazed by her question and continued to walk on as he replied, looking only at the route ahead of him.

'Once the wreags have been ordered by their masters to track a certain smell, they'll do so without question. They can store and pass that smell on to other wreags within the packs, even if they're fifty miles away. Each of them mentally records prey they've been stalking recently or scents they've been told to watch out for.'

Louise stared at him in disbelief. 'So even though they probably weren't the same patrol that chased me a few days ago, they still knew my scent and still knew to pursue me!'

'That's right. It's one of the reasons wreags are such perfect hunters.'

There was a moments silence, as Louise tried to

comprehend what she had just been told. She already considered the wreags to be formidable and forbidding foes, but now she knew that no matter where she went, a wreag patrol would instantly be able to identify her. This was a terrifying concept.

Whilst she remained absorbed in thought, he continued, 'The vial I gave you contains a liquid that masks your basic scent. It's not strong enough to notice it yourself, but it changes it enough to make your scent unfamiliar to the wreags.'

'Wow, surely Brisheit and his men wouldn't allow such a substance to exist? Where did you get hold of it?'

'To be honest, very few people even know it exists. I got it from an old magic woman. If Brisheit knew about it, both she and the potion would be quickly and quietly destroyed.'

Louise found herself smelling her wrists, curious to see if she would be able to identify a difference. She didn't smell anything and it had absorbed completely, leaving no trace.

'So, Louise,' Jamsen asked, 'what happened the last time you encountered wreags? Were you in the woods?'

Louise felt panic rising within her. She was beginning to wish she'd thought of a more thorough cover story. That way she would have been able to answer all questions put to her with total confidence.

'I was just on my way to the woods,' she replied hastily, trying to think what to say next. 'I was on a path and saw them coming. It turned out that they saw me and began hunting me down.' She paused, hoping she sounded sincere, subconsciously raising her hand to her neck as she made sure that the Whisper was still securely hidden under her shirt. As she did, Louise noticed the bandage that still covered the symbol on her hand was starting to peel back. She hurriedly pressed it down with her other hand. Louise slowly realised that Jamsen was watching her every move and so, to distract him from the bandage on her hand, she continued to make up her story. 'I didn't really know why they were chasing me, but it was terrifying. Barney and I simply ran as fast as we could.'

'And how did you get away?' Jamsen asked, still watching her closely, clearly intrigued by what she was doing to her hand.

This was the question Louise was truly dreading and her mind raced as she desperately tried to think of a feasible way in which she could have escaped a wreag patrol. 'I was far enough away from them when they started the pursuit and I managed to outrun them. I didn't know it at the time but going in the opposite direction to the Whalsp Woods must have helped!'

Louise watched him intensely, looking for any indication that he may not believe her story. Instead, he looked forward, concentrating on the path he was following, his expression neutral.

'That was very fortunate, although obviously unfortunate that they began to track you in the first place,' he said, turning his head to smile at her sympathetically.

She smiled back, uncertainly. He faced forwards and they continued in silence, brushing against the thick leaves that dangled down from the crops. Despite the intense fear she had been subjected to ever since arriving back in Calaresp, Louise was beginning to find that this world was becoming inexplicably comfortable and somehow familiar, which was strange considering she had so few memories of this place.

They continued walking and as they reached the end of the field, Louise was able to get a look at the landscape. She could make out a few more fields in front of them and further back in the distance, darker than the night's sky, stood the shadow-like forms of large mountains. The gentle sound of trickling water soon penetrated her ears and although she couldn't see a great deal in the moonlight, Louise observed a small indent in the ground on her right, seemingly running alongside all of the fields. She deduced that this was where the trickling sound originated from and so knew there must be a small river or a large stream running nearby.

'Is the village we're going to your home?' Louise asked Jamsen, overwhelmed with curiosity regarding her companion.

Jamsen quickly turned his head to look at her, a hint of suspicion flashing across his face. However, it wasn't long before that familiar smile returned.

'To be honest, I travel so often I don't consider any place to be my home.' Jamsen paused, contemplating for a moment. 'Although my family once lived near Fortor. So, if anywhere was home, that would probably have to be it!'

'Are your family still there?' She could feel her curiosity spiking.

The smile on his face immediately disappeared and his mood seemed to darken.

'No,' he replied in a quiet voice. 'My family died when I was just a young boy.' He looked away and stared into the distance; Louise took this as a hint that their discussion was over and so said no more. Instead, she turned to her side to check on Barney and she couldn't repress a smile when she saw him trotting happily at her side. He occasionally turned his head as an intriguing smell struck his nostrils, but never strayed from Louise, which was of great comfort to her.

Chapter Nineteen

Once they reached the end of the second field, Jamsen stuck his hand out to indicate she should stop, and both she and Barney obeyed. Louise followed his gaze and saw there was a wide dirt path just in front of them. She realised that he had stopped them in order to check whether anyone was travelling along it and found herself scanning both ends of the path too. She couldn't see anything and it seemed neither could Jamsen, who visibly relaxed as he whispered, 'Right, let's get going.'

Slowly and steadily, they crossed the path and went onto a grass verge, just beyond which was yet another wood. This time the trees stood a fair distance apart and much to Louise's relief, they were completely different from each other. Looking to her left, she noticed that the large stream followed them into the woods as the comforting trickling of the water stayed with them the entire way.

They walked another twenty minutes before Jamsen spoke to her again.

'Follow me,' he said, finally turning back to give her a brief smile. 'I think it's about time we had a rest!'

Now he'd mentioned it, Louise realised just how exhausted she was, and so gave no objection. She'd been so caught up in the drama of escaping the patrol and the wonders of her new environment that she'd barely noticed. She looked down at Barney, he too had slowed considerably, and his long tongue lolled out the side of his mouth.

They headed towards the large stream steadily making a shallow path through the wood. Jamsen led them over to one of the largest trees hugging the edge of the stream, and Louise got the distinct impression that this was a resting point he was very familiar with. The tree he had selected had a tremendously large trunk and, on the side, closest to the stream, a section of the trunk stood indented, creating a small but sufficient shelter. Louise found herself smiling, impressed with her guide's infallible knowledge of the land.

Once Jamsen reached the tree, he stood back and gestured for Louise to settle herself in first. He then turned and scanned their surroundings, making sure the coast was clear and that they hadn't been followed. Thoroughly exhausted at this point, Louise obeyed without objection. She carelessly dropped her bag to the ground and rested her back against the back of the tree. She immediately shut her eyes and took a deep breath, feeling every inch of her body scream out in relief and pain as she finally stopped. She watched as Barney made his way over to the stream, took a long drink, then returned to slump down by her side.

Feeling a slight chill, she pulled her bag towards her and rooted inside it for the warm and comforting blanket she knew she'd packed. As soon as she'd found it, she threw it over herself. Then curiosity swept over her as she wondered about the whereabouts of her travel companion. It took her a few moments to locate him, but she finally noticed him a few metres away; a dark figure amid the tall dark trees. He was picking up objects off the ground and then cradling them in one arm. He then repeated the action several more times. When he eventually returned, Louise realised that he was holding a selection of sticks and branches. He carelessly dumped them on the ground and started building them up into a pyramid, underneath which he placed some dried leaves and moss. He then picked up two larger sticks that he'd collected and began to rub them together.

Louise had the distinct impression that he'd done this before, and as he settled himself on the ground, she knew he didn't expect it to light immediately. She watched him for a moment or two longer before she pulled her bag over and from a secure pocket, pulled out a box of matches. Pushing off her blanket, she made her way over to Jamsen and held them out to him.

'Here,' she said, so overcome with exhaustion that even forming words seemed impossibly difficult. 'These may help.'

Jamsen looked up at her and once he saw the small box held in front of him, his expression changed to one of bewilderment. He took the box and examined it, then slid it open, removing a single match to examine it. Raising an eyebrow, he looked back up at Louise.

'And what exactly is it?' he asked.

Louise was taken aback for a moment and then cursed herself, deciding that in future, she would need to be far more careful about introducing unusual items to her companion, or anyone in Calaresp. Her mind raced as she considered the best way to deal with the situation.

'You've never seen matches before?' she finally asked.

'Matches?' Jamsen replied, shaking his head.

'We have them in my village.' Louise took the box back from him and pulled a match out. 'We use them, as we have for years, to light fires.'

As she struck the match against the side of the box, fire burst into life and Jamsen gave a quiet gasp of surprise. Louise then placed the flame at the bottom of the sticks, in the midst of the dried leaves and moss, and a small fire erupted.

'Incredible,' Jamsen said in a quiet voice as he took the box back and mimicked her actions, lighting another match. He allowed it to burn right down to his fingers and dropped it to the ground in surprise as the heat burned him. 'I can't believe I've never seen them before! What an incredible creation!'

Jamsen went to light another match but Louise grabbed for them just before he could do so.

'They aren't easy to get hold of, even in my village. I would rather you didn't use them all up.' She smiled at him apologetically and placed the matches back into her bag. He acknowledged this with a quick smile and nod before reverting his attention back to the ever-growing fire between them.

Once the fire was successfully lit, Jamsen held his hands out in front of him, his face immediately portraying the satisfaction of the heat that was warming him. Louise meanwhile, still had her blanket wrapped around her, with her back pressed against the tree. She felt the warmth of the fire on her feet — a sensation most satisfying.

Having had a hectic and dramatic day, Louise was finally able to let herself go and she felt a sense of great ease spread right through her. She looked over at Jamsen and felt a moment of empathy as she saw him situating himself as close to the fire as possible, so as to absorb the heat. Louise felt a pang of guilt as she pulled her warm blanket right around her, Barney snuggled against her legs. For a moment she considered offering to share her blanket with him but as soon as the thought had popped into her mind, she realised how awkward that would be. To be in such close proximity with a man she barely knew and wasn't even sure if she could trust, made her feel instantly uncomfortable. So instead, Louise remained quiet.

Jamsen let out a long sigh. Louise watched as he pulled over his satchel and took out a thick cape. Before he pulled it around himself, Jamsen glanced over at her. Louise, suddenly feeling guilty that she hadn't offered to share the blanket, got the distinct impression that he was about to offer her the cape itself or at least to share it with her. When he saw her tucked up cosily with her own blanket, he simply smiled and pulled his cape further around himself.

Before she could say anything, he moved up towards her. Maintaining a reasonable distance, he too slumped back against the tree and stretched out his legs so that they were warmed by the fire.

'We still have a long way to go tomorrow,' he said, looking over at her with a friendly smile. 'We should get some sleep.'

'Do we need to keep watch or anything?' Louise asked.

'We'll be fine, this side of the tree can't be seen from the road. Even the fire is hidden.' His gaze fell on Barney as he lay between them; he was quite obviously keeping half an eye on Jamsen. 'Besides, I think your dog will be keeping one eye open at all times!'

Louise smiled and gently stroked Barney's back. 'Fair point. Well, I guess I'll see you in the morning. Goodnight.'

'Goodnight,' Jamsen replied, lying back onto the ground and pulling his cape around him.

Louise lay back on the ground too. She had expected it to be hard and uncomfortable but was surprised to find it quite pleasantly soft. Placing her hand on it, she realised that the ground in the hollow of the tree was covered with a thick layer of moss. As she pulled her blanket right up to her face, ensuring she remained as warm as possible, she let out a quiet sigh of satisfaction. Before she could give any thought to her situation and their precarious resting place, Louise was fast asleep.

Chapter Twenty

The sun shone brightly through the widely spread trees, creating sparkling reflections on the stream. Louise awoke to the gentle sound of the water trickling. Feeling well-rested, she stretched, satisfied and content. She slowly opened her eyes and experienced that inevitable momentary panic as to where exactly she was and why she was sleeping on the ground. As the events of the day before caught up on her, Louise felt a surprising surge of dread pass through her. Had she made the right decision to come to Calarep? The threat of the unknown path in front of her was a terrifying prospect and she suddenly ached and longed for the comfort of her own bed and the security of her own home.

These concerns were soon forgotten as she heard quiet footsteps approaching her. Turning around, she decided that the sounds were coming from the other side of the large tree. Moving faster than she had ever believed herself capable of, she spun around, simultaneously pulling the small knife out of her pocket and flicking it open. Louise found herself breathing heavily and she bit her lip to try and stifle the sound so that the person approaching wouldn't realise she was lying in wait. She allowed herself to look back, keen to locate Barney, certain that if she were under any threat, he would help protect her. Barney, however, was still lying on the ground where she'd been just moments before, looking up at her with a quizzical look. Louise was immediately puzzled but was more aware of the imminent danger she was in. She focused her attention back on the approaching footsteps.

Due to the direction of the sun, the figure was immediately draped in shadow when they emerged from the other side of the tree. However, she could tell by their sheer size that the person was a man. There was also something faintly familiar about them. She blinked as the brightness of the sun seemed to almost blind her; the shape stepped out of the light of the sun and into the shade of the tree. Her eyes recovering, Louise recognised Jamsen standing in front of her, that familiar grin spread across his face.

'You need to be more careful,' he said. 'If you think someone's trying to creep up on you, you really should position yourself so that you have the advantage. By blinding yourself, you're practically offering yourself on a plate.'

Louise could feel the red blush flare-up in her cheeks as embarrassment coursed through her body.

'I'm sorry, I didn't realise it was you.'

'Evidently not,' he replied, still smiling. He then dropped more sticks on the ground and just as he had the night before, he began to construct a small fire. 'Now, would you like some breakfast?'

Louise studied him for a moment and before she

knew it, a smile spread across her face too. Despite the uncertainty she had felt the night before, she found his smile strangely comforting and her instincts were increasingly telling her to trust him.

She nodded and settled back to the ground, putting away the knife and pulling out the box of matches, which she passed to him.

Quickly and efficiently, he built and lit the fire. Then, pulling his satchel towards him, he drew out the animal which he had caught the day before. Now, however, it was stripped of its fur, its internal organs disposed of. All that was left was the frame and the meat. Pulling out a small but sharp knife, Jamsen, with four very quick motions, took the creature apart so that the legs and breast meat were separated. He then placed one of the legs on the end of his knife and held it above the flames. He remained like this for a while, pulling it back every now and then to gently squeeze the cooking meat between his fingers. Having done this five times, Jamsen was clearly happy that the meat was now cooked.

He brought out a small metal plate from his pack and placed the piece of meat onto it. He continued to do this until all the meat was cooked, then he placed the plate between himself and Louise.

'Here, help yourself,' he said, flashing one of his charming smiles at her.

They quickly consumed all of the cooked meat and as soon as she'd finished, Louise leant back, stomach full of the surprisingly delicious meat. But as she sighed contentedly, Jamsen stood up, gathered his belongings, and kicked at the ground just in front of the fire, immediately extinguishing the flame.

He looked over with an apologetic look. 'I'm sorry, I know how tired you are but we really need to keep moving. We have a long way to go.'

Louise sighed and slowly got up. As she got to her feet, she half-expected to be overwhelmed with aches and pains from her exhausted legs. However, Louise felt surprisingly refreshed and prepared for another day of walking. Barney, who had been grateful to receive some of her breakfast, now got up and slowly stretched. He then trotted a few paces ahead as if to let Louise know he was ready to go.

She quickly stuffed her blanket into her bag and a few other items that had worked their way out. She threw it onto her back and scraped her messy, unbrushed hair back into a ponytail. Straightening out her clothes, she looked to Jamsen with a smile.

'Okay then, let's get going.'

Having arrived in these woods in the dead of the night, Louise hadn't been able to truly appreciate the beauty of their surroundings. Now, as she looked around her, she was able to take it in.

They were completely different from the eerie woods in which she'd first arrived. The trees stood a fair distance away from each other, allowing the warming beams of the sun to penetrate the ground. This had enabled a beautiful blanket of flowers to grow, some of which were prettier than anything Louise had ever seen. They came in all colours and sizes and were truly awe-inspiring. Through this carpet of colour ran the beautiful stream, the sound of which was gentle and relaxing; the water glistened, sparkled, and danced in the light of the sun. Louise smiled as she found herself immediately relaxed; the memory of the night before seemed like a distant nightmare that she'd now awoken from.

Jamsen placed his hand on Louise's waist to gently gesture her forwards. At his touch, Louise felt her heart flutter. She hadn't missed the fact that he was an incredibly handsome man and as his well-toned arms and gentle, comforting hands touched her, she became even more aware of it.

'The coast is clear,' he said, his hand remaining on her waist. 'We'll stay in the woods for the moment and head east, just following the stream. That should lead us into Shorot.'

'Will we actually go into the village? I mean, is it safe there?' Louise asked, glad they weren't leaving the striking woods straight away.

'With me there, you'll be perfectly safe. I've supplied them with goods from the Whalsp Woods for several years now. They wouldn't ever vocalise it, but they aren't particularly fond of Brisheit and his regime.'

Louise was intrigued. If this village didn't support Brisheit, perhaps some of the rebels were based there. Perhaps there was a slim possibility that they were loyal supporters of her family. She was desperate to ask Jamsen more but was wary about being too obvious or giving him any reason to question her.

'If they don't vocalise it, how do you know they don't support Brisheit?'

'They quietly grumble and I have occasionally heard them questioning his methods and brutality.'

Louise mulled this over for a few minutes and decided that the best method would be to wait until they got there—then she could assess the situation herself. However, she couldn't stop herself from asking one more question.

'How about you then? What are your feelings towards Brisheit and his regime?'

Still walking, Jamsen looked back at her and studied her for a few moments, expressionless. He looked away as he replied, 'Considering the fact you met me in the Whalsp Woods, what do you think?'

Louise couldn't help but smile as she considered his reply. Jamsen caught it as he turned to give her a quick look. He too smiled and then continued to talk.

'I don't like the violence of Brisheit and his army, their brutality and hostility towards the people of Calaresp over the last twenty years is unforgivable. But since there is no one else to challenge him for the throne, there's no other choice.'

Louse had been contemplating whether or not to ask him about the rebels. As he spoke, the question danced on her tongue, desperate to come out. Eventually, she had to say something.

'In my village, we heard rumours of rebels fighting back against Brisheit. Is that true?'

As he turned around, he raised an eyebrow and gave her a scrupulous look. 'My,' he said, not taking his eyes off her, 'has the gossip spread as far as your village?'

Louise felt an instant jolt of paranoia, certain that he must know her to be lying. She didn't want to go into too much detail, certain that the more she lied, the more likely it was he would find her out. As such, she simply nodded, which seemed to appease him. He gave an appreciative nod and continued to talk.

'Well, I suppose it isn't too great a surprise. There have always been rumours of a rebellious group;

bodyguards, fighters, and friends of the Royal family. Whether it's true or not, I couldn't say—they've never been particularly active for rebels. They've never really made their presence known to either prove or disprove the rumours.' His expression suddenly drew dark, 'Not once,' he said quietly 'have they stopped the brutal acts committed by Brisheit and his army, so they may as well not exist.'

She studied him for a few moments, realising the expression of pain that had spread across his face. For a moment she was tempted to ask him what was wrong, but the fact that they were still strangers stopped her. She had been grateful that he hadn't asked her anything too personal yet and didn't want to seem inconsiderate by expecting that level of detail from him. So instead, she looked away and continued admiring their surroundings.

They continued through the woods and with every step, Louise found her tired spirit lifting. Each and every flower—colourful and entirely unique—leapt out to her as if screaming for her attention. Their vibrancy pushed out every concern and doubt she had experienced since having arrived in Calaresp. The collection of flowers moved rhythmically as if there were a gentle wind, when in fact, the air around them was completely still. It made it seem as if they were dancing and Louise could feel her own spirit doing the same. For the first time, she felt as if she were home; as if her spirit had been calling out, yearning to be reconnected with the world in which she'd been born, the world in which her own family had ruled for centuries.

It wasn't too long before Barney strayed away from

Louise's side and ran ahead of them, leaping and bounding, taking every opportunity to sniff everything and anything. She hadn't realised that as she walked and admired all her surroundings, a wide grin spread across her face. At least not until Jamsen turned to look at her, mouth open as if he were about to say something. On seeing her joy, he too smiled and gave an appreciative look around.

'I forgot, you won't have seen the beauty of this part of the land before,' he finally said, gesturing to their surroundings. 'A nice contrast to the Whalsp Woods at least.'

'It truly is breath-taking!' Louis replied. 'Is all of Calaresp as beautiful as this?'

Jamsen shrugged, his expression becoming bitter. 'As with all lands, there are parts with incredible natural beauty, left completely untouched, that reward us with scenes such as this.' He sighed and took a few moments before continuing. 'Then there are lands that have been rampaged, bearing witness to the horrific inhumane deeds of Brisheit's army. They are barren and burnt lands where nothing can grow because of the crimes committed there, the hurt inflicted on the people that once lived there. It is completely unforgivable.'

Sadness welled up deep within Louise as she thought of such beauty being destroyed beyond repair by such monstrous acts. 'Can they truly never be repaired?'

Jamsen looked at her closely as if trying to decide how much to tell her. After a while, he turned looked away absentmindedly. 'I have heard it said that when the Clarest family ruled, with their goodness and their magic, the land thrived. Their magic and the kindness they showed to both people and their environment were reflected by the incomprehensible beauty of the land. At Brisheit's touch, it has gradually begun to decay. Some believe that the only way for it to heal and once again truly flourish would be for someone with the Whisper's magic to rule.' Jamsen chuckled quietly to himself. 'But Brisheit made sure that would never happen when he wiped out the Clarest line.' Once again, he gave Louise a somewhat suspicious look. 'Not that we're meant to talk about the time before Brisheit, of course. But I think I can trust you?'

Louise didn't quite know what to say in reply to that. So instead, she gave him a warm smile and a slight nod of her head. She didn't believe he needed her to say anything else.

Following this conversation, the silence between them resumed as Louise allowed herself to get lost in her thoughts. She had so many questions she longed to ask him, but logic stopped her, as she was aware that too much of an interest would seem suspicious. Also, if he began to delve too much, he could discover her true identity. Subconsciously, she began to gently rub her right hand, pressing down slightly on the fabric plaster that stuck there. It created quite a satisfying contrast to her smooth skin, and it comfortably covered the mysterious scar that lay underneath.

Jamsen turned back, his mouth open as if he were about to say something. His glance went to her hand and his unspoken words vanished from his lips. A curious look spread across his face and his brow creased. He then looked up at Louise and clearly noted the fearful expression that flashed across her face.

'What's that on your hand?' he asked quietly.

At first, all she could do was look back at him as she tried to force her scattered brain to think of a reply.

'Oh, this? Well, it's nothing!' She struggled with her words and as if her feet were mocking her, they too stumbled, catching on a small tree root, sending her flying forwards through the air. She saw the ground growing ever closer and braced herself for impact. Instead, she found large arms gripping her shoulders tightly, taking her weight and drawing her back away from the ground, swinging her with some force into his arms.

He grunted slightly. 'There we go,' he said. 'You almost hit the ground that time!'

Louise immediately backed away, awkwardness washing over her as she found herself so close to Jamsen. He didn't seem to notice, merely laughing at the situation. Once he was sure she had regained her balance he turned and continued onwards, his curiosity regarding her plaster forgotten.

Jamsen had only taken a few steps before he stopped once again. As he did so, she saw his entire body stiffen. Barney did the same, then he stuck his nose in the air and his hackles slowly began to rise. Whilst she'd been watching Barney, Jamsen had crossed back towards her and gently grabbed her arm, just above the elbow. Barney defensively moved closer to her and to keep him near her, Louise held onto his collar. All three of them surveyed their surroundings.

For a while, Louse remained silent, unsure if talking would draw unwanted attention to them. She was filled with confusion and uncertainty, and eventually, she couldn't contain herself any further. In as quiet a voice as she could, Louise whispered into Jamsen's ear,

'What is it? Another patrol?'

He didn't reply immediately and Louise began to wonder whether her gentle whisper had perhaps been a little too quiet. Just as she was about to repeat her question, he turned to look at her. She was so taken aback by his expression of sheer shock that she gasped involuntarily. In an even quieter voice, she asked, 'What?'

Jamsen bit his lip, his eyes flickering from one direction to another. He forcefully pulled on her arm, causing her no pain but leading her onwards at a much faster pace. She followed him without further questions, a decision reinforced by the look of sincere concentration set upon his face as he glanced behind them. After they'd quietly run for a while, he pulled her up next to him and slowed their pace.

'It's not a patrol. In some ways, depending on how many there are, it could be far, far worse,' he whispered. Maintaining his grip on her arm, he made sure she was close enough to hear his softest whispers. Then he continued, 'When the wreags in Brisheit's army reach a certain age, they are deemed unsuitable for service. They are brought a reasonable distance away from the palace and set loose, free to roam the wilderness to fend for themselves. You thought that Brisheit's wreags were bad? Wild wreags are even worse. They don't have handlers holding them back, they don't have restrictions placed upon them or consequences for their disobedience. The wild wreags are hungry, desperate, and more violent than you could possibly imagine.'

With her spare hand, Louise slipped out the small knife from her pocket. She gripped the handle so firmly in her hand that it pushed deep into her flesh, but her panic left her unaware of the pain it was causing her. With her other hand, she fumbled at the top of her shirt, pretending to straighten out the collar whilst in actual fact, she was subtly fumbling for the pendant. Finally, she found it and clasped it in her other hand. Somewhere deep inside her, she realised that the knife gave her no comfort. Whilst the pendant, which had once again beginning to glow, calmed her. It wasn't, however, quite strong enough amidst the fear that was coursing through her. It was like a child's voice quietly calling out in a room full of adults that were screaming and shouting.

They came to a sudden stop and Jamsen looked around. He must have sensed her fear as he gently found and held her clenched knife-wielding hand in his, firmly and comfortingly. As she became aware of herself again, she knew a red flush was creeping through her cheeks as she concentrated on his large, warm, gentle hand holding hers.

She forced herself to look up at him, concerned that he might have noticed her blushing. Much to her relief, he was still scanning the trees around them. Forcing herself to regain her composure, she began to wonder why they still weren't moving. Surely, they were making it considerably easier for the wild wreags to catch them?

As if reading her mind, he leant in closer to her and whispered, 'Most of the time they'll only hunt in very small packs, or occasionally alone, depending on how they were treated when in Brisheit's army. There is, however, one larger pack that is known to roam near these woods; they are formidable and kill everything and anything they come across. We don't have a chance if they are the wreags hunting us. It's unlikely though, as they've always roamed near these woods, but never normally in them.'

He paused for a few moments, still scanning his surroundings. Eventually, he let out a deep, long breath. He looked at her, a reluctant smile on his face. 'I don't think it is the large pack, I have a feeling it's just the one, but I wouldn't swear by it. Either way, we need to get moving.'

They continued through the woods and Louise began to believe that they were gradually leaving the wild wreag behind. She felt herself regaining control, her pounding heart beginning to remember its regular beat.

That was until Jamsen suddenly spun around at such a speed, he almost sent her flying to the ground. He stood between them, one arm suspended in her direction and the other tightly gripped his bow, as if he were expecting something to pounce at any second. She stared at him incredulously, but he held a hand to his lips and frantically signalled for her to remain quiet. The look of concern that had spread across his face was enough to tell her that they were still in danger. The fear that had ebbed gently away from her now sprang back into action.

He bought up the hand that had been pressed to his lips and used it to indicate to his left. Without the need for communication, she instantly began walking in that direction. Barney, who hadn't left her side since they'd acknowledged the presence of the wild wreag, now crouched low, his hackles raised, as he followed Louise.

Louise reached a large tree and heard a low whistle

from Jamsen. She turned back quickly and saw him indicating for her to remain by the tree. She crouched low, next to the tree, and placed an arm on Barney's back. She tried to convince herself that it was for his protection when in actual fact, it was a selfish move to make herself feel better.

As she looked up, she saw Jamsen cautiously moving towards her. When he was only a few steps away, an all too familiar sound rang through every one of them, penetrating their hearts and freezing the blood in their veins. The horror of the wreag's howl slowly brought Louise to her feet and as it howled for a second time, she flew her hand out to clumsily grab his. He firmly gripped hers, acknowledging one and others fear and providing whatever comfort they could to each other. He moved beside her and they stood for a moment, backs against the large tree, Barney standing just before them. Then, as the wreag's howl spread through the woods for a third time, it was joined by another. Jamsen gripped her hand even more firmly as if reminding her that he was there. Moments later, trying to penetrate the ear-splitting howls, he shouted, 'Run Louise!'

She was only just able to hear him. He didn't let go of her hand as he whipped her around the tree.

They ran noisily through the woods, moving much faster than they had done before. It wasn't long before they reached a small river.

Louise looked back as they ran, trusting Jamsen to continue to guide her whilst her gaze was diverted. She quickly scanned the horizon to ensure their pursuers weren't yet visible. She was temporarily relieved to see they weren't. Any thoughts of the hunting wreag soon swept from her mind, as her foot sank into cool water, instantly soaking through her boots and drenching her socks. The shock made her spin her head around and she stared at Jamsen in confusion as she saw he had led her directly into the river. Instinctively, she began to resist plunging further into the cool water and so drew back from him. Without glancing back at her, he tightened his grip on her hand to the extent that it was almost painful and pulled her further into the water.

Reaching the other side, Louise's legs were bogged down with the weight of the water. She shook them as they climbed up the slight incline now in front of them. Just as they reached the other side, another howl came crashing through the trees; branches and leaves trembled as the horror of the sound spread through them. Jamsen twisted his head back in the direction of the sound and abruptly dropped her hand, whisking it behind him to whip out his bow, the other grabbing an arrow which he readied to fire. He pointed it downwards and scanned their surroundings, then whispered to Louise, 'They've picked up on our scent and at least one is on our trail. If there's another wreag following us, that last howl will have alerted him to our position.' There was a pause as he continued to survey their surroundings. 'We need to keep moving.' Once again, the pair found themselves running desperately through the woods, Barney loyally by her side. The pursuing howl came ever closer, becoming increasingly deafening.

Eventually, they reached a large, well-formed tree and it was here that Jamsen came to a stop. Louise swung herself in all directions looking for the wreag, her mind filled with panic, uncertain as to why they'd stopped. She was concerned that Jamsen had given up hope. Whilst Louise looked around her, Jamsen seemed more intent on studying the tree above them and its low-hanging branches. It stood high and full, allowing the trunk to disappear around a third of the way up, swallowed by branches and leaves.

'Climb up,' Jamsen instructed in an urgent voice as he looked back at her, his left-hand gesturing to one of the lower branches. It took a moment for Louise to fully register what he'd said and once she understood, her first thought was Barney. As if he'd read her mind, Jamsen looked down at Barney before asking, 'Can you get Barney to crouch low and stay by the trunk of the tree without moving, no matter what happens?'

Louise nodded, still uncertain as to what was going on.

'Then do it!' Jamsen said, panic and fear seeping through in his tone.

She quietly called Barney over and indicated for him to move next to the tree and lie down.

'Down and stay,' she whispered in a quiet, stern voice. He obeyed without hesitation.

Louise then diverted her attention back to Jamsen, desperate to know his intentions. Before she could say anything, Jamsen turned back to her and with a flash of anger and a tone of deep frustration, he gestured to the tree and snapped, 'Up the tree! Now!'

As the ever-nearing howl reached her ears, she turned and flung herself clumsily onto one of the low hanging branches. Without looking back and as quickly as she could, she began to make her way up the tree. It had been many a year since she'd climbed a tree, but her childhood experiences allowed her to do it fairly well. She climbed high enough to be concealed by the branches and yet low enough that she could still see what was going on beneath her.

Having expected Jamsen to follow her up the tree, she was surprised to see that he was still stood on the ground, bow and arrow raised and ready. She averted her attention from Jamsen for a second as she double-checked Barney had remained where she'd left him. She was quietly impressed with him as she saw he was still there.

Jamsen took a few steps away from the tree and Louise felt panic spread through her, uncertain as to what he was going to do next. She was just about to ask him why he hadn't climbed up the tree with her when yet another howl reached them. The second he heard it, Jamsen crouched low to the ground, his bow still drawn. It was at that moment that Louise realised his intention; it was as if a light had been flicked on. Now it had picked up on their scent, there was no chance they could escape the ever-approaching beast. The thought that he had hidden Louise and Barney away, leaving himself to face the wreag alone, was a concept she found beyond comprehension.

'No Jamsen! You can't think of fighting that thing alone!'

He didn't reply. Instead, his attention was fixed on a point just ahead of him. Louise was just about to say something else but then she followed Jamsen's line of vision and saw movement. Simultaneously, out of the corner of her eye, she saw Jamsen tense his body as if preparing himself. It was at that point she noticed, just across from them, between two trees, a set of red eyes framed by a large dark body. Its form was dark and foreboding in comparison to the beautiful woods surrounding it. It looked like the devil himself staring out from a serene bed of flowers.

Louise felt her body tense and as the wreag began to stalk forwards, she held her hand to her mouth, concerned that she might involuntarily cry out. At closer proximity, the beast was even more terrifying than Louise could ever have comprehended. Its sharp teeth protruded from the long muzzle and as before, the ends were darkly stained with blood. It had a long dark scar across the right-hand side of its face, as if a knife or a sword had slashed through it. She could instantly see the age of the wreag as, unlike the ones she'd seen in the Scottish woods, this one had white streaks throughout its fur and right across its muzzle, presumably indicating a slightly older beast.

It stared at Jamsen, and he stared back, never taking his eyes off the approaching predator. Not too far away from him, the wreag came to a halt. They remained like this for a few minutes, until suddenly, as if a silent voice had given them a countdown, they each sprang into action. The wreag forced its giant hind legs into the ground, projecting his body forwards, forcing the flowers and grass surrounding it to collapse, folding over like a piece of paper.

As it sprang forward, Jamsen crouched lower, and with inconceivable speed, shot an arrow. Silently piercing through the air, it quickly flew towards the wreag and penetrated the thick skin of the beast, just a few centimetres shy of its left eye. The creature didn't seem to acknowledge it. Moments later, Jamsen released another; this flew just as fast as the previous one. The second one, however, was a more successful shot, the sharp point piercing and passing into its eyeball. Louise watched with bated breath, expecting the creature to yelp in pain or to fall backwards. Instead, the wreag let out a ferocious roar and gave it's head a quick shake as if trying to dislodge the protruding arrow. When this was unsuccessful, it continued towards the crouching archer.

Louise barely had time to take all of this in before Jamsen had fired yet another arrow; this one was just as successful as the second, hitting the creature in the other eye. This shot hadn't been quite as clean and instead of entering straight through the eye, it ripped past it and entered the skin just to the side. It caused such a considerable amount of damage that the eye seemed to completely disappear, replaced by a mass of destroyed skin, fur, and black blood.

At this point, the creature stopped in its tracks and fervently shook its head from side to side. It was a futile action as the arrows remained where they were. When it finally stopped thrashing its head, it faced Jamsen, and roared once again. Even though two of the arrows had destroyed the creature's eyes, it still seemed to know exactly where Jamsen was and so began to move towards him. The closer it came to them; the clearer Louise could see the damage that had been done to the beast. Black blood gushed from the three wounds, most fervently from the two arrows that had entered the wreag's face; the one that had entered straight through the eye had a small stream of black blood mingled with a strange white substance.

Louise, who had initially been impressed by the accuracy of Jamsen's shots, suddenly felt a sense of foreboding and began to doubt whether they had any weapon that could take the creature down in time. It launched itself into the air. She saw Jamsen preparing himself, throwing his bow and remaining arrows to the side. Darkness began to cover him like a cloud casting a shadow on an otherwise beautiful day. Moments before he vanished completely, Louise saw a flash of light pass between them. As the wreag landed on top of him, Louise heard a roar of pain and suddenly realised that the flash of light had been the reflection of a dagger and that this was what had caused the creature to cry out. It reeled backwards, moving a few paces away from him, panting heavily. It only took a few seconds for the wreag to recover and it stalked forwards, ready for yet another attack. As it pounced again, Jamsen reacted even faster and this time, Louise was able to see him thrust his dagger deep into the beast's chest.

This second attack again seemed to weaken the creature, but not stop it. It reinforced its position and tried snapping at him. Jamsen used one of his hands to desperately keep the creature's mouth and sharp, blood-stained teeth away from him. He was only able to do so by continuously thrusting his dagger into its body, gradually weakening it. As Louise watched, she knew that Jamsen would tire long before the creature and that once he did, it wouldn't take long for it to tear him to pieces.

Louise felt hopeless and eventually, it became too much for her. She began to make her way down the tree. As soon as she reached the ground, Barney raised his head; she held out a hand to ensure he remained exactly where he was. With the other hand, she pulled out her small knife, suddenly uncertain as to exactly what she could do to help. The beast thrashed around so desperately that she found it very hard to approach without risking a bite from those sharp, deadly teeth.

Jamsen visibly weakened in front of her and all of a sudden, Louise knew exactly what she had to do. Without the slightest hint of hesitation, she faced the wreag, grabbed the arrow protruding from its eye, and the second one situated just slightly to the side of it. She used all her strength to try and force the two arrows further into the wreag's skull. Louise was certain that pushing the arrows further in would cause them to pierce the brain, immediately killing it. Initially, they didn't budge; no matter how hard she pushed, they wouldn't sink further into the thick skin. She made so little impact that the wreag didn't even divert his attention from Jamsen.

Standing over him, Louise could see Jamsen beginning to struggle, his arms seemed to fail him occasionally, as he lost his grip and each time he did, the snapping beast on top of him came ever closer. Louise began to panic, suddenly unsure as to whether she would have the strength to force the embedded arrows further into the creature's face. Images of the wreag ripping Jamsen to pieces flashed through her mind and with that, her breath quickened. As desperation welled up inside of her, she forced herself to concentrate solely on the two arrows, focusing all her strength on those two points. Had she seen the pendant tucked neatly away under her shirt, she would have seen that its centre was beginning to glow. Although it was small, it shone as brightly as the fiercest flame. As it did so, small veins of light seamlessly left it and entered into Louise's body, creating a bond between the two and joining them together. Her chest was practically alight with the particles from the pendant. The same light veins passed from her chest to her arms, then vanished underneath her skin. The only part of this process Louise noticed was when her hands began to tingle, then to her great surprise. the two arrows finally began to move.

Louise felt a cry, force its way through her mouth as she tripled her efforts, oblivious as to where her true strength was coming from. The sounds coming from the beast's face as the arrows pushed ever further inwards were nauseating. A thick black substance with small white streams ebbed from the ever-worsening wounds and covered Louise's hands, but she kept pushing as Jamsen kept fighting against the powerful creature. A hand suddenly clasped on top of hers, and between them, they forced the remainder of the arrow into the wreag's head.

Barney, meanwhile, had leapt forwards and began snapping at the wreag's legs. Instantaneously, the creature's head reeled backwards as if disorientated, blood oozing down its face. It remained standing for a few moments longer and Louise feared that even with the two arrows penetrating its brain, it wouldn't be enough to stop it. She found herself wondering whether this formidable creature could ever be killed. Just as this thought struck her, the wreag stopped. It froze on top of Jamsen as if it had been stuffed. Then it violently threw up a vile combination of blood and mucus which landed straight on his face. The Wreag gagged as if choking and finally stepped back. Jamsen, immediately wiped some of the revolting substance out of his eyes so that he could see. The beast had only taken a few steps back before collapsing to the ground with an earth-shattering crash. Its legs jerked dramatically and then lay flat on the ground. It didn't move again. The wreag's mouth lay open and, a small pool of black blood appeared before quickly soaking into the ground.

Chapter Twenty-one

Jamsen barely gave it a second glance before getting up, wiping more of the pungent mess from his face. His gaze fixed on Louise as he spat out a little bit of blood that must have managed to get into his mouth. He gazed at her, then gave her a quick nod before saying in a quiet voice, 'Thank you.' He then abruptly turned away and walked off. Louise hesitated for a moment, giving the dead wreag one last suspicious look before following Jamsen. He grabbed the bag he'd discarded on the farthest side of the tree before making his way down to the nearby river. Louise followed suit and collected her own discarded possessions, Barney loyally at her side.

The second Jamsen reached the water, he threw his bag to the side and pulled out a piece of cloth, a little larger than a flannel. He dunked his head and as Louise approached, she saw the water around his face turn black. She could see him rub his face with his hands, splashing water at the sections not completely submerged. Slowly lifting his head, he brought the cloth up to his face and used it to ensure every inch of his face was clean. When he was finished, he tied the cloth to the side of his bag—presumably to dry—and stood up. He still averted his gaze from Louise, which made her feel increasingly nervous and uncomfortable. When he eventually did look at her, those emotions didn't disappear; his gaze was vacant, uncertain, and she couldn't decide whether he was angry with her or not.

'A wreag's skull is notoriously difficult to penetrate, that's why my arrows made little difference. I shot at the eyes as I thought it was the best chance I had.' He paused as if collecting his thoughts, then he looked back at her with an intense stare. 'How did you get those arrows through with just your hands!?'

Louise could do little more than just stare back at him, she hadn't thought she'd done anything that impressive. Having said that, she hadn't known the density of the creature's skull. As her mind raced, Louise had to remind herself to breathe. Something deep within her told her to conceal her own theories as to what happened.

She forced a grin onto her face and chuckled, 'I'm sorry to disappoint you but those arrows of yours did far more damage than you realised. By the time I started pushing them, they were already through the skull. I actually had to do very little.' She smiled apologetically whilst Jamsen continued to watch her with an unreadable expression on his face.

They simply looked at one another for a while until, the smile which usually frequented his face returned. 'Well, regardless of what happened, the wreag is dead and it was your intervention that saved my life. For that, I am beyond grateful.' He gently touched her arm and once again Louise could feel that gentle blush spreading in her cheeks.

He looked back at the spot the wreag had died and gave a deep, heartfelt sigh. 'We need to get moving before another one appears. You smelt how poignant the blood was—any other wreags in the area will be here in minutes to devour its remains. We need to be miles from here so they don't pick up on our scent as well.'

Jamsen placed his equipment and bags back onto his back and gestured for Louise to do the same. She quickly followed suit and it wasn't long before they were on their way.

Louise found herself suddenly longing to find some sort of civilisation, certain that it would offer some security from the preying wreags. Although she had no recollection of the towns, villages or cities of Calaresp, she longed to be surrounded by people.

As they walked onwards, she barely acknowledging the beauty surrounding them. Her mind was racing as she tried to recall exactly what had happened when she'd pushed those arrows through. She wasn't sure whether the strange sensation in her hands had been her imagination or if it were merely caused by the strain of pushing with such intensity. No matter how hard she tried, she couldn't explain it. Instead, she found her mind drifting to the pendant around her neck, to the ever-intensifying scar on her wrist.

She continued walking, completely absorbed by her thoughts. When she eventually did take in her surroundings again, she realised it was beginning to dramatically change. The grass was growing patchy and yellow; further ahead, she noticed it had completely disappeared, to be replaced with wet and boggy mud. The flowers had completely vanished and the trees began to disappear, creating a large barren circle in the middle of the flourishing woods. The luscious and colourful beauty that had surrounded them for so long was now becoming bleak and dead.

Louise furrowed her brow as she scanned the scene in front of her and she felt her stomach churn. It wasn't until Jamsen turned to look at her that she realised she'd let out a quiet gasp. Looking up at him, she saw a grimace on his face.

'What happened here?' she asked in a quiet voice.

He didn't reply straight away. Instead, he surveyed the land in front of him and sighed deeply.

'This particular section of the woods, believe it or not, used to be a point of remarkable beauty. There was once a huge Koa tree right in the centre, with incredible wide overhanging branches. The ground was laden with hundreds of dramatic and colourful flowers. It was a truly magical spot.' He stopped talking and stared intently ahead, a reminiscing smile spreading across his face. 'No one knows exactly what happened. All we do know is that hundreds of people were massacred. To be honest, it's always been a mystery as to how they were killed and why they were here in the first place. Ever since it happened, this section of the woods began to die.'

He continued talking but as he did, Louise began to feel lightheaded. She abruptly stopped walking but the world around her continued to spin. She didn't notice herself placing an unsteady hand on Jamsen's arm, causing him to stop in his tracks. He instantly turned towards Louise with a look of concern on his face. A crippling wave of nausea washed over her. She was certain that she was about to collapse and so sank to the floor, not noticing Jamsen and Barney disappearing from view. She held her face in her hands, desperate for the ordeal to end.

When she reopened them, her surroundings had completely changed. The bleak circle of land that she'd been staring at moments before had vanished. Instead, there were a circle of small trees and a beautiful larger one right at the centre. She soon noticed, however, that it didn't look real. The trees, the flowers and the grass weren't solid objects — they were transparent, the rest of the woods just about visible through them. They seemed to be made up of a serene blue mist, creating in front of her a spectre-like dimension that she found profoundly surreal.

Louise suddenly looked beside her, desperate to ask Jamsen where they were, but was startled to find he wasn't there. Instinctively, she turned to her other side, where Barney had been mere moments before. She felt her entire body turn cold as she realised that he too had vanished.

'Barney,' she whispered, desperately hoping he would simply pop up beside her. Deep inside, however, she wasn't surprised when he didn't.

She suddenly saw something move out of the corner of her eye and she swung her head back to the transparent tree. When her eyes finally fixed on the scene in front of her, Louise's mouth fell open. When she'd first observed her new surroundings there hadn't been a soul in sight — she'd been alone. Now, the woods in front of her were full of people. Just like the trees, they were made from the same blue mist, with an eerie transparency that filled Louise with uncertainty. She was taken aback by just how many people there were walking through the woods. She noticed masses of large tents surrounding the tall tree in the centre. Scattered between them were campfires and a collection of pots and pans, some with large wooden cooking spoons sticking out of them.

Some of the figures strolled leisurely through the camps whilst others warmed themselves by the small fires, chatting merrily. Even from where she sat, Louise could see that they looked happy, smiling and laughing as they relaxed together. Some were crafting makeshift weapons as they talked, whilst others looked at maps. Louise was utterly absorbed by it all. A part of her was certain that it had to be an illusion—a dream of some sort—too surreal to be anything else. A stronger part of her knew however that this was real. She felt a flash of realisation as it dawned on her that this camp, these people, were scenes from the past, from before the massacre and the mysterious destruction.

Louise suddenly felt an intense pain in her hand, where the small scar had appeared. She rubbed it absentmindedly but kept her eyes on the camp in front of her. She could see multiple conversations going on, but the woods were completely silent. Instinctively she turned around, and as she did, she saw a sight that terrified her. Sneaking through the trees, drawing ever closer, were Brisheit's men. Louise gasped before she could stop herself and automatically began backing away. She soon noticed, however, that they were tainted with the same blue mist and so knew they couldn't be real, like the others they shouldn't be able to see her, let alone hurt her. She longed to shout out, to warn the unsuspecting, innocent people camping just metres away from her. Instead, Louise remained exactly where she was, a gut-wrenching feeling of guilt overcoming her as she sensed what she was about to witness.

Brisheit's men finally came to a stop not far from the edge of a clearing. They crouched low behind some trees, deep in the shadows so they wouldn't be seen. Louise could see a line of men standing on the opposite side of the wood, making a complete circle, surrounding them. A formidable man to the right of Louise raised his hand and immediately the men lifted bows into the air, arrows ready to be fired.

Abruptly, the man, with his hand still raised in the air, brought his other hand up and clapped them together. The moment that he did, Louise felt the sound reverberating around her, the vibrations passing through her entire body as if thunder had erupted inside of her. The ends of the arrows all spontaneously caught on fire. The unsuspecting victims in the centre had also heard the thunderous clap and looked up in surprise and alarm, just in time to see the fiery arrows being released, aimed straight for them. People instantly fell to the ground; some of the arrows landed in the tents and erupted into flames.

The fire burnt with the same blue tinge as the rest of the scene in front of her. Whether it was her imagination, or a trick caused by whatever magic allowed her to witness the scene was uncertain, but she could feel the intensity of the fire as it caused an unbearable heat on her face. The woods had previously been silent but now they were filled with the harrowing screams of those suffering horrific deaths. Then she noticed that those who had survived the initial attack were heading away from the fire, desperate to escape. In that same moment, wreags appeared as if from thin air, they launched themselves straight at the hopeless, helpless fleeing victims. There was no other way to describe it—the scene in front of her was a massacre. The wreags ripped them apart, devouring them quickly and ruthlessly.

Louise felt it was all becoming too much for her; the urge to throw up and the desire to run away were fighting one another, each desperate to be acted upon. It was at that moment she realised the blue scene in front of her was beginning to darken, like the flame of a candle flickering before it gets blown out. Eventually, all that was left was a small collection of tiny, glistening blue lights dancing in front of her, until they too disappeared into the seemingly dark background.

Chapter Twenty-two

When Louise opened her eyes, she was relieved to find that her surroundings had returned to normal. The clearing—which she now knew had been caused by ferocious fire—stood before her. The barren land, a graveyard for the hundreds of people that had brutally lost their lives.

It gradually dawned upon her that she could feel a hand tightly gripped around her shoulders and as she looked up at Jamsen's concerned face, Louise was comforted, as warmth and safety washing over her. Barney rested his head on her knee, looking up at her anxiously. Louise felt the urge to rise, to get as far away as possible from what had been a site of such horror and misery.

'Careful there!' Jamsen said in a soft and gentle voice. 'I don't think you're quite ready to get up yet!'

Louise desperately wanted to protest but as he slowly lowered her half-risen body back to the ground, she could feel relief surge through her.

'What just happened? Are you unwell?' he asked.

Her eyes widened as a multitude of options

whizzed through her mind. No matter what way she looked at it, she knew that revealing what had really just happened would simply result in more questions. That could lead to him finding out more about Louise's true identity than she wanted him to. So instead, to allow herself a little bit more time, she held her head in her hands as if she were still experiencing a dizzy spell.

Once she felt she had regained control of herself, she looked up at him and mustered a smile. 'I think it must just be exhaustion, and I've not exactly been eating all that much. It just gave me a bit of a dizzy spell. I'll be okay now.'

Jamsen briefly eyed her with a look that said he didn't quite believe her. Instead of questioning her further, however, he rooted around in his pack and brought out a leather flask full of water and a small piece of rather stale-looking bread. Louise took them gratefully, trying to ignore the lump that remained in her throat from witnessing the massacre of so many.

Raising the bread with her right hand, it shook violently, whilst the left hand holding the flask was only a little better. She was aware of Jamsen watching her and she finished the food and drink as quickly as she could in the vain hope, he wouldn't notice just how badly she had been affected. She handed back the flask and Jamsen turned away as he placed it back into his pack. Now her hands were empty, Louise was all too aware they were still shaking, so she tightly grasped them together, hoping he wouldn't notice.

When he turned back, his expression was full of concern.. 'You just sat there, not moving, not talking, just staring into the distance,' he said. 'Then you started breathing unnaturally fast. You grasped your right hand as if you were in immense pain and you screamed.'

Louise watched as his gaze went to her hand; the hand on which her scar had appeared. It was still hidden rather pathetically by the plaster, constantly losing its stickiness.

There was a moment's silence—an incredibly awkward moment.

'What is that on your hand?' Jamsen eventually asked, watching her so closely that Louise felt he was looking right into her soul.

Instinctively, Louise pressed down on the plaster, ensuring it was still stuck to her skin. She had always known that when lying, the best way not to get caught was to remain as close to the truth as possible.

'It's just a plaster. I cut my hand before I left and I'm just making sure it doesn't get infected.'

Jamsen furrowed his brow. 'So that strange piece of fabric is what you would call a plaster?' He peered at it curiously, then moments later, he seemed satisfied, flashing her one of his grins and standing up. She followed his example, experiencing a moment of dizziness as she did so. Jamsen thrust his arm out and steadied her. Her gaze fell on Jamsen and she saw the look of deep concern on his face.

'I just don't understand what could have made you scream as horrifically as you did.' His voice was quiet as if he'd been reluctant to bring it up again.

'I passed out. Perhaps I had some sort of dream that triggered a scream. I really don't know; all I do know is that I'm fine now. I promise.' Understanding he was concerned; Louise placed a reassuring hand on his shoulder. He acknowledged her touch by placing his own hand on top of hers. He then looked down at her, smiled, and moved away.

'We need to get moving, I want us to be in Shorot before night. I know someone there who will give us shelter.'

They walked in silence for around half an hour. Then without anything to initiate it, Jamsen launched into conversation. Louise did her best to listen as he told her a hunting story. He told her of an occasion in which he had been sheltering beneath a Theto, when he was awoken by the grunting of a Gren, watching him, waiting to make its move. As he said the word Gren, a vision of a large boar-like creature with a longer snout and an array of sharp teeth flashed through her mind. For a moment, she wondered how she knew what a Gren was. Then she decided that considering the day's events, it mattered little. It was most likely a lost memory from her childhood.

As Jamsen launched into a description of how he fought the Gren unarmed, Louise found herself being absorbed by her thoughts. She vaguely heard Jamsen laughing as the story became increasingly comical. Louise chuckled absentmindedly, hearing none of what he had said. Instead, images of the innocent, unarmed men, women and children being murdered without mercy kept flashing through her mind.

Rubbing her eyes, she forced herself to concentrate on Jamsen's story, to let the horrors she'd witnessed remain in the past. It was at this moment that she realised Jamsen had stopped speaking. He was still chuckling quietly to himself as he let the memory of that day sweep him away. For a moment, she pondered whether she should reply, to imply that she'd been listening, but instead, she simply smiled. They continued like this for a while, one thriving reminiscently in a humorous memory whilst the other remained haunted by the faces of ghosts long dead.

Chapter Twenty-three

Eventually, they came to the bottom of a hill and as they began to climb it, they left behind the wood, the trees becoming increasingly sparse. As they reached the crest of the hill, they were able to see a large village in the distance, sitting comfortably in a valley.

'That is Shorot. It's a quiet village—most there keep themselves to themselves. However, I have a friend who owes me a favour or two. He'll shelter us for the night, and we can see whether we want to move on tomorrow or stay and rest for another night.'

Before Louise had the chance to reply, Jamsen started his descent down the steep hill. She promptly followed him and before long, they were able to join up with a large, well-laid dirt path that led straight to Shorot. From where they'd stood at the top of the hill, Shorot hadn't appeared to be too far away. However, it was a good few hours before they finally reached it.

As they approached the outskirts, they passed a few small, isolated houses and an occasional farm. As they came closer, the dirt path they'd been walking on, made way to a cobblestone road. Either side of which stood beautifully built red brick houses joined together in a long terrace, occasionally breaking to allow for a small side street. The streets became increasingly busy the closer they got to the centre. The houses remained fundamentally the same, only growing in size and grandeur. Some of these houses became well-presented shops that were selling a whole manner of things, ranging from books and clothing to luxurious-looking food. Louise studied one of the clothes shops as they passed and the fashions inside. She was relieved to see that her own outfit wasn't too outlandish for this new world. As the streets became busier, she was able to study women passing her by on the street; many wore black trousers like her, topped with simple shirts of various designs. Others, however, wore beautiful long skirts made from thick, elaborately decorated material. The most popular of which were flowers, snowflakes, and something that looked like orange cat's eyes. They were elegantly fitted from the waist to the middle of the hip, then the rest of the skirt fell gracefully down to their feet. On top of this, they wore simple long-sleeved shirts that were tucked into their skirts, and an array of colourful shawls.

Jamsen hadn't spoken since they'd arrived in Shorot and Louise had the distinct impression that this had been intentional—it meant that they could pass through the town more or less unobserved. He then led her down a small, dark and cobbled alleyway. At first glance, it didn't look as if there was anything of any consequence there, but then Louise looked to the very end of the alley, where there was a dark, dilapidated door. Above which there was an equally neglected sign; under the dirt, Louise was just able to make out the words *'The Alley's End'*. There was also a painting of some sort but Louise couldn't quite work out what it was. Jamsen paused for a second and checked the entrance to the alley, making sure no one was watching them. Once he was certain the coast was clear, he opened the door and they stepped inside. It took a few moments for Louise to adapt to the darkness that engulfed her. Once this happened, a surprisingly large place spread out in front of her and although it was dark—only lit by torches and a roaring fire—it was a cosy setting.

Along the right-hand side stood a basic wooden staircase leading to an even darker second floor. A few tables and chairs were scattered across the area in front of them. Most of the chairs were empty; those that weren't were occupied by dark, featureless shapes. Directly opposite them was the bar, behind which stood a small portly man, his face covered by a thick greying beard which matched the receding hair on his head.

Jamsen raised his hand in greeting and the man behind the bar promptly put the pint he was drinking down and waved back in delighted acknowledgement. Jamsen approached and they were soon shaking hands. Moments later, their heads came together and they whispered an inaudible conversation. Louise suddenly felt awkward, as if she were intruding, so she looked away from them and back into the near-empty room behind them. Her attention returned to the two men when Jamsen reached across the bar and subtly took a large metallic key from the bartender. He gave him a quick nod and then returned to his pint.

Jamsen then turned away and took Louise's arm,

gesturing for her to walk towards a table in the corner. They sat down and he surveyed the room, his gaze lingering on the dark figures. Louise watched him and felt herself mimicking him, a feeling of unease spread through her as she looked around. Jamsen, on the other hand, gave a satisfied sigh and looked over at Louise with a smile. Barney lay on the ground next to Louise, observing the room, clearly as sceptical as she was.

'It may not be the best-looking pub in the world but folk here keep themselves to themselves and they make an incredible stew!'

As if Jamsen had summoned him, the landlord appeared with two metallic bowls, both full of a delicious smelling stew. He also placed a wooden board on the table with freshly homemade bread on it. Louise hadn't realised just how hungry she was until she saw the food in front of her. With little grace or care for how messy they got, Louise and Jamsen dug in. The food vanished within minutes, Louise having shared some of hers with Barney, who sat patiently under the table.

They relaxed at the table for a while, making small talk. The more time that passed, the more Louise found herself enjoying Jamsen's company. The evening went by quickly and by the time they decided it was best to get some rest, she felt as if she'd known him her entire life. Guilt nibbled at her as she knew she wasn't telling him the whole truth. There were many moments where she was tempted to divulge all but she was still reluctant; something still forced her to hold back.

Eventually, the two of them noticed that the pub had now emptied, the fire just glowing embers. A wave of exhaustion rushed over Louise as the trials of the last few days and the late hour became a little too much for her. It must have been written across her face, as he rubbed her shoulder sympathetically.

'I think it's about time we got some sleep, I imagine it'll be another long day tomorrow.'

'That sounds like a great idea,' Louise replied, smiling back at him. The two looked at one another for a few seconds longer, before she suddenly felt awkward, her usual blush rising up into her cheeks. Turning her head away, she forced herself to yawn.

They left their table and began making their way up the dark staircase, Jamsen leading the way. The landlord was dozing at the far end of the bar and so they decided not to disturb him. The dark corridor was even darker than it had seemed from the bottom of the stairs, but Jamsen knew where he was going and lead them down the dark corridor. When they reached the door at the end, he whisked a key out of his pocket.

The room was small and relatively simplistic; against the far wall was an oak double bed with an inviting green duvet that immediately called out to Louise. On its right, a window, hidden from view by a set of dark green curtains. On the wall opposite, there was a large fireplace with a roaring fire which must have been lit by a member of staff.

Instinctively, Louise made her way across to the bed, next to which she dumped her pack. It suddenly hit her as she turned around to survey the room that there was only one bed. She looked over at Jamsen with the now-familiar flush spreading across her face. He looked up at her and before she had the chance to say anything, he smiled.

'You sleep in the bed, I'll grab a few of the spare

blankets and will sleep in front of the fire.'

'That doesn't seem fair. After all you've done for me, you should be the one who gets to sleep in the bed.'

Jamsen gave her an indignant look, then wandered towards her and took a spare blanket and two spare pillows from the bed. He went back to the fire and made himself a rather comfortable-looking bed just in front of it. Propping himself up against the armchair just in front of the fire, Jamsen pulled off his leather boots and placed them beside his bow and arrow, which as always remained within his reach.

'Thank you,' Louise said smiling at him.

He looked up at her and gave her a warm smile back, 'You need to get some sleep — we still have a fair way to go.'

Louise pulled off her boots and put them at the bottom of the bed, then pulled the covers back and crawled inside. As her body was enveloped by the soft, warm bed, she let out a small sigh, overwhelmed with relief. Tucking the covers all around her, she lay looking at Jamsen; he too was now lying down, wrapped up in his blankets. He looked at her and smiled again.

'Night,' he said quietly.

'Night,' Louise replied before instantly falling into a deep and dreamless sleep. Barney settling on the floor next to her.

Chapter Twenty-four

Light streamed into the room and flooded onto Louise's face, gently waking her from a full and satisfying sleep. She gradually opened her eyes whilst stretching her entire body in all directions. Turning her head towards the source of the light, she saw Jamsen was standing by the small window. Curtains that had been drawn through the night were now open and swaying gently in the breeze of the open window. Barney had positioned himself between her and Jamsen, prepared in case he tried to attack her.

Jamsen still hadn't noticed that Louise was now awake, even when Barney turned his head back towards her and gave his tail a few wags. Instead, he was leaning out of the window, looking at something just out of sight. Without warning, he threw himself backwards out of the spotlight. Even from where she sat Louise could see the look of panic that had spread across his face. She jumped out of the bed and quickly joined him over by the window.

'What? What is it?' she asked in a quiet voice.

Jamsen drew one of the curtains over and used it to

hide himself as he looked back out of the window. After a while, he stepped back and indicated for Louise to take a look.

'Brisheit's men arrived in Shorot at some point this morning. A friend of mine came by to let me know they were searching all buildings up and down the main street. They've just reached the buildings opposite the alley.'

Louise looked out of the window, using the curtain to hide herself from public view as Jamsen had. The window overlooked the alley they had walked down the previous night. At the far end, she saw a terrifying sight — Brisheit's men creating a blockade up and down the street. A few others had entered a house directly opposite the alley. They roughly pushed a man, woman, and two young girls out onto the street. One soldier grabbed the mother by her hair and held her tightly, slowly drawing a knife up to her throat and holding it there. Louise could see his mouth moving as he spoke to the woman's husband, who was pleading on his hands and knees. Meanwhile, men had entered the house and could be heard ruthlessly searching it.

'What are they looking for?' Louise asked in a shaky voice.

'I couldn't say for sure,' Jamsen replied. 'But I have a suspicion they're looking for you.'

Louise stopped watching the scene and turned to look at him, dread and fear spreading through her.

'For me! What makes you think that?'

'It's the only explanation I can come up with. The wreags we encountered were so intent on finding you, so centred on your scent. It's too great a coincidence that we arrived last night and they arrive here the very next day.'

Louise didn't know what to say and so turned back to the window. The second he had said it, she had known he was right. They knew who she was, they knew she was here, and they would do anything and everything to find her. She felt a pang of guilt as she watched the family on the street. The woman was still being held at knifepoint. The husband, who must have tried to help her, was now being kicked and punched by some of the soldiers, the two little girls crying hysterically as they watched.

For a moment, Louise was filled with the urge to hand herself in. She couldn't stand the thought that people were being beaten and threatened on her account. Then the men who had been searching the house came back out, shaking their heads. The man holding the knife let the woman go; she collapsed next to her husband and he rested his head in her lap as he writhed in pain. The two little girls joined them and the family embraced one another.

One of the soldiers indicated to one of the houses at the entrance to the alleyway and men ran out of sight, presumably forcing their way inside. Louise moved away from the window, suddenly realising they were getting closer to entering the alley and searching the inn. She looked back into the room to find Jamsen hurriedly putting his gear back together again.

'Quickly get your stuff together, we need to get out of here,' he said, meeting her gaze. 'We'll have a little bit of time as very few actually know this pub exists. They'll obviously find it but not straight away.'

Louise didn't need telling twice, she grabbed her bag and began pulling her boots back onto her feet. She was ready in minutes and began making her way across the room. Jamsen was shoving a jacket back into his bag. He hadn't noticed that as he'd grabbed his bag, he'd knocked his quiver over, sending one of his arrows across the floor. Louise bent down to pick it up and held it out to him. He gave her a hurried smile as he reached out to take it. As he looked at her outstretched hand, however, his expression changed to one of shock and disbelief.

For a moment they both held onto the arrow, until, feeling awkward, Louise lowered her hand. As she did, Jamsen reached out and grabbed it roughly. He turned it in his hand, looking closely at it.

Louise slowly followed his gaze, dreading what she knew she was going to see. The bandage that had covered the mysterious scar had fallen off during the night. It had been a while since she had looked at it herself and she was amazed at how much it had changed over such a short period. It was now so deeply indented in her skin that it looked as if it had been there for her entire life; it looked the same colour as the rest of her skin, but every now and again it seemed to glow a golden colour and flicker the deep reddish-orange of fire. Both Jamsen and Louise stared at it in equal amazement.

She abruptly pulled her hand away from his grip and it caught him completely unaware, giving him no chance to hold onto her. As pointless as it was, she pulled her jumper down so that it covered her wrist. For a moment, she looked down at the ground, trying not to look at him. He began to stammer as he tried to work out what he was going to say.

'You can't be, surely not,' he said, his gaze not

leaving hers for a second. 'I never actually thought it was true. You're the lost daughter of the Clarest family, the missing princess of Calaresp.' A smile spread across his face as the true extent of her identity dawned on him.

Louise looked away from him, distracted by sounds from just outside the window; the searching soldiers seemed to be drawing ever closer. She was filled with panic, unsure as to what was the greater threat at this point — Brisheit's men or the only man who knew her true identity. She considered for a moment, then looked at Jamsen and made a split decision.

'Are you still willing to help me?' she asked, looking at him intently.

He paused, clearly still processing all he had just learnt. 'You can't be though, it's impossible!'

Louise remained quiet, simply watching him, an expression of sheer desperation on her face. He looked back at her, took a deep breath, and nodded, 'Of course I'll still help. Come on, let's get out of here. But later, you owe me an explanation!'

They made their way towards the door and Jamsen was about to grab the handle when he abruptly placed his pack on the ground and began rooting around inside of it. He brought out a stretch of tatty red material that was around the size of a scarf. He held it out towards her and she took it, a confused expression on her face.

'You'll need to keep that covered,' he said, indicating towards Louise's new scar. 'Wrap this around it. If any of Brisheit's men or supporters see it, we'll both be dead instantly.'

She nodded and wrapped it around her hand.

Jamsen opened the door and they both waited with bated breath. Then, they took a few tentative steps into the hallway. They both froze when the sounds of raised voices echoing from downstairs.

'Quick! Follow me!' he whispered, slipping into the hallway.

Louise followed him but was surprised to see he was walking in the opposite direction of the main staircase, and instead was heading off towards the end of the corridor, to a dead end. She stood for a moment, confused, certain that he was making a mistake. Suddenly, she heard screams piercing through the pub; screams of people pleading for their lives.

By now, Jamsen had reached the end of the corridor and stood with his hand resting on the doorknob. He looked back, aware that Louise and Barney hadn't followed him. He let out a light whistle which, although it reached Louise's ears, was too quiet to go any further. As she looked over, he urgently beckoned for her to follow him. Instincts took over and she quickly made her way towards him.

It proved to be the right decision as Louise could hear the sound of armour shuffling towards the staircase and footsteps as they began making their way up the stairs. Louise, aware that her pursuers were drawing ever closer, increased her pace. Jamsen, meanwhile, was stood with the door open, his hand outstretched towards Louise. As soon as she was close enough, she reached her hand out and he grabbed it, pulling her inside, Barney close at her heel. Jamsen promptly closed the door, just as the soldiers had reached the landing. Through the closed door, Louise could hear a woman's voice briskly shouting out instructions; her voice was shrill with a cruel edge to it.

'Start with these rooms, I want everything searched quickly and effectively! She must be in this damned village somewhere.'

Louise turned and observed the room in which they were now taking refuge and she was immediately filled with dread. They seemed to be completely trapped.

They stood in a small sitting room, well-lit, with beautiful large windows overlooking the main street. Spreading right across the far wall stood a large bookcase, brimming with colourful, old books. Louise navigated past a few old and tatty sofas situated in the centre of the room and headed towards Jamsen, who was stood looking at some of the books.

'We don't have time for you to look at books,' she whispered harshly. 'I thought you said you were going to help me escape?'

Jamsen simply raised a hand, indicating that he needed a moment of silence. 'Ah here we are!' he said, opening one of the books. As he opened it, Louise realised that rather than pages, the book held a secret compartment, from which Jamsen took a brown leather pouch. He promptly opened it and poured a green powder into his hand, then placed the pouch back inside the book and returned the book to the bookcase. He looked over at Louise and gave her a wink. The sound of the searching soldiers getting ever closer to them.

Jamsen moved across to the end of the bookcase, where a small section of the wall was left bare. He lifted the hand containing the powder and using his other hand, he removed several small pinches which he flicked at the wall. As the powder touched the wall, it was instantly absorbed, then the entire wall flashed green. He did this until there was no powder left and instead of just a wall, there now stood a green glowing door.

'Come on,' Jamsen said, ripping it open. Louise hesitated for a second, amazed at what he'd just done. Then she followed him, entering into a dark and narrow corridor. As soon as she and Barney were inside, Jamsen closed the door, which continued to glow for a moment before it gradually went out, plunging them into darkness. Louise lifted a hand and pressed it against the wall, expecting to feel the same door they had passed through moments before. Instead, her fingers met cold brick.

Just as she was about to ask Jamsen what had happened to the door, she felt him gently gripping her arm.

'Are you okay?' he whispered.

'I'm fine, but how did you do that?' she replied.

'It's Willoper. A friend of mine keeps a stash of it in certain hideouts so he can make a quick escape. He won't mind us borrowing some,' he said quietly.

'So, what do we do now?'

They could hear movement in the room they had just been in and so both remained silent for a while. Louise then felt Jamsen moving closer to her, and he brought his head right next to hers,

'Well,' he said, whispering right into Louise's ear. 'This is actually a secret passageway; it stretches out through four houses. There is then a flight of stairs which will take us back to street level.'

'Do you have any sort of light?'

There was a moment's silence and in a defensive

voice, Jamsen replied, 'Well, I didn't exactly have time to plan ahead. Trust me though, I've used this passageway several times, I know it pretty well.' He gently grabbed her hand, 'I can lead you safely through.'

As it often did, the feel of Jamsen's touch sent a rush of happiness through her entire body. His hand tightened around hers — large, comforting and strong — giving it a gentle squeeze as he began to lead her onwards through the darkness. Louise forced herself to suppress a smile, chastising herself for having such a girlish reaction.

They continued through the pitch-black passageway, an experience Louise found increasingly disorientating. Her spare hand reached out and found the wall. Gingerly, she ran her hand against it, a sensation which gave her some sense of control. As she walked, she could feel Barney occasionally bumping against her legs as he remained as close to her as he could.

It seemed as if they'd walked for ages and eventually Louise became so absorbed by the dark corridor that she completely forgot about the murderous army in pursuit of her. All she could think about were her surroundings, as she began to wonder whether they had been continuously walking in a straight line or if the corridor had diverted at all. It certainly felt longer than four houses worth of walking.

'Careful, we've reached the stairs,' whispered Jamsen, so quietly that Louise didn't take in what he'd said. She realised just a few seconds too late and taking her step forward, she was shocked to realise that she'd run out of floor. She jerked forward, missing the first step and landing awkwardly on the second, which caused her to begin falling down the stairs. Fortunately, Jamsen, with his incredible reflexes, was able to twist around and catch her in his strong arms before she had fallen too far. She was now so close to Jamsen she could feel his breath against the side of her face, his arms wrapped tightly around her waist. Much to her embarrassment, she let out a small gasp which had very little to do with the fact she'd fallen.

'You alright?' he said, still holding her close to him. 'I did warn you there were stairs.' There was something about his tone that told Louise he was smiling and she found that she was too.

Louise laughed. 'I'm okay, I just didn't hear you in time. Thanks for catching me though.'

He loosened his grip on her and steadied her before completely removing his arms from her waist. For a moment, Louise was alone on the dark staircase and she felt a mild panic spread through her.

'You're still there, aren't you?' she asked in a quiet voice.

She suddenly felt his hand touching her arm and then his hand found hers. 'Of course, I am.'

He slowly guided her down the remaining stairs, allowing her to take one step at a time. Abruptly they came to a stop and Louise could hear Jamsen moving something. Then he opened a door and the stairwell was flooded with natural light. Louise found herself blinded and blinked wildly as she tried to adjust herself as quickly as possible.

Chapter Twenty-five

They stepped out into a narrow, empty alleyway. It was small and littered with old wooden crates and rubbish, the entrance to it was small and partially blocked keeping them hidden from the main street. She turned around at the sound of Jamsen shutting the door and was amazed to see how closely it matched the remainder of the wall. She felt fairly certain that if she were to look away, she would struggle to locate it again.

'Stay here,' Jamsen said, drawing her attention away from the hidden door.

He silently edged his way to the far end of the alleyway and crouching low, he peeked out onto the street. He scanned it in both directions and then made his way back to Louise.

'They've moved on from the pub and are slowly making their way down here. They seem to be fairly distracted with one of the larger shops on the street. We should go now, as we should be able to get away unnoticed.'

A noise in the street interrupted him and they both

turned towards it. There was nothing there.

'Just to be on the safe side,' Jamsen said, turning back to Louise, 'we should leave the alley and walk separately. I expect they've been told you are travelling with a man and a dog. So, Barney and I will head out first. Then you can head out about twenty seconds later. That way you should still be able to see us, but there will be a reasonable distance between us, so we shouldn't arouse suspicion.

'Okay, I'm not sure if Barney will go with you willingly though, so you'd best put him on his lead.'

Jamsen nodded at her and mere moments later, he and Barney had casually stepped out onto the street. Louise stood totally alone and felt utterly panic-stricken. She slowly took a breath and forced herself to count to twenty. When the time was up, she took another deep breath and stepped out onto the street. She walked away from the soldiers, staring straight ahead, ignoring the desperate temptation to look back.

The street was noticeably quieter than before, those that remained kept their heads down and scurried on their way. It only took Louise a few moments to spot Jamsen ahead of her and she felt her fear slightly subside. He gave a brief glance backwards and nodded when he saw her, then turned around and kept walking.

Louise felt incredibly self-conscious as she walked down the quiet street, and her eyes were drawn to the windows of the buildings on either side of her. Everywhere she looked, she saw curtains twitching, and eyes staring out nervously. Those that she did pass on the street, began looking at her with accusatory eyes and hard faces. The guilt she'd felt at seeing innocent people suffering because of her began to intensify. Without intending to, Louise began to quicken her pace, and soon she had caught up with Jamsen.

'Okay?' he said, keeping his eyes on the street ahead, still not looking at her or showing any signs of knowing her.

'I can see eyes watching us everywhere. Even the people we pass on the street suspect me, blame me.'

'You're a stranger; my face is vaguely known but yours is completely new.' He suddenly grasped her hand and held it tightly. 'Change of plan, they may be less suspicious if they think you're with me. We do need to get out of here quickly though.'

He led Louise across the street and they went down a side road. As soon as they had left the main street, they quickened their pace, desperately trying to escape the betraying eyes that followed them. Then they ran, trying to keep each footstep quiet, despite their speed. The town wasn't quite as large as Louise had initially thought, and before she knew it, the houses became sparse and isolated. When they eventually stopped, they were well clear of the centre of Shorot. They took a moment to catch their breath and check the road behind them, making sure that they hadn't been followed.

They didn't linger too long and were soon walking along a country road leading into yet another forest. Even though they had eased their pace, they glanced back countless times, paranoid that they may yet be followed and found.

So, obsessed with ensuring the soldiers weren't following them, they didn't notice four men and two women stepping out from the trees. They stood confidentially in the middle of the road, blocking it. Louise and Jamsen came to an abrupt stop as they realised that the greater threat stood before them and not behind.

Those in front of them held a variety of weapons, including sharp knives and bows, and Louise was startled to see that one even held a very sharp axe.

'Please remain where you are and do not touch your weapons,' said one of the women in a curt voice. She wore plain dark clothing and her long black hair had streaks of white throughout which was emphasised by the way she'd tightly tied it back. Louise judged her to be around forty-five, but she couldn't be certain, as the scars marking her face made it difficult to tell.

They stopped obediently, Jamsen standing protectively in front of Louise, who held down her bandaged hand as if concerned that they may be able to see through the material. Jamsen flicked his head from side to side, clearly looking for an escape route. The woman ahead of them realised that her prey was preparing to fly so she suddenly flicked her hands to the air. As she did, the sound of footsteps surrounded them and she could see more people stepping out from all directions until they were completely surrounded.

Barney's hackles raised and a low growl escaped from him. Louise placed a reassuring hand on his collar, just in case he suddenly decided to attack.

'Who are you and where are you going?' asked the woman, her tone suggesting that she found the situation somewhat tiring. Her gaze moved to the bow and arrow tightly gripped by Jamsen's side. In response to this, she brought her hands to her back and drew two incredibly sharp, slightly curved blades, gracefully flicking them around in her hands and holding them up for Jamsen to see. As if echoing her movements, the rest of the group brought up their own weapons and stood ready to attack. The woman made a subtle gesture with one of her blades towards Jamsen's bow and arrow.

Jamsen grimaced as he looked around, clearly frustrated by the trap that had so quickly swallowed them up. Maintaining eye contact with the woman in charge, he loosened his grip on his weapon and gently dropped it to the ground.

'We're just passing through. My partner and I have been hunting and we are now heading home,' he said in a low voice. Louise was sure she detected anger in his answer.

The woman studied them for a moment, took a few steps closer, and then began pacing from side to side. She looked up at them and smiled with a look of mock sympathy. 'Now that's a line we've heard a few times.'

'Well, it's the truth,' Jamsen interjected.

'As I'm sure you're aware, the soldiers of Calaresp have been searching these woods for traces of rebels — those trying to cause trouble for General Brisheit's reign.' She paused, looking at them, her face filled with anger and hatred. 'Now, we aren't rebels, nor do we have any association with them. The soldiers have decided, however, not to believe that and so send their men into these woods to find us and kill us. They weren't successful until they started sending spies; normal people who usually would pass us by without drawing even a hint of attention.' She looked back with sadness at the men and women in her party. 'We welcomed people into our groups; they would eat with us, sit by our campfires, and laugh with us. Then they would report our location the next day and we would be hunted like dogs.' She spat on the ground. 'Some did even worse.'

Those surrounding her muttered threats to Louise and Jamsen—insults and expressions of their own hatred. The woman raised a hand to calm them. Then, regaining control of her group, she looked back at them with a slight smile spreading across her mouth.

'We are no longer naïve; we are no longer gullible. Now we think of none but ourselves, our own protection. These are our woods now. We take any who are even remotely suspicious captive and we torture them. It's remarkable how often our instincts have proven to be accurate.'

She approached Jamsen, lifting one of her knives and placing it underneath his chin. Louise could see an indentation in his skin, threatening to pierce through it.

'Now,' the woman said in a quiet voice, 'you say the two of you have been hunting, but I see no signs of you having caught anything. And judging by the quality of your bow, I would imagine you are a reasonably good hunter.' She moved the knife so that the blade rested right across his throat as if she were about to cut it open. 'To me, that makes you two suspicious.' She took the knife from his throat and turned to walk away. 'Take them,' she instructed her companions.

Jamsen instinctively stepped in front of Louise—which did little good, as they were completely surrounded. He tried to fight a few off as they drew closer, but they were soon overwhelmed by hands, fists and nails. Soon they were both restricted, hands tightly tied behind their backs. Dazed and disorientated,

Louise frantically looked around, searching for Barney. In the chaos, he seemed to have completely disappeared.

'Barney? Barney! Where are you, boy?'

He was nowhere to be seen and Louise found this of strange comfort—it meant that he hadn't been hurt or captured, otherwise there would be a trace of him. Nevertheless, as they were pushed forwards, Louise couldn't help but survey her surrounding, hoping to see him somewhere. This caused her to stumble and trip a few times, which soon began to frustrate her captors. They'd pick her up off the ground harshly, pushing her onwards.

Eventually, they came to a stop and Jamsen was brought to her side. Two guards remained with them, weapons raised. Whilst the others, huddled in a small group, had a heated discussion. Jamsen took this opportunity to lean in towards Louise.

'Don't worry,' he whispered. 'I saw Barney escaping. When they grabbed us and tied our hands, I saw him sneaking off and making a run for the woods. He got away; they didn't notice.'

At this news, Louise battled with a mix of emotions. She was relieved he had escaped, but the thought of him alone in this strange new world was an equally terrifying prospect. This concern must have translated in her expression and Jamsen looked at her encouragingly.

'Don't worry, he's a smart dog. He'll be fine.'

Louise knew this was true but the thought of being without her trusted friend made her feel more alone than she had in years. But before she could dwell on the matter, the huddled group dispersed and were making their way back towards them. Without a word, they shoved black hoods over both of their faces, plunging them into darkness.

Chapter Twenty-six

One of the captors placed his hands roughly on Louise's shoulder and began pushing her forwards. Beside her, she could hear Jamsen's heavy footsteps as he too was guided through the woods. It wasn't a comfortable journey and Louise tripped and stumbled on several occasions. The muffled curses near her told Louise that Jamsen was experiencing similar difficulties. When they came to a stop, somebody suddenly grabbed Louise's hands, and she could hear the sound of chains. When the hood was pulled off her head, she realised that her hand restraints had now been attached to a chain wrapped around a tree. Just to her right, Jamsen was thrown into a second tree, his head smacking into the trunk, causing him to fall to the ground.

    He must have done something to have angered his captor as he now treated him with ruthless brutality, kicking him in the stomach every time he tried to stand up. Louise cried out in sympathy and Jamsen looked at her. On seeing the distress in her expression, he stopped struggling. His captor took this opportunity to attach his hand restraints to a chain surrounding the second tree and then, with one final kick, he glared at both of them and stalked away.

Straight away Jamsen began to struggle against the chains, flinging his arms around wildly. Louise gave a gentle tug and wiggled her hands to see if she could slip them free but was unsuccessful. She gave in and slumped to the ground, exhausted and concerned about what would happen to them next. Jamsen now had his foot resting against the tree, using it to pull as hard as he could against his chains. When this didn't work, he let out a cry of anguish and frustration before following Louise's example and slumping to the ground.

Louise took this opportunity to take in her surroundings; they were chained up on the outskirts of a reasonably large and busy camp. There were large tents scattered in front of her and all-around people bustled, making and sharpening weapons, cooking, talking, and even resting. No one looked over at the two prisoners and they were too far away for Louise to hear any of their conversations.

After a long silence, Jamsen raised his head and looked at her.

'Why didn't you tell me who you really are when we first met?' he asked in a quiet voice.

'Given the type of people who are after me, can you blame me for holding back?' she replied. 'I wanted to trust you, but I couldn't take that risk, at least not straight away.'

He didn't reply at first, but studied her face intently. Then, after a few awkward minutes, he gave the slightest hint of a smile and nodded.

'So, where have you been all these years? Were you telling the truth about being in a village on the outskirts?' he asked.

Louise sighed and looked away from him, resigned to the fact that she was better off telling him the truth. She opened her mouth to reply, but before she could form a single word, she noticed a large, unpleasant-looking man making his way towards her. He looked at her with an expression of such deep resentment and hatred that she was momentarily taken back. He leant forwards and pulled Louise to her feet, roughly unchaining her hands from the tree. Jamsen let out a huge roar of anger and fought ferociously against his own chains.

'Leave her alone!' he screamed. 'Take me instead, question me!'

The man ignored him and pulled Louise away with such force that she could feel her restraints digging deep into her skin, causing warm blood to trickle down her hands, dripping to the ground. Jamsen's screams followed her. She was dragged into a large green tent, the inside of which was unnervingly dark. The ground was a combination of dry mud and sand and Louise was certain she could see old, dried-out pools of blood. In the very centre of the space stood a tall wooden pole driven deep into the ground, around which was a large collection of bloodstains. With nothing else in the room, Louise kept her eyes fixed on the pole, dreading what would happen next. The man pulled her over to it and finally undid her restraints. She felt an inexpressible relief, but this disappeared moments later as he pulled her arms behind her and placed new restraints on them, attaching her to the pole. Louise fought against it as best she could, but her efforts went practically unnoticed by her remarkably strong guard.

As soon as her restraints were secure, the large man stepped back and stood just to Louise's left. In the distance, Louise could still hear Jamsen's shouts echoing through the camp, then a familiar voice nearby shouted harshly: 'Will someone shut him up!'

Straight away, Jamsen fell silent. Louise's mind filled with the horrible things their captors might have done to shut him up so quickly and she was desperate for him to make another noise, just to let her know he was okay.

Moments later, the woman whose voice she had heard — they had first met on the road — entered the room. She gave Louise a pleasant smile, as if they were meeting for a coffee or a casual job interview. She nodded at the man beside Louise and approached her captive.

'Now, you are going to tell me why there are suddenly so many of Brisheit's men around. Why they are searching Shorot and why they've been searching the woods so thoroughly. What or who are you looking for?'

'I don't know, we aren't with Brisheit and his army. We were just passing through; we don't mean you or your friends any harm.'

The woman nodded and gave her a forced smile that didn't quite reach her eyes. 'Rogers,' she said, her eyes not leaving Louise's face.

Without the need for any further instruction, the man stepped forward and stood in front of Louise. He drew his right hand back, his fingers curling up to form a fist. Louise saw it moving forwards, going so slowly that it almost looked as if it were moving in slow motion. Before she knew it, his fist had smashed full force into her face. Pain erupted in her left temple and her head flung backwards, smacking hard against the wooden pole she was stuck to. Before she had the chance to recover, another blow hit her hard in the ribs, causing her to double over as best as her restraints would allow. Another blow hit her again in the same spot, then two more times. The world around her began to darken, strange spots of light flickering in her eyes.

Rogers took a step back and looked over at the woman, who gave a single shake of her head. As she did the man stepped away, returning to his position at her side.

Louise coughed as she struggled to catch her breath. Pain like she'd never experienced before coursed through her entire body. Meanwhile, the woman stood watching her, clearly allowing her time to recover. Eventually, she took a step closer.

'I'll ask you again. Why did Brisheit send you here?'

Louise coughed, took a deep breath, and then forced herself to look directly into the woman's eyes. 'I've already told you,' she said bitterly, wheezing breaths between each word, 'we don't work for Brisheit, we don't have anything to do with him. We were just passing through these woods.'

The woman sighed dramatically and took a few steps closer, bending over so she could look Louise in the face. 'Look, why not make this easy on yourself? Just tell us the truth.'

Louise glared with an expression of disgust and hatred. The woman sighed again as she gestured her hand, causing Rogers to step forward. He smiled at her maliciously as he drew back his clenched fist. As Louise prepared herself, she suddenly felt a strange sensation begin to spread through her body. Seconds later, a bright light appeared in the pendant hanging around her neck. This was instantly absorbed by her body, creating golden veins through her skin. Just as Rogers' fist was about to strike Louise's face, she looked up at him. With power coursing through her, she was filled with a renewed strength.

'Stop!' she screamed ferociously. As she did, a blinding light spread like a wave from her body. When it reached Rogers, he was thrown backwards with such force that he crashed into one of the wooden poles supporting the tent. The light continued to spread through the small space, striking the woman, who flew backwards into the far side of the tent. She, unlike Rogers, was cushioned by the material of the tent. For a few moments, they both lay motionless. Louise felt her tensed body relax and she took a few deep breaths, now completely exhausted.

The woman rolled onto her front, then slowly lifted her head and stared at Louise, with a look of shock and wonder on her face.

Meanwhile, Rogers staggered to his feet. Once he had steadied himself, he let out a bloodcurdling roar of anger and stomped towards Louise.

'How the hell did you do that?' he asked in a low rattling voice, his face now right next to Louise's. He raised his hand a few times as if he were going to punch her again but thought better of it. He spat at her, then let out a continuous stream of curses and threats. Louise simply stared back at him, struggling just to keep her head up but determined to look him in the eyes. This seemingly didn't help his temper, as he let out another roar and suddenly thrust his hand outwards and clasped it tightly around her throat.

Louise choked and spluttered, her exhausted body struggling to fight back against the man's strength. She desperately tried to move her head away, to wriggle out of his grip, but it didn't make any difference. She tried to muster the same power that had blasted him away mere moments before, but her body felt hollow, tired. As he squeezed harder, she felt as if her lungs were going to explode in their desperation to find oxygen. Rogers stared at her with an expression of hatred and overwhelming fear.

'Rogers!' the woman shouted from behind him. 'Let go of her right now!'

He gave another squeeze, glanced back at the woman briefly, made a sound like an angry bull, and finally let go. He stalked off, clearly still furious at Louise's mysterious act of retaliation. He left the tent, leaving the two women alone.

The woman paid him no attention, keeping her gaze firmly fixed on Louise. Slowly she approached her with a look of great awe on her face. She studied Louise for a moment and then smiled.

'It's you, isn't it? I can't believe it, but it must be!' she said in a quiet voice, almost as if she were talking to herself.

Louise didn't reply, she too was blown away by her own display of power, She was also suspicious, unsure as to what the woman would do with her now.

'You're Princess Louise aren't you, the rightful heir of Calaresp?'

Something in Louise's face must have given her away as the woman suddenly gasped and her arms reached out to clasp Louise on the shoulders.

'Oh, so that means, it means, she did it! Clarris found you, didn't she!'

The fact she knew the name *Clarris* gave Louise a rush of different emotions. It sparked a flicker of hope inside her which mingled with relief at the prospect she may have just found an ally. At the same time however, she had to question whether she would want an ally willing to cause as much harm and pain to a stranger as she had just done.

'Who are you?' Louise said, her voice hoarse and maintaining an unfriendly tone.

The woman didn't seem to notice her tone and had a joyful smile on her face, arms now back at her side. 'My name is Ballie. Clarris was my very dearest friend, we've known each other since we were children. I saw her about three weeks ago and she told me that you were alive and that she was going to find you and bring you back.' She let out an almost hysterical laugh. 'I actually didn't believe her! Where is she? I wouldn't have thought she'd have ever left your side.'

Ballie came to an abrupt stop as she saw the expression on Louise's face, and the smile quickly disappeared. 'She didn't make it did she?' she asked, her voice suddenly very sombre.

Louise studied her face and decided to finally tell the truth. She shook her head. Ballie's eyes filled with tears and a sob escaped her as she turned away from Louise. She remained like this for a few moments then took a few deep breaths and brought her hands up to her eyes, where she seemed to wipe away a few silent tears. When she turned back, her eyes were slightly reddened, but she had managed to regain her composure. As she looked at Louise properly for the first time, a look of genuine shock spread across her face.

'Oh, I'm so sorry, I've not even untied you yet!' She rushed over to Louise and unlocked the chains behind her back.

Louise eased her hands forward and took a nervous step. She hadn't quite realised how big a part the restraints had played in keeping her upright following the beating, and now without them, she fell gracelessly to the ground. The pain in her ribs and head intensified and she let out a low and piteous groan as she rolled onto her back, hands wrapped around her waist protectively.

Ballie rushed over to her, an expression of guilt spreading across her face, 'Are you okay? Oh, I am so sorry! Here, lean against this,' She pulled Louise backwards until her back leant against the pole, her hands still wrapped around her waist.

Ballie sat down beside her, 'I had no idea, no idea at all it was you. None of us did. We've been tricked and betrayed so many times.' She hesitated and Louise once again saw tears forming in her eyes. 'I'm just so sorry.'

Despite the extent of her pain, Louise was surprised by how much she sympathised with Ballie. She knew and understood the difficulties of not knowing who you could trust and could only imagine how that would get amplified when you were betrayed multiple times. A small part of her, however, still resented them for the pain they'd inflicted on her.

She held her hands up to cradle her head and

pressed gently on her temples. Ballie stood up and went across to the entrance of the tent. 'Hey, Jenny! Bring me the medical supplies and a cloth with some warm water. Quickly.' She returned to Louise and sat beside her, not wanting to touch her for fear of causing any more pain. It wasn't long before another woman, presumably Jenny, entered the tent, arms full and a wide bowl of water balanced precariously in the crook of her arm. Ballie rushed to help her before she had the opportunity to drop anything and the two women carefully laid out all the supplies on the ground. Once this was done, Jenny stood beside Ballie, clearly uncertain as to what she was meant to do next.

'I'll tend to her, you can go,' she said, not giving her a second glance.

As soon as Jenny had left the tent, she set about dealing with the wounds she had indirectly inflicted on her. She dug out two small brown bottles, a little pot of a strange clumpy green sludge, two long stretches of white cloth, and the bowl of water. First, she placed one of the strips of cloth into the water, then she dabbed Louise's head with it, causing another spasm of pain to ripple through Louise's body. Using the same cloth, she then poured a measure of liquid from each of the bottles and held them to Louise's head for a while. They didn't speak whilst she dealt with her injuries as Ballie seemed totally absorbed in what she was doing. After a while, with the cloth still pressed against her head, Louise felt the stabbing pain subside as it was replaced by a mild throb and her surroundings began to stop spinning. Ballie tentatively took the cloth away for a moment and seemed happy with the effect. She placed it carelessly back on the ground.

She reached for the strange pot of green sludge and coated her right hand in it. 'Can you lift your top a little for me, just high enough for me to get to your ribs? That was the other main impact point, wasn't it?'

Still feeling dazed and confused Louise nodded and lifted the left-hand side of her shirt, revealing her swollen and reddened waist.

'This cream won't stop it from hurting, at least not as well as the ointments did on your head, but it will, over time, heal the internal injuries. Sadly, I can't use the cream and the ointment together so you may have to deal with a little bit of pain for a few days.' Ballie began to spread the cream at the point in which Rogers' fist had impacted. Through the pain she was already experiencing, Louise felt a tingling, sharp shooting pain spreading through her side. Instinctively, she went to rub the cream off to stop the pain. But with an apologetic smile, Ballie held her hands down to prevent her.

'I'm sorry, I know that it's painful but it'll do so much good, I promise.'

Reluctantly, Louise stopped wriggling and was soon amazed to see that the cream was already being absorbed into her skin. Eventually, it looked as if it had never even been there. Finally, Ballie sat back and smiled at Louise, clearly satisfied with her work.

'There, you should start feeling a little bit better in a few hours.' She hesitated for a few seconds before she continued, 'It means you'll be stuck with the bruises for at least a day though. There wasn't much I could do about that.'

With the pain and confusion finally beginning to subside Louise was able to regain control of her thoughts. 'You need to release my friend, Jamsen. Right now.'

Before she could say any more, Ballie had let out a stifled gasp of shock and jumped to her feet. 'Oh! I had completely forgotten about him. Of course, if he's a friend of yours we'll release him, straight away.' She dashed out of the tent, left for a few seconds and then returned, giving Louise a nod to let her know Jamsen was being released.

Louise smiled with relief, realising just how desperate she was to be reunited with him.

'Also,' Louise said, giving her surroundings a reproachful look, 'could we possibly move to another tent? One that's perhaps a little more comfortable, where I haven't had the crap beaten out of me?'

'Oh, I am so sorry! I should have thought of that!' Ballie replied, an instant look of panic spreading across her face.

'It's fine!' Louise gave her a small, reserved smile as Ballie helped her to her feet.

Moments later, with the support of Ballie's arm, she entered another tent. Unlike the previous one, this had no pole in the centre and the ground was covered with a beautiful blue rug. In the very centre of the room was a long wooden table, with six chairs set around it. In the corners were books and chests. On top of many of these were various scattered scrolls, quills, and types of ink.

Ballie gently lowered Louise into the seat at the top of the table, then placed a mug in front of her. Inside of this was a light pink substance with three very small purple flowers floating in it. An incredible aroma hit Louise and the second it did, she felt an instant lift. The drowsiness caused by the beating almost dissipated. Amazed by how much of a difference the smell alone had on her, before she could stop herself, she'd taken a long and satisfying sip. When she put the mug back down, she let out a sigh of appreciation and sat back in her seat.

'It's good, isn't it?' Ballie smiled. 'The drink itself is made up of Manipolies and Lilioc, whilst the little flowers on top are Bestros. Each of them has great healing powers, and when soaked in warm water, they create the perfect revival drink. They've been used for centuries after battles or attacks.'

Moments later, the flaps of the tent opened up and Jamsen walked in, being roughly escorted by two of the men that had captured them earlier. He had a deep red slit on his bottom lip and a trail of dried blood that had leaked right down to his chin, causing a few drops on his shirt. He also had a dark bruise appearing at the corner of his right eye. He looked angrier than Louise had ever seen him and something in his stature made him look incredibly intimidating. As he looked at her, he quickly took in her multiple injuries. And as he rushed over to her, his expression changed to one of deep concern.

'Are you okay?' he asked, crouching beside her, his large hand gently touching the side of her face. The other went to her waist, where she still held her ribs as if concerned, they would fall out. 'What the hell did they do to you?'

'I'm okay, honestly,' she replied, smiling. She couldn't even begin to express the relief she felt at seeing him and forcibly had to stop herself from throwing her arms around him and drawing him into a tight hug. Instead, she let out a small laugh. 'You don't look too much better. Are you okay? Here, have a sip of this, it should help.' She held out her mug.

Jamsen gave the mug a suspicious look and held it at arm's length.

'It's okay, I've had some and it's incredible.' She placed her hand over his and pushed the mug back towards him. He took a tentative sip and as soon as he had, she could see the effect it had on him.

Ballie brought over a second mug and placed it in front of him. Jamsen clearly hadn't noticed Ballie was in the room and as soon as he did, he stepped in front of Louise defensively.

'It's okay, Jamsen,' Louise said, placing a reassuring hand on his arm. 'She knows the truth, she knows who I am, and she's actually on our side!' He looked at her with a look of concern and confusion but allowed Louise to guide him into the seat beside her. 'Ballie knew the woman who gave me the means to return to Calaresp, the woman who helped me to remember who I truly am.' Louise smiled at Ballie and then looked back at Jamsen. 'I think it's about time I gave you the full story and explain to Ballie exactly what happened to Clarris.'

Louise gestured for Ballie to sit down as Jamsen glared at the woman. Taking a deep breath, Louise told them all she knew. They both sat as Louise explained her day-to-day life before she'd entered the portal, and how she'd had no idea who she was or where she'd actually come from before Clarris's visit. When she reached the point in her tale where Clarris was ripped apart by the wreags, she looked over at Ballie. Having learnt of the pain her friend had suffered, she had turned away from Louise and Jamsen, refusing to make eye contact with them. Louise looked away from her, allowing Ballie a few moments to recover, then took hold of the woman's hand and gave it a gentle squeeze. Ballie took a few deep breaths, then looked up and smiled at Louise.

'It's okay,' she said in a quiet voice. 'Please, go on.'

Louise gave her a weak smile in return and continued. Eventually, Louise sat back and gave her overwhelmed audience time to process her story.

'So, are they still pursuing you?' Ballie asked, her eyes transfixed on Louise.

'That's who we were trying to escape from before we bumped into you.' Jamsen said darkly.

'They must know who you are, otherwise, they would have lost interest a while ago.' Ballie said with a look of shock. 'That means they'll do anything to get to you. You need to keep moving or it'll be too easy for them. I'll also need to get my camp moved otherwise the wreags will lead the soldiers right here.'

Louise promptly felt the need to apologise for the potential trouble she had brought upon Ballie and her people. Then she remembered that despite their protests, these people had taken her and Jamsen captives. The situation had been entirely out of Louise's control.

'I'll send them in the opposite direction to us, it might even help to mask our trail,' Ballie said quietly to herself.

Both Jamsen and Louise looked at her in surprise. 'You're coming with us!?' they asked at the same time.

Ballie looked at them. 'Oh, yes of course! Clarris would have wanted me to. Also, I can help you find the rebels.'

Jamsen looked at her scathingly, 'How do you think you'll be able to help?'

She gave them both a patient smile. 'Although I'm not one of them—I have my own people, my own family to look after—I do nevertheless know them very well, and some of their key members are my closest friends. Like Clarris, for instance. Anyway, after what we put you through, the least I can do is help you get to them safely.

'That would be great!' Louise said, suddenly filled with renewed hope and enthusiasm, which instantly began to ebb away when she saw the dark and frustrated expression on Jamsen's face. Ballie, on the other hand, didn't seem to notice this and went to leave. Just before she bustled out of the tent, muttering about what preparations would be needed, Louise sat bolt upright and desperately asked, 'I don't suppose you've seen a dog hanging around, have you?'

Clearly distracted, Ballie shook her head. 'What? A Dog? No, sorry.'

As Ballie left the tent, Louise felt crestfallen.

Jamsen leant in towards her. 'He'll be okay, don't worry. Now, do you really think we can trust her?' he asked in a quiet voice, as if worried they would be overheard. 'After all she's done? I mean, look at your face.' His voice softened as he surveyed her injuries.

His hand was resting on the table and Louise placed her own on top of it; he gripped her fingers and gently held them in his own.

'The woman who sent me here, Clarris—she trusted her. And as soon as she realised who I was, she let me go and has been kind to me ever since,' Louise explained.

'We aren't the only ones she's done this to though. In fact, we've been pretty lucky. I'm fairly certain that they kill most of the people they take hostage. As for her kindness on realising who you are... what if she works for Brisheit and intends to lead us straight to him? She may have even told Brisheit about Clarris's mission in the first place, it may be her fault she's dead.'

Louise paused for a moment, having never considered this option. She delved deep within herself as she tried to decide whether or not to trust Ballie. No matter what way she looked at it, however, a strong voice deep within her was telling her that although misguided, Ballie could be trusted. Louise looked up at Jamsen, her expression resolute.

'I can't explain why, but I trust her and I think we should go with her.'

Jamsen watched her for a few minutes, a look of deep concern on his face, then he nodded his consent and Louise felt a huge wave of relief pass through her. She would never have gone with Ballie if Jamsen had refused to join them. She felt herself needlessly blushing as she realised that whatever happened, she wanted to stay by Jamsen for as long as she could.

He leant back in his seat, clearly only now allowing himself to take the opportunity to relax.

'So, you don't remember anything about Calaresp, about your family, your heritage?' he asked, arms crossed and feet stretched out in front of him.

Louise considered for a moment, 'Not at first, no, but after I'd met Clarris and she'd given me the Whisper, something changed. That night I saw flashes of my parents and the castle, and it all seemed so familiar. It's like my memory is a jigsaw, gradually being put together.' She laughed at her own analogy. 'At the moment, it's still a pretty bare jigsaw, I can tell you that much!'

Jamsen chuckled and let out a low whistle in amazement. 'Well, no wonder you've been so clueless at times! It does explain a lot!' He shot her a cheeky smile and Louise couldn't help but laugh. As she looked at him, she suddenly realised how worried she'd been that he would desert her when he discovered the truth. The fact that he had stayed by her side filled her with such tremendous relief.

'Do you know much about my family? About the abilities we have?' she asked dubiously.

'Not a great deal. I was about the same age as you when your family were, well…'

'Murdered,' Louise interjected coldly.

'I don't remember all that much about them, or you. I do remember my mother telling me a little bit. She said that although the powers were hereditary, you could only fully use them if you had the Whisper, as if it acknowledged your right to rule.' Jamsen smiled as he looked at Louise before continuing, 'She told me that the lost princess had shown signs that she would be incredibly powerful right from birth; possibly as powerful as the original royal who first took control of the Whisper's power. My mother had also heard that the little princess had a mark on her hand, a small scar that matched the markings that could be found on the Whisper. This was something that had never been seen before and many prophets and mystics claimed she was destined to do great and wonderful things.' Jamsen paused for a second and he looked up at Louise earnestly. 'I do remember how Calaresp mourned when your family were killed. Especially for you — the lost princess. Brisheit had boasted so fervently about how he had killed you. Obviously, he didn't want anyone to know he had failed. But as I say, I was only a young boy at the time, I'm sure the rebels will be able to tell you much more.'

There was a short silence as Louise tried to force herself to remember more of her childhood, of her parents. It seemed that she couldn't force the flashbacks, they revealed elements of her childhood only when necessary. As a thought popped into her head Louise's gaze flashed up to Jamsen in mild alarm.

'Are you still willing to come with me?' she asked, trying to sound as calm and casual as she could.

Jamsen smiled and took her hand in his, 'Of course I am.' There was a moment's silence which became almost awkward and Louise found herself giving his hand a squeeze, then pulling it away. 'Anyway, I haven't anything else to do,' he said teasingly. 'And I must admit it has been quite an adventure so far.'

Louise smiled in reply and nodded her head in gratitude. Then without having to say a word to each other, they rose from their seats and went to see what progress Ballie was making with her preparations.

Chapter Twenty-seven

Less than an hour later they were ready to go. Ballie had brought together a team consisting of one woman and three men, all of whom looked at Louise with alarm and amazement. Almost instantly, a man and a woman approached her hand in hand, clearly a couple. They both had kind, friendly faces. The woman was well-rounded with dark red hair framing a pale face whilst the man was well-built, with grey, thinning hair despite his young appearance.

As soon as they had reached her, they offered to shake her hand.

'Hello, it's such a pleasure to meet you! My name is Pascen and this is my husband, Trevel,' said the woman.

The man beamed at her as he said, 'We both used to work at the castle in Calaresp when your parents ruled, and although we didn't know them very well, we can tell you they were incredible and very kind to everyone.'

Before she could stop herself, a wide smile spread across Louise's face. These were the first people she'd met who had known her parents since Clarris and she found herself desperate to know more.

'I was the stable mistress and my husband was a chef in the kitchens, it was such a wonderful time.' Pascen smiled to herself. Then she took hold of Louise's hand and gave her an earnest look as she said. 'Your parents were remarkable people, what happened to them was beyond appalling.'

Louise couldn't think what to say and so simply nodded. The couple gave her one last smile before moving on.

The other two men didn't approach Louise, nor did they seem particularly pleased to be there. They looked incredibly alike and Louise presumed them to be brothers if not twins. They looked sullen and unfriendly, both had dark, greasy unkempt hair and large, well-muscled bodies. On realising that she was staring at them they simply nodded, expressionless. Louise nodded back and uncomfortable looked away.

'Ah, there you are!' Ballie appeared from behind Louise, resting a friendly hand on her shoulder. 'Ready to get going?'

Louise looked around at her escort, then at Jamsen, before looking back at Ballie. 'I think so. At least as ready as I'll ever be!'

'I've only told this group who you truly are; I thought it would be too dangerous for the rest of the camp to know. It's safer for everyone if we keep your identity a secret for now. Many of the camp don't even know we're leaving, they're too busy getting ready to go in the opposite direction. So, we should try and leave as quietly as we can.'

They left the camp completely unobserved and soon

it was out of sight as they made their way further into the woods. Louise began the journey walking with Pascen and Trevel as they told her all about their time in Calaresp, before the uprising. They told her how they'd sometimes see her mother walking around the castle, singing to herself with a gentle and delicate voice that would warm the hearts of all she met. As they spoke, Louise could hear it—a distant echo of a beautiful voice drifting through her memories. Trevel also told her how he would often see her father working away in the castle gardens. It seemed that her parents loved everything about Calaresp, from the land itself to the smallest creature.

As they spoke, fractions of memories flashed through Louise's mind of her parents laughing, smiling, and dancing with one another, and it caused a wide grin to spread across her face. Little did she know that as she reminisced, the Whisper safely tucked underneath her shirt glowed slightly as memories of her past began to unlock in her mind.

Eventually, after a full day of walking, they decided to stop and set up camp for the night. They each went about pitching small tents, large enough to hold just two people. Once they were up, Ballie approached Louise and gestured to the small tent behind her.

'Louise, would you like to share a tent with me?' she asked. 'One of us has to sleep alone and I don't think it would be safe for that person to be you. I want you with someone so that we can ensure you remain safe.'

Louise hesitated and without meaning to, looked towards Jamsen, who was closely watching the exchange.

'You are also welcome to come in my tent?' he said

in a quiet voice only meant for her. 'Wherever you feel most comfortable, and safest, especially considering I have never had anyone beat you.' He gave Ballie a begrudging look which she returned with an angry one of her own.

'I think I'll stick with Jamsen if you don't mind Ballie,' Louise replied without a moment's hesitation. 'He's been pretty good at keeping an eye on me so far.'

Ballie smiled at her and nodded, 'It's okay, I understand.'

They all settled down fairly quickly, and a blazing fire was made in the centre. Which Trevel used to make them delicious and warming meal. Afterwards, they sat around the fire and allowed themselves to relax. The two sullen men situated themselves as far from the group as possible, whilst still benefitting from the heat of the fire. They smoked small cigarettes that emitted bright red and black plumes of smoke that danced and mingled together. They made quiet conversation and practically ignored the remainder of the group. Pascen and Trevel sat closely together, his arm wrapped protectively around his wife as they laughed and joked. Jamsen, Louise and Ballie sat just to the side of them and discussed the route they would take the next day.

Halfway through the conversation, Louise thought she saw a light flash very faintly out of the corner of her eye. She quickly turned her head in that direction but there was nothing there. Jamsen followed her gaze.

'What?' he asked anxiously. 'Did you see something?'

Louise ignored him for a few moments as she continued to watch. The woods remained still and dark and she eventually averted her gaze back to her companions.

'No, it's fine,' she said quietly. 'It must have just been my imagination. What were you saying?'

They continued with their conversation, but soon Louise found her attention wavering back to the trees to her side. For a while, she drifted in and out of the discussion, certain that it hadn't been a mistake, certain that something had moved out in the wood. She hoped it was Barney but instinctively knew it wasn't. Then all of a sudden, she saw the light again, a faint blue object moving quickly between two large trees. There was something remarkably familiar about the form and without a word to her companions, she rose to her feet and began moving towards the spot she'd been staring at. She was so consumed with curiosity, she didn't notice Jamsen and Ballie's exclamations of surprise and confusion.

Louise completely ignored her companions, so absorbed by the visions ahead of her. As she grew closer, another blue shape appeared, followed by another, moving gracefully between the trees. Louise felt a wave of dizziness pass through her and before she knew it, she had collapsed to the ground, her hand breaking her fall. Behind her, Jamsen let out a cry of alarm, but the sound seemed to pass right by her and she wasn't even aware when his arms gripped her shoulders, lifting her back off the ground until she rested in his lap. Instead, Louise found herself being absorbed into this new blue world, and just as before, she passed into a scene from the past.

Louise found that she seemed to have a lot more control over this vision than the last time and with a great effort, she pulled herself to her feet. She looked back at where she'd been and was instantly filled with alarm as she saw herself lying lifelessly in Jamsen's arms. He gently touched her face, trying desperately to wake her. She looked down at her own body and realised that, like the people in front of her, she was no longer a solid form. Instead, there was now a blue, cloud-like shape outlining her frame. She tried to place a hand on her arm but instead of making contact, it simply passed through it as if it were made of smoke. She looked at the Whisper hanging around her chest and realised it was glowing a warm orange light that seemed to spread in delicate lines through her body.

A small part of her wanted to study her own body, but something drew her attention upwards and she began to observe the scene before her. Much the same as her last vision, Louise saw there was a camp set up in the centre of the wood. However, this one was considerably smaller than the last and this time the occupants were lying around the fire, fast asleep. The blue forms moved and snored lightly in their sleep, and Louise picked her way between them, carefully studying their sleeping faces. Although she was fascinated to see this vision of the past, she couldn't help but wonder why she was being shown it. She had understood that the last vision had been intended to show her the mystery of the barren land — how the blood of so many innocent people had been spilt so mercilessly that the land, like the victims, would never live again.

On this occasion, however, nothing seemed to be happening and she hadn't noticed any barren sections of the wood to mark any murderous acts. She continued to walk through the sleeping bodies, searching her surroundings for the slightest sign of an attack. All of a sudden something moved, and Louise was surprised to find her attention being drawn into the centre of the camp. A small girl, no older than seven, had stood up out of her makeshift bed. She looked at those sleeping around her and when she was content that no one else was awake, she knelt back to her bed, from which she drew out a single arrow. Louise watched with curiosity as the little girl raised it to the sky, and to her amazement, without the assistance of a bow, it shot upwards into the darkness of the night. Louise's eyes followed it upwards and she let out a small gasp as it suddenly exploded into a ball of light, spreading outwards like a firework. A few seconds later, it vanished and the camp went dark. Louise looked back down and was amazed to see that everyone in the camp was still asleep. She was even more surprised when she looked back at the young girl, only to find she was now back in bed.

Louise edged closer to take a better look at the seemingly sleeping child. Her innocent and angelic face rested lightly in her pillow, a small strand of hair resting gently against her nose. Her small hands held onto the blankets, wrapping them tightly around her. The girl moved her hand very slightly and as she did, Louise saw that she was holding onto something underneath the covers; the top of it glistened slightly. Louise moved to get a better look but before she could, an explosion of movement erupted around her.

Looking up, she saw people quickly approaching the sleeping camp; soldiers with their weapons bared. They stabbed and slashed at the sleeping figures, who were gradually starting to wake — for many of them, it was far too late. Screams of pain began to fill the air around her as people woke to find swords slicing through their unprepared bodies. Eventually, those in the camp began to organise themselves and started fighting back. Louise rushed forwards, desperate to try and help. Then she remembered just how powerless she was. Suddenly she twisted around, worried about the safety of the small girl. The horrific sight that met her once she'd located the girl, made her heart skip a beat. Clutched tightly in the girl's small hands was a long sharp dagger. Holding it out in front of her, she moved towards a young woman of about seventeen who was just rising from her bed, clearly confused and very frightened. Without hesitation, the younger girl lifted her dagger and with her spare hand, grabbed the other girl's hair and held her head back. With remarkable ease, she drew the dagger slowly and deeply across her throat, leaving behind a trail of blood as she sliced open the girl's throat.

Louise's blood turned cold at the sight, the horror of the scene intensified when she noticed the smile of deep satisfaction that had spread across the child's face. Without hesitation, she moved on to a man who was cradling the limp corpse of a woman in his lap; he wept over the motionless body, three arrows sticking out from her bloodied chest. Louise wanted to shout out, to warn the man as the little girl approached, but she could do nothing as the child moved behind him. Clearly uncertain as to whether she would be strong enough to hold his head back, she instead stabbed the dagger into the side of the man's neck. With remarkable speed, she stabbed the dagger back into his neck another four times. She didn't stop to see if the man was dead. Instead, as if bored of an old toy, she flicked her head around and trotted off in the other direction.

Louise continued to watch and with horror, she realised that the man wasn't quite yet dead. The woman in his lap was temporarily forgotten as he held a shaking hand to the side of his neck in a desperate attempt to hold back the heavy stream of blood now escaping him. He then collapsed to the ground and in his last moments, he released his grip on his throat and moved his bloody hand across to the woman, until his hand intertwined with hers. As she forced herself to turn away, Louise wiped the tears that streamed down her cheeks. She looked around at the chaos and bloodshed occurring all around her and soon found herself feeling increasingly lightheaded.

Soon, the blue figures began to disappear and as everything around her began to change, she couldn't stop herself from collapsing to the ground. Louise became vaguely aware of hands tightly grasping her shoulders and she realised she was leaning against a large warm form, their arms tightly and comfortingly wound around her. She was shaking uncontrollably and the strong arms rubbed her shoulders, spreading warmth back into her body. Eventually, she was able to open her eyes, and as she did, she looked up to see Jamsen holding her, a look of concern spread across his face. She attempted a smile and he did the same.

'Seriously,' he said in a quiet voice, resting his chin on the top of her head, 'you have to stop doing this to me.'

Despite the exhaustion that still spread through her body, Louise laughed slightly.

'I will certainly try my best,' Louise replied.

Jamsen let out a single soft laugh as he held her tightly. Louise could feel the steady beat of his heart as her head lay against his chest and his fast-panicked breaths left and entered his body. Suddenly, as if awakening from a dream, she sat up and looked around her, making sure that the visions of the past had truly gone, that the murderous little girl had left.

For the first time, she remembered Ballie, who was knelt just in front of her. 'Are you okay?' she asked, her eyes not leaving Louise. 'What happened?'

Louise didn't answer. Instead, she held her head in her hands as she tried once again to get a full grip on her surroundings. Ballie looked over to Jamsen for an answer and Louise heard him clearing his voice. 'I don't know, but I think it's happened to her before, a few days ago.'

'Look!' Ballie interrupted before Jamsen could say any more. She pointed a finger to Louise's chest.

Louise looked down and realised that the Whisper had fallen out from underneath her shirt and was now dangling below her, gently swaying. She lifted the Whisper to her face and looked closely at it. Most of the time it consisted of an endless darkness but now, it had a faint blue glow, the same colour as the people from the past. Instinctively she clutched it in her hand, hiding it from the others, her fingers wrapped tightly around it. Jamsen, however, didn't pay any attention to the Whisper. He continued to watch Louise with a look of apprehension.

'Is that… Is that the Whisper?' Ballie asked in a quiet, awed voice.

Louise looked at her for a moment and then

begrudgingly nodded. She hadn't shown anyone the Whisper before and until now it had remained hidden under her shirt. For a reason she couldn't quite explain, she felt very exposed. Meanwhile, Ballie's eyes had widened as they rested where the Whisper had been, a smile spreading across her face in amazement at having seen such a renowned pendant.

'Here, lean against this,' Jamsen interrupted, seeing that Louise was still feeling weak and faint. He indicated to the trunk of a tall tree beside her and held her arm as she half-walked, half-crawled over to it. When she finally leaned against the tree, she let out a small sigh of satisfaction as she felt her body begin to relax. She forced herself to take deep breaths to calm herself and almost instantly, she began to feel better and became more aware of her surroundings.

'Are you ready to talk?' Jamsen asked in a quiet voice and Louise knew that he was hoping to get some sort of explanation. 'Can you tell me what happened?'

Louise nodded and took a moment to try and process everything she'd seen. The main image that flickered continuously through her mind was that of the little girl, so brutal and ruthless.

'I think…' she said in a quiet voice, 'I think I see flashbacks of the past. It happened when we were in the woods. When I had said that I had merely fainted, I actually saw Brisheit's men murdering an entire camp full of innocent people. It's the reason why the land never recovered, never regrew. What had occurred was so brutal, so cruel, it just couldn't. The same thing happened here.' And with this, Louise pointed to the centre of the trees that sat around them. Just as before, she could now see there was a large barren spot where the forest floor was black as if rotten. It wasn't as easy to see as the first spot had been, as a lot of debris had fallen from the trees above to cover it.

'What did you see this time?' Jamsen prompted.

'Well, it was another camp, albeit a lot smaller. Everyone was asleep, lying on the ground, in blankets. There were no tents and only a single spot in which a fire had been made and put out. A little girl was sleeping in the centre.'

But before she could continue, Ballie gasped and her hand shot up to cover her mouth as if belatedly stifling the sound. Louise looked at her, surprised by her reaction.

'I know what you saw,' Ballie said in a shaky voice. Jamsen looked at Ballie, a mild look of surprise on his face.

'I told you before that we've been infiltrated by Brisheit's men on several occasions. It happened to us, right here—it was my camp you saw. We had found a young girl, alone in the woods. She was a ragged, miserable-looking thing who had seemingly suffered a horrific shock. She told us that her parents had been killed by soldiers and we knew straight away it would have been Brisheit's men. We took her in, intending to take her to one of the nearby towns where we knew a family that would be overjoyed to look after her.' Ballie stared off into the distance for a moment and then took a deep breath as if preparing herself for what she wanted to say next. 'That night, we were attacked. Brisheit's men took us completely by surprise as we slept, overpowering those on watch. They killed twenty-nine of us in total—I was one of only ten that escaped. We were lucky that the rest of our group had camped elsewhere, otherwise many more of us could have died.'

'How many did that little girl kill?' Louise quietly asked.

Jamsen looked at her in disbelief. Clearly shocked, he laughed, 'The little girl? She can't have killed, surely not?' He trailed off, losing confidence in his disbelief.

'Fifteen,' Ballie replied numbly. 'She killed fifteen men and women.'

Jamsen put his head in his hand and when he brought it back up, he couldn't make eye contact with either of them.

'Before I realised what had happened, before I knew what she had done,' Ballie continued, her eyes glistening, 'I saw the girl walking through the horrors, the bloodshed. All I could think about was saving her.' She paused, taking a deep breath before continuing. 'Before I could get to her, however, I saw my partner Petrie. He got to her before I could, also intent on getting her out of there. I watched as he knelt in front of her, checking her over to see if she was okay. All I remember was the girl laughing lightly as if he had told her a funny joke. Then she drew a bloody dagger and with one swift motion, she… she…' Ballie's words became interjected with sobs. She took a few moments to control herself before she continued. 'The little girl slit his throat. There was nothing I could do to save him.'

There was a long silence in which Jamsen stared at the ground. Louise continued to look at Ballie, a sympathetic look on her face, her mouth open as if to say something. She found however, that no words could express what she felt.

'By the time I reached him he was already dead, so then I did what was necessary.' Ballie looked at Louise with a look of forced confidence on her face. 'The little girl had already wandered off, so I grabbed Petrie's bow and arrow and I shot her. I killed her with two arrows.' Ballie's breaths became heavy and arduous and she looked away.

Louise felt utterly helpless; she felt desperately sorry for Ballie, knowing how difficult a position she'd been placed in that night. She hesitated for a few moments, unsure as to how she could comfort her. She then took hold of Ballie's hand and gave it a gentle squeeze. A few seconds later, Ballie squeezed back and looked up at Louise, seemingly regaining control of herself.

'I'm sorry,' she said with a slight hiccup. 'It was such an awful night, not only because I lost Petrie, but also because I had to kill a little girl. I've never had to do something so awful; I don't think I can ever forgive myself.'

'I saw the girl, I saw what she did. You couldn't have done anything differently,' Louise said soothingly, remembering how bloodthirsty the girl had been.

'I just can't stop wondering what we did to that little girl to have made her betray us in such a horrific way. I keep wondering whether Brisheit's men could have bewitched her somehow, maybe possessed her. In which case, instead of killing her, I should have tried to help her.'

'Ballie,' Louise interjected, knowing that she was becoming overwhelmed with guilt. 'I saw the girl, remember? She wasn't bewitched or possessed. I don't know why she did what she did, but it was her own choice, she enjoyed it, you could see it in her eyes. You did the right thing, otherwise, she would have carried on killing.'

There was a moment's silence, then Ballie looked up, gave her a brief smile and then looked off into the distance, not wanting to discuss the matter further.

'How is it you can see these visions of the past?' Jamsen asked.

Over the past few days, Louise had given this matter a lot of thought and she finally felt that she was ready to discuss it with him. 'To be totally honest, I don't know. I don't really understand anything that's happened over the last few weeks. I have no idea how I'm seeing visions of the past, or how I managed to throw Ballie and Rogers across the tent. I sometimes feel as if a strange power is welling up inside of me, which scares me as I don't know how or if I can control it. I know and understand that it's my heritage, my family's gift bestowed upon me. But it's so difficult to even begin to comprehend.'

She paused to collect her thoughts, feeling as if her mind was racing. Ballie and Jamsen watched her, not interrupting. 'Only a few weeks ago, I was in my little cottage, a writer living alone with my dog. Now, I've crossed over into an entirely new world where I seem to have magic and there is an entire army determined to spill my blood to unlock the greatest evil ever seen. It's all so much to take in. I wish I understood even just a small part of it.'

There was a long silence. Louise suddenly felt somewhat awkward at having finally revealed her own turmoil and confusion regarding the situation.

Eventually, Ballie began to speak in a quiet,

uncertain voice. 'I might be able to help you with a small portion of what you've been experiencing.' Louise looked up at her and she could tell that Ballie felt a little uncomfortable and unsure of herself. 'As I've told you before, I was good friends with Clarris and she often spoke about your family. I remember her telling me once that the Clarest family had a very strong bond with this world, this land. They respected it and always seemed to understand it. The legend is that when your great-great-great-grandmother began to change, the land reflected that; everything turned to darkness and died. It wasn't until she was usurped that it began to recover. Clarris told me that the kindness and love felt by whoever holds the Whisper will help the land to flourish, whilst cruelty and evilness destroy it.'

Louise watched her expectantly, 'I still don't understand what this has to do with me seeing visions of the past.'

'This is where my own theories come into play, so bear with me! I think the land is aware you've returned and that you've been united with the Whisper. I think that the earth, the air, the grass and the trees all recognise you.'

Louise couldn't stop a snort of disbelief escaping her. She looked at Jamsen, who looked back at her and grinned wildly at the absurdity of Ballie's statement. Ballie merely smiled at them, understanding their reaction and realising that it sounded ridiculous, if not a little bit crazy.

'I know, I know, but please just bear with me. You have seen visions in locations where acts of horrific brutality have occurred. Places wherein innocent blood has been spilt, absorbed by the land itself. I think it's telling you its story and in doing so, it's connecting and bonding with you, which I believe is helping it to heal. You are helping it to heal.'

Louise simply stared at her, speechless. Although Ballie's explanation felt farfetched, something about it seemed right and the more she thought about it, the more sense it seemed to make. She thought about how drained she'd felt on the two occasions it had happened. Her mouth fell open when she looked across to the spot in which the camp had been and slowly got to her feet. She wandered over and as she reached the point in which the little girl had slept, she knelt and looked at the ground.

Moving some of the debris that was lying on the forest floor, she was astonished to see that something remarkable. The decay was beginning to disappear, and in a few places, she could even see small green sprouts of grass poking through.

Having followed her, Jamsen looked over her shoulder and let out a small gasp of shock.

'That was all decayed before, wasn't it?' he asked in a quiet voice. Louise simply nodded in reply. She was beginning to feel overwhelmed and she was so exhausted, a headache was beginning to bother her.

'So, what do you think about what Ballie said, about you being connected to the land?'

'I don't know,' Louise replied, holding an exhausted hand up to her head as she tried to elevate some of the growing pain. 'It's been a long day though and I think I'm going to have to get some sleep.'

'Of course,' Ballie said approaching them. 'You must be exhausted.'

Louise nodded and without another word, she

turned around and made her way back to the camp. In the time they'd been away, the remainder of their team had put the fire out and gone to bed. Louise was relieved that the camp was empty as it meant she didn't have to talk to anyone and could go straight to bed. Inside the tent she was to share with Jamsen she found two bundles of bedding, one in each corner. Louise practically collapsed into the one on the right, pulling the blankets over herself and remaining completely motionless. She was instantly relieved as the pain in her head eased.

Chapter Twenty-eight

It wasn't long before she heard the sound of footsteps approaching the camp and she knew that Jamsen and Ballie had returned to camp. One pair of footsteps moved away from Louise's tent, whilst the other stopped just outside. Jamsen seemed to pause for a moment then entered, slumping down into his bed and letting out a tired sigh as he settled himself. Louise turned and looked at him. Feeling chilled to the bone, she kept the blankets wrapped closely around her. Jamsen noticed she was watching him and returned her gaze with a smile.

'You alright?' He asked, pulling off his boots and settling into his bed, still looking at her.

'I guess so. I'm just exhausted.'

Jamsen nodded, still smiling. 'I'm not surprised. When I first met you, I had no idea what you were going through. Now, after having heard your tale, I'm pretty impressed.'

Louise gave him an appreciative smile and pulled the blanket closer, she could feel sleep beginning to take over.

'Was it difficult? Learning who you really are? You've spent a large part of your life thinking you were one thing, only to discover that you were royalty – with magic, of all things!'

'I suppose so. But it was strange – as soon as Clarris gave me this,' she pulled out the Whisper and cradled it delicately in her hand, 'I've been having flashbacks of what I knew to be my real past. Memories that had been locked away in my mind. Since then, everything – from the magic to the land itself – has felt familiar. It's difficult and overwhelming but, weirdly, it's also quite comforting.' She lay back, feeling a little awkward revealing so her innermost thought to someone she had only known for a few days. 'Although I loved my life before all of this, I always felt as if something was missing. As if something wasn't quite right. Ever since I've been here, that feeling has completely vanished.'

A small, understanding smile spread across his face. 'Well, if it had been me, I don't think I could have coped as well as you have!'

There was a prolonged silence as the two of them looked at each other. It was at that moment Louise realised how much his presence had helped her to deal with her arrival in Calaresp.

'Thank you,' Louise said quietly.

'What for?'

'For sticking with me, even when you realised, I hadn't been honest with you.'

Jamsen shrugged and finally looked away from her. 'Well, I wasn't going to just abandon you. You're quite good company really!' He gave her a cheeky smile. He then pulled his bow beside him and began to adjust the string.

Louise laughed and felt a fraction of the tension that had built up within her ease considerably. She looked up at him again and smiled as he worked on his bow. He then looked up at her, catching Louise staring at him. She immediately blushed. Jamsen, however, merely returned her smile.

'We should get some sleep.' he said, watching as she yawned widely.

'That's probably the best idea I've heard all day.'

They each nestled into their separate beds and before she could stop herself, Louise placed a hand by her side to find and stroke Barney. She felt a wrenching in her stomach as she remembered he wasn't there.

'Don't worry,' Jamsen said. 'I'm sure Barney's fine and will work his way back to you.'

Louise sighed and gave a slight nod, then stretched her hand out and extinguished the lantern sitting between them. As she did, Jamsen stretched out his own hand and took hers.

'I'll do everything I can to get you home, and to keep you safe. I promise,' he said quietly.

Before Louise could reply, he had put out the lantern for her and settled back into his bed.

Chapter Twenty-nine

The next day, Louise woke up feeling more refreshed and optimistic than she had in days. With renewed enthusiasm, she helped Jamsen to dismantle their tent. It wasn't long before the camp was packed up and they were on their way, everyone chatting cheerfully with one another. Louise walked alongside Pascen and Trevel and they told her stories of their past, how they'd met and the difficulties their love had been forced to endure over the last few years.

The group spent the day trudging through the woods, only stopping to check they were still heading in the right direction or to take quick breaks. As they finally approached their destination, they could hear the distant sounds of people living their day-to-day lives. Then, before any of the group could react, they heard the metallic swipe of a sword being drawn. They stopped, only to discover that they were surrounded. Men and women appeared; their weapons pointed at the small group, each wearing a strange mix-match of armour.

A tall, broad man with a grey beard and neat hair

stepped forward. Unlike his companions, his armour matched perfectly, although it did show some tell-tale signs of age. Louise was even able to see several impact points, presumably from fierce weapons. His face was cold and hard as he surveyed them and raised his longsword. He used it to point at the intruders, taking in the different statures and weapons of the little group.

'Who are you and where, may I ask, are you going?' he said in a stern and distrusting voice.

Ballie stepped forward from the back of the group, weaponless hands raised in the air.

'Zalan!' she said in a friendly, welcoming tone. 'It's Ballie.'

As Zalan looked at the approaching woman, an instant flash of recognition passed across his face. A friendly smile transformed him almost immediately and he lowered his sword. He held a hand in the air and flicked it, signalling to his men to lower their weapons and back down.

'Ballie!' he said, his voice now deep, warm and welcoming. 'How wonderful to see you! What brings you all the way out here? Last we heard; you were based in the Flirest woods.'

He held out his arm and Ballie followed suit. They clasped each other's outstretched arms and beamed.

'Well,' Ballie said in a satisfied voice, 'I've brought you a visitor.'

She turned around and gestured to Louise. Louise hesitated for a moment, then stepped forward. She placed a reassuring hand on Jamsen's back as she passed, having noticed how he bristled in protest. The closer she got to Zalan, the more her initial fear and apprehension ebbed away and a strong sense of familiarity grew.

When he first laid eyes on Louise, his expression became one of absolute shock. Then a smile spread across the weathered soldier's face and much to Louise's surprise, he knelt to the ground in front of her, holding the hilt of his sword, the blade sinking slightly into the ground. Louise stopped in surprise and stared at him, unsure as to what to do next.

Zalan looked up at her, beaming, 'Your, your Majesty!' He stuttered slightly, as if he were battling to get the words out. 'I cannot tell you what an honour it is, how long I have waited and hoped for this day.'

Louise looked around, feeling awkward, 'Please get up, you really don't have to.'

He smiled and got back to his feet.

Louise found herself simply staring at him. 'Do I know you, you seem familiar.'

Zalan placed his large, gloved hands on either side of her shoulders and Louise could see Jamsen out of the corner of her eye, stepping forward protectively.

'My name is Zalan, I was once a captain in your father's army. I was a member of his personal guard, and I often escorted him and your mother around the kingdom. I was on duty the night you were born. I was always by your side, as well as your mother's. I doubt you'd remember but I was teaching you to fight with a sword, you were very good!' He smiled, obviously caught in a fond memory.

'It was a small wooden sword,' Louise said quietly as once again, long-forgotten memories of her childhood flashed through her mind. 'It had a small L carved at the hilt and a symbol just like this one.' She lifted her hand and looked at the mark carved deeply into her skin.

Zalan nodded eagerly as he too looked in amazement at the mark on her hand. He gestured towards it, 'I remember how surprised everyone was when you were born with that mark on your hand — the mark of your family's magic. Your parents knew the prophecies and were so immensely proud.'

Louise smiled at him, 'I don't remember an awful lot, but the memories are slowly coming back. I do know I liked you very much, you were always very kind to me.'

Beaming back at her, Zalan finally took in the rest of the group. 'Come,' he said in a welcoming voice. 'Let's get you and your friends back to our village, then we can get you all settled in and we can talk properly.' He gestured to them and they followed him.

Louise and Zalan were walking side by side with a watchful Jamsen closely behind. Louise noticed Zalan watching her with a small smile on his face. She looked back at him curiously.

'Sorry, Your Majesty. I didn't mean to stare.'

'Please, don't call me that. Louise will be fine!'

Zalan nodded and then continued to talk, 'I was just noting how much you look like your parents,' he paused as he took in her features. 'You have your mother's hair and much of her face, but your smile and your expressions are exactly the same as your father's. He often showed much of what he was thinking without realising.'

Louise smiled in return, then looked away. 'I have so few memories of my childhood but more are coming back to me as time goes by.'

'I'm sure getting closer to your home will help!'

Zalan said, smiling as he placed an encouraging hand on her back.

Louise was soon distracted by a man perched on a branch halfway up a tree. He watched them approaching, a bow and arrow raised and ready to fire. As they got closer, Zalan gestured to the man, who nodded, lowered his weapon, and went back to surveying his surroundings.

Moments later, Louise saw a small collection of stone and wooden houses set right in the middle of a circle of trees. People bustled around, going about their day-to-day business. As the group approached, all eyes fell on Louise and it wasn't long before they had come to a complete standstill. Zalan ushered them towards a small stone building on the far side of the village and without hesitation, they entered.

A woman sat at the far end of a large table situated in the very centre of the room. There was only one room in this building and every wall was filled with boxes and bags; some had weapons sticking out, others had clothing and material. The woman stood up, surprised by their entrance, then a look of shock spread across her face as she stared at Louise. An expression that must have been mirrored by Louise, as the woman in front of her was the spitting image of Clarris and for a moment, Louise considered the possibility she was in fact alive. As she looked closer, however, she was able to notice certain small differences that made her realise she was not the dead woman. She was clearly a good few years older than Clarris, her nose was narrower, and her hair was darker and shorter.

The woman approached; her arms outstretched. She clasped Louise's hand and smiled.

'Louise, it's so wonderful to finally meet you.'

From behind her, a dog suddenly came running forward. Louise's heart was instantly filled with such overwhelming joy that a breathless gasp escaped her.

'Barney!' she yelled, and as she knelt down, her old companion jumped around her, sniffing and licking her face.

'He arrived a few days ago,' the woman explained. 'We had heard that a young woman was being tracked by Brisheit and his men, that travelled with a dog, we weren't sure if it was you though. But Barney here found us and since then we've been waiting for you to arrive.'

Louise spent some much needed time making a great deal of fuss over Barney, before eventually getting back to her feet, smiling uncertainly at the woman. Before she could stop herself, she asked, 'Are you related to Clarris?'

The woman smiled and nodded, 'She was my sister. My name is Darty.'

Louise looked at her in surprise. '*Was!*' she said, louder than she had meant to. 'So, you know? But how?'

Darty lowered her head. 'Well, I had heard reports that she'd been injured by Brisheit himself. It's known by all that he poisons his daggers. When she didn't appear at our arranged rendezvous point, I knew she hadn't made it. We weren't even sure if she'd made it to you. That was until Brisheit's men began to search and scour the countryside. Then we knew she had succeeded.'

'I'm sorry I couldn't help her, save her.' Louise said, full of guilt.

'It's fine.' Darty retorted with such a blasé attitude Louise felt a flash of anger ripple through her. 'We knew the dangers involved,'

Darty sat back down in the chair. Louise, Jamsen, and Ballie followed suit. Barney ensured he was as close to Louise as possible. The rest of their group had remained outside or dispersed into the camp, welcomed by old friends. Louise was full of questions and the second she sat down, she spun towards Darty. 'Clarris told me to find you, but she said you'd be in Pologor. How come you're here instead?' This woman may have looked a lot like Clarris, but there was something about her Louise didn't like and she could feel a wave of anger and frustration towards her steadily intensifying.

'We had to leave Pologor about a week ago. Brisheit's men were getting closer to finding us. We had no choice but to leave, so we've scattered throughout the local countryside.'

'Well, I guess it's a good thing we ran into Ballie,' Louise said, aware they could have aimlessly walked into Pologor, and headed straight into Brisheit's hands.

'We had spies instructed to watch out for you. Had they found you, they would have brought you straight to me.' Darty replied, as if this should have been obvious.

'So, what's the plan now?' Louise asked. Ever since she'd met Clarris and decided to return to Calaresp, she had been so intent on finding the rebels that she had given very little thought to what they would do afterwards. How they would deal with Brisheit.

'Well, his army may be large, but only the elite soldiers who are always with him and the wreag handlers are loyal. Only they kill and carry out Brisheit's orders willingly. The remainder are forced to, either because of threats to their families and loved ones or because they are poor and alone. They would fight for you and your heritage if they thought you were alive. But as so many have lost hope, they don't think there is an alternative. We need to take you through our underground network, let people see you alive, and rally them to the cause. They won't believe it through word of mouth, they'll need to see you for themselves. When we have the right numbers, we'll launch our attack against the unlawful usurper.'

Louise contemplated this for a second. Although she didn't want to delay the suffering the people of Calaresp were already experiencing, it made sense for them to take their time and do it properly.

'We'll also have a huge advantage with your magic!' Darty continued with a satisfied look. 'Brisheit has few that have mastered magic and even then, they don't compare to you.

'My magic?' Louise replied, confused. She had only just begun learning about it herself, she wasn't sure how long it would take her to fully understand it.

'Well of course!' Darty replied with an incredulous look. 'You do have magic, don't you?'

'Well, yes,' Louise said, feeling awkward.

'There we go then!'

Louise looked at Darty and felt a pang of annoyance at her frustratingly confident smile.

'Well, I'm not sure how much help my magic will be just yet.'

'It was predicted you would have magic unlike any seen in Calaresp before. Even by now, you should be more powerful than your ancestors ever were.' Darty replied, a smile still spread across her face. still had a smile on her face.

'Well, I'm sure that would have been the case if Brisheit hadn't killed my parents and I hadn't been sent to an alternative world.' Louise could feel her temper rising as she looked at the woman in front of her. Darty seemed so confident that Louise already had full control of her magic, and she was being frustratingly dismissive of Louise's honesty, presuming she was simply being modest. 'As it stands, I only found out that I had magic a few weeks ago, and I've only started using it in the last few days. Even then, it's not been intentional!'

Darty looked at her in surprise, an incredulous expression on her face, suggesting she thought Louise was winding her up. 'What do you mean, you haven't done it intentionally yet?'

'Well, I've only been aware of myself doing magic twice, and on both occasions, it was when I felt personally threatened.'

There was a moment's silence and Darty looked over at Ballie with a confused expression.

'We just presumed you would have control of it by now?' she said quietly, clearly disappointed.

As Louise stared at her, she felt herself finally boiling over. 'Oh, well, I'm sorry to be such a disappointment to you! Look, you have no idea what I've gone through over the past few weeks. You have no clue how it feels to have learned your entire life was a pretence, to have memories of your childhood locked away from you. To have those same memories slowly unlock themselves years later, one-by-one! To find out the man that killed your entire family is still trying to hunt and kill you. To find out that you have magic, let alone comprehend how to use it or the fact you're destined to be more powerful than anyone in history.' Louise was now standing, a furious expression on her face. As she finished her sentence, she slammed her fist down on the table. As it impacted on the hard surface, several golden lightening-like shapes spread down the table, causing cracks as they went. Louise stared at it for a moment and then, expression still furious, she looked back at Darty with a sarcastic smile on her face. 'Well, there you go, there's a little bit of magic for you!'

Darty stared back at her in surprise, 'I'm sorry, I didn't mean to.'

Before she could finish, Louise had walked away from the table and out of the stone building, Barney following close behind.

As soon as she was outside, Louise slammed the door shut and leant against the cool stones of the building. She could hear the faint voice of Zalan and Jamsen speaking in curt voices to Darty, their tones implying that Darty's expectations of Louise had been unfair and unrealistic. Louise forced herself to take deep, calming breaths, her fists still clenched. She could still feel the strange sensation of power buzzing within her. She was becoming increasingly powerful and she knew it, but she was equally aware that she hadn't learnt how to control it yet.

The door beside her opened and she looked over, her temper prickling as she anticipated Darty. As Jamsen stepped outside she felt herself relax.

'You alright?' he asked in a quiet, gentle voice.

Louise gave him a quick smile, then turned away

and nodded.

'Don't pay any attention to that Darty woman,' he reassured. 'She doesn't know what she's talking about. She realises now that she's expecting a little bit too much, too soon. I don't like her, but I do think she regrets how naïve she's been.'

Louise didn't answer. Instead, she allowed her gaze to drift off into the distance, watching the bustling village in front of her.

Chapter Thirty

A man suddenly came running through the small makeshift village. Louise watched as he headed straight for them. He was wrapped tightly in a dark cloak with only his eyes and nose visible. Louise and Jamsen watched him curiously, Jamsen's hand resting at the hilt of his dagger. The closer he came, the more Louise realised something was desperately wrong. He passed them without even a glance, intent on his destination as he flung himself into the building.

Jamsen and Louise hurried in after him. Even though they were only a few seconds behind, they found that he had already collapsed into one of the chairs at the table. His heavy breathes were interrupted by sobs as he carefully removed his cloak, revealing a truly horrific sight. His top had seemingly once been long-sleeved, but the sleeves of his shirt had been carelessly ripped off. Where his skin should have been, all Louise could see was a mass of blood and exposed muscle. It was obvious he had been flayed. The sight was so revolting that Louise had to stop herself from turning away. Instead, she looked up at his face but was equally shocked by what she saw; one of his eyes was bloodied and swollen and as she looked closer, she wasn't even sure if it was still there. His other eye didn't seem that damaged but the white of it was a dark red colour. His nose was bloodied and snapped to the side, clearly broken. There were deep bleeding gashes on either side of his cheek running down to his throat.

Louise and Jamsen stared at him and then at one another in amazement. Darty and Zalan, meanwhile, had rushed to the man's side and both were looking for ways to deal with his wounds. The stranger simply brushed them aside.

'Stop it,' he said weakly.

'Get help,' Darty said, looking up at Zalan.

But before Zalan could leave, the man let out a wail of protest. 'No, we don't have time. Stay!'

Zalan hesitated, and then both he and Darty sat down in the seats on either side of him.

'What happened?' Darty asked in a quiet, concerned voice.

'I'm so, so sorry,' he said, beginning to weep.

'Tell me,' Darty asked patiently. As Louise watched, she could feel a lot of her frustration and dislike towards the woman ebb away.

'I'm so sorry,' he gasped through sobs. 'They tortured me. They peeled off the skin on my arms and fed it to wreags. I've never experienced pain like it before. They kicked me and punched me.' He raised a reluctant, shaking hand to his head. 'They... They even set my hair on fire.' And sure enough, instead of hair, the man had a black charred mess on the top of his head, through which a few bloodied blisters were visible.

The injured man broke down into tormented sobs and the entire group waited patiently for him to compose himself. 'I'm so sorry,' he whimpered again and Louise felt a lump forming in the back of her throat, dreading what he was going to say next.

'I told them,' he said quietly, looking away from Darty and Zalan.

'You told them what?' Zalan asked, clearly keen to learn how much the man had revealed.

'I told them where you're hiding. I told them that we were the ones who sent Clarris and I told them that this would be where the princess would be brought as soon as she was found. I told them about our spies. They've captured and killed all of them already.' As he continued the sobs intensified, 'Now they're on their way here. They let me go just a few hours ago, I don't think they thought I'd make it here alive. Or perhaps they don't think my warning will help you at all! I don't know, but they intend to kill everyone.'

The man began to weep so intensely that it caused his entire body to convulse. Darty gently rubbed his back, being careful not to hurt him. 'It's not your fault,' she said with a sympathetic smile. 'You were tortured, nobody blames you.'

It was obvious that she was trying to sound calm, but Louise could see the fear and panic in her eyes. Darty gave the man one final reassuring pat and then stood up and turned away. She walked over to Zalan and spoke quietly to him. Zalan then left the tent quickly, without even a backward glance.

As soon as he was gone, Darty returned to the sobbing man and as she reached him, two old men entered the building.

'Come on,' Darty said quietly to him. 'You need to go with these two, they're going to help you and tend to your wounds. Then they'll get you out of here before the soldiers arrive.'

The sobbing man barely seemed to be listening, it was as if all energy had left him since he had passed on his message. The men helped him to his feet and practically had to drag him out of the room.

As soon as they had left, Darty stalked over to Louise. 'We need to get you out of here as quickly as possible,' she said, looking at her intensely.

Louise nodded, understanding that they needed to leave, appreciating the urgency. Nevertheless, a thought at the back of her mind was holding her back and stopping her from moving. 'I can't leave just yet. I want to help the rest of the camp get out of here first. I can't just run away when I know Brisheit is coming here, looking for me. I've seen what he does to people!'

Darty smiled sympathetically, 'Everyone in the camp is being dealt with. They're being evacuated as we speak. They'll be split up into small groups and sent off into different directions — as they know these woods, I'm confident everyone will get away. At the moment, my priority is you. If we don't get you out of here safely, everything we've been fighting for over the past twelve years will have been pointless.' She turned away from her and headed towards the door. 'Zalan has put a team together, they should be ready and waiting for us to leave.'

Louise was still reluctant to leave without helping, but was also aware that Darty's words were reasonable. Eventually, she nodded and the three of them sprang into action.

Just as they were about to leave, Ballie gently touched Louise's arm, 'This is where I'm going to have to leave you.'

'Oh Ballie, aren't you coming with us!' she asked, surprised at how hard this news hit her. She had become surprisingly close to Ballie.

'I can't,' she replied, giving Louise a sad smile. 'I have to get back to my group, make sure they're alright. I've been away from them too long as it is. I'm sorry.'

Louise nodded in understanding and gave Ballie a quick hug 'Thank you, for everything you've done.'

Ballie squeezed her tightly and smiled. 'Stay safe, I know a lot is expected of you, but I want you to make sure you look after yourself. You know where we are if you ever need us.'

Then she shook hands with Jamsen and made her way out. Louise stared at the closed door for a few seconds before they continued getting ready. Louise grabbed Darty's arm and pulled her to the side.

'I'm sorry for my reaction back there.' she said sincerely. 'It's just been an exhausting few days.'

Darty smiled. 'I understand. I'm sorry too, I was foolish and inconsiderate.'

'Can I ask a favour?' Louise asked gingerly.

'Of course!'

'I want my dog, Barney as far away from trouble as possible. Which currently means as far from me as possible. I don't want him to get hurt.' Louise's hand absentmindedly found Barney's ear and stroked it. 'But once this is over, he must be returned to me straight away.'

Darty gave a knowing smile, 'I was hoping to tell you this under better circumstances.' She paused as she looked down at Barney. 'Have you never wondered how your dog was able to guide you so reliably? How he knew how to find us?'

'I, well, I haven't had much time to dwell on it. I suppose it is a little strange, but he's such a clever dog, it's not that big a surprise.' Louise replied, eying Darty suspiciously.

'It's very simple, he too comes from Calaresp.'

Louis stared at her in disbelief. She opened her mouth to reply, but nothing came out.

'It's true.' Darty said with a smile. 'We sent him to look after you and when the time was right, to guide you home.'

Staring down at him, Louise considered everything that had happened, everything Barney had done. It gradually began to make sense.

Darty called a woman over from a nearby house. 'This is Kari, she is the one who bred him and trained him. She's been looking after him these past few days. You can trust him with her, and she'll return him as soon as it is safe to do so.'

The woman beamed at Louise as Barney's tail wagged at Kari. Louise smiled back in astonishment.

'Don't worry, I'll take good care of him, and I'll return him as soon as it's safe.' Kari said, patting Barney gently.

Louise knelt and gave her old companion a long hug. 'So, this has been a homecoming for both of us! You clever old boy!' She kissed the top of his head. 'I'm sorry I have to send you away now. It's the safest option, but I promise I'll get you back. It's the best thing for you right now my old boy.' She felt tears filling her eyes. Barney licked her as if to tell her he understood and with a reluctant look back, he followed Kari as she and her family disappeared into the woods.

Forcing herself to look away, Louise followed as they made their way to the far end of the village. She noticed a small group of people, patiently waiting. As they approached, Louise recognised Zalan grinning at her from the centre of the group. The remainder turned to look at her and she felt an immense amount of pressure as they watched her expectantly. Louise felt a wave of relief as she recognised Trevel and Pascen, and they both gave her reassuring smiles. Stood next to them was a young man with shoulder-length light blonde hair, who strode forward confidently with his hand outstretched. He gave her a charming smile and as she gave him her hand, he kissed it with dramatic flair.

'Delighted to meet you,' he said in a smooth voice.

'This is Enik,' Zalan said, stepping forward and rolling his eyes. 'Despite the fact he comes across as a bit of a fool he is one of our very best archers.'

At these words, Enik bowed with obvious exaggeration and stepped back, grinning. Beside her, Louise could feel Jamsen bristling and when she looked over at him, she saw him giving Enik a distrusting look. Louise subconsciously smiled to herself.

'This is Toln,' Zalan continued, indicating to an older man with a long white beard that reached a good way down his chest. His small beady eyes gave him a stern look which initially intimidated Louise a little, but when he flashed her a smile, his expression completely changed and his face lit up. He gave Louise a curt nod and a brief handshake.

'This is Shelt. She's Enik's older sister.' Zalan indicated to a very tall woman with incredibly short, light blonde hair. She stepped forward and looked Louise up and down, then turned away as if disgusted by what she saw. Louise gave Zalan a surprised look. He merely shook his head at her as if telling her it was of no concern.

'Finally, this is Matok.' A muscular man with short black messy hair and startling green eyes gave her a smile and a nod.

'This is the team who will escort us to our next safe house and from there, we will start making everyone aware that the princess is back,' Darty said, stepping out in front of Jamsen and Louise so that she stood in front of the team. She had a proud expression on her face. 'Right, let's head off.'

'Do you not think there should be more of us?' Jamsen asked, observing the relatively small group. 'You know, safety in numbers.'

'Technically, yes, but we'll be far less conspicuous if we travel in a small group. If there were a lot of us, Brisheit and his men would know it was us and they'd be on us in a heartbeat,' Zalan said in a solemn voice.

Jamsen seemed reluctant to agree as he considered the people in front of him for a moment. When he looked at Louise, she gave him a nod, letting him know that she thought Zalan was right. Jamsen nodded back in agreement and with that, they set off.

Chapter Thirty-one

They walked at a steady pace, and before long, they had left behind the sounds of the busy, panic-stricken village. Enik scouted at the front of the group, his silent footsteps made him the perfect candidate. The team had been made aware that the wreags had previously picked up on Louise's scent and had tracked her on more than one occasion. Because of this, Matok stayed at the back of the group, ensuring that they weren't followed.

When they were certain that there were far enough from the village, they stopped to rest and eat, intending to then walk through the night, using the darkness to remain as hidden as possible. Louise and Jamsen sat down, whilst Darty and Zalan sat opposite them, staring intensely at Jamsen. He looked back at them expectantly, his eyebrows raised as he waited for one of them to speak.

'We need to know who you are and why you've been travelling with Louise,' Darty said in a cold voice.

'He saved me!' Louise replied, amazed at the tone in which they were addressing him. 'When I first arrived in Calaresp, I was alone and I had no idea where to go. He saved me from a patrol of Brisheit's men.'

'Well, that's very convenient isn't it?' Darty retorted without averting her gaze from Jamsen.

'What are you implying?' Jamsen replied, his voice indignant.

'That you are using her position. No doubt when she is returned to her rightful place as ruler of Calaresp, you will use your forced friendship with her for your own gain.'

'Now come on Darty,' Zalan interrupted. 'We don't know that. I thought we were just supposed to be asking him a few questions not making unsubstantiated accusations.'

Louise turned to Darty, a furious expression on her face. 'How dare you, Darty. You have no idea what he's gone through in trying to help me. He didn't even know who I was for the first few days.'

'So how did he work out the truth?' Darty asked, her expression hadn't changed.

'He saw this,' Louise retorted, raising her hand to show the small scar on it. 'I can assure you he was more than surprised when he saw it, yet he continued to help me. If that's not the sign of a loyal friend, I don't know what is.'

Darty finally looked away from Jamsen and looked at Louise. 'You have that much trust in him?' she asked.

Louise nodded and a wide smile spread across Zalan's face.

'Well, thank goodness for that! You must understand we had to check. So many people these days have an ulterior motive and so many others would readily give information away to Brisheit's men. I had a good feeling about you though, young man, and I'm glad to see I'm right.'

'We simply can't be too careful,' Darty interjected, giving Jamsen an apologetic smile.

Jamsen studied the two of them for a few seconds, then his contagious smile spread across his face and he gave Zalan a friendly pat on the arm.

'Of course, I understand,' he replied with a light-hearted laugh. 'I'm glad Louise has found people who care for her so deeply.'

The mood between the four of them instantly relaxed, although Louise still felt a little bit of animosity towards Darty. There was something about her attitude and her distinct lack of respect for others that frustrated her.

'So, where have you come from Jamsen? What took you to the Whalsp Woods?' Zalan asked. His tone no longer that of an interrogator; instead, one of sheer curiosity.

Jamsen seemed to have noticed the difference in tone and he replied in a friendly voice. 'I spend my time travelling across Calaresp. I have friends all over that I often stay with and when that's not possible, I get money from hunting. That's why I was in the Whalsp Woods—I'd heard a rumour that a Gnok had been spotted there and I went in search of it, as they sell for quite a considerable amount.'

'Where in Calaresp were you born?' Darty asked, tucking into a biscuit.

'Balniso,' Jamsen replied.

'Oh, so not far from Fortor!' Zalan replied, a broad smile of recognition on his face. 'Are your family still there?'

Jamsen shook his head, his gaze now staring fixedly at the ground. 'No,' he replied. 'They were killed in an accident when I was a child, I grew up in an orphanage.'

'Oh, well, I'm sorry to hear that,' Zalan replied awkwardly.

Jamsen merely shrugged and looked away. Louise was filled with sympathy for Jamsen. Whenever she had asked about his family, he had always abruptly changed the subject. Now she understood why. There was a prolonged silence, eventually broken by Darty, announcing they should keep moving. Without another word, they all stood up and went on their way.

'I'm sorry about your family,' Louise said as she walked alongside Jamsen.

'Thanks,' he replied.

'Was it hard growing up in an orphanage?' she asked, watching his face, looking for the slightest hint he didn't want to discuss his childhood. Instead, he simply smiled grimly.

'Before Brisheit, the orphanage was actually a pretty great place. It didn't compare to having a home of your own, but the kids were nevertheless happy there. When Brisheit took over, everything changed. The couple who ran it mysteriously disappeared. Many believed they were killed because they spoke out frequently against Brisheit's regime. An old man took over, he was cruel and treated us more like soldiers than children.'

'That must have been awful,' Louise replied. 'How did you manage to get away?'

Jamsen looked off into the distance for a moment, and Louise thought a darkness had spread across his face. However, it quickly vanished and Jamsen looked at her, his usual smile across his face. 'I ran away,' he said with a laugh. 'It was difficult at first, but I got by.'

Louise smiled back at him with admiration and the subject soon changed to their surroundings as Jamsen began to tell her what type of land they would be walking across.

Chapter Thirty-one

They travelled for a few days through woods and farmlands, across small hills, and through small, picturesque valleys. Louise became very fond of her small group, including the over-confident Enik. The only person she was unsure of was Shelt—the woman barely spoke to her and when she did, it was normally in a brash, disdainful tone. She couldn't work out what the woman had against her but after a few attempts at conversation, she decided she was better off staying away from her. Jamsen remained aloof with the majority of the group, although he seemed to have a natural connection with Matok. The two of them had numerous discussions regarding hunting and their preferred techniques.

For the last few days, rain had fallen on them fairly consistently and it had severely dampened their spirits. As they trudged through a thick wood, Louise came to an abrupt stop. All her senses on alert, as she tried to work out whether she'd heard something. She heard the sound again and this time she distinctly saw the features of a face looking out from behind the leaves of

The Whisper of Calaresp

a tree. Alerted by her tense stature, Jamsen was soon by her side followed by the rest of the group.

'What's wrong?' he asked in a low voice, concern ebbing through with every word. Louise, merely pointed to the branch as she took an involuntary step back. Matok, who was now standing the closest to the branch, gave it an apprehensive look and cautiously approached it, his sword raised before him. Something suddenly leapt out, jumping carelessly past him, landing on the ground just before Louise. Matok almost fell to the ground in alarm. As he turned around, he cursed quietly to himself.

Before Louise stood a small figure who barely reached her knees. It wore an outfit made entirely of green leaves, seemingly the same kind as the tree in which it had been taking refuge. It had a pointed and unforgiving little face as it stared around at the group, its fiery red hair covering the entirety of its body as well as its forearms and knees. There was something vaguely recognisable about the little figure and Louise found herself wanting to laugh with relief, all fear quickly leaving her.

'Great,' Shelt said, 'that's exactly what we need. A heril.'

'A heril!' Louise exclaimed. 'Well, it doesn't look especially threatening!' She looked around at the group, a wide smile on her face as she tried to share the hilarity of the creature standing in front of them. She was surprised to see how serious everyone else looked and that they still held their weapons in their hands.

'This is serious, they might not look threatening, but they are notoriously difficult to catch and with their speed, they can cause a considerable amount of damage. I would also be careful that it doesn't touch you on the top of your forehead,' Jamsen said, only sparing Louise a very quick glance. 'Also if there's one, there's inevitably more lurking somewhere in this area. They like to stay in groups.'

Louise looked back at him with surprise and incredulity. She couldn't decide whether or not he was winding her up. Then with alarming speed, the heril moved, leaving behind a blur of green and red.

'Stand together!' Zalan said in a deep, commanding voice.

They promptly did as he said and Louise found herself automatically conforming, still finding it difficult to believe that such a small creature could cause such panic.

The blurred form of the heril seemed to be running circles around them, screaming a strange incomprehensible cackle of words.

'It's calling to the rest of its pack,' Darty said, her eyes flickering through the branches of the trees around them.

'Why do I need to watch out for them touching my forehead?' Louise asked Jamsen, still thoroughly confused.

'By touching your forehead and saying the right words they turn you into a golden statue, then if they touch you for a second time, you break into tiny little pieces. They then collect those pieces, put it into a cauldron, and eat it,' Jamsen replied as he tried to manoeuvre himself just in front of Louise. 'Myth has it that even though you've been turned into gold, you can feel everything right up until they cook you. They're quite rare, so many don't believe they actually exist.'

The Whisper of Calaresp

The creature finally came to a stop just in front of them, looking at them with a wide grin across its face. With remarkable speed, Enik raised his bow and arrow and took a shot at it. Despite his speed, the heril moved just in time.

'Damn it!' Enik said, getting another arrow ready, clearly waiting for another opportunity.

Subtly, Jamsen raised his own bow, and with the arrow, he followed the heril's path as it continued to run circles around them. He suddenly took a shot. Louise was almost certain that he had missed, however, it promptly stopped running and collapsed to the ground.

Enik looked over at Jamsen with surprise and admiration. He let out a short whistle. 'That was some shot!' he said, smiling at him.

Most of the group then relaxed, except for Zalan, who remained as he was. 'Keep formation,' he hissed. 'Don't forget, others are coming.'

Just after he had spoken, the sound of rustling came from a tree just beside Trevel and another near Shelt. Everyone sprang back into action, weapons at the ready. Before anyone else had the chance to do anything, Jamsen had released another arrow and another red-haired heril fell to the ground, motionless. Jamsen twisted around to take another shot but this time, Enik released his arrow first. Another, smaller heril fell to the ground.

'I had to get at least one of them,' Enik said with an apologetic shrug to Jamsen. 'You've been showing me up here!' The two men grinned at one another.

'That seems to be all of them,' Zalan said, sighing in relief. 'Let's get moving.'

The group took one last look around and then started making their way back through the woods. Louise lingered for a few minutes, looking over the first dead heril which was now lying at her feet. Jamsen came over, placing a hand on her shoulder.

'You alright?' He glanced to his side as Darty joined them.

'Clarris told me that when the windows appear between Calaresp and Earth, sometimes some of the creatures and beasts from this world get seen in mine. Because they aren't native to Earth, they've been the source of a number of myths and folktales'.

'That's right,' Darty said, looking down at the heril. 'For hundreds of years, we've tried to keep the windows a secret from the people of Earth. When the windows were first discovered, our ancestors sent spies through to Earth, not only to learn more about the people there but to see whether there would be any opportunity for a partnership. Our spies reported back that the people of Earth were power-driven and ruthless. We heard accounts of how they treated each other and realised that if they knew about our world, they would probably deem us a threat and wage war on us. So, we've been keeping Calaresp a secret, at least to the best of our abilities. Restrictions were created in terms of who could create the windows, and if any opened for a particularly long time, we would set guards around them. Obviously, there have been occasions in which people from Earth have glimpsed a window into Calaresp. Luckily, they seem to be quite a cynical race, and rather than believe what they've seen with their own eyes, the subject becomes some sort of fairy tale they tell to their children.'

Realisation and recognition spread through Louise as she stared down at the heril. Suddenly, before she could stop herself, a laugh burst out of her. Both Darty and Jamsen stared at her in surprise. Louise covered her hand over her mouth and looked at them sheepishly.

'I'm sorry,' she said. 'But I've just realised why this heril is so familiar!'

Jamsen raised his eyebrows questioningly and Louise couldn't stop another laugh leaking out from her.

'Leprechauns!' she cried.

'What?' Jamsen asked, thoroughly confused.

'On Earth, there is a myth about little men with red hair who wear green suits. They're supposed to live in Ireland.' The others stared at her in amusement. 'I think they're based on these guys! Although on Earth, they're considered to be lucky. Legend says that if you find the end of a rainbow, you'll find a pot of gold with one sitting on it!'

'That's crazy!' Jamsen said, in a disbelieving voice. 'They think these murderous, carnivorous little monsters are a sign of good luck?'

Darty seemed to be in deep thought. When she finally looked up, she had an expression of comprehension on her face. 'I would imagine that one of the herils crossed over to Earth, got stuck there, turned someone into gold, broke them down into pieces, and then something happened to it before it had the opportunity to eat its prey. Someone probably caught a glimpse of it and found the gold. Quite a few of Earth's myths have been founded on those types of situations.'

'That's bizarre,' Louise murmured.

'Come on, we need to catch up with the others,' Darty said and without another word, the three of them turned around and walked away from the lifeless bodies of the herils.

Chapter Thirty-two

A few hours later, much to their relief, the rain finally came to a stop. Despite this, the atmosphere in the woods remained dark and dreary. They soon approached a line of trees that looked like they had been severely burnt and as Matok prodded one with his sword, charred fragments fell to the ground.

Jamsen let out a small gasp and as Louise turned to look at him, she was surprised to find that all the colour had drained from his face as he stared up at the trees ahead of him. His grip on his sword was so tight that his knuckles had turned bone white.

'Jamsen, what's the matter?' she asked.

He didn't seem to hear her at first and it wasn't until Louise repeated herself three times that he drew his eyes away from the trees. At this point, the rest of the group were also watching, confused as to why the eerie trees had managed to have such a distinct impact on him.

He looked intently at Louise for a few moments and then, as if only just remembering they were there, he looked over at the rest of the group. His expression was riddled with concern. Jamsen awkwardly raised his hand to his head and brushed it through his unkempt hair. 'Sorry, I just...' He stopped and turned away from the group, looking back at the trees. 'I've heard rumours that Brisheit has used his magicians to create a creature, a horrifying thing that he uses to hunt down his prey.'

'A wreag,' Trevel said in the sort of tone you'd use with a small child.

'No,' Jamsen snapped back. 'This is a creature unlike anything he's ever made before. It's far worse.'

'What do you mean?' Darty asked, clearly getting a little frustrated by the delay.

'I don't know, I've never seen it. His magicians are said to have only recently created it. He's not put it to use yet. I just heard that he had created a gigantic monster that he uses to trap, corner and destroy. It's said to cause death and destruction to anything that it touches.'

At these words, the rest of the group looked over at the blackened trees.

Darty moved directly in front of Jamsen. 'And if he hasn't actually used it yet, if it hasn't actually been seen, how do you know about it?' Her voice was riddled with suspicion and her gaze even made Louise feel uncomfortable.

'A friend of mine knows a soldier in Brisheit's army,' Jamsen replied instantly, staring indignantly back at Darty as if challenging her. 'He said that they had been testing it on Brisheit's men and that his friend had seen it with his own eyes. Apparently, it was one of the most horrific sights he'd ever had to witness. And that's coming from someone who works for

Brisheit.'

The two continued to stare at one another for a while, neither of them wanting to back down. Darty eventually gave him a slight nod, clearly willing to accept his source.

'Well, regardless, I know these woods like the back of my hand and this is the fastest way to our destination. These trees aren't dead — I imagine they've been damaged by a fire of some sort. Whether or not Brisheit has created some new monster is irrelevant, none of us has spotted it yet and we cannot avoid the quickest route merely because of a wild rumour. We need to keep moving. At this point, Brisheit's men are more likely to be behind us than in front of us.'

The rest of the group looked at each other dubiously, their gazes flickering between the blackened trees and the confident Darty in front of them.

'Come on, let's get going,' Matok said, giving Jamsen an apologetic look. A smile spread across Darty's face as he followed her between the trees. The others, satisfied that there was no immediate threat, followed suit. Louise was the only one to hesitate. She trusted Jamsen and his instincts and he seemed genuinely frightened to cross into this section of the woods. She looked at Zalan with a pleading expression, as she struggled to find a way to word her dilemma. Seemingly picking up on this, Zalan walked over to Louise, looking at her intently.

'Come on,' he said calmly, 'we need to keep moving. I know you trust Jamsen, so do I. But Darty knows this wood very well and her people are constantly patrolling it. If such a creature were here, we would have had reports by now.'

He looked at Jamsen, 'I believe you—I believe that the creature you speak of exists—but is it not feasible that these trees have been damaged by something else, like fire? Is a hunch worth a two-day delay?'

Jamsen, his face riddled in concern, pondered for a few minutes before answering. 'I suppose not.'

'Right then,' Zalan said, flashing them both a smile. 'Let's get going. We all need to remain extra vigilant. Any sign of the creature Jamsen has spoken of and we get away from this stretch of wood as quickly as possible.'

Everyone seemed satisfied, except for Jamsen and Louise, who shared a concerned look before following the rest of the group. Eventually, the trees went back to normal in terms of both colour and formation, and as they did so, Darty gave Jamsen a triumphant look. He merely nodded in reply, clearly accepting that she may have been right all along. Regardless, Jamsen remained close by Louise's side. She occasionally tried to make conversation with him, but his replies were fairly monosyllabic, his mind seemingly on something else.

They continued walking until nightfall, then they found a spot in which to set up camp. The group was exhausted, and there was something rather contagious about Jamsen's sombre mood. As a result, there was very little conversation and it wasn't long until the entire group had made their way to bed, Trevel and Matok taking the first watch.

Louise fell asleep almost instantly, worn out by the day's walking. Her sleep, however, was interspersed with dreams both good and bad. Firstly, she saw vague memories of her parents, her past. These soon altered into flashes of a dark night, the air around them alive with screams and shouts of warning. Then she was running through the woods, holding tightly onto the hand of a cloaked woman, wreag's howling in the distance. She woke up in a panic, covered in sweat as if she had been running. At her sudden movement, Jamsen sat bolt upright, a dagger in his hands at the ready. When he realised they were still alone, he turned to Louise, concern sweeping across his face.

Still absorbed by the terror of her dream, Louise barely noticed him.

He placed a hand on the side of her face and looked at her closely as if checking for injury. 'Are you okay?'

It took a moment for Louise to come to her senses, to fully wake up. When she did, Louise took a deep breath as if she were finally coming back to life. 'I'm fine, I'm okay,' she said in a small voice, forcing a smile. 'I just had a bad dream.'

He visibly relaxed and he sank back into his bed. 'Can you remember what happened?' he asked her in a gentle voice.

'It was the night my parents died, how I fled from the castle. I couldn't see anything distinctive, just fragments.'

'That must have been such an awful night,' he replied compassionately.

Louise smiled and slowly sank back into her bed, exhaustion sweeping through her. Unable to keep her eyes open, she fell asleep, not even taking the time to reply to Jamsen.

Chapter Thirty-three

The next morning, they quickly packed up and continued on their way. Louise was silent as she walked, forcing herself to remember the better parts of the dream. How the corner of her mother's mouth would dimple as she laughed, or the sheer happiness on her father's face as he watched Louise learning to fight with a sword. She was so absorbed by her thoughts that she almost walked straight into Shelt, who had come to an abrupt stop in front of her. It was with a shock that Louise realised the entire group had stopped moving. One at a time, they slowly raised their weapons and closed ranks so that they were stood together.

Louise opened her mouth to ask what was wrong. Before she had the chance, Zalan moved to her side and raised his hand, signalling for her to stay quiet. Louise looked around, desperately trying to understand what was threatening them. Then Louise heard it. At first, it was merely a twig snapping, then it was the sound of several. This was mingled with the dull echo of distant voices.

Louise felt her heart stop for a second, only to have it burst back into action as a screech cut through the woods like a knife. It was a low sound, not of terror but of unquenchable hatred. The sound carried effortlessly towards them, reverberating through Louise's ears. As the terrifying screech continued, Louise realised that it wasn't just one voice, underneath the anger was a multitude of small cries of terror, mingled with pleas for help. As if hundreds of people were being held prisoner by that unearthly cry.

Everyone in the group lifted their hands to their ears, trying to block out the sounds surrounding them. They looked at one another with alarmed expressions, their faces pale and strained.

When the scream finally stopped, the woods around them felt unnervingly quiet. They all slowly brought their hands down from their ears, then raised their weapons and prepared themselves for whatever was approaching. Before any of them could say a word, another sound penetrated the silence, one Louise knew all too well—a wreag's howl. It struck fear right into the very centre of her heart, a feeling which intensified when it was joined by another eight or nine howls, coming from every direction. They knew they were completely surrounded.

'We need to get out of here,' Jamsen said, looking around in a panic.

'But which way!' Toln asked. 'The howls are coming from all around us.'

'We need to come back the way we came! Quickly!' He grabbed Louise's arm and began pulling her in that direction.

'No!' Matok cried out, swinging an arm out to stop

them. 'The wreag's are almost certainly coming from that direction, they'll have tracked our scent. We're better off going this way.' He pointed in the opposite direction. Then as if on cue, a wreag's howl came from the exact spot he was pointing to.

'It's too late, they've surrounded us,' Louise said in a quiet voice.

The group spun around in circles, certain that one of the creatures hunting them was going to appear at any minute. Louise had her back turned when she heard a quick intake of breath. Turning, she saw Pascen taking a step back, then looked past her, eyes widening in alarm

A cloud of thick dark smoke was slowly moving towards them, curling around the trees, scorching them the moment it touched them. The large cloud of smoke came to a stop, then grew upwards, whilst small tentacles edged out at either side.

'There's something in it,' she said squinting to get a better look. 'Something in the centre of the smoke.'

Before anyone could reply, Enik let out a shout. 'Wreags, all around us.'

Louise turned and gave a jolt as she realised that he was right—wreags had formed a perfect circle around them, except for the areas engulfed in the dark, ominous smoke. As if they had hit an invisible wall, the wreags stopped, snarling and growling at them. Instinctively the group turned their backs to one another, ensuring that they didn't leave a single one of their enemies unwatched.

'We have no other choice, we need to stand our ground and deal with the biggest threat, which at the moment is whatever is in the smoke. The wreag's don't seem to want to approach, maybe whatever is in the smoke is keeping them at bay.' Zalan said, standing at Louise's side with his weapon raised.

Louise tightly held her knife, fear and terror fighting to be the most prominent within her. Then, they finally saw what was lurking in the smoke. It was quite unlike anything Louise had ever seen and she felt her body begin to shake with fear. Beside her, she knew the others were equally as shocked, as they let out small gasps and stifled screams.

Through the smoke loomed a giant, white, skull-like head, with sunken eye sockets that held nothing but endless pits of darkness. Its mouth was a line of sharp pointed teeth set in a fixed grin and where there should have been a nose, there were two small slits. Its body was enshrouded in the smoke and it was difficult to differentiate between the two. When Louise looked closer, however, she was able to make out a shapeless solid form thriving within the smoke. As it drifted towards them she could see long, skeletal arms reaching out, with huge sharp claws. They gripped the nearest trees, causing a low ripping sound to emit through the woods as the large trunks tore in two, sending them crashing to the ground where they immediately disintegrated. The sound as they landed reverberated through Louise's entire body; the effects of the impact were so great, she almost felt as though she'd been severely winded.

The looming creature stopped just in front of them and its grotesque head moved to look down on them. It opened its eerie, grinning mouth very slightly, revealing even more darkness. As it did, the same screech they'd heard earlier spread around them, far louder and more horrifying than it had been before. Everyone in the group raised their hands to their ears again, desperately trying to block out the sound. No matter how hard she pressed her ears, Louise couldn't rid herself of the terrible noise, and this time the screams and pleas for help mingled within the screech were even more prominent.

Looking ever closer at the abyss that seemed to be its body, Louise thought she saw peaks of movement from within the smoke. It took her a few moments to realise that the shapes moving within the beast were the silhouettes of humans pressing against their prison, trying to reach out for help, desperate to escape.

Without a word, both Jamsen and Enik raised their bows and each released an arrow. At the exact point in which the arrows should have penetrated, they simply passed straight through. Where there had once been a solid form, there was now only smoke, as if the creature had recognised the threat of the arrows. Once that threat was gone, its body became solid again.

Jamsen and Enik glanced at one another momentarily, then without a word they released another arrow, this time aiming straight for its head. This time, before they even came close to impact, two small clouds of smoke appeared in front of its face and as the arrows passed through them, they simply disappeared along with the smoke.

'What the hell is going on?' Enik murmured. 'How are we supposed to defend ourselves?'

'I don't know,' Jamsen replied, looking around. 'But there is something I think we can try, fire.'

Louise nodded, understanding immediately understanding his plan. She grabbed her bag and began rooting through it. Eventually, she felt the box beneath her fingers and quickly grabbed it, passing it to Jamsen, who took it with an appreciative smile.

He grabbed a shirt from his bag and used his knife to tear it into small strips, promptly wrapping it around the end of his arrow. He passed the matches back to Louise and set his arrow.

'Can you light the material for me?' he asked Louise, staring intently at the creature before them.

Louise pulled out a match, lit it, and set the flame below the material. It caught on fire and without a moment's hesitation, he released it. He once again aimed the arrow at the creature's body but unlike the last time, the arrow didn't simply pass through. Instead, it impacted and seemed to explode; for a split second, its entire body was on fire. The creature, which had started moving again, came to an abrupt stop. The smoke that had been continuously spreading towards them flinched backwards for a moment. Then as if nothing had happened, it began moving once again, the smoke continuing to edge around them.

'Fire,' Jamsen said with a tone of immense satisfaction. 'It doesn't seem to damage it but it does at least slow the creature down!'

Zalan flung his bag down to the ground and started rummaging within it. He pulled out a blanket and a piece of clothing. He immediately began ripping them into strips which he piled up onto the ground.

'Here,' he said, passing them to Matok. 'Start wrapping these around as many of the arrows as you can.'

Matok quickly did as he was told, then as soon as the arrows were ready, Jamsen and Enik fired two of them, slowing it down very slightly. Just as they were about to fire another, a shout made them all come to an abrupt stop.

'The wreag's are getting closer!' Pascen screamed in a terrified voice.

They pulled their eyes away from the monster and sure enough, the wreags had moved considerably closer. They closed the circle around them, although they made sure that they weren't too near to the monster or the smoke emanating from it.

'I think they're frightened of this thing,' Louise said, studying the wreags who had stopped again.

'Now we're completely stuck!' Shelt shouted in a slightly manic tone. She turned to Louise, 'Do something!' she screamed. 'Use your magic!'

Louise froze, panic suddenly spreading through her. She looked at Jamsen beseechingly, but he was firing another arrow at the monster, it's smoke now even closer to them.

'I-I-I...' Louise stammered, looking desperately around. 'Well, I'll try,' her voice was uncertain. She raised her hands very slightly, directing them at the monster, and then she shut her eyes, forcing herself to concentrate. She remained that way for a few minutes, willing her magic to come to light. She did everything she could to try and awaken her magic, but nothing worked. She heard a loud grunt of annoyance from Shelt and as she opened her eyes, she realised that she was watching her closely.

'I'm sorry, I don't know how to control it yet!' Louise said, desperately trying to excuse her failure, overwhelmed with guilt. The rest of the group didn't seem aware of the exchange between the two women, or Louise's failed attempt at magic.

Although the monster had come to a stop, its smoke had begun spreading around them, stopping metres from the waiting wreags. There was a temporary stalemate and then clearly too desperate for a meal, the beasts began to edge closer, snapping at the air.

One particularly brave wreag that was closest to the smoke edged itself towards the group and Pascen and Trevel immediately stepped forward to fend it off. The smoke was slowly surrounding them, blocking out the wreags. It silently moved behind the lone wreag that Trevel and Pascen were fighting, trapping it along with Louise and the rest of the group.

The wreag leapt and flung Pascen down to the ground and Trevel lunged forward, trying to get it off his wife. Louise pulled out her small knife and followed suit, stabbing at the wreag repeatedly. It tried to shake its two attackers off, allowing Pascen to pull herself out from under its grip. Just as she was about to escape, the wreag twisted its large mouth back in her direction and sank its teeth into the top of her left leg. Pascen screamed in pain as she twisted her body, her leg still trapped in the wreag's teeth. Tolt, Matok and Darty had now rushed forward to help, but the wreag, ignoring Louise and Trevel, began to drag Pascen backwards, away from the group. She clawed desperately at the ground, writhing in pain, the beasts' teeth still firmly gripping her leg.

Louise jumped forward and grabbed Pascen's hand tightly. She tried to hold on and pull her away from the wreag but this just caused more tension on her leg, making her scream out in pain. Louise stopped pulling, easing her grip very slightly. The wreag in the meantime was drawing ever closer to the smoke, completely unaware it was lurking behind it. Its back paws suddenly touched the very edge of it, the wreag stopped dead in its tracks as it realised what had happened. It let go of Pascen's leg and Louise took this chance to pull her away from the creature, Trevel leaping forward to help. She shook uncontrollably in her husband's arms as he cradled her.

The wreag stood motionless for a moment, then it dramatically arched its back as it let out a high-pitched whine. Then through the smoke, long skeletal arms stretched out. They grabbed hold of the wreag's back legs and effortlessly pulled the creature backwards into the dense, smoke. It was enveloped with remarkable speed, and although the wreag itself was no longer visible there was a large bulge, which began to move through the smoke towards the skeletal creature. When it finally reached its destination, Louise saw a brief flash of the wreag and was shocked to see that where there had been thick fur, it now had bald patches, through which she could see flashes of flesh and even the white of bone. She heard a final howl, which was more terrifying than any sound it had made before. It was filled with pain and complete terror, and as it rang through her ears, Louise couldn't help but feel sorry for the creature. It seemed to be absorbed into the creature's body, and then there was complete silence.

Louise watched with horror, slowly beginning to understand exactly how dangerous the smoke surrounding them was. She wasn't able to dwell on it for much longer, however, as Pascen was now hyperventilating, almost overcome with pain. It was at that point that Louise realised the others had been too distracted by other threats to see the terrible fate of the wreag.

'The smoke is now completely surrounding us,' Louise said quietly, almost to herself. She looked over at Trevel and as his eyes met hers, she saw the fear in them as his injured wife lay in his arms. 'We need to move her into the centre, we need to stay as far away from the smoke as we can.' She said this in a louder voice, trying to get the attention of the rest of the group.

'I agree!' Zalan said without hesitation and the group then huddled together, placing Pascen in the centre.

'Don't let the smoke touch you,' Louise said. 'That's what killed the wreag, it didn't have a chance.'

'We need to get out of here,' Enik said, panic evident in his voice. 'But how!'

'There is no way out,' Toln replied sternly. 'We have no choice; we have to try and defeat this thing or else we may as well just give up.'

'Everyone, stand around Pascen, she's the most vulnerable right now.' They sprang into action at Jamsen's words. 'Then we need to use fire to keep the smoke at bay. Place as much material around us as possible, in a continuous circle. We can then set it alight—it should keep it away, at least for a little bit.'

Once the circle around them was complete, Jamsen began looking around frantically. 'Louise, where's the box of matches?'

Louise looked over at her bag which had been knocked over in the mayhem of the attack. Her belongings scattered across the ground; the matches were nowhere to be seen. Everyone started looking around, desperately trying to find it.

'There!' Enik shouted. 'Is that it? I think I can see it!' he pointed to the ground just a few feet away, just outside of their makeshift circle. Before any of them could do anything, Enik had jumped over the line of material, being careful not to get too close to the smoke. He snatched up the matches and turned back to them with a satisfied look, holding it up in the air triumphantly. He started making his way back over to the others but just before he reached the circle, he came to an abrupt stop. A small slither of smoke, like a skinny arm, had stretched out and reached towards Enik. Boney fingers wrapped around his ankle; the smile only left his face when he was suddenly and forcefully yanked backwards.

It all happened so quickly that nobody had the chance to react. A little too late, the entire group (with the exception of Pascen and Trevel) had lunged forwards, arms outstretched. None of them able to reach him in time and it wasn't long before they were able to hear his muffled screams as his bulging shape began to travel through the smoke. They stood watching for a second in stunned silence, only managing to glimpse him when he had almost reached the mouth of the creature. His body was red and bloody and at this point, he had stopped screaming. Just before he vanished forever, all they could hear was a quiet cry of 'Shelt! Please help me!' Then as he disappeared, he let out a final scream.

As his voice finally went quiet, Shelt took up the mantle, a harsh scream of anger escaping her.

'Enik!' Shelt screamed. 'Enik! I'm coming!' She surged forward, her sword raised, a frightened anger spread across her face.

Zalan and Matok grabbed her by either arm and dragged her backwards. As strong as she was, she wasn't quite a match for the two burly men. She thrashed against them, desperate to get to her brother; a pointless act as he had now completely disappeared into the smoke. She fell to the ground, tears streaming down her face as she stared at the skeletal creature above them. Shelt's body shook as she cradled her head in her hands and silently sobbed. Above her, Zalan and Matok looked at each other uncertainly. Matok rested a hand on her back in reassurance, which seemed to go completely unnoticed as she just continued to sob.

Chapter Thirty-four

A pit formed deep in Louise's stomach as sympathy for the woman seeped through her, and she felt tears of her own forming in her eyes as she watched. Then she noticed something just in the corner of her eye; lying on the ground, just outside of their circle, lay the box of matches Without hesitation Louise lunged towards it, careful not to get too close to the smoke that lurked by the perimeter of the circle.

Retreating back into the circle, she looked over at Jamsen with a look of quiet triumph. Whilst the others tried to comfort Shelt, Louise and Jamsen crouched eagerly by the far side of the circle of material. She pulled out a match and as she flicked it against the side of the box it burst into light. Louise was full of uncertainty as to how well the material would burn once lit. This question was soon answered as the closest section of the material lit for only mere seconds before it went out again.

'It's not working,' Jamsen said in a low voice. 'What are we going to do?'

Louise felt fear and uncertainty spreading through

her and in her panicked state, she continued to try lighting the material with a second match. With a cry of frustration, she threw the matches to the ground. As she threw them to the ground, something sparked on her hand, she stared at the spot in which the light had appeared with startled disbelief. Jamsen hadn't noticed, his attention instead set upon the ever-approaching smoke. She very slightly moved her hand outwards and palm up. She shut her eyes and pleaded with her body to allow the magic to flow once again. She still felt nothing and in desperation, her other hand clasped tightly around the Whisper as if appealing for its help.

It took a few minutes but eventually, she felt something in response. A slight tingling spread through her body which vanished almost as soon as it had appeared. Opening her eyes, Louise let out a gasp of delight; resting in the very centre of her hand was a small ball of flames, constantly curling and twirling around in a small circle. She stared at it in amazement and lifted her other hand to examine it further. Although she felt no warmth underneath her hand, as she held the other one over it, Louise was startled as to just how much heat was being emitted from it.

'Wow!' Jamsen cried from beside her and Louise lifted her head slightly to see him staring intently at her hand. He shot her a wide grin which Louise instantly returned. She then looked back to her hand and eased the ball of flames forwards towards the ripped material in front of her. At first, the flame didn't leave her hand and a flickering of panic spread through her as she desperately tried to think of how she could move it. She took a few deep breaths and forced herself to calm down. Then, with a new surge of confidence Louise forced herself to concentrate on the material in front of her, then carefully she flicked her hand down towards it and the flame flew forwards. The second it touched the material it set it alight. Jamsen cried in celebration and startled by the noise, the others spun around to see what was wrong. They all let out cries of surprise and delight.

'Fantastic!' Zalan roared, rushing over to them. 'Can you keep doing it? Can you set them all alight?'

Before she had the chance to try, however, Shelt had come racing over to her with indecipherable shouts of anger. She launched herself at Louise, knocking her to the ground. Louise felt the air rushing out of her lungs, leaving her body feeling empty and a feeling of nausea spreading through her as she gasped for air. Breathing became even more difficult as Shelt placed her hands around Louise's throat, thwarting her attempts to refill her lungs. Instead, an involuntary rasping sound came from her throat. The world around Louise went in and out of focus as she frantically tried to push the large woman away.

'You did have magic! You do know how to use it! You let Enik die!' Shelt screamed. Louise then felt the other woman's grip begin to slacken as the rest of the group tried to prise her hands apart.

As soon as Shelt's grip slackened Louise gasped and with immense relief, she felt her lungs fill with air. She inhaled so quickly that she began to cough and splutter and she rolled onto her front as she tried to recover. A few moments later, she looked around to see where her attacker had gone. Shelt was lying on the ground, Jamsen standing over her, dagger in his hand.

'I had no choice. She was trying to kill Louise,'

Jamsen said as everyone stared at him. It quickly became clear that he had knocked her out using the hilt of his dagger as she now lay unconscious on the ground. The rest of the group nodded in agreement.

'Matok, can you help me to restrain her, we don't know when she'll wake up again or how she'll act once she does,' Darty said as she brought a stretch of rope out of her pack. They moved Shelt's arms and roughly tied them together.

Meanwhile, Jamsen and Zalan knelt beside Louise, looks of concern spread across their faces.

'Are you okay?' Jamsen asked, his arm wrapped around her shoulder as he helped her to sit upright, her breathing once again regular and under control.

Darty approached, looking at the smoke that was threatening to enter the circle. 'I know you're still recovering,' she said quietly, 'but do you think you can try using your magic on that creature. Your fire may be able to penetrate that smoke. Then could you try and set the remainder of the material alight? We're running out of time.'

'Okay, I'll give it a try.' Louise's voice was meek.

She forced herself to concentrate and as before, she gripped the Whisper in her hand. This time, however, nothing happened. Her body felt exhausted, she found herself struggling to concentrate and despite various attempts, she knew that she wasn't going to be able to do it again.

'I'm sorry, I'm not quite sure how I did it before. I can't do it again,' she said in an apologetic tone. 'Let's try using the strip that's already on fire to set the rest alight.' Zalan nodded in agreement and the two of them rushed forwards. He drew his sword and Louise drew her small knife; they both then used the blades to move the material closer to the strip beside it. This too caught on fire.

'Please, someone help me!' Trevel cried out. Pascen's body began to convulse and Jamsen rushed over to help hold her down. The two men's faces were pale as they gripped her arms and their grips didn't slacken until her body stopped shaking. When it finally did, they looked at each other with concern. Pascen now lay motionless, clearly unconscious. Trevel sat back and stared at his wife's bloody and severely damaged leg.

'She'll be alright.' Jamsen said, staring intently at the other man.

Louise felt a wave of dizziness pass through her and she sat back, holding her head.

'Go and sit down for a minute,' Zalan said, resting an arm gently on her shoulder. 'Jamsen and I'll light the rest of this.'

Louise didn't have the strength to argue and obediently moved over to Pascen. She grabbed a spare bit of material and pressed it against Pascen's bleeding leg, allowing herself the opportunity to sit back and rest. Meanwhile, Jamsen and Zalan went about lighting the rest of the circle. Trevel still cradled his wife's head, whispering gently in her ear.

Toln and Matok had finished restraining Shelt and rushed to help Zalan and Jamsen to complete the ring of fire.

Resting her head in her free hand, Louise closed her eyes for a few seconds as she tried to force the dizziness to pass. When she looked back up again, the circle was almost complete, only three strips were remaining. It was evident that the fire circle was helping, as the smoke was no longer approaching and now just lingered at the edges. Her gaze landed on Jamsen as he lit the remaining strips of material. Then she looked past him and her heart stopped—the smoke was still very active where there wasn't any fire. As Jamsen moved, she realised a slither of the smoke had formed into an arm and was now stretching through the gap, reaching towards him without his knowledge.

'No!' Louise screamed out, instantly jumping to her feet. Moving with a speed she didn't know she was capable of, she darted towards him and without a moment to spare, she pushed him out of the way. She only had enough time to see Jamsen falling to the ground, before she felt something gripping her around her waist. Looking down, she realised the smoke had wrapped itself around her stomach, a skeletal hand appeared gripping her with surprising strength. She was suddenly wrenched backwards with such ferocity and speed she was immediately disorientated. Through the smoke, claws began to cut through her skin, causing excruciating pain to spread through her. She would have screamed but the creature's grip was so tight that her lungs felt like they had stopped working.

As she was being pulled away, she looked up and was able to see Jamsen; he had gotten back to his feet and with a shout of terror, he was running towards her, desperately trying to reach her. Moments later, everything went black as Louise was surrounded by the smoke.

The clawed hand abruptly released her and she floated gently in the smoke as you would in a pool of water. Then without warning, Louise experienced pain, unlike anything she'd ever experienced before. The smoke penetrated every part of her body and she felt like she was slowly being ripped apart, her skin stripped off. Even her eyes felt like they were being pushed out of their sockets. She threw her head backwards as she thrashed around in the smoke. She began to scream; a harrowing, pain-ridden sound. She was vaguely aware that she was slowly travelling through the smoke and that, like the wreag and Enik before her, she was heading to the skeletal creature's terrifying and grotesque body.

She forced herself to concentrate, to try and think, or to find a means of escape. Whilst doing so, she looked down and was horrified when she saw what had become of her body. Large patches of her clothing had vanished and the skin underneath was visible. Then moments later, right in front of her eyes, she saw her skin begin to disappear, dissolving as if acid were being poured onto it, revealing the raw flesh and bone underneath.

Tears gushed down her face, causing excruciating pain as they reached patches of her skin that had disappeared. The pain was gradually becoming too much and she felt her body begin to convulse and spasm. She knew at this point that there was no way she was going to be able to escape from this torture, desperation and exhaustion began to take over. Subconsciously, her hand had reached down and had somehow found the Whisper. At this point, she almost welcomed death—thoughts of being returned to the place of her birth, of helping to release the people of Calaresp from Brisheit's tyranny, immediately fled her mind. All she wanted was to sleep, to leave this world and the pain that had now consumed her. The world around her began to darken and she slowly felt her consciousness slipping away.

Louise became vaguely aware of a warmth in the centre of her chest, where the Whisper hung. All of a sudden, something began to erupt from within her and the darkness around her filled with a bright golden light. As the darkness vanished, so too did the pain that had spread to every crevice of her body.

As power from the Whisper coursed through her and she began to regain control of her body, her mind was still not quite her own as it filled with flashes of memories and emotions long forgotten.

She saw herself as a little girl playing in wonderful gardens with her father, singing with her mother. Other flashes filled her mind and Louise saw herself being taught to ride a horse, fight with a sword, and even master her magic. She saw herself sitting upright in her bed, her parents sat either side of her, her mother reading aloud whilst Louise and her father sat transfixed. Louise remembered a stormy night in which her sleep was interrupted by the sounds of screams and the clashing of swords. She remembered seeing a much younger and less worn-out Clarris rushing into the room with her mother and with a few others, they left the castle through secret and hidden passageways, fleeing her much-loved home. Louise saw her younger self asking where her parents were. She remembered the pain and how bitterly she cried when she was told that they had been killed and that Clarris and the others needed to send her somewhere safe.

When the flashes of her past finally stopped, Louise remembered everything. Her mind reeled as she processed all the unlocked memories. Then she gradually remembered the life-threatening position she now found herself in. With very little effort she felt her power building up within her. Her body healed itself as she moved into an upright position and flung her arms out to the side. As she did, there was an explosion of golden light, which chased the darkness away. She felt hundreds of life forms rush past her, finally freed from their eternal prison. The smoke tried to regain control, claws desperately trying to rip her apart, but Louise's magic was too strong. She saw the skull-like face writhe in pain, then slowly vanish as her magic overcame it. Seconds later, Louise's feet touched the ground. The light vanished and the smoke dissipated, it took a few seconds for her eyes to adjust. When Louise finally looked up again, she saw Jamsen rushing towards her. His mouth was opening and shutting and she knew he was calling her name but Louise couldn't hear it.

Finally reaching her, Jamsen grabbed her shoulders and looked her up and down, clearly searching for injuries.

'Are you alright?' he asked in a desperate and frightened voice. 'What happened, how did you...'

Before he could say any more, Louise—feeling strangely detached from her body—walked straight past him. She barely noticed Zalan and the rest of the group reaching out to her, her attention set solely on the woman lying on the ground. When Louise finally reached her, Trevel fell away from his lifeless wife, staring up at Louise.

She could feel Jamsen following her closely, she could feel his need and desire to touch her, to make sure she was okay. She knelt on the ground and with extreme care, she rested her hands on Pascen's bleeding leg. Louise barely noticed the flashes of golden light streaking through her body, just underneath her skin. Or the mark on her wrist as it erupted into golden light. She shut her eyes and forced herself and her body to concentrate on the wound. Remaining like this for a while, she could feel the power surging through her and into Pascen's. Then, with startling abruptness, she felt the energy leave her and without warning, she collapsed to the ground, almost as if she were a discarded string puppet. As she fell, her hand went to her thigh where she suddenly felt a strange and overwhelming burst of pain. Louise was vaguely aware of an explosion of shouts and cries; before she could register anything else, she passed out.

Chapter Thirty-five

When Louise next awoke it took her a few minutes to work out where she was. She gradually recognised the wall of the tent she'd been sharing with Jamsen. She felt the reassuring presence of warm blankets wrapped around her, so comfortable and content that she found herself reluctant at first to move. With surprise she realised that she wasn't alone in the tent — a form lay on the ground just beside her, clearly asleep, snoring lightly.

Louise slowly sat upright, the haziness beginning to dissipate. She forced herself to take it slowly, worried that any sudden movements could overwhelm her body, which had already taken on so much.

Awoken by her movement Jamsen jumped up, his eyes scanning the room as if he were expecting an attack. His gaze finally settled on Louise and his pale face flushed with colour. Louise couldn't stop herself from grinning as a familiar smile spread across his face.

'Louise!' he said, his voice choked with emotion. 'Are you okay? How do you feel?'

'Okay, I think.' Louise replied in a small voice. 'A

little tired. What exactly happened?'

Jamsen sat back on his feet, watching her closely. 'Well, you saved me. You sacrificed yourself to the smoke for me.' He stopped and stared at her for a few seconds. 'You shouldn't have done that,' he continued. 'You are so much more important, more valuable than I am.'

'That's not true, not true at all,' Louise said so quickly she even surprised herself.

Jamsen raised his eyebrows, challenging this statement.

'I would do it again without a moment's hesitation,' she said sternly.

'You were consumed by the smoke. You just vanished, there was nothing I could do.' His voice broke and he looked away from her. Louise could tell by the tone of his voice that he was riddled with guilt and remorse. 'I saw you travelling towards the skeletal creature and I could see it was ripping the flesh off your body. I tried to run and save you, but the others held me back. The next time I saw your body you weren't moving and I thought you were dead. I started throwing everything I could, to see if it made a difference, but nothing worked.'

He placed his head in his hands, still avoiding eye contact with her. He seemed reluctant to go on but he eventually did, his voice subdued. 'I couldn't see you anymore, you'd vanished. An incredibly bright light appeared within the skeletal creature; it was small to begin with, and then suddenly, it exploded. None of us were able to look directly at it. When it finally went out, I looked back and the creature was gone, the smoke had vanished... Heck, even the wreags had vanished.'

He laughed gently and finally looked at her. 'You were just stood there, where that thing had been.

'I vaguely remember that,' Louise said as she forced her sleepy brain back into action, to remember everything that had happened.

'I ran over to you and although you seemed unharmed there was something strange, something surreal about you.' He hesitated struggling to find the right words. 'You had these streaks of light flickering through your body, it was almost like a golden lightning storm under your skin. It was terrifying and incredible at the same time. Even your eyes had changed, they seemed to be glowing with the same light. You walked over to Pascen, put your hand on her leg…' He paused for a second, looking at her with complete admiration. 'As soon as you touched her, you started healing her. It was amazing! Then once you'd finished, you collapsed. Darty noticed that there was blood on your trousers and when she looked closer, she realised that Pascen's leg injury had transferred to you. You healed her and took the injury yourself.'

Instinctively, Louise placed a hand on her right thigh—it was slightly sensitive to her touch, like a slowly healing bruise.

'It's still there,' Jamsen said comfortingly. 'It looks like a scar you've had for years. It's strange.

Louise pulled the blankets down and found that her trousers had been removed and folded carefully just to the side of her bed. Her mind was buzzing and she didn't feel the slightest bit self-conscious about being trouserless in Jamsen's company. Where there previously been smooth skin, there was now a deep scar running down the side of her thigh. It looked like she'd had it for her entire life and Louise tentatively placed a finger on it. To her relief, it wasn't even remotely painful. She traced the outline of the scar and stared at it for a few seconds longer.

Slowly and carefully, Louise moved out of the bed and pulled her trousers back on. Jamsen turned away respectfully as she did.

'How's Pascen?' Louise asked as she moved to leave the tent. 'Is she alright? Can you take me to her?'

'She's fine, whatever you did, fixed her completely. It's as if she was never even attacked,' Jamsen replied, smiling broadly at her. 'Come on, I'll take you to her.' They left the tent and Jamsen continued to talk as they walked. 'We set up camp a few miles from where we were attacked. With both you and Shelt unconscious, we were limited as to how far we could go.'

The camp was strangely quiet apart from the very far end, where a small campfire was burning merrily. It was relatively dark but the fire gently lit the silhouettes of the rest of their group. They promptly made their way towards it but before they got too close, Jamsen grasped Louise's hand and gently pulled her back, looking at her with an intensity she hadn't seen before.

She looked back at him; aware a blush was again appearing on her cheeks. He placed his hands on either side of her head, resting messily in her hair. He gently pulled her face towards his own and she obeyed as if hypnotised. Then he kissed her with a passion she didn't know was possible. Her body immediately responded and as they kissed, she placed her hands on his muscular chest.

When they finally pulled apart, they stared hungrily at each other for a few seconds.

'I've been wanting to do that for a while,' he said breathlessly.

They kissed again, this time Jamsen ran his fingers through her hair, using his other hand to pull her closer to him. When they stopped, they remained where they were, their faces close together, both longing for more.

'We should go and join the others,' Jamsen said, tenderly kissing the palm of her hand.

They reluctantly pulled apart and stepped into the light of the campfire. Zalan, Trevel, and a fully-healed Pascen rose to their feet as soon as they saw her. Darty, Matok, and Toln, on the other hand, remained where they were but looked up at her with broad grins. Everyone seemed happy to see her except for Shelt, who remained seated, her face turned away. Before Louise had any time to dwell on the animosity exuding from the large woman, Pascen let out a sharp gasp of relief and rushed to Louise, hugging her tightly. Jamsen stood back, smiling.

When she finally let go, Louise barely had time to take a breath before Trevel took his wife's place, hugging her just as tightly.

'Thank you for saving my wife,' he whispered in her ear. Trevel pulled away, a huge smile on his face. 'I can never repay you for what you did, I will forever be in your debt.'

'We both will,' Pascen interjected, wrapping her arm around Trevel's waist. He looked down at his wife as if she were the most precious thing in the world. 'Thank you, I don't know how you did it, but thank you.'

Louise felt herself smiling and nodding. She was consumed with intense relief at finding Pascen alive and well and this feeling was so overpowering, she couldn't think of anything to say. Trevel and Pascen seemed to understand her inner struggle, gave her another warm smile, and then sat back down again.

Zalan stepped forward and smiled at her. As Louise looked at him, all the recently returned memories of him came to the forefront of her mind. As a child, she had loved him dearly, almost as if he were an uncle to her. She now understood how hard it must have been for him when she couldn't remember him, how difficult it would have been to restrain himself from hugging and holding her. Instinctively Louise stepped forward and hugged him. For a moment he was surprised, but then he barked with laughter and returned her embrace.

'What's that for?' he said with a chuckle.

Louise stood back and smiled at him. 'When I was inside that creature, that monster, I used my powers as I've never used them before. As I did, all my memories came back. I remember everything — I remember you!'

Once she'd said this, Louise realised that for the first time in her life she felt truly complete, like she knew and fully understood herself.

Before she could say anything else, Zalan had stepped forward and hugged her again, clearly relieved and delighted.

'You remember me,' he said quietly, more to himself than anyone else. 'It's great to have you back, Louise. To have you back completely. Your parents would be so proud of you.'

Everyone sat around the fire and Louise looked around at their faces as they glowed gently in the firelight. She noticed Darty looking at her in admiration and when they finally made eye contact, she simply gave her an approving nod.

'So, you have your magic again, do you? Shame you couldn't bring yourself to use it to save Enik,' Shelt said in a harsh and brittle voice.

'Shelt, I am so sorry about Enik but there was nothing I could have done to save him. I didn't understand my powers then. I had to practically die before I finally remembered how to use them, to understand them.'

'Liar!' Shelt screamed, staring intently at the fire. 'Right after that... that thing killed my brother, you were able to make a ball of flame in your hands. If you had done that earlier, you could have saved him! You just didn't care about him!'

'Shelt!' Zalan and Darty said in unison, staring at the woman with shock.

Shelt pushed a small strand of greasy hair behind her ear and smiled benevolently.

'I would have saved Enik if I could have. If I'd known how,' Louise replied, anger combining with sorrow as she answered.

'Stop pretending! Stop pretending to feel bad that he's dead! You didn't care about him, you didn't know him. All you care about is yourself!' Shelt screamed, rising to her feet.

'Shelt!' Darty shouted, standing up, dwarfed by the other woman. 'It wasn't her fault, you can't take this out on her! You know who she is! You have no right talking to her like this!'

This statement made Louise feel awkward and uncomfortable. She knew it had been the wrong thing to say before Shelt even had time to fully process it.

'Of course, I know who she is!' Shelt drew close to

Darty. 'She's a naïve little princess who hasn't been in Calaresp since she was a child. She hasn't had to fight every day, to see the ones you love die for a pointless cause.'

'Of course, my parents dying was a wonderful experience, growing up in an entirely different world with no friends, no family was easy. Always feeling like you didn't belong, that something was missing. Then to discover the truth and that the man who killed your parents is still, to this day, desperate to see you dead,' Louise found frustration and anger bursting out of her and before she knew it, she too was up on her feet.

A bizarre sound of indignation erupted from Shelt's mouth and she slowly stalked towards Louise. 'I should just hand you over to Brisheit myself. Perhaps then I can guarantee my safety and the safety of the family that I have left.' Her hand rested on the hilt of her sword and a satisfied look spread across her face. 'I never wanted to help you, I couldn't care less about you or your stupid family. Enik was the one who wanted to be here. I just came to make sure he didn't get hurt, and because of you, I failed.'

As Shelt drew closer to Louise the rest of the group rose to their feet, their hands placed on their weapons, preparing themselves. Louise stood her ground confidentially, now very aware of her own capabilities. Without being entirely conscious of it, a small smile spread across her face as she stared at Shelt. 'I would like to see you try and hand me over to Brisheit.'

This seemed to be a step too far for Shelt, who quickly pulled out her sword and with an animalistic roar, rushed towards Louise. Calmly, Louise raised her right hand. With her memories restored, she remembered all the time her mother had spent teaching her how to properly use and control her magic. Every lesson was fresh in her mind, alongside a further understanding of her powers and those of the Whisper that came with having been so close to death.

Louise held her hand upright and flicked it forwards in a fluid motion so that the palm was facing the ground. Shelt was immediately sent flying backwards, where she smashed into a tree and fell limply to the ground. She recovered with remarkable speed and jumped back to her feet. Louise could see the anger in Shelt's eyes pushing her to attack again.

Raising her sword again, Shelt moved forwards but before she could do anything, Louise simply clicked her fingers. As she did, Shelt's legs locked together, holding her firmly in place. Shelt tried jerking her legs forwards, confused. When she finally understood what Louise had done, a thunderous look spread across her face.

Louise merely smiled sadly, 'Well, you didn't give me much of a choice, did you!'

The rest of the group looked at Louise with mingled expressions of surprise, admiration, and even amusement.

'Well,' Darty turned to Shelt. 'I hope that's put you in your place. It's about time someone did.'

Shelt let out a harrowing scream of anger as she kept struggling to move her legs. 'Let me go!'

Louise lifted her hand and this time she flicked her fingers apart. Taken completely by surprise, Shelt's legs collapsed beneath her. She remained on the floor for a few minutes, breathing heavily. When she looked up again her eyes were filled with sheer hatred, but she seemed to have regained control over her emotions.

'I've had enough. I never wanted to be here in the first place. You won't defeat Brisheit regardless of what pathetic party tricks you can do. You simply aren't strong enough.'

With that, Shelt stood up and glared at the group. She then grabbed her possessions and left.

There was a momentary silence as the group processed everything that had just happened. Jamsen turned to Louise, breaking the awkward silence. 'Wow, you really know how to use your powers now, don't you!'

Louise took a deep breath, feeling resoundingly awkward. She had hated using her powers on Shelt; although she had never liked the woman. She had still been a member of the rebels and she had just lost her brother. Louise took a few seconds to compose herself and then turned to address Jamsen and the rest of the group.

'My mother and an old Warlock started teaching me to use my powers when I was incredibly young. The Warlock didn't have any powers himself, but he came from a long line of Warlocks who knew and understood the Whisper and its potential powers. The two of them taught me a lot. When my memories were unlocked, when I almost died, it was like the Whisper opened up to me, unveiling everything. Now it seems to be more instinctive than anything else.'

Jamsen smiled back at her and the rest nodded in understanding. Darty and Zalan stared in the direction Shelt had disappeared. From where Louise stood, she couldn't quite make out their hushed whispers. Moving up beside them, she was finally able to hear what they were saying.

'I didn't know she'd do this! She's an incredible fighter, that's why I let her come!' Darty said defiantly.

'But we knew she had no loyalty to us, to Louise. It was Enik who believed in our cause; he fought and died for it. I've even heard people say she spoke quite flatteringly about Brisheit and his methods,' Zalan replied gruffly, giving Darty a cold look.

They both nodded at Louise, acknowledging her presence but continuing to look at where Shelt had disappeared.

'I'm sorry I had to do that to her,' Louise said, making the most of the lull in the conversation.

'If you hadn't, one of us would have had to fight her,' Zalan flashed her a comforting smile. 'She's an incredible swordswoman and I'm certain somebody would have died. I don't think she would have accepted anything less.'

'You had no choice,' Darty said, placing a comforting hand on Louise's shoulder. She gave a deep sigh. 'Now you're better, we should probably set off again. We've remained here for far too long and it's not safe. Also, I'm keen for us to reach the safe house by tomorrow night.'

The rest nodded and in next to no time, they were packed up and heading through the woods. They moved along in silence, each consumed by the events of the last few days. Jamsen and Louise walked alongside one another, so close that their fingertips occasionally brushed. Despite all that had happened, every time they looked at each other she was filled with an unexpected burst of happiness.

Chapter Thirty-six

Zalan always remained behind Louise, where he could keep an eye on her at all times. He smiled to himself as he noticed the new level of closeness between Jamsen and Louise. Darty remained at the front of the group, maintaining a keen eye on their surroundings. She was closely followed by Trevel and Pascen, who had their arms wrapped tightly around each other. Matok wasn't too far behind, swigging quick sips from a small hipflask. Meanwhile, Toln brought up the rear.

Jamsen leant in close to Louise, a comforting hand on her back. 'It must have been a real relief to finally get your memories back. So, do you remember absolutely everything?'

Louise nodded. 'It's bittersweet, to be honest. Before, when someone mentioned my parent's deaths, it wasn't too difficult because I didn't feel that strong a connection to them. I knew they were my parents, but I couldn't really remember them. Now that I remember them and my childhood, it's utterly heartbreaking. It's like it's all happening again. They were so wonderful, my childhood itself was simply perfect.'

'Can you tell me a little bit about them?' Jamsen asked with an encouraging smile.

Louise looked up at him, took a deep breath and then delved into her past. She told Jamsen about the incredible love her parents had for each other, how happy they had been as a family. The days they spent exploring Calaresp, or simply relaxing within the castle itself. How she'd been told about her ancestors, the meaning behind her scar, and how it had been prophesied that she would one day be the most powerful ruler ever known. How it was said that she was destined to be the rightful and true owner of the Whisper.

After walking for what seemed like hours, the group began to relax. Then without warning, cutting through the atmosphere like a knife, there was the sound of a wreag's howl. They all came to an abrupt stop and formed a circle with their weapons raised.

'I think it came from that direction,' Jamsen whispered.

The group momentarily shifted their attention to the direction in which he was pointing. Then more howls pierced through the woods; by now, they seemed to be coming from every direction.

'I think we're surrounded again,' Darty said quietly, clearly frightened.

Suddenly, as if a large curtain had been drawn back, a line of Brisheit's men appeared right in front of them, encircling them. Restrained at their sides was an overwhelming number of wreags.

'Prepare yourselves,' Zalan said, lifting his weapon.

'We can't take all of them!' Trevel replied in a hiss.

'Can you use your powers?' Darty looked at Louise

with desperation.

'I think so.' Louise quickly tallied up just how many men and wreags were now surrounding them. 'Although I don't think I've entirely recovered my strength. I think, however, that I have an idea.'

Without another word she raised both her hands and then closed her eyes, blocking out the immediate threat of the men standing mere metres away. Louise could feel the steady beating of her heart and with the Whisper sitting right next to it she felt the undeniable bond between them. It began to feel as if her heart and the Whisper were synchronised; one pumping life through her body, the other pumping magic. Louise felt the power rushing through her and when she opened her eyes again, she glanced downwards. As she did, she saw streaks of gold flashing through her body like small bolts of lightning. She took a few seconds to admire how spectacular a sight it was. She moved her hands upwards, the mark on her wrist glowing brightly, she paused for a second and then brought them back down so that they were either side of her. A golden bubble had spread around the group, separating them from Brisheit's men. It shimmered for a split second and then disappeared.

'What was that?' Pascen asked, amazed. 'Where did it go? Is it still there?'

'I-I-I put a sh-shield around us. You c-c-an't see it anymore b-but I can assure you, it's st-st-still there.' Louise stuttered as she spoke, as all of her efforts were being put into maintaining the shield. She was still weakened from recent events and although she now knew how to use her powers, her body was still adapting and getting used to them.

Then, all at once, the wreags were released and at least thirty of the horrible creatures lunged forward, unaware of the shield. When they hit it, they shrieked and howled in pain, their bodies flung backwards. As soon as they hit the ground, they leapt back onto their feet and tried again. The invisible shield surrounding them soon became visible, smeared with blood. Despite their injuries, the beasts kept desperately trying to reach their prey. At first, the group inside the shield had flinched each time they made impact. Now they stood, almost relaxed, weapons very slightly lowered as they stared in amazement at Louise's creation.

'Are you okay?' Jamsen whispered in her ear, placing a supportive hand on the small of her back.

Louise was breathing hard; maintaining a shield so powerful that it could withstand the power of the wreags was proving to be incredibly difficult. She could feel her power and energy seeping away from her with every passing moment.

'It's difficult to keep it up, to make sure it's strong enough.' Louise said in gasps. 'I don't think it's going to last too much longer! They can't get in but you should be able to fire weapons outwards.'

'I understand. Just do what you can.' Jamsen turned to the rest of the group, 'The shield should allow our arrows to pass through it. We need to take out as many of the soldiers as possible, she can't keep it up for too much longer.' Without hesitation, Jamsen raised his bow and began shooting arrows out into the mass of wreags. One or two of them had already injured themselves by battering into the shield, so a few arrows from Jamsen were enough to either kill them or significantly injure them. Matok, meanwhile, had brought out a collection of daggers from his pack and went about throwing them into the beasts. His blows were less successful than Jamsen's but he eventually took one down.

A low whistle echoed around them and as if they had been pulled backwards, the wreags turned away from Louise and her group. Sporting various levels of injuries, they limped and dragged themselves back behind their holders. The group looked at each other in confusion and fear, uncertain as to what had controlled them so easily. This question was soon answered when the soldiers stepped to the side, allowing a large shape to make its way towards them.

Soon Louise was looking straight into the eyes of the man she had spent such a large part of her life hiding from. Brisheit towered above them with a malicious grin on his face. He stared straight at Louise, clearly not having eyes for anyone else.

'It's wonderful to finally see you again, young princess,' he said in a quiet growl, a self-satisfied grin spreading across his face. 'It's been such a long time!' He walked right up to the blood-smeared edge of the shield, a dying wreag lying by his feet. 'My, oh my, has anyone told you how much you look like your parents? I can see a little bit of both of them in you. It's uncanny.'

He laughed deeply, staring at her intently. 'I have to tell you, it was so tedious, so frustrating when your parents were alive. They were such pathetic rulers — weak and unworthy. Treating the poor, the lower classes as if they were equal. Those of us with money suffered as a result. They were such a pleasure to kill.'

Louise felt uncontrollable anger rising through her

body, as if her blood were boiling inside her. There was a desperate urge to hurl the full force of her power straight at him, to wipe that revolting self-adoring smile from his face. She knew, however, that if she did, she would leave her friends utterly defenceless.

'Get your weapons ready—if the shield comes down, we need to prepare ourselves,' Zalan whispered to those around him.

Brisheit didn't seem to hear, he had gently placed his hand on the shield and pressed against it. Then with an alarming amount of power, he calmly slammed his hand against it. His strength, unlike the wreags', caused tremors throughout Louise's shield, followed by a loud, echoing thud.

'How did they find us?' Pascen asked in a quiet voice.

As soon as she spoke, Brisheit's head flicked to the side, like a predator that's just located its prey.

'I would bet anything that Shelt had something to do with it. It wouldn't surprise me if she had betrayed us,' Darty said confidently.

He let out another booming, piercing laugh. He turned and raised his hands dramatically. 'Well, then this must be Shelt!'

The men behind him started moving and a lone man stepped forward. He held something in his hands and as he drew close to Brisheit, he lifted it into the air.

Pascen's screams pierced through their surroundings and the rest of the group reeled in shock as they recognised the decapitated head of Shelt, her hair covered in blood and large parts of her cheeks missing, having been ripped off her face. The right side of her mouth was gone, revealing her teeth and gums as they glistened with blood. Her eyes were open, staring directly at them with an emptiness that reached right into Louise's soul.

'We found her a few hours ago, she didn't even hear us coming. To be honest, she barely put up a fight, it was pretty dull. Both my men and the wreags enjoyed her though.'

Louise had to look away, overwhelmed by a feeling of complete revolution. As her emotions began to take over, she could feel the strength of the shield waver momentarily.

'She wasn't the only one who betrayed you though,' Brisheit continued. 'She was just a chance discovery.'

The group all looked up, the horror of Shelt's decapitated head forgotten, pushed aside by the revelation that one of their number had deceived them.

With a sharp flick of his head, Brisheit looked in Louise's direction, a wide grin spread across his face.

'I'm so glad to see you again, Captain. I must say, you've done a marvellous job. As instructed, you have safely delivered the young princess to us. I can assure you that you'll be fully rewarded for your success, your loyalty.'

Louise turned to her side, following Brisheit's gaze. As her eyes reached Jamsen, her whole world came to a complete standstill. She slowly lowered her hands as she stared in disbelief at the man who she had trusted so completely. She didn't even notice as the shield disappeared.

'You!' Darty screamed in a shrill voice, anger flashing across her face.

Zalan turned with the same anger and quickly drew a long dagger, pointing it towards Jamsen whilst keeping his long sword towards Brisheit. He edged closer, clearly intent on putting himself between Jamsen and Louise.

Jamsen ignored the group. Instead, he flung his bow to his shoulder and turned towards Louise. He stared at her and she stared back, a large lump forming in her throat as she tried to comprehend what this meant.

'Is it true?' she asked in a quiet, unsteady voice. 'You're with Brisheit? It wasn't a coincidence when you met me just after I had arrived in Calaresp, you knew who I was from the start. You weren't actually helping me. It was all lies.' Her voice grew louder and angrier with every word.

'Louise, please, just let me explain. I was indeed sent to find you, with the intention of leading you to Brisheit.'

With these words, Louise turned away from Jamsen, keen for him not to see the tears that were forming in her eyes.

He looked at her desperately as he continued, 'Listen, you have to understand, as soon as I had spent time with you and had gotten to know you, I knew what I was doing was wrong. On that first day, I decided that I was no longer part of Brisheit's army. I have genuinely been trying to protect you.' He tried to grab her hands but before he could, she wrenched them away aggressively. 'I'm on your side,' he pleaded. 'I didn't lead you to into this, I promise!'

Louise simply stared at him, so taken aback by this betrayal that she couldn't even begin to form a reply.

'Well now, that is a shame,' Brisheit said, his voice cutting through the silence. 'You were a great addition to my army and I would have to say, an often-ruthless

Captain. However, regardless of whether you had wanted to remain with us or not, we no longer need you.'

Before he had finished speaking and before Louise even had the chance to acknowledge what was happening, an arrow pierced through Jamsen's shoulder. He inhaled sharply; his eyes wide as he looked down at the arrow penetrating him. His face had become frighteningly pale. He raised his shaking hands and clearly in a state of shock, he rested them on the arrow and pulled it out. He let out a deep, agonising roar of pain. He brought the arrow to his face and looked closely at the tip; it was coated with a dark purple, clumpy substance.

'Poison,' Jamsen croaked, his gaze flickering from side to side as if he were finding it difficult to focus. He then sank to his knees and collapsed face-first into the ground.

'Jamsen!' Louise screamed. All thoughts of betrayal left her as she rushed to his side. She gently lifted him so he lay on his back, but he winched with pain at each movement. 'Are you okay, Jamsen? What should I do?' she asked, panic coursing through her, her voice cracking as she spoke.

When Jamsen's gaze finally fixed on hers, tears began to form in the corner of his eyes. 'I'm so sorry,' he whispered, a desperate look on his face as poisoned blood, splatter with streaks of purple gushed from the wound on his shoulder. 'I really didn't betray you; I would never do that.'

Louise pressed her hand against the wound in a desperate bid to stop the bleeding. He placed his hand over hers, more interested in expressing his remorse to

Louise than dealing with his wound. A single tear trickled down his face as he stared at her.

'It's going to be okay. You're going to be okay, I promise,' she whispered as she frantically searched for a way of helping him, paying no attention to the sniggering soldiers, or the fact that they were starting to close in on them.

The rest of the group had their weapons raised, ready to try and fight them off. Louise manoeuvred herself and pulling his shirt back, she rested both of her hands across Jamsen's wound. Golden streaks began to flash through her body, primarily across her arms. Where his wound had been gushing blood and poison, it now glowed with the same golden shine. Louise could feel intense and incredible power streaming through her.

She was vaguely aware of voices in the distance as she desperately tried to heal Jamsen. She heard Brisheit screaming, 'I want the princess, that old, poor excuse for a soldier, Zalan and the tall woman alive. They are still of use to me. Kill the others. Now!'

There was a sudden eruption of movement all around her as the soldiers rushed forward to attack. They had clearly decided that the wreags were too dangerous to release as they would have just killed everything in sight. Louise was vaguely aware of intense fighting going on around her as her group of friends battled a continuous onslaught of soldiers. She couldn't dwell on this for too long, however, as her priority was to save Jamsen. As soon as she was sure he was going to be alright she would use her powers to help the others.

Suddenly, out of the corner of her eye, she saw a

large revolting man creeping up on Trevel as he fought two other soldiers. He had raised a large, blood-covered axe, ready to swing it at Trevel's head. Louise was torn for a second and then before she could stop herself, she raised one hand, keeping the other on Jamsen. She mustered even more power and sent a ball of light towards the large man, sending him flying backwards. Trevel continued to fight the other two men but was aware of what had happened and gave Louise a small nod. In quick succession, Louise did the same for both Matok and Zalan, still healing Jamsen at the same time.

Louise soon felt her energy and powers beginning to dwindle. Although she had reconnected with the Whisper, her body was still adapting to the powers and she was currently limited as to how much of it she could actually use.

As she healed Jamsen, she felt a sharp stabbing pain building up in her shoulder. The pain intensified; each breath became increasingly difficult to draw. She began to struggle to see, shapes and colours merging together as she faded in and out of consciousness.

When Louise finally took her hands away from Jamsen she sank to the ground just beside him. She was vaguely aware of Jamsen stirring very slightly beside her and when she was sure that he was okay, she felt a surge of relief.

She felt his hand weakly touch her face, 'You shouldn't have wasted your powers on me. I'm not worth it.' he whispered.

It took all of her energy to force her head up to look at Jamsen. She only had a second to take in his face before she saw large hands grabbing him around the throat and pulling him backwards. This was met with shouts of triumph and mockery. Instantly, faces loomed in front of her; toothless bloody grins and acrid smells that were able to seep through her exhaustion. With Jamsen no longer within sight, she struggled to muster even just an ounce of energy to save her friends, Jamsen and herself. Nothing happened, however, and seconds later the world around her lurched and began to move as they ruthlessly lifted her and carried her away. She tried to look around to locate the others but she had reached the end of her tether and the world faded into nothing.

Chapter Thirty-seven

Louise slowly began to wake up. She kept her eyes shut as she struggled to overcome the extreme exhaustion coursing through her body. Beneath her, she felt a cold, hard, damp surface. As memories flooded back she scrunched her eyes, desperately trying to shut out all that had happened, trying to block out the horrific reality that was waiting for her.

When she did finally open her eyes, the sight that met her was even worse than she could have possibly imagined. She was in a small dark cell, the only light coming from a tiny, barred window at the top of the far wall. From what she could see, the walls and floor were covered with a light blue, mould-like moss. She could just make out a door on the far wall; it was made of iron and had no windows or handle.

There was an overwhelming smell of rot and urine in the cell which made Louise want to throw up. She slowly pushed herself upwards and leant her back against the cold and wet wall. Her hand went absentmindedly to her shoulder, where she could still feel flashes of pain. Carefully pulling back her shirt, she wasn't surprised to find that she had a prominent scar exactly where Jamsen had been shot with the arrow.

Subconsciously, her hand moved to her chest to grasp the Whisper. Since having it, the Whisper had become a great source of power and confidence. Where the small pendant should have been resting, there was nothing—her hand was met with air and her cold clammy skin. She began frantically searching her body for the missing Whisper, fear trickling through her as she realised, she may have lost it. As her search continued without success, a void began to appear within her—the Whisper was gone. A more frightening prospect began to dawn on her; there was a very good chance that the Whisper had been taken by Brisheit and his men when she was captured.

Her mind reeled with this realisation, she couldn't even begin to comprehend how disastrous this was. Brisheit had managed to obtain the one object that the rebels had kept away from him for years, at the cost of countless lives. As this thought began to consume her, the guilt intensified as she considered the number of innocent people who had died for her. Now, in just a matter of weeks, Louise had let them all down. She had failed.

Brisheit had captured both her and the Whisper in one sweep—the two things he needed to unlock the power for himself. She knew that once he had taken her blood and bathed the Whisper in it, he would not only be unstoppable but would unleash horrors unlike any Calaresp had seen before. If her ancestor—who had begun as a kind and caring person—had been corrupted by it, then she could only begin to imagine what it would do to someone who was already, incomprehensibly evil.

Louise slowly got to her feet, steadying herself against the wall. She carefully moved around her dimly-lit cell, desperately trying to find a means of escape. She even tried to lift herself up to the barred window, her fingertips scrabbling against the bricks of the wall. However, she was too weak and the window was just a little too high. She still felt unsteady on her feet, so she gave up and slumped back against the wall, despair spreading through her. Slowly and with a tearless sob, she sank back to the ground, her head resting in her hands.

Louise couldn't fully recall what had happened. She had been so engrossed in healing Jamsen that she had only seen fragments of the fight. A memory suddenly flashed into her mind. The last thing she could remember seeing as she was dragged away was Jamsen, slumped on the ground, men hitting and kicking him. Behind him, she remembered two shapes, two bodies lying lifelessly next to each other.

'They can't all be dead,' she whispered to herself. Nevertheless, despair began to spread through Louise like wildfire and tears streamed down her face. She had failed everyone, from Jamsen and her parents to the rebels who had sacrificed themselves to return her to her throne. She would never be able to fulfil the expectations of the people of Calaresp. The sobs began to explode from her involuntarily as she waited for her fate.

Louise remained this way for what felt like hours. She continued to cry until she felt that there was nothing left to come out of her. At this point, she was overcome by exhaustion, and with little thought to the filthy conditions of the ground below her, she lay down. Intent on blocking the world out until they came to take her.

As she tried to sleep, she was distracted by a sharp pain in her chest. Initially, she thought it was a result of the injury she had taken from Jamsen, but on further investigation, she realised something was sticking into her as she lay on the ground. She forced herself upright and began fishing around in her shirt pocket. Her fingertips brushed lightly against something hard in the corner; it was caught in the seam of her shirt and when she first pulled at it, she found she couldn't get a grip on it. After a few failed attempts, she finally managed to pull out a small dark purple bead. She recognised it straight away and promptly delved further into her pocket as she searched for more. Using the tips of her nails, she managed to find another two beads. These were smaller than the first.

Louise sat in her dark cell, her findings resting securely in the palm of her outstretched hand. Her mind raced a mile a minute as she considered her options. Eventually, Louise placed two of the beads back in her pocket and positioned the remaining one between her fingers, rubbing it in one direction and then another. A small smile gradually began to spread across her face and she suddenly knew what she was supposed to do.

Standing up, she prepared herself.

Chapter Thirty-eight

Once the window was fully formed Louise stepped through. She was instantly blinded by the intensity of the natural light now surrounding her. She blinked desperately trying to adapt to her new surroundings. Once she had, Louise was amazed at the sight in front of her. Despite being back in Earth, she was clearly no longer in Scotland; let alone the woods she'd been in when she had first left.

Louise was now stood in the alley of an old, cobbled street that was lined with colourfully painted, quaint little shops, creating a picture book scene. There were a variety of signs and banners advertising the goods and offers available, and the people wandering about created a vibrant and friendly atmosphere. A stark contrast to the dark, dank cell she'd been stuck in moments before. She turned just in time to see the window to Calaresp vanish.

Still feeling shaken and weak, Louise began to make her way down the street, barely noticing the people she passed. She slowly became aware that some of the shoppers around her were noticing her dishevelled state; they whispered and some even pointed with unsubtle fingers. Louise began to feel incredibly self-conscious and without her Whisper, she felt powerless and vulnerable.

As soon as the opportunity arose, Louise darted down a side road, leaving behind the busy shopping street. She hoped to find a quiet spot in which she could open another window and return to Calaresp. With her magic and memories restored she hoped she could now control where the windows opened. Her escape from the bustling street was short-lived, however, as she soon came to the entrance of another, busy street filled with even more shops. The sounds of seagulls pierced the air and as she followed their flight through the sky. Louise noticed a large estuary, situated on one side of the town. Struck by the smell of fresh sea air she could see that the estuary in front of her led out into the sea. It was filled with boats of all shapes and sizes, some docked whilst others were either leaving or arriving. Fishermen, locals and tourists were everywhere and despite her distraught state, a small part of Louise was still able to acknowledge the beauty of this charming seaside town.

To open another window, to get back to Calaresp, she'd have to find somewhere quiet and secluded. Looking around her, she desperately tried to find somewhere suitable. She finally noticed a sign opposite her that pointed right through the centre of the town. It read: *'Coastal path to Stoke Fleming'*. A flash of hope filled Louise as she felt sure that a coastal path would be far more likely to offer seclusion.

She started off, ensuring that she followed the signs. Eventually, the road she'd been following brought her to a relatively small castle situated on the water's edge, where the estuary met the sea. It was fixed right into the corner of the landscape, neatly hidden by trees. Fully aware that she was short on time, Louise rushed past the castle car park and hesitated momentarily, then a grim smile spread across her face. She'd found the perfect spot. She clambered down a rock face until she was on a tiny — and most importantly — totally secluded pebbled beach.

Taking a few seconds to regain her breath and composure, she began to consider her options. She desperately wanted to get back, to find her friends, and to try and help them. She was also desperately keen — Whisper or not — to help the people of Calaresp and to try and rid them of Brisheit's presence.

A sudden thought struck Louise and she held her hand, palm upright in front of her. Even though she didn't have the Whisper, she was certain that she still retained a little of its magic within her body. She forced herself to concentrate on that small light within her, shutting her eyes and gritting her teeth as she willed her body to create a flame in her hand. However, when she finally opened her eyes again, her palm was still empty. Frustration and desperation flooded through her and she felt the small flash of magic she had detected edging even further away from her consciousness.

Trying to force herself to remain strong, Louise held her head in her hands. Despite her best efforts, her emotions started to get the better of her and an angry, growl-like scream erupted from within her. As it did, she flung her hands away from her dramatically and at that moment, a small ball of light appeared in the centre of her palm, floating just above her skin, rotating furiously. Louise looked at it, relief surging through her body. A few seconds later it vanished, but its very presence had been such an immense comfort to her, confirming that she did still have a little magic. It filled her with a tiny yet comforting flicker of confidence. She did it again, just to prove it wasn't a fluke.

Then, without hesitation, she pulled out the small bead that she had returned to the safety of her pocket. With a final glance around her, she smiled, satisfied with her decision, happy at the prospect of returning. She concentrated on Calaresp, on the castle, her home and soon a small window had opened just in front of her.

Chapter Thirty-nine

As soon as she became aware of her surroundings Louise's senses fled back to her. She surveyed the room, trying to decipher where in the castle she had appeared. She was now in a small, dusty sitting room. Judging by the damp smell of neglect and the tatty moth-eaten armchairs scattered around the room, she felt certain that the room hadn't been used for a very long time. With a small triumphant smile, she knew she was back in the castle, she cast her memory back as she tried to work out where she was.

She pieced together a memory of a room containing large bookcases full of beautifully colourful and well-read books. She remembered a roaring fire, and in front, two beautiful dark red armchairs. Louise immediately looked over at the tatty remains of the chair she had noticed moments before. Her hand instinctively reached down to touch, the memory of her father sitting in it flashed through her mind. She scanned the room once more and felt angry as she thought of her happy, loving family, who Brisheit had so cruelly extinguished. All for the need and want of power and bloodshed. This anger quickly turned into a determined resolve. This was her home and she was going to take it back from him. She was going to return Calaresp to the wonderful place it had been when she was a child.

Noticing a large arching window to her right, Louise wandered over and looked outside. She gasped as she looked out onto a landscape she suddenly remembered and loved with a burning passion. She was able to identify every inch of the castle grounds and when she saw what used to be her father's much loved and pristinely kept garden, she clenched her fists, nails digging into her skin.

The once beautiful space was now filled with small and presumably rather young wreags. Around their necks were thick and powerful chains that were attached to solid, sturdy poles. The ground was now mud, with no trace of the lush grass that had once covered it. Scattered across the mud were the remnants of mauled meals, blood, and scraps of skin and fur. As she looked closer, Louise realised there were a significant number of human skulls in the mud too, none of which were without considerable damage. Louise forced herself to look away, determined that she was going to return every inch of the castle to its former glory.

Taking a deep breath, Louise pushed aside the memories that were forcefully resurfacing and made her way over to the door. Opening it very slightly and with considerable care, she peeked out into the hallway. She was terrified that there would be soldiers or a patrol waiting right outside. Heart beating fast, Louise looked both left and right and was relieved to see that there was no one there.

She quietly made her way down the hallway, knowing it would eventually take her to one of the many staircases that led straight to the Main Hall, where Brisheit would inevitably be.

As she crept along, every single one of her senses was on high alert, the slightest sound setting her heart racing. Her feet itched in their readiness to run. As she tiptoed along, her feet instinctively picked their way across the floorboards, avoiding the areas which would creek and potentially draw attention to her.

The staircase had wooden bannisters that framed two small balconies on either side of the stairway. They reached right the way down to the bottom, where they curled gracefully into small circles. The stairs were covered in a dark green carpet which stopped on the last stair. Louise edged her way onto the staircase with considerable care, making sure no one was around.

As she placed her foot on the first step, a tentative hand on the bannister, Louise heard something that made her stop in her tracks. She took a deep breath as a sound echoed from the hallway opposite to the one she had just emerged from. Louise paused, listening closely, not even daring to breathe. At first, she heard nothing. Then the murmur of multiple voices reached her. Cutting through them, there came a deep and heartless bark of a reply that Louise recognised as belonging to Brisheit.

Louise froze for a second, unsure as to what she should do. She was half tempted to run down the stairs whilst the rest of her body seemed to be frozen to the spot, incapable of moving. With barely a moment to spare, Louise regained control of herself, she darted back down the corridor she had left. She threw herself through the first door she came to, quickly and quietly closed the door behind her. She scanned the room to make sure no one was in there and instantly recognising it, she pushed aside the memories that leapt into her mind. Instead, she leant against the door, opening it a fraction so she could see what was going on.

Seconds later, she saw a group of men arrive at the top of the stairs, all walking carefully around a central figure. Six men were surrounding him, five of whom almost equalled him in size and wore various styles of battle-worn armour. The sixth, standing closest to Brisheit, was considerably smaller and very lanky. Despite the failings in his stature, the smallest man seemed to be the most confident and at ease. The rest seemed to be extremely agitated as Brisheit's tone grew louder and louder.

'So, what you're telling me,' Brisheit said, the anger clear in his tone, 'is that not only did you let the Whisper slip through your grasp when it was served to you on a plate, but now you have also lost the princess. She was in a locked cell! How did you lose her?!'

Even from her hiding place, Louise could feel the anger and the tension radiating from him. One of the large men mumbled a reply but Louise couldn't quite make it out. Brisheit turned towards him with a look of sheer hatred that made all but the small man shrink back in fear. An older, well-built man stepped up from the back of the group, he wiped the small beads of sweat from his brow with the back of his hand before he spoke.

'The cell was locked. We don't know how she

managed to escape it, let alone the castle.'

The small man snorted, a look of disdain on his face. 'I would imagine someone helped her.' He then turned to Brisheit, 'Someone within the castle helped her to escape my Lord — they betrayed you.'

Brisheit seemed to contemplate this for a second before grunting his support for the theory. 'In which case you need to question everyone who had access to the cells, everyone who could have helped her. Use whatever methods necessary to get a confession. Then I want you to take them out into the courtyard and torture them in front of everyone, let them all see the consequences of helping the Clarest princess. In the meantime, I want you to split the men into two teams; one to pursue the princess whilst the others scour the woods for the Whisper. Search everyone you come across. If I don't have both before the sun sets, I will cut off one arm from each of you and feed it to my wreags. You know how they obsess once they've had just a little bit of their prey. They'll wait until you're alone, vulnerable, probably sleeping, and finish off what they started.' He glared maliciously at the men around him. 'Now GO!' he bellowed before turning around and making his way down the stairs.

The small man followed him with a superior look on his face.

'How are you progressing with the portals?' Brisheit asked him in a quieter voice.

'Very well, my Lord,' the small man replied in a sharp-pitched voice. 'We need to make a few alterations, then they'll be ready. Then once they are activated, they should force Calaresp and Earth to merge into one. There will be some destruction and I'm sure some deaths, but that's inevitable.'

'Have you found a way to keep my armies and I safe during the transition?'

'We are very close to a solution. If all are kept within this castle, we should be able to minimise casualties, although I can't say the same for anyone outside of these walls, in either world.'

Brisheit laughed, 'I couldn't care less what happened to them, as long as I can take control of both worlds. Then with the unlocked power of the Whisper, I should be unstoppable.'

At this point, they went too far down the staircase for Louise to hear anymore. However, she had heard enough for all the colour to rush out of her face. The fact that he intended to merge the two worlds was incomprehensible. The act itself would kill thousands and those remaining would be forced to live under Brisheit's cruel and ruthless dictatorship.

Creeping out of the room, Louise made sure the halls were clear before she made her way to the balcony framing the staircase. She was there just in time to see Brisheit and the small man enter the Main Hall to their left, whilst the soldiers walked straight past to the castle entrance.

She was filled with hope as it dawned on her, they didn't have the Whisper either. Judging by his comments, Louise felt fairly certain that Brisheit believed her to have hidden it somewhere. She knew this to be false, although the only other option she could think of was that it had fallen to the ground and had been lost during her capture.

Thoughts whizzed through her head as she considered what to do. She quickly decided that her best option would be to see if she could hear more, to find out exactly what was going on. That way she might be able to get an idea as to what happened to the rest of her group and the Whisper. Either would give her a better chance of defeating Brisheit. This was mingled with the somewhat selfish desire to know what exactly had happened to Jamsen. She was fairly certain he was dead, but she just had to know for sure.

Edging out of the door, she made sure that the coast was clear and then crept out into the hallway. She became instantly aware that she was alone, the silence around her almost oppressive.

Forever observing her surroundings, she began creeping down the stairs. When she reached the bottom, a memory suddenly shifted in her mind as she saw the wooden panels at the side of the staircase.

Moving towards them, she crouched down and gently fingered the top right corner of one of the panels. Lightly etched into the wood was a small rose. A smile spread onto her face as she remembered her father bringing her here, late at night, when the rest of the castle was asleep.

'Here,' he had whispered to her, pointing to the rose. 'Your grandfather and I drew that rose — both here and in a few other places throughout the castle. Behind it, there are secret passageways. Your mother and I, and now you, are the only people who know about them.'

Louise traced the rose with her finger and then pressed the largest petal. As she did so the whole panel gently swung inwards. It revealed a small passage leading into darkness. As she stared into it, new memories came flooding back to her as she remembered all the routes hidden behind the walls.

She heard the sound of approaching footsteps and without hesitation she climbed into the darkness, using a small piece of string on the inside of the door to click it shut. As darkness consumed her, the footsteps drew closer and she remained silent, not wanting to draw any attention to herself. Once they had gone, she raised her palm and placed all her concentration into forcing the flow of her magic. As she did, a small ball of blue light appeared, illuminating the passageway. It was clear that no one had been here for a very long time, as there were spiders' webs everywhere.

Louise cringed slightly as she spotted a few spiders slinking along the thin silver strands. Although she wasn't necessarily frightened of spiders, the thought of them crawling across her skin was not a pleasant one. She made her way forward, aware that her mission was far more important. She pushed through them, the light still in the palm of her hand.

As she reached the end of that passageway it split into two directions and she hesitated for a moment. As she looked both ways, a map of the secret tunnels popped into her head. Turning her head to the right she knew that if she were to follow this route, she would be able to sneak into the Main Hall.

Quickly and without allowing herself the opportunity to change her mind, Louise took the passage to her right. She soon lifted the light to the wall and began to study it. She knew there was another small panel that would open up into a door. Using her spare hand, she gently brushed it against the wall, searching for any abnormalities in the wood.

Eventually, Louise's finger touched upon a small,

barely noticeable nook in the top corner of the panel. Lifting her hand to shroud it in light, Louise noticed the vague outline of a small flower. It had been distorted by woodworm and worn down by general degradation.

She pushed the flower and with a small click, it swung in towards her. The second it opened, Louise was hit by the sound of Brisheit's harsh voice, shouting and threatening. The voices that replied were quiet and subdued. She remained where she was for a few minutes, extinguished the light in her hand, then nervously stepped into the same room as the man who had murdered her parents and thousands of others. All of a sudden, she heard them mentioning the 'Whisper', but the secret passage was just a little bit too far away and when Brisheit wasn't shouting, she couldn't make out exactly what he was saying.

With a great deal of care, she pulled the small door further open, peeked out, and was relieved to find that the passageway was still covered by the same tapestry that had been there when she had been just a girl. This particular tapestry ran down a large section of the wall and if she remained behind it, she knew she could get closer to Brisheit without being detected. She eased her way out and paused for a moment, ensuring the passage door remained slightly open in case she needed to make a quick escape.

Taking care to be as quiet as possible, she crept between the wall and the tapestry, trying her best to make sure she didn't cause the latter to move. She pulled out her small knife, which the guards had fortunately not taken from her before her imprisonment, presumably not acknowledging it as a weapon. She gripped it tightly in the same hand that moments before had held the ball of light. She didn't intend to attack but felt it was sensible to be prepared for anything. When she had gone as far as she could, Louise knelt low to the ground and now found she could hear everything. With considerable care, she peeked out from behind the tapestry. Brisheit was instantly in her sights, sat slumped in a grand throne that had once belonged to her father. When she had last seen it, the throne had been a beautiful green with dark blue symbols embroidered along it. Now it had become a dirty brown, with a few dark red stains that looked uncannily like blood. The armrests had scratches and cuts all along them, as if they had been hacked at with a knife or sword. Louise shuddered as the wonderful memories of her father in this room were overlapped by the horrific scene in front of her.

Chapter Forty

Brisheit was flanked by two large guards standing on either side of his seat. In front of him was the small man that had been on the staircase along with two other men of similar stature. They were all staring at two large, wildly frightened soldiers who only had eyes for Brisheit.

'So, are you or are you not certain that Captain Jamsen was dead when you left him? Brisheit asked in a quiet voice that was full of anger and aggression.

Louise felt her heart flicker for a second and an internal conflict flared up within her as the hope of him being alive mingled with the anger she still felt at learning his true identity. She found herself almost holding her breath as she desperately listened to the interrogation unfolding in front of her.

'Well,' said a gruff, terrified voice. 'Your shot was a good one, the poison was fully absorbed and he was covered in blood. I mean, I looked to see if he was breathing...' The man paused as if trying to collect his thoughts. 'He wasn't, I'm sure that he wasn't.'

At these words, Brisheit slowly moved forwards in

his seat, his expression darkening.

'We both kicked him and beat him badly, and he still didn't react,' the man promptly said, sensing the danger he was in. 'I even kicked him in the head a few times, but he didn't budge. With your perfect shot and the blows he got from us, he couldn't have survived. And anyway, he's been left out in the woods, alone and seriously injured. No one's going to find him apart from hungry beasts.' The man dared a grin as he looked up to Brisheit.

There was a moment's silence and it was as if everyone was holding their breath, waiting to see how Brisheit was going to react. He studied the two men in front of him for a second and then let out a harsh laugh. 'Good!' he said loudly.

The small man raised a hand shyly to the air and let out a small cough, clearly keen to get Brisheit's attention. Brisheit signalled the man over.

'What is it, Alonx?' he asked in an almost respectful tone that Louise hadn't believed him to be capable of.

'Well, we must keep in mind that the young princess was trying to use her magic on him before we were able to capture her. It may well be she was trying to heal him.'

Brisheit considered this for a moment. 'If she were, do you think she could have been successful?'

Alonx hesitated for a moment and then an impertinent smile spread across his sly-looking face. 'Although there is a slight possibility, I would very much doubt she has either the capability or the power to wield the magic that would be necessary.'

'She managed that damned shield though?' Brisheit asked.

'Indeed, but that wouldn't have taken as much effort, and you saw how quickly it fell once she was distracted. We must keep in mind that she's been without her powers on Earth all this time.'

'Yes, but remember the prophecies. You were the one who told me how powerful she was going to become. That's why we had to take action when we did — before she could become a threat to us.'

'I know and had she remained in Calaresp, no doubt she would have been the most powerful woman to have ever lived. But because she left and has spent most of her life on Earth, her powers won't have developed in the same way. She should be capable of a few minor acts of magic, nothing more.'

Brisheit nodded in understanding, 'And you're sure of this?' he asked.

'Yes,' Alonx replied. 'Have I been wrong yet, my Lord?' he said with a sickening smile.

Brisheit considered him for a moment and then turned back to the two soldiers. 'Just in case, I want you to return to the bodies we left behind and to burn them. You can help in the search for the Whisper whilst you're there.'

There was a moment's hesitation, which Brisheit observed with evident anger. 'GO!' he shouted, frustrated by the delay. There was a sudden clatter of footsteps as the two men burst into action and left the room.

A tremendous sense of disorientation swept over Louise — a sensation that was becoming all too familiar. She looked around in trepidation, fully expecting to see mysterious blue figures drifting around, reflecting events from the past. She began to hope it was simply her imagination, her terrified self-conscious playing tricks on her. Then she heard distant shouts and screams edging ever closer. Then, without opening the doors, the blue ghostly shapes Louise had been expecting entered the room.

A second version of Brisheit — one with a blue tint — stormed through the hall. He was followed by a troop of men, all of whom had bold, triumphant looks on their faces. With a bolt of shock, Louise saw that a man and a woman were being dragged ruthlessly into the room. Brisheit sat on the throne, the prisoners were thrown down in front of him. As they looked up at their captor, Louise clasped a hand to her mouth, the prisoners in front of her were her parents.

Forced onto their knees, her mother and father looked up at Brisheit with defiance. Despite the strength they were trying to portray, Louise was sure she could see tears streaming down her mother's face. She was aware that Brisheit was speaking, but she couldn't hear a word; her attention was set on her parents and nothing else. Analysing every inch of their faces, carving every detail into her memory.

As Brisheit let out a cruel laugh, Louise's attention finally drifted to him. He had moved to Louise's father, a long-bloodied blade held in his hand.

'Now,' he said, his voice echoing through the hall. 'Now, I'm going to stab you. But I'll make sure you live long enough to see your wife die, and as you die yourself, you'll fade away in the knowledge that I'm also going to kill your daughter. Then this entire Kingdom will be mine and eventually, I'll get to Earth and that too will fall under my rule.'

He raised his sword and with a blur of blue light,

forced it into Louise's father's side, just below his ribs. Her mother screamed as her father groaned and collapsed to the floor in pain. Louise was certain that she could hear her father rasping and gasping for breath. Brisheit then moved over to Louise's mother. She could see her father's attempts to cry out, to move forward to save the woman he loved. But he was too injured — there was nothing he could do and he knew it. Brisheit pulled her mother's hair, forcing her to raise her head. As she did, he took his sword and slowly drew it across her neck, the sharp blade leaving behind a trickling trail of blood. As she began to choke and gasp for air, blood bubbling out of her mouth, Louise could see her father wailing in misery.

Brisheit threw her mother's dead body to the ground and went close to her father, laughing at him cruelly. Louise's father went quiet. Then slowly and painfully he pushed himself up and with surprising speed, he drew out a very small dagger and clumsily lunged at Brisheit. His injuries were too severe and as she watched, Louise knew that her father had no chance.

With a mocking grin, Brisheit simply stood back, leaving Louise's father to collapse to the ground. He laughed at him and without hesitation, lifted his sword once again and gracelessly hacked her father's neck, brutally decapitating him.

The scene remained as it was for a few seconds; her parents lying dead on the ground, Brisheit standing over them with a delighted smile on his face. It slowly began to fade, the blue becoming lighter until it was completely gone. The hall reverted to how it had been moments before. Brisheit sat at his chair, flanked by two men, whilst Alonx and a group of others held conversation she no longer had any interest in hearing.

In a state of complete shock, Louise once again fully hid behind the tapestry. Tears were silently flowing down her face. She held her hand over her mouth to disguise the hiccupping gasps involuntarily escaping her. She tried to process exactly what she had seen, but couldn't get the image of her dying parents out of her mind. She shut her eyes, but they were still there, and the cries from her father when her mother had died still echoed through her mind.

With a strength she didn't know she was capable of, Louise cleared her mind, knowing that she would never forget those images but that she had to put them aside until she was safe. She peeked out from her hiding place to once again get a better look at what was going on. As she looked out, she immediately noticed Alonx pausing in his conversation as if a loud noise or a bad smell had caught his attention. She thought for a minute that his gaze flicked in her direction and she was terrified he was going to spot her. She flung herself back into her hiding place and took a few quiet deep breaths to try and calm herself. Aware that she was being slightly reckless but unable to stop herself, she looked out once more, desperate to know whether she had been seen.

Much to her relief, Alonx was once again quietly talking to the group of men. Brisheit was now eating a chicken leg from a plate that was being held out by the soldier beside him.

Deciding that had been too close a call, she thought it would be best to leave before her luck ran out. Just as she started to make her way back behind the tapestry, she noticed Alonx walk over to Brisheit and whisper in his ear. The cruel man grinned slightly and took another swig of his drink, which had been balanced on the arm of the throne. Louise felt a slight temptation to see whether Brisheit had just learnt something of any significance but decided she was still better off leaving.

Louise turned herself around and began her escape, comforted by the continued conversations surrounding her. She slowly made her way back to the entrance to the secret passage.

When it was eventually within sight she subconsciously sped up, every inch of her desperate to leave the room. Out of nowhere, she heard a sound, unnervingly close and before she even had time to react, she saw the tapestry in front of her moving. A spear penetrated the fabric and wedged itself into the wall; this was followed by a second in almost exactly the same place. Instantly blocking the passage.

Chapter Forty-one

A cruel voice she was becoming unnervingly familiar with suddenly echoed through the hall, 'It was so kind of you princess, to save us the trouble of finding you. I must admit I didn't think you'd make it quite as easy as this.'

Dread coursed through every inch of her body and her mind raced as she considered any possible means of escape.

'Are you going to come out and join us? You don't have any other way out,' he continued, his voice almost lazy in tone.

She was aware that she didn't have any other choice at this point and that her best bet would be to confront him and reassess her options. She had to force her reluctant body to move back towards the end of the tapestry.

When she finally came out, she felt remarkably small in the large hall, well aware of the silence now surrounding her. She ignored the additional men in the room and looked directly at Brisheit, desperately hoping that she was successfully hiding her fear.

Brisheit looked back at her with a malicious grin spread across his face. He raised an index finger and gestured for her to move closer.

Alonx was now stood beside Brisheit, looking at Louise with considerable self-satisfaction.

Following her gaze, Brisheit grinned and gestured to Alonx that he had permission to speak. The latter responded with a small nod.

'It's a pleasure to see you again, princess, although I'm sure you won't remember me. Let me introduce myself, my name is Alonx, I was a servant to the Warlocks who schooled you. At the time, nobody noticed me, and nobody realised exactly how much I was able to learn just by watching the Masters at work. So, I absorbed and learnt until I was just as powerful as they were, if not more so. I realised how much potential Commander Brisheit had, and how effective he would be at leading Calaresp — unlike your weak parents! So, I swore my loyalty to him and did all I could to help him achieve his destiny.'

'Alonx here,' Brisheit said with little concern as to whether Alonx had finished speaking, 'has mastered the art of magic very successfully. He was the one who was able to detect you were in the room.' He looked at Alonx once again as if giving permitting him to speak.

'It is of course different to the type of magic you have, but it is nevertheless powerful enough. You have no control over your limited magic and it pulses from you like a heartbeat. Oozes out of you carelessly,' Alonx sneered. 'You had so much potential. In a way, it's such a shame it's been wasted. You are nothing now.'

Louise was vaguely aware that she was now

standing almost exactly where she had just witnessed her parents die. She felt a sudden surge of strength, an almost comforting sensation that told her that she wasn't alone. She felt strangely certain that some element, some trace of her parent's spirits, now stood beside her.

She met Alonx's gaze and before she knew what she was doing, she gave him a small smile. 'I'm not as weak as you think I am,' she said in a quiet yet strong voice.

Brisheit looked angered by the fact she had the audacity not to be frightened.

Louise saw him glance at Alonx as if looking for confirmation as to whether this confidence was unfounded. Alonx maintained his arrogant smile.

'Restrain her, just in case.' Brisheit said to him firmly.

Without hesitation, Alonx pulled out a green powder from a small bag at his side. He whispered inaudible words over it and then blew it in Louise's direction. It all happened so quickly that Louise barely had time to react. As it reached her body, she felt a strange tingling sensation spreading right across her. She felt the remnants of power that remained within her beginning to ebb away and her body locked in place.

She panicked as a weakness spread throughout her, leaving her feeling helpless and pathetic. Brisheit and Alonx looked at one another gloatingly. As she watched them, a burst of anger spread through Louise and this fuelled her. She closed her eyes and forced herself to concentrate. Slowly her body began to fight back and she could feel herself gradually regaining control.

With a surge of warmth, she felt her powers spreading through her body, even stronger than they had been before, almost as strong as when the Whisper sat around her neck. She flung her hand in Alonx's direction and the green powder which had disappeared into her reappeared, suspended in the air. She slowly pointed a finger towards Alonx and as she did, a bright flash occurred and the green powder was flung back towards him. It penetrated Alonx, immediately freezing him in place, his expression stuck between an arrogant smile and a look of shock.

Brisheit rose to his feet and drew out his sword. He glared at Alonx with an expression of utter fury, then with even more anger, he looked at Louise. Some of his men stepped forward, also with their weapons raised, but Brisheit held his hand out.

'Stay where you are,' Brisheit said in a deep voice. 'She's mine.' He began to move towards her. 'You may have some power, but I know you haven't got the Whisper. Even when you had it, all you were capable of were a few party tricks. I am not threatened by you.'

Louise simply smiled in reply, hoping she looked a lot more confident than she actually felt. She raised her hand and created a ball of flames. At the sight of it, Brisheit's eyes widened and he cautiously raised his sword. She forced the flame in his direction and at first, it looked like it was going to hit him. However, it vanished before it reached him, as if it had run out of power.

Brisheit stared at her with a look of surprise, then delighted amusement. 'Well, well, not as powerful as you thought, are you?' he asked in a mocking tone.

Not allowing herself to be phased by her failure,

Louise raised her hand again. He was now cackling and moving closer to her, the sword ready in his hand. This time nothing happened and she began to feel herself panicking. She tried to snap his legs together to disable him as she had done with Shelt, but again, nothing happened.

Brisheit was now clearly able to see her dilemma and his laugh became increasingly wild and ecstatic. Before she was able to do anything else Brisheit had reached her, a large hand grabbing her ruthlessly around her throat and raising her from the ground so that her feet wriggled desperately in the air. Louise found all the oxygen immediately leaving her body; her mouth opened and shut in desperation and her hands scrabbled pointlessly at his. Her lungs felt like they were about to explode and she felt the world around her beginning to waver and spin.

An idea suddenly reached through the buzz and pointless noise that had filled her brain. She reached down to her pocket and with desperation, she pulled out her small knife. Clutching it in her hand, she used any remaining strength to plunge it into the top of Brisheit's chest.

The effect was instantaneous. He quickly let go of her, sending her plummeting to the ground like a forsaken doll. Louise smashed into the floor, her body filled with an instantaneous pain.

Brisheit looked at the knife that was embedded just under his collar bone. He stared at it with a look of confusion for a second, then with little pause, he pulled the dagger out and threw it to the ground. Blood flew out of his wound but he seemed to barely notice.

Meanwhile, Louise had slowly begun crawling

away from him, still gasping for breath. In two steps, however, Brisheit was able to catch up with her and he knelt over her, blood now dripping on her from his open wound.

'Nice try,' he mocked as he grabbed her arm. He dragged her across the room back towards the throne, behind which Alonx still watched, frozen in position. Brisheit flung her body to the ground. 'I'm not going to kill you, at least not until I have the Whisper. But that doesn't mean I can't grievously injure you. Almost kill you. Put you into a state that will make you wish you were dead. Then this idiot,' he said, indicating to Alonx, 'will preserve you so that your blood remains nice and fresh for the Whisper.'

Louise desperately tried to think of a means of escape, but her choices seemed limited.

'The irony,' Brisheit continued, 'is that one way or another, your life is going to end in the same spot your parents both died.' He knelt to the ground and drew out a long sharp sword, alarmingly similar to the one that she had seen him using on her parents. 'Where to start,' he said quietly, as if almost talking to himself.

He pushed the point of the sword into Louise's cheek and she instantly felt the pain as he dragged it across her face. A warm trickle followed the movement of his sword as blood began to descend down her cheek. As pain and fury pulsed through her, Louise was only vaguely aware that her right hand was rising upwards. With a gasp of effort, Louise felt power flowing through her body and before Brisheit knew what was happening, she flung him away from her, sending his body unceremoniously across the room.

Louise watched Brisheit as he lay on the ground. He

didn't get up straight away and Louise's instincts kicked in, suddenly aware that this could be an opportunity to escape. She forced herself to her feet and scrambled across the room, intent on getting underneath the tapestry and forcing open the door of the secret passage. As she ran, she could hear a clattering sound as Brisheit got to his feet, he let out a small roar and she could hear him running towards her. It became clear that he was quickly catching up on her and with a horrible realisation, she knew she wasn't going to make it. Making a flash decision, she quickly turned, changing direction so she was now heading towards the main door.

Out of nowhere, a bolt of air hit her with such force that it winded her, and she was flung across the room. She hit the ground painfully and gulped to regain her breath. Looking around her, dazed, it didn't take her long to work out what had happened — Alonx had somehow freed himself and had used a pot of blue powder to create a bolt of air. Some small particles of it still floated in the air just in front of him. He had a triumphant grin on his face as he pulled out another pot, this time filled with a dark red powder.

Before Louise could move out of the way he had flipped the lid off and raised it to his lips. He mumbled a few words above it before tipping the powder out and blowing at it gently. With remarkable speed, the powder travelled the distance between them and clung to her. Almost immediately, she lost all feeling in her body, her arms and legs involuntarily pulled outwards and she was raised into the air until she was suspended.

Confusion and fear spread through her as quickly as

her own blood. This intensified as she saw Brisheit slowly approaching her, a thunderous look on his face. As he saw Louise frozen in place a quiet laugh rumbled out of him, although the expression on his face never actually changed.

'Well done, Alonx,' he said, his gaze never leaving Louise's. 'Looks like we've got you now, princess.'

Walking right up to her, he drew his dagger, but he didn't linger as he had before. Instead, he plunged it deep into her right thigh. Even though she had no control over her body, it seemed that it didn't block out pain. Louise let out a long, agonising scream as unbearable pain spread through her. Brisheit watched on in satisfaction and then pulled the dagger out again, causing another wave of agony. He played with the knife for a few seconds and before she knew what was happening, he had stabbed her in the other thigh. Louise screamed again.

Brisheit turned away and walked closer to Alonx, laughing. 'You're right, she isn't nearly as powerful as I had expected. Just a few simple, weak tricks.'

Anger rippled through Louise's body mingling with the agonising pain. She knew that if she'd had the Whisper, she would have been far more powerful than in her current state. She let out short, sharp breaths as she tried to regain control of herself. Aware that the situation wasn't looking particularly hopeful.

All of a sudden, they all turned their heads as the main doors flung open, slamming harshly into the stone walls surrounding them. A lone figure stood in the doorway staring in at them, followed by the shouts and cries of outraged soldiers. Louise was beginning to feel lightheaded, because of this, it took her eyes a few seconds to identify the figure ahead of her. Brisheit had experienced no such problem, letting out a growl as he recognised the intruder.

Then Louise realised who it was—Jamsen. He remained where he was for a few seconds as he assessed the room. Then as the men pursuing him got closer, he turned and slammed the doors shut behind him. Using a rope from his pocket, he tied it around the door handles, temporarily securing them.

Louise felt a strange mingle of emotion as she watched him. She was overjoyed to find him still alive but a nagging doubt at the back of her mind made her wonder who exactly he was here to help. Her own heart answered this question as it filled with such overwhelming joy as he made his way towards her.

Brisheit watched on with an expression of amusement. Jamsen looked at him warily but his concern for Louise was too overwhelming to stop him. In the meantime, the soldiers outside the Main Hall had already managed to force the door open. They were about to run to Jamsen but Brisheit raised his hand.

'It's fine, we can deal with both of them,' he said with an arrogant tone. The men did as they were told and retreated to the entrance of the room.

Chapter Forty-two

Louise, still suspended in the air, looked at Jamsen as he approached her, the wide smile on his face igniting a flicker of hope within her. His smile soon disappeared as he realised the condition she was in and as he looked at her bloodstained legs, the colour drained from his cheeks.

'Louise, are you alright?' he asked in a gentle voice. 'I'm so glad I found you.' He grasped at her, searching for ropes or any sign of restraints. When he found none, his gaze turned to Alonx and Brisheit. 'What have you done to her?' he growled at them.

'I would say your goodbyes now, Captain. You'll both be dead soon enough,' Brisheit barked a laugh as he looked at Jamsen incredulously. 'Look at you both, without any weapons. I mean, you're powerless. The pair of you are easy pickings now!'

In a flash, Jamsen turned to her, a small smile spreading across his face. He studied her for a moment as if he were trying to take in every detail of her face before the end. He grabbed her hand and although she couldn't move it, Louise felt him place a small smooth

The Whisper of Calaresp

object within it. He wrapped her fingers around it and squeezed it shut.

'Here, I believe this is yours,' he said in a whisper. 'I managed to get it before they took you away.'

At first, she looked at him in confusion, then she felt a strange, warming sensation in her hands. She could feel the warmth beginning to spread through her body as she felt the Whisper's power being restored to her.

Meanwhile, Jamsen turned to face Brisheit.

'So,' Brisheit asked. 'Just out of curiosity, how did you survive? I thought my men had beaten you to death, and my arrow's shot had been clean and effective.' He was obviously only mildly interested; his tone was one of sheer boredom.

'Louise was able to heal your arrow shot with her powers. I think some of her magic was left within me when your men beat me, as I was completely healed about an hour later.'

Brisheit gave a small uninterested grunt, clearly unfazed by the minor bump in his plan. 'Enough talk now, it's time for the two of you to die.'

He nodded at Alonx, who with remarkable speed drew out another vial of red powder, opened it, and blew it away. Moments later, Jamsen was also suspended in the air as he struggled with all his might to move.

'Now, seeing as my men weren't able to take you out the first time, I may as well do it myself. And I'm glad that I can do it in front of you, princess,' Brisheit said with a malicious grin.

He walked towards Jamsen with his dagger held upright in his hand. He held it close to Jamsen's face and looked over at Louise.

'Say goodbye to the Captain.' He raised the dagger, held it at the edge of Jamsen's throat, and pushed it inwards ever so slightly, causing a small trickle of blood to appear.

Louise felt a pang of panic at the very thought of losing Jamsen again. She tightened her grip on the Whisper. She was starting to feel the full extent of her power returning to her, every inch of her body full of that tingling warmth. She shut her eyes and visualised forcing the poisonous red powder from her body. She slowly returned to the ground and turned to Brisheit, anger burning within her. The pain in her legs was overridden by the power now pumping through her body.

Brisheit slowly turned to look at her. For a fraction of a second, a look of fear and surprise spread across his face, quickly replaced by anger. 'Don't you think it's time you gave up? I've seen the extent of your power and it's not exactly something to be concerned about.'

'Perhaps,' Louise replied with a smile. 'But that was before I had this.' She held up the chain of the Whisper and let the pendant dangle.

'Where did you get that?' Brisheit growled, trying with little success to control his anger. Before she had the chance to reply, he continued to talk. 'It doesn't matter, I doubt it'll make much difference. You'll never live up to that stupid prophecy.'

Nevertheless, he raised a finger and signalled to the soldiers at the door. The men ran inside, their weapons raised and aimed at Louise and Jamsen. He moved away from Jamsen, as if bored. This was clearly a signal to his men as four of them raised crossbows and in quick succession, fired arrows aimed at Jamsen.

The Whisper of Calaresp

Calmly, Louise raised her hand and the four arrows simply fell to the ground. Brisheit stared at her uncomfortably and Louise's smile widened in reply. Alonx stepped forward, pulling out another vial from his pocket. Without even looking at him, Louise flicked her hand to the side and Alonx was sent flying across the room until he smashed into the wall, where he crumpled to the ground and ceased moving. She raised her other hand and with her palm upright, she simply waved her hand downwards and Jamsen was freed, his body returning to the ground.

Bisheit's expression became increasingly angry, as a dark shadow spread across it. 'You will never be more powerful than me,' he hissed. 'I deserved this throne and so I took it. You, like your parents, aren't strong enough. Those two wounds in your leg are only a taster of what I'm going to do to you.'

With this, he let out a wild roar and with his dagger raised, he rushed at her, his large body making the ground shake with every step. In this time, Louise had put the Whisper back around her neck. Calmly and with complete composure, she raised her hands and held them out before her. Her entire body was now infused with the golden light from the Whisper. She pushed her hands forward and a flash of golden light flew towards Brisheit and came to a sudden stop; his body wavered for a second and then as if he had been punched, he was forced to the ground. He tried to get up but before he could take even another step, Louise flicked his legs together, locking him in position.

'Get them!' Brisheit screamed, humiliated and angry. 'Get them now!

There were now even more soldiers in the room and

some had brought wreags. At Brisheit's words, at least six of them were released, pounding towards Louise and Jamsen. Jamsen, who had armed himself with Brisheit's discarded dagger, stepped between Louise and their enemies, ready to fight. But before he could do anything, Louise had once again raised her hand and as she did, a purple light appeared within it. She let it loose towards the approaching wreags; it passed harmlessly through Jamsen but when it reached the wreags it wrapped around them, covering them completely. It then disappeared taking the wreags with it. She then sent a second light and using both hands, spread it across the entire far side of the room; when it made contact with the soldiers, they all stopped exactly where they were. She waved her hand out one last time and with a flash of light, the soldiers all disappeared.

Jamsen stood beside her and watched in sheer amazement. She spared him a quick smile and then turned back to Brisheit, whose face was now almost completely red, spit flicking out of his mouth as he let out hisses of anger.

'Your men are all gone, Brisheit. I am also going to destroy each and every wreag that you have created. They are cruel and unnatural beasts, whose nature can never be changed.' Louise slowly approached Brisheit, the power still pulsing through her body. She felt an almost uncontrollable sense of anger and she was surprised at the number of different ways in which she was now imagining killing Brisheit. 'First,' she said, almost in a whisper. 'I'm going to have to deal with you!'

Louise flicked her index finger upwards and as if he were a puppet, Brisheit got to his feet. Brisheit roared with anger and outrage that Louise was controlling him with such ease. She could see him struggling against her powers but to no avail.

'You killed my parents, and you've destroyed Calaresp, killing thousands of innocent people.' Louise moved ever closer to her captive.

'You're weak and pathetic,' Brisheit spat in reply. 'Just like your parents.'

'It's your turn to die, and I'm going to make sure it's slow and incredibly painful. Just as you had intended for me.'

Louise raised her hands, becoming increasingly aware of the extent of the power pulsing through her body. She knew that if she did want to kill him quickly, all she had to do was click her fingers and it would happen. She felt a moment's doubt, something deep within her telling her that she didn't need to kill him at all. It was an awareness that if she were to kill him, something within her would change forever. The power pulsed through her again, and as it did the doubts left her mind.

Louise raised a finger towards Brisheit and slowly moved it upwards. As she did, a piece of skin from Brisheit's face began to peel away. He screamed in agony and outrage. Louise carried on, moving to the other side, taking another strip of skin.

Unbeknown to Louise, as she tortured her captive, the once golden glow that spread through her body and the Whisper began to darken, and dark purple vein-like streaks appeared across her skin. Her eyes turned into endless, black pits. As it did, her vision, her heart, and even her intentions darkened. She soon found herself thoroughly enjoying her revenge. One side of his face was now almost entirely without skin, his flesh glistening with fresh blood. His eyes bulged with pain and anger, prompting Louise to consider taking his eyes out next.

All of a sudden Louise felt a hand tightly gripping her arm and pulling her away. Louise spun around, the power coursing around her. She felt overwhelming anger at whoever had dared to interrupt her.

'Louise,' a familiar voice said loudly, piercing through the darkness. It made Louise hesitate for a split second. As she did, a hand gently touched her face, the voice once again reaching her. 'Look at me Louise, you need to come back to me. This isn't you; this is the Whisper.'

Louise was filled with confusion as an internal battle ensued within her between the darkness and the light. Out of nowhere, Louise felt Jamsen gently kissing her. As he did, love and hope filled her heart and as they shone, it banished all of the darkness. The hatred and the anger simply vanished and as she looked into Jamsen's eyes, she felt dawning horror as she realised what she had been about to do.

'I don't know what happened,' Louise croaked in a barely audible whisper.

'It's okay,' Jamsen replied, holding her tightly. 'I think it was the Whisper, I think you allowed its power to take over you. It's always been said that the Whisper is capable of incredible good and evil. You and your great-great-great-grandmother are the only two people strong enough to have used it to its full potential. It destroyed her, but you've managed to overcome it.'

This time Louise was the one who kissed Jamsen, gently placing a hand on his cheek as she did. For her, it was the kiss of a lifetime and filled her with the love and happiness that had temporarily been absent.

'You'll be okay,' he whispered. 'You just need to remember who you are.'

She stared at him for a second longer and then turned around to look at Brisheit.

'Just kill me. You may as well do. Whilst I live, I will do all I can to find a way to kill you, to take back my rightful place as ruler,' Brisheit hissed at her. 'So just kill me! Or are you not strong enough?!'

Louise merely stared back at him; all anger having left her. All she felt now was pity. 'I'm not going to kill you, I won't be like you.' Brisheit spat a combination of blood and saliva just in front of her feet. Louise gave him a small smile. 'That doesn't mean, however, I'm going to let you get away with all of the awful things you did.'

Louise flicked her hand and all of the missing skin returned to Brisheit's face as if nothing had happened. His expression didn't change. Instead, he just looked at her with a look of sheer hatred. With a wave of her hand, his mouth closed, and despite his best efforts he couldn't utter another word. She waved her hand again and he stood motionless, his eyes staring straight ahead as if hypnotised.

The sound of footsteps approaching the Main Hall echoed towards them. Both Louise and Jamsen turned around in anticipation, both readying themselves for another attack. Instead of soldiers, however, the people who worked in the castle came racing into the room. They came with makeshift weapons, axes and sticks raised and ready to attack. They came to an abrupt stop as they saw Louise and as it dawned on them who she was, they let out small cries of surprised delight.

Louise turned to Jamsen with an expression of complete confusion which he immediately returned. Two people pushed their way through the crowd and began to approach them. Louise recognised Zalan and Darty making their way towards her and she felt overwhelming relief to see them alive and well. With a gasp of happiness, she rushed forward and embraced them.

'I'm so glad you're both okay,' Louise gushed. 'What happened to you? I was worried you were dead.'

'We've been in the prison cells,' Zalan explained, looking exhausted. 'When the castle realised you were here and fighting Brisheit, they overthrew his soldiers and released us from our cells. We took out as many soldiers as we could, sent word to the rebel camps, and came to help you.' He gave her a small smile. 'It doesn't look like you needed it though.' He said nodding at Brisheit with a surprised look on his face.

'What do you want us to do with him?' Darty asked, looking at Brisheit with both satisfaction and fear.

Louise spared a glance for the people crowded around the doorway, watching her expectantly. She took a deep breath to calm herself down.

'We need to put him in our most secure cell. I'll then place a series of magic traps around it to prevent him from ever escaping or being helped to escape,' she said confidently. As quickly as the words had come out, four men and two women stepped forward and approached Brisheit. With him under Louise's magical influence, they escorted him out of the room.

They all watched him leave. When Louise turned around, she found Zalan was looking at her with an expression of love and admiration.

'We need to rid this land of everyone who was ever loyal to Brisheit, either through imprisonment or banishment,' Louise said to him.

Zalan nodded to a group standing nearby. 'Spread those orders throughout Calaresp. We can lock them up for now and deal with who to banish later.'

They immediately left the room, which was becoming increasingly full as more and more people from the castle came to see their lost princess. Darty looked at Louise with an expression of admiration and then turned to the people.

'I would like you all to welcome home our rightful Queen, the rightful ruler of Calaresp, Queen Louise Clarest.'

A loud cheer immediately erupted throughout the Main Hall and as it did, the room seemed to brighten. Louise looked around her, completely overwhelmed. Her gaze fell on Jamsen, who looked back at her with such a look of love that Louise was instantly calmed.

When the cheers finally settled down, they looked at her expectantly. Louise knew she had to speak, she owed it to them. 'Thank you for being here, and thank you all for your loyalty. Now Brisheit and his evil regime are gone, we have the chance to return Calaresp to what it once was. A safe place where we can all live, without fear, without the hatred Brisheit brought into our world. It's going to be difficult and it won't happen straight away but together we can get there.' She paused and beamed a smile at them all. 'I'm so glad to be home at last.'

The room erupted as the crowd shouted their agreement and joy. Louise made her way over to Zalan.

'What about the rest of the team? Where are they?' Louise asked, the question had been burning within her.

Zalan's cheerful mood quickly vanished. He lowered his head. 'Sadly, they didn't survive. Brisheit's men ensured there was nothing left of them.'

Louise felt her tears well up. 'We have to do something, to mark their sacrifice, their courage. So, we always remember them.'

Zalan nodded, a small smile spreading across his face. 'That's a terrific idea.'

Louise spent the next hour meeting those who had come to fight for her, the normal people who had picked up whatever weapons they could to defend her. Then, with help from Zalan and Darty, she set about putting people to task, clearing any and every sign of Brisheit from the castle. She also gave the order that they should have a great feast, to celebrate, which was met with considerable enthusiasm. The Main Hall was soon half-emptied as everyone got to work.

Zalan moved to Louise's side. 'Now,' he said in a commanding voice. 'You must be exhausted so why don't you get some rest and we'll sort out this mess of a castle.' There was an instant ripple of laughter and gradually the great hall emptied. When they were finally left alone, Jamsen, Darty and Zalan turned to look at Louise with expressions of delight.

'You did it!' Jamsen said, taking her hand in his, squeezing it gently. Flashing her that familiar smile that made her heart skip a beat.

'Are you injured at all?' Zalan asked her, his happiness mingled with concern as he looked down at her blood-stained thighs.

'I'm fine,' Louise replied calmly. 'I healed myself.' She pulled back the ripped material to show unmarked skin.

'Impressive!' Darty replied. She stood up and looked around. 'Look at all you've done. You're even more powerful than the prophecy said.'

Jamsen placed a hand gently on her back, beaming with pride. Zalan looked at him with uncertainty and distrust. 'Are you sure we can trust him, Your Majesty? He already tricked us once.'

Louise looked at Jamsen and smiled, 'Yes, we can. It's because of Jamsen I was able to defeat Brisheit, he's the one that returned the Whisper to me.'

Zalan nodded. 'Well, I think we should give them a bit of time alone.' He said, looking at Darty. 'There's plenty of things for us to crack on with.'

Darty nodded and the two of them gave Louise a quick hug, both grinning from ear to ear as they left the room.

Just as she reached the door, Darty stopped and turned back to Louise. 'I think there's one last surprise for you!'

Louise frowned, about to ask her what she was talking about when Barney bounded into the room. On seeing him Louise let out a sob of delight. He ran forward and she crashed to the ground as her loyal companion jumped into her arms, licking her face. Louise laughed. 'Oh, good boy Barney!' A huge grin spread across her face. 'How I've missed you.'

Jamsen came forward and he too knelt to the ground to greet Barney, whose tail wagged uncontrollably. 'You've put on weight boy.' he said, rubbing Barney's stomach.

Louise watched the others leave and then eventually got up and turned and made her way to the window on the far side of the room. Jamsen and Barney followed her and they looked outside the window. From there, they could see a beautiful lake, surrounded by large trees and rolling hills.

'Well,' Jamsen said in a quiet voice. 'Can you believe how far we've come? Especially you.'

Louise laughed, 'Not really, no! Although being here does feel so right, so natural.'

Jamsen turned her until she was facing him, his expression now riddled with guilt and concern. 'I'm so sorry that I lied to you. I honestly didn't mean to betray you. I stopped working for Brisheit straight after I met you. I knew there was something about you, something so wonderful that I knew I could never do anything to hurt you.'

'It's okay,' Louise placed an arm on his shoulder.

'It's not,' Jamsen interrupted. 'I lied to you and I have to explain. Brisheit often sent men to take children from the orphanages to train for his army. He felt that this would make them more loyal, more likely to follow his lead without question. I was recruited with no other option.' He looked away from her, clearly ashamed. 'I did some awful things, and although I was very good at it, I hated every second. In fact, I hated my life in general. But it was my life, it was all I knew. I didn't have anything to live for until I met you.'

Louise placed a hand on his cheek and slowly turned his face to make him look at her. 'Honestly,' she said in a gentle voice. 'It's okay, I don't blame you. You didn't betray me. You've saved me more often than I could ever repay you.'

They kissed and Louise felt an overwhelming sense of happiness, aware that this life, this place, and this man had always been her destiny.

They stood looking out of the window arm-in-arm for a few seconds. Louise raised the Whisper and looked at it.

'I don't know if I want to keep this,' she said in a quiet, shaky voice. 'I don't know what it did to me — the power, the sensation of it flowing through my body was terrifying. I didn't have any control over it.'

'You did control it,' Jamsen replied. 'You'll always be able to control it. For a few seconds, you simply forgot who you were, that's how it was able to overpower you. All you need to do is remember who you are.'

'What if I get lost in it again?' she asked, uncertain.

'Then I will be there, I will always be there to remind you who you truly are.'

They looked at one another and embraced once more, his strong arms wrapped around her, then they turned to look at the magnificent scene in front of them. Barney stood by her side and she gently stroked the top of his head.

'What now?' Jamsen asked, holding her tightly.

'Now, the daunting task of restoring Calaresp has to begin. Returning it to what it once was, how it should be. I'm home now and I'm ready to make my family and my people proud.

THE END

Printed in Great Britain
by Amazon